Escape to...

a glamorous world of sun-drenched passion, rising temperatures and romantic destinations...

Revel in those long, lazy summer days...

Drift away to a land of tempting azure seas, pure white beaches and divine 'Greek Gods', in
Escape to Greek Affairs,
two scintillating bestselling romances in one volume.

Available in the

Escape to

Collection...

19th May 2006

16th June 2006

21st July 2006

18th August 2006

Escape to...
GREEK AFFAIRS

Containing

Smokescreen Marriage
by Sara Craven
&
The Mediterranean Tycoon
by Margaret Mayo

Harlequin Mills & Boon Limited, Eton House,
18-24 Paradise Road,
Richmond, Surrey TW9 1SR

ESCAPE TO GREEK AFFAIRS

Smokescreen Marriage and *The Mediterranean Tycoon* were first published in Great Britain by Harlequin Mills & Boon Limited in separate, single volumes.

ISBN 10: 0 263 85081 1
ISBN 13: 978 0 263 85081 9

055-0706

Printed and bound in Spain
by Litografia Rosés S.A., Barcelona

SMOKESCREEN MARRIAGE

by

Sara Craven

Sara Craven was born in South Devon, and grew up surrounded by books in a house by the sea. After leaving grammar school she worked as a local journalist, covering everything from flower shows to murders. She started writing for Mills & Boon® in 1975. Apart from writing, her passions include films, music, cooking and eating in good restaurants. She now lives in Somerset.

Sara Craven has appeared on the Channel Four game show *Fifteen to One* and in 1997 was also the last ever winner of the *Mastermind of Great Britain* championship.

Sara Craven has a new novel, *Bride of Desire*, available in Mills & Boon Modern Romance® in September 2006.

CHAPTER ONE

THE room was in deep shadow. Moonlight pouring through the slats of the tall shuttered windows lay in thin bands across the tiled floor.

The whirr of the ceiling fan gently moving the warm air above the wide bed was barely audible against the ceaseless rasp of the cicadas in the garden below the room.

Once, she'd found these sounds alien. Now, they were the natural accompaniment to her nights in this house.

As was the firm masculine tread approaching the bed. The warm, husky voice, touched with laughter, whispering 'Katharina *mou*.'

And she, turning slowly, languidly, under the linen sheet that was her only covering, smiling her welcome, as she reached up to him with outstretched arms, her body alive with need—with longing…

With a gasp, Kate sat up in the darkness, throat tight, heart pounding violently.

She made herself draw deep calming breaths as she glanced round the room, seeking reassurance. Her bedroom, in her flat. Curtains masking the windows, not shutters. And, outside, the uneasy rumble of London traffic.

A dream, she thought. Only a bad dream. Just another nightmare.

At the beginning, they'd been almost nightly occurrences, as her stunned mind and bruised senses tried to rationalise what had happened to her.

She had never really succeeded, of course. The hurt, the betrayal had cut too deep. The events of the past year were always there, in the corner of her mind, eating corrosively into her consciousness.

But the bad dreams had been kept at bay for a while. It was now almost two weeks since the last one.

She had, she thought, begun to heal.

And now this…

Was it an omen? she wondered. Tomorrow—the next day—would there be some news at last? The letter—the phone call—that would bring her the promise of freedom.

God knows, she'd made it as easy as she could, going right against the advice of her lawyer.

'But, Mrs Theodakis, you're entitled…'

She'd stopped him there. 'I want nothing,' she said. 'Nothing at all. Kindly make sure the other side is—aware of that. And please don't use that name either,' she added constrainedly. 'I prefer Miss Dennison.'

He had assented politely, but his raised brows told her more loudly than words that no amount of preference could change a thing.

She had taken off her wedding ring, but she couldn't as easily erase the events of the past year from her tired memory.

She was still legally the wife of Michael Theodakis, and would remain so until she received his consent to the swift, clean-break divorce she had requested.

Once she was free of him, then the nightmares would stop, she told herself. And she could begin to put her life back together again.

That was the inner promise that had kept her going through these dark days and endless nights since she'd fled from Mick, and their charade of a marriage. From the images that still haunted her, waking and sleeping.

She drew her knees up to her chin, shivering a little. Her cotton nightgown was damp, and clinging to her body. She was tired—her job as a tour guide escorting parties of foreign tourists round the British Isles was a demanding one—but her body was wide awake, restless with the needs and desires she'd struggled so hard to suppress.

How could the memory of him still be so potent? she wondered despairingly. Why couldn't she forget him as easily as he seemed to have forgotten her? Why didn't he answer her solicitor's letters—or instruct one of the team of lawyers who served the mighty Theodakis clan to deal with them for him?

With all his money and power, it was the simplest thing in the world to rid himself of an unwanted wife. He was signing papers all day long. What would one more signature matter?

She lay down again, pulling the covers round her, in spite of the warmth of the August night. Cocooning herself so that the expanse of the bed beside her would not seem quite so empty—so desolate.

And knowing that nothing would ever make any difference to the loneliness and the hurt.

It was nearly eight when she reached home the following evening, and Kate felt bone-weary as she let herself into the narrow hall. She had spent the day showing a party of thirty Japanese tourists round Stratford-on-Avon. They had been unfailingly polite, and interested, absorbing information like sponges, but Kate was aware that she had not been on top form. She'd been restless, edgy all day, blaming her disturbed night for her difficulties in concentration.

Tonight, she thought grimly, she would take one of the pills the doctor had prescribed when she first returned from Greece.

She needed this job, and couldn't afford to lose it, even if it was only temporary, filling in for someone on maternity leave.

All the winter jobs for reps with tour companies had already gone when she came back to Britain, although her old company Halcyon Club Travel were keen to hire her again next summer.

And that's what she planned to do, although she'd stipulated that she would not return to any of the Greek islands.

On her way to the stairs, she paused to collect her mail from the row of rickety pigeon-holes on the wall.

Mostly circulars, she judged, and the gas bill—and then stopped, her attention totally arrested as she saw the Greek stamp.

She stared down at the large square envelope with its neatly typed direction, her eyes dilating, a small choked sound rising in her throat.

She thought, 'He's found me. He knows where I am. But how?'

And why was he making contact with her directly, when she'd made it clear that all correspondence was to be conducted through their lawyers?

But then, when had Mick Theodakis ever played by any rules except his own?

She went up the stairs slowly, aware that her legs were shaking. When she reached her door, she had to struggle to fit her key into the lock, but at last she managed it.

In her small living room, she dropped the letter on to the dining table as if it was red-hot, then walked across to her answerphone which was blinking at her, and pressed the 'play' button. Perhaps, if Mick had written to her, he'd also contacted her lawyer, and the message she was hoping for might be waiting at last.

Instead Grant's concerned voice said, 'Kate—are you all right? You haven't called me this week. Touch base, darling—please.'

Kate sighed inwardly, and went across to the bedroom to take off the navy shift dress, and navy and emerald striped blazer that constituted her uniform.

It was kind of Grant to be anxious, but she knew in her heart that it was more than kindness that prompted his frequent calls. It was pressure. He wanted her back, their former relationship re-established, and moved on to the next stage. He took it for granted that she wanted this too. That, like him, she regarded the past year as an aberration—a period of temporary insanity, now happily concluded. And that when she had gained her divorce, she would marry him.

But Kate knew it would never happen. She and Grant had not been officially engaged, when she'd gone off to work as a travel company rep on Zycos in the Ionian Sea, but she knew, when the season was over, he would ask her to marry him, and that she would probably agree.

She hadn't even been sure why she was hesitating. He was good-looking, they shared a number of interests, and, if his kisses did not set her on fire, Kate enjoyed them enough to look forward to the full consummation of their relationship. And during her weeks on Zycos she had missed him, written to him every week, and happily anticipated his phone calls planning their future.

Surely that was a good enough basis for marriage—wasn't it?

Probably Grant thought it still was. Only she knew better. Knew she was no longer the same person. And soon she would have to tell him so, she thought with genuine regret.

She unzipped her dress, and put it on a hanger. Underneath she was wearing bra and briefs in white broderie anglaise, pretty and practical, but not glamorous or sexy, she thought, studying herself dispassionately.

And totally different from the exquisite lingerie that Mick had brought her from Paris and Rome—lacy cobwebby things that whispered against her skin. Filmy enticing scraps to please the eyes of a lover.

Only, there was no lover—and never had been.

She slipped on her pale-green gingham housecoat and tied its sash, then put up a hand and removed the barrette that confined her red-gold hair at the nape of her neck during the working day, letting it cascade down to her shoulders.

'Like a scented flame,' Mick would tell her huskily, his hands tangling in the silky strands—lifting them to his lips.

She stiffened, recognising that was a no-go area. She could not afford such memories.

She wanted to move away from the mirror but something kept her there, examining herself with cold critical attention.

How could she ever have imagined in her wildest dreams that she was the kind of woman to attract and hold a man like Mick Theodakis? she asked herself bleakly.

Because she had never been a classic beauty. Her nose was too long and her jaw too square for that. But she had good cheekbones, and long lashes, although the eyes they fringed were an odd shade between green and grey.

'Jade smoke,' Mick had called them...

And she was luckier than most redheads, she thought, swiftly refocusing her attention. Her creamy skin didn't burn or freckle, but turned a light, even gold. The tan she'd acquired in Greece still lingered. She could see quite plainly the white band of her finger where her wedding ring had been. But that was the only mark, because Mick had always encouraged her to join him in sunbathing nude beside their private pool.

She froze, cursing inwardly. Oh, God, why was she doing this to herself—allowing herself to remember these things?

Well, she knew why, of course. It was because of that envelope ticking away like a time bomb in the other room.

Her throat tightened uncontrollably. She turned away from the mirror and went into the kitchen and made herself a mug of coffee, hot, black and very strong. If she'd had any brandy, she'd have added a dollop of that too.

Then, she sat down at the table, and steeled herself to open the envelope.

It was disturbing to realise how easily he'd been able to pinpoint her whereabouts—as if he was demonstrating his power over her from across the world. Showing her that there was nowhere she could run and hide. No refuge that he could not find.

Only he had no power, she told herself fiercely. Not any more. Not ever again. And she tore open the envelope.

She found herself staring down at an elegantly engraved

white card. A wedding invitation, she thought in total bewilderment, as she scanned it. And the last thing she'd expected to find. She felt oddly deflated as she read the beautifully printed words.

So—Ismene, Mick's younger sister was marrying her Petros at last. But why on earth was she being sent an invitation?

Frowningly, she unfolded the accompanying note.

'Dearest Katharina,' it read. 'Papa finally gave his permission and I am so happy. We are to be married in the village in October, and you promised you would be there for me on my wedding day. I depend on you, sister. Your loving Ismene.'

Kate crumpled the note in her hand. Was Ismene crazy, or just naïve? she wondered. She couldn't really expect her brother's estranged wife to be part of a family occasion, whatever rash commitment Kate might have made in those early days when she was still living in her fool's paradise.

But I'm not that person any more, Kate thought, her face set, her body rigid. I'll have to write to her—explain somehow.

But why had Mick ever allowed the invitation to be sent? It made no sense. Although the wilful Ismene probably hadn't bothered to seek his permission, she acknowledged with a faint sigh.

And she was astonished that Aristotle Theodakis, the all-powerful patriarch of the family, had agreed to the marriage. While she'd been living under his roof at the Villa Dionysius, he'd been adamantly opposed to it. No mere doctor was good enough for his daughter, he'd roared, even if it was the son of his old friend and *tavli* opponent. And slammed doors, furious scenes, and the sound of Ismene's hysterical weeping had been almost daily occurrences.

Until Mick had flatly announced he could stand no more, and had insisted that he and Kate move out of their wing of the main building, and out of earshot, down to the comparative seclusion of the beach house. Where they'd remained…

She drank some of the scalding coffee, but it did nothing to melt the ice in the pit of her stomach.

Those weeks, she thought, had been the happiest of her life. Day had succeeded sunlit day. Night followed moonlit night. Raised voices were replaced by birdsong, the whisper of the breeze in the pine trees, and the murmur of the sea.

And, above all, Michael touching her—whispering to her, coaxing her out of the last of her natural shyness, teaching her to take as well as give in their lovemaking. And to be proud of her slim, long-legged body with its narrow waist and small high breasts.

And she'd been an eager pupil, she thought bitterly. How readily she'd surrendered to the caress of his cool, experienced hands and mouth, sobbing out her breathless, mindless rapture as their naked bodies joined in passion.

So beguiled, so entranced by the new sensual vistas that Mick had revealed to her, that she'd mistaken them for love.

Whereas all she'd really been to him was a novelty—a temporary amusement.

The smokescreen he'd cynically needed to divert attention from his real passion.

The coffee tasted bitter, and she pushed it away from her, feeling faintly nauseous.

She couldn't afford to tear her heart out over Ismene, she told herself curtly. They'd become close over the months, and she knew that the younger girl would be missing her company with only Victorine to turn to. In fact, the note had almost sounded like a cry for help.

But she couldn't allow herself to think like that. And in particular she couldn't permit her mind to dwell on Victorine, the Creole beauty who now ruled Aristotle Theodakis, without releasing any of her hold over his son.

She would write a brief and formal expression of regret,

and leave it there. Keep it strictly impersonal, although Ismene might be hurt to have no response to her note.

But then, Kate thought, I also have the right to some reaction to my request for a divorce. After all, it's been a month since my lawyer sent off the papers.

Impatiently, she pushed the invitation away and rose. It was no wonder she was feeling flaky. She ought to have something to eat. She'd only had time to grab a sandwich at lunch time, and there was cold chicken and salad in the fridge, only her appetite seemed to have deserted her.

And she had a hectic day tomorrow—a group of reluctant French schoolchildren to chivvy around the Tower of London.

Perhaps she would just have a warm shower, wash her hair, and go to bed early. Catch up on some of that lost sleep.

Her bathroom was small, and the shower cubicle rather cramped, not tempting her to linger. She towelled down quickly, and resumed her housecoat before returning to the living room with her hair-drier.

She was just plugging it in when, to her surprise and irritation, someone knocked at the door.

Kate sighed, winding a towel round her wet hair. It was bound to be Mrs Thursgood, the elderly widow who lived on the ground floor, and accepted parcels and packets intended for other tenants who'd left for work before the mail arrived.

She was a kindly soul but gossipy, and she would expect a cup of tea and a cosy chat in return for her trouble of trailing up to the top floor with Kate's book club selection, or whatever.

I really, truly, don't want to talk, Kate thought grimly, as she pinned on a smile and flung open the door.

And stood, lips parting in a soundless gasp, eyes widening in shock, feeling the blood drain from her face.

'My beloved wife,' Michael Theodakis said softly. '*Kalispera*. May I come in?'

'No,' she said. Her voice sounded hoarse—distorted above the sudden roaring in her ears. She was afraid she was going to faint, and knew she couldn't afford any such weakness. She took a step backwards.

'No,' she repeated more vehemently.

He was smiling, totally at ease, propping a dark-clad shoulder against the doorframe.

'But we cannot conduct a civilised conversation on the *door*step, *agapi mou*.'

She said thickly, 'I've got nothing to say to you—on the doorstep or anywhere else. If you want to talk, speak to my solicitor. And don't call me your darling.'

'How unkind,' he said. 'When I have travelled such a long way at such inconvenience to see you again. I'd hoped some of our Greek hospitality might have rubbed off on you.'

'That isn't the aspect of my life with you that I remember most clearly,' Kate said, her breathing beginning to steady. 'And I didn't invite you here, so please go.'

Mick Theodakis raised both hands in mock surrender. 'Easy, Katharina *mou*. I did not come here to fight a war, but negotiate a peaceful settlement. Isn't that what you want too?'

'I want a quick divorce,' she said. 'And never to see you again.'

'Go on.' The dark eyes glinted down at her from beneath hooded lids. 'Surely you have a third wish. All the best stories do, I believe.'

Kate drew a quick, sharp breath. 'This,' she said gratingly, 'is not a fairy story.'

'No,' he said. 'To be honest, I am not sure whether it is a comedy or a tragedy.'

'Honest?' Kate echoed scornfully. 'You don't know the meaning of the word.'

'However,' he went on as if she hadn't spoken. 'I am quite certain I am not leaving until you have heard what I have to say, *yineka mou*.'

'I am not your wife,' she said. 'I resigned that dubious honour when I left Kefalonia. And I thought I'd made it clear in my note that our so-called marriage was over.'

'It was a model of clarity,' he said courteously. 'I have learned every word of it by heart. And the fact that you left your wedding ring beside it added extra emphasis.'

'Then you'll understand there is nothing to discuss.' She lifted her chin. 'Now, go please. I have a heavy duty tomorrow, and I'd like to go to bed.'

'Not,' he said softly. 'With wet hair. That is something that *I* remember from our brief marriage, Katharina.' He stepped into the room, kicking the door shut behind him.

There was no lock on her bedroom door, and one dodgy bolt on the bathroom. With nowhere to run, Kate decided to stand her ground.

'How dare you.' Her face was burning as she glared at him. 'Get out of here, before I call the police.'

'To do what?' Mick asked coolly. 'Have I ever struck you—or molested you in any way, *agapi mou*, that you did not welcome?' He watched the colour suddenly deepen in her shocked face, and nodded sardonically. 'Besides, all police are reluctant to intervene in domestic disputes. So, why don't you sit down and dry your hair while you listen to what I have to say?'

He paused, then held out his hand. 'Unless you would like me to dry it for you,' he added softly. 'As I used to.'

Kate swallowed convulsively, and shook her head, not trusting her voice.

It wasn't fair, she raged inwardly. It wasn't right for him to remind her of all the small, tender intimacies they'd once shared.

The way she'd sat between his knees as he blow-dried her hair, combing it gently with his fingers, letting the soft strands drift in the current of warm air.

And how her efforts to perform the same service for him had always been thwarted, as he loosened the sash on her robe, and drew the folds slowly apart, pressing tiny sensuous kisses on her naked body as she stood, flushed and breathless, in front of him. Until her attempt at hairdressing was forgotten in the sweet urgency of the moment.

Oh, she did not need to remember that.

Her cotton housecoat was long-sleeved and full-skirted, buttoned chastely to the throat, but she was still blazingly aware that she was naked under it—and that he knew it too, and was enjoying her discomfort.

The room seemed suddenly to have shrunk. His presence dominated it, physically and emotionally. Invaded her space in the worst way. Dried her throat and made her legs shake under her.

Even as she turned away and walked across to the dining table, every detail of him was etched on her mind, as if she'd touched him with her fingers.

Yet she did not have to do that—to remember.

She knew that the black curling hair was brushed back from his face with careless elegance. That his dark eyes were brilliant, but watchful beneath their heavy lids, or that the cool, firm mouth held a hint of sensuality in the slight fullness of the lower lip.

It was a proud face, strong and uncompromising, but when he smiled, its charm had twisted the heart in her body.

He was formally dressed, the charcoal business suit accentuating the tall, lean body which moved with such arrogant grace. His olive skin looked very dark against the immaculate white shirt. His tie was silk, and there were discreet gold links in his cuffs matching the narrow bracelet on his watch and, she noticed with a sudden painful thud of her heart, the plain band on the third finger of his right hand.

The ring which matched hers, inscribed inside with their names and the date, which she had slipped on to his finger on their wedding day…

How could he still be wearing it? How could he be such a hypocrite? she asked herself numbly.

He said, 'Aren't you going to ask me to sit down—offer me some coffee?'

'You're not a guest,' Kate said, keeping her voice level with an effort. 'And this is not a social call.' She frowned. 'How did you get in, anyway?'

'A charming lady on the ground floor.' He paused. 'She seemed pleased you were having a visitor.'

Mrs Thursgood, Kate thought, grinding her teeth. Who normally guarded the front door like Cerberus at the gates of Hell.

She said, 'She allows her imagination to run away with her sometimes.'

She loosened the towel that was swathed round her head, and her damp hair tumbled on to her shoulders. Then she switched on the drier, and picked up the brush.

Mick stood by the old-fashioned fireplace watching every movement, his whole body very still, except for a muscle flickering at the side of his mouth.

He said at last, 'You've received Ismene's invitation.' His tone was abrupt, and it was a statement rather than a question.

'It came today.'

'So you haven't had time to reply.'

'It won't take much time,' Kate said shortly. 'Naturally, I shan't be going.'

'Ah,' Mick said gently. 'But that is what I came to discuss with you. It would mean a great deal to my sister to have you present, so I hope you will reconsider.'

Kate switched off the drier and stared at him, pushing her hair back from her face. 'That's impossible.'

'I hope not. Ismene has missed you very badly, and this is a special time for her.' He paused. 'I would regard your attendance as a favour.'

Kate gasped. 'And that's supposed to make all the difference?' she demanded furiously.

'I thought it might.' He leaned an arm on the mantelshelf,

looking hatefully assured and relaxed. 'In fact, I believed we might exchange favours.'

There was an uncertain silence, then Kate said, 'What do you mean?'

'You want a simple, consensual divorce.' He smiled at her. 'Which you can have—at a price.'

There was another tingling silence.

She said, 'And if the price is too high?'

He shrugged. 'Then I refuse to consent, and we let the legal process run its course.' He added casually, 'I understand it can take several years.'

'That's—blackmail.' Her voice shook.

'Is it?' he said. 'But perhaps I do not agree that our marriage has "irretrievably broken down" as you allege in that document.'

'But you must. It has.' Kate drew a deep breath. 'And you're bluffing. I know you are. You don't wish to stay married any more than I do.'

His mouth twisted. 'You're mistaken, *agapi mou*. I am in no particular hurry to be free.'

No, she thought, with a stab of anguish. Not while your father is still alive, and Victorine is nominally his…

She said slowly, 'So I have to attend Ismene's wedding if I want a quick divorce.'

'Is it really such a hardship? Kefalonia is very beautiful in September.'

'Kefalonia is beautiful all the year round.' Her tone was curt. 'It's only some of the people there who make it ugly.'

'A word of advice, *pedhi mou*.' His smile was mirthless. 'It is better to win an opponent over than to antagonise him.'

Kate lifted her chin. 'I think it's a little late to worry about that.' She hesitated. 'But everyone must know by now that our marriage is over. Won't they find it strange if I'm at the wedding?'

'I am not interested in what people think.' His voice was suddenly harsh. 'Besides, they only know that we have been separated for a short time. You might simply have come back to this country to attend to some family business.'

'Is that what you've been telling people?' She shook her head. 'My God, you can't even be honest about our marriage breaking down.'

'They will know soon enough, when the wedding is over.'

'Well, I hope you don't expect me to take part in some spurious reunion,' Kate said acidly. 'I'm not that good an actress.' She paused. 'Why do you want me there?'

'Did I say wanted?' Mick drawled. 'Don't flatter yourself, my sweet one. I am here on Ismene's behalf, not my own.'

She did not look at him, staring instead at her gingham-covered knee. 'Then I'd be there—just as an ordinary guest? Nothing more?'

He said mockingly, 'Why, Katharina, did you think you had left me all these weeks to sleep alone? That I've been burning for your return. What an innocent you are.'

'Not,' she said, 'any more.' She was silent for a moment. 'I need time to think about this.'

'You have twenty-four hours. I am staying at the Royal Empress Hotel. You remember it?'

'Yes.' It was a painful whisper.

He nodded. 'You can contact me there with your answer.'

He walked to the door, and paused for a final swift look round the room.

He said, 'So this is what you left me for. I hope it is worth it.'

'I don't have to live in the lap of luxury to be happy,' Kate said defiantly.

'Evidently,' he said. 'If happy is what you are.' He looked her over, slowly and thoroughly, a smile curling his mouth.

He said softly, 'Eyes like smoke and hair like flame. What a waste *agapi mou*. What a tragic waste.'

And was gone.

CHAPTER TWO

FOR several long moments Kate stood like a statue, staring at the closed door, pain and disbelief warring within her for supremacy.

Then she gave a little choked cry and ran to her bedroom, flinging herself face down across the bed, her hands gripping the covers as if they were her last hold on sanity.

She said aloud, 'Fool.' And again, more savagely, her voice breaking, '*Fool*.'

Had she really thought she could escape so easily? That Michael Theodakis would simply allow her—the girl he'd taken from nowhere—to walk away from him?

Not that he cared about her, or their marriage, as she had bitter cause to know, but the fact that she'd chosen to expose the hypocrisy of their relationship by leaving, had clearly damaged his pride. And that, of course, was an unforgivable sin.

Her own pride, naturally, didn't count.

He hadn't even asked her why she had left, but then he didn't have to. He already knew. He would have been told…

Nor had he offered one word of apology or explanation for the actions which had driven her away.

No, she was clearly the one who was at fault because she'd failed to turn a blind eye to his cynical infidelity.

After all, she'd had the Theodakis millions to enjoy, and she could not deny Mick had been generous. There'd been the house outside Athens, and the sumptuous apartments in Paris and New York as well as the clothes and jewellery he'd given her, all of which she'd left behind when she fled.

But that had been her choice, and Mick, no doubt, felt he

had bought her silence—her discretion, and, in his eyes, she had reneged on their unwritten bargain.

A bargain she had not realised existed until that terrible afternoon…

She shuddered, pressing her face deep into the bed until coloured sparks danced behind her closed eyelids.

But nothing could drive the image from her brain. Mick sprawled naked and asleep across the bed—their bed. And Victorine sitting at the dressing table combing her hair, clad in nothing but a towel.

And now, in spite of that, he required her to stand meekly at his side during Ismene's wedding celebrations, playing the dutiful wife. As if she owed him something.

But she'd only have to role-play by day, she reminded herself. At least she would not be asked to pretend at night.

And neither would he. Not any longer.

How could a man do that? she wondered wildly. How could he make love to one woman, with his heart and mind committed to another?

And all those precious passionate moments when the dark strength of his body had lifted her to the edge of paradise and beyond—how could they have meant so little to him?

But perhaps sexual fulfilment had also been part of his side of the bargain along with the designer wardrobe and the money he'd provided. One of the assets of being Mrs Michael Theodakis.

But it wasn't enough. Because she'd wanted love. And that was something he'd never offered. At least he'd been honest about that.

Probably, he'd found her inexperience—her naïvete amusing, she thought, lashing herself into fresh anger against him.

Because anger was good. Safe. It kept the frantic tears of loneliness and betrayal at bay. And she couldn't afford any more tears. Any more heartbreak.

She'd wept enough. Now, somehow, she had to move on.

But she couldn't begin to build a new life while her brief

marriage still existed, trapping her in the old one. She needed it to be over, and left far behind her. But for that, of course, she had to have Mick's co-operation. Oh, it would be so good to tell him to go to hell. That she would die sooner than return to Kefalonia and play at being his wife again for however short a time.

Because that meant she would become once more the smokescreen against his father's jealous and totally justified suspicions. And how could she bear it?

Or stand seeing, yet again, the triumph and contempt in Victorine's beautiful face? The look she'd turned on Kate, standing ashen-faced in the doorway that afternoon only a few agonised weeks ago.

'How tactless of you, *chère*.' Her honeyed drawl was barbed. 'Perhaps in future you should knock before entering your husband's bedroom.'

Kate had taken two shaky steps backwards, then run for the bathroom down the passage, her hand over her mouth as nausea churned inside her.

She was violently, cripplingly sick, kneeling on the tiled floor while walls and ceiling revolved unsteadily around her. She had no idea how long she'd stayed there. But eventually some firm purpose was born out of the sickness and misery, making her realise that she had to get out. That her brief marriage was over, and that she could not bear to spend even another hour under any roof that belonged to the Theodakis family.

She had to force herself to go back into that bedroom, bracing herself for another humiliating confrontation, but Victorine had gone.

Mick was still fast asleep. Exhausted by his labours, no doubt, she thought, rubbing salt into her own bitter wounds. And how dared he sleep while her heart was breaking?

She needed to confront him, she realised. To accuse him and see the guilt in his face.

She put her hand on his shoulder, and shook him.

'Mick.' Her voice cracked on his name. 'Wake up.'

He stirred drowsily, without opening his eyes. '*S'agapo*,' he muttered, his voice slurred. 'I love you.'

Kate gasped, and took a step backwards, a stricken hand flying to her mouth. At last he'd said them—the words she'd yearned to hear ever since they'd been together.

Only they were not meant for her, but his secret lover—the woman he'd been enjoying so passionately in her absence. The mistress he'd never actually discarded. It was the final—the unforgivable hurt, she thought as she turned painfully and walked away.

She packed the minimum in a small weekend case, then scribbled him a note which she left on the night table with her wedding ring.

'I should never have married you,' she wrote. 'It was a terrible mistake, and I cannot bear to go on living with you for another moment. Don't try to find me.'

No one saw her go. She drove to the airport, and managed to get a seat on a plane to Athens, and from there to London.

She had sworn that she would never go back.

And I can't, Kate thought, a shudder crawling the length of her body. I can't do it. It's too degrading to have to face her. To see them together, knowing what I know.

But what real alternative did she have?

She couldn't wait for years in limbo until Mick finally decided to let her go.

And, while his father lived, he had no real reason to end the marriage.

She had humiliated him by her precipitate departure, and she was being punished as a consequence. That was what it was all about. She had to be returned to the scene of her anguish—her betrayal—and made to endure all the memories and misery that it would evoke.

She burrowed into the quilt like a small wounded animal seeking sanctuary, her mind rejecting the images forcing themselves relentlessly on her inner vision.

Oh, how could he do this? How dared he simply—appear in her life again and start making demands?

Because he's without shame, she told herself, bitterly. And without decency. He's rich enough to do without them.

But I'm not. And somehow I have to find my way through this, and keep my own integrity in the process. And lying here with my eyes shut isn't going to change a thing.

She sat up slowly, pushing her still-damp hair back from her face with a slight shiver.

Meanwhile she had a job to do tomorrow, and preparations to make for that. Normal life was there to be got on with, even if the safe wall she'd thought she'd built around herself had suddenly come crashing down.

She trailed back into the living room, and switched on her hair-drier, staring unseeingly into space as she dealt with the tangled red waves, restoring them to some kind of order.

As, in the fullness of time, she would restore her life. Find a new calm—a new security.

There had never been any safety with Mick, of course. He'd appeared on her horizon like some great dark planet, and she'd been the moon drawn helplessly into his orbit. And by the time she'd realised the danger she was in, it was already too late.

But from the first time she'd seen him, she'd been in too deep, out of her depth and sinking.

As the drier hummed, Kate let her tired mind drift back over the months to where it had all begun…

'Oh, come on, Katie, don't let me down. It'll be a laugh.' Lisa's tone was cajoling. 'After all, when do we get a chance to get inside a hotel like the Zycos Regina? Don't you want to see how the other half live? Besides, I really need you to make up the foursome.'

Kate bit her lip. It had been a long season on the Greek island of Zycos, and, although on the whole she'd enjoyed being a tour rep for Halcyon Club Travel, she felt bone-weary now that it was over.

All she wanted to do that evening was complete her packing for the following day's flight, have a hot shower, and an early night. But Lisa, the fellow rep with whom she'd shared a small apartment all summer, wanted a night on the town.

She said cautiously, 'Who did you say was going?'

'His name's Stavros,' Lisa said. 'And he's the disc jockey at the Nite Spot down on the waterfront.'

'Oh,' Kate said. 'That place.'

Lisa tossed her head. 'You're such a snob,' she accused.

Kate sighed. 'Not at all. It just hasn't got a very good reputation, and you know it. It's always being raided.'

'Well, we're not taking clients there,' Lisa said. 'And Stavros just plays the music. He's gorgeous.' She rolled her eyes lasciviously. 'The other guy's his cousin Dimitris from Athens.'

Kate began, 'I don't think…' but Lisa cut across her.

'Oh, come on, Katie. Let your hair down for once. It's an evening out, not a lifetime commitment, for God's sake. And we'll be out of here tomorrow.'

Well that was true, Kate acknowledged. It was just one evening, and she could always invent a diplomatic headache if things got heavy.

Besides, if she was honest, she'd always had a sneaking curiosity about the Zycos Regina, the largest but also most exclusive hotel on the island, and set in its own private grounds well away from the lively coastal resorts favoured by the majority of tourists.

She knew that it was part of a chain of equally prestigious hotels dotted round the Mediterranean, their standards of luxury and service putting them out of the reach of the package tour market.

It might be fun, she thought, not just to see how the other half lived, but join them too for a brief while.

She smiled at Lisa. 'All right,' she said. 'You talked me into it.'

She chose carefully from her limited wardrobe that evening, opting for a black linen shift, knee-length, sleeveless and discreetly square necked. Lisa, blonde and bubbly, favoured the outrageous look out of uniform, and would be wearing something skimpy and cut-off, but Kate felt that restraint was her best bet.

For that reason, she twisted her hair into its usual tidy pleat instead of leaving it loose on her shoulders, as she'd originally intended. And she applied just a modicum of makeup, darkening her long lashes, and applying a light coral glow to her mouth.

She slipped on a pair of strappy sandals, then stood back to view herself in the mirror.

The evening was warm and still, but she suddenly found herself shivering as if a small chill wind had penetrated the shutters of her room.

And heard a warning voice in her head say quietly, 'Be careful.'

Oh, for God's sake, she thought impatiently as she turned towards the door. What can possibly happen in such a public—and eminently high-class—place?

Stavros, she disliked on sight. His coarse good looks might attract Lisa, but held no appeal for her. He looked her up and down smilingly, and she felt as if she'd been touched by a finger dipped in slime.

And Dimitris, with his flashy clothes and abundance of gold jewellery, set her teeth on edge too. As did the way he looked at her, as if he was mentally stripping her.

Oh, well, she thought with a mental shrug. The evening won't last forever. It will just seem like it.

The club at the Zycos Regina impressed her immediately with its understated elegance, and subdued lighting. The clientele, mostly couples expensively dressed, were seated at tables set round an oval dance floor, and, on a corner dais, a quartet was playing soft dance music interspersed with interesting jazz.

'It's not very lively,' Lisa complained loudly, twisting round in her chair to survey the other patrons. 'If they're all so rich, why aren't they happier?'

Kate, uncomfortably aware of raised eyebrows and disapproving glances from adjoining tables, winced as she took a sip from the lurid cocktail that had been served to them all by an impassive waiter, and thought how much she'd have preferred a glass of wine.

It embarrassed her to see Dimitris flourishing a wallet full of notes, and clearly believing an extravagant tip allowed him to treat the staff like dirt.

It crucified her too to see Stavros stroking Lisa's exposed skin with a proprietorial hand and leering into her cleavage, then finding Dimitris leaning towards her, murmuring throatily with a suggestive smile, and reaching for her hand.

Deliberately, Kate edged her own chair away, feeling as if she'd woken to find herself in the middle of her worst nightmare.

We don't belong here she thought, with a sigh, as she began to plan her own strategic withdrawal. And we'd better leave before they ask us to go.

She wasn't sure of the moment when she knew she was being watched, but she felt the impact of the glance like a hand on her shoulder.

She drank some more of the unpleasant cocktail, then risked a swift look round, wondering resignedly if the management had already been summoned.

It was a corner table, set slightly apart from the others, and occupied by three men.

And the man watching her sat in the middle. In his early thirties, he was clearly younger than the other two, and, equally obviously, he was the one in control.

Even that first lightning assessment told her that he was good-looking, although not classically handsome. The dark face was strong, the lines of nose and jaw arrogantly marked. But more than that he exuded power, a charismatic force that could reach across a crowded room and touch its object like the caress of a hand.

She knew she should look away, but it was already too late. For an electrifying moment their eyes met, and locked, and Kate felt her breathing quicken and her throat tighten in an odd excitement.

But there was no warmth in his gaze. His expression was cool and watchful, his brows drawn together in a slight frown, as if something had displeased him.

And no prizes for guessing what that was, Kate thought, as she turned back to her companions, her face hot with embarrassed colour.

'Who's that?' Lisa had noticed the direction of her gaze, and was staring herself with open interest. 'Do you know him?' She giggled. 'Have you been holding out on me, Katie?'

'Not in the least,' Kate said crisply. 'Nor do I want to know him. I think he feels we're lowering the tone of the establishment.'

The fact that she thought exactly the same herself seemed paradoxically to increase her resentment.

'But I know him.' Stavros leaned forward, eyes gleaming. 'That is Michalis Theodakis. His father owns the whole Regina chain of hotels, and a great deal more, but the son now runs the company.'

Kate's brows lifted. 'Really?' she asked sceptically. 'What's he doing here?'

'He visits all the hotels,' Stavros explained. 'Checking them at random.'

'So who are the guys with him?' Lisa questioned.

'Who knows?' His minders probably.' His tone was envious. 'He is already a multi-millionaire in his own right, but he will be even richer when he gets control of all the Theodakis holdings. If he ever does,' he added, grinning.

'They say he and his father have quarrelled and Aristotle Theodakis would do anything to prevent him stepping into his shoes.'

He sent Kate a sly glance. 'Do you want him, *kougla mou*? Many women do, and not just for his money. He is quite a stud. You would have to stand in a long line, I think.'

'Don't be absurd,' Kate said coldly, aware that her flush had deepened. 'And do keep your voice down. I think he's planning to have us thrown out.'

That icy considering look had thrown her badly. He had seen her companions and judged her accordingly, so naturally she was honour bound to prove to him that his low opinion of her was entirely justified.

Teeth gritted, she reached for her drink, only to find the whole nasty concoction cascading down the front of her dress as her arm was jogged by a passing waiter.

She gasped and jumped up, shaking her skirt. Stavros and Dimitris were on their feet too, shouting angrily and gesticulating at the waiter, who was apologising abjectly and proffering a clean napkin.

'I'd better go to the powder room,' Kate interrupted, embarrassed at the attention the accident was attracting.

She turned, and cannoned into a tall figure standing behind her. As his hands grasped her arms to steady her, she realised it was Michael Theodakis.

'Allow me to make amends for the clumsiness of my staff, *thespinis*.' He spoke excellent English, she thought, with just a trace of an accent which, allied to his low-pitched drawl, some women would undoubtedly find sexy. 'If you will come with me, my housekeeper will attend to your dress.'

'There's really no need.' She freed herself, and took a small step backwards, her face warming. Because, close to, he was formidably attractive—over six feet in height, broad shouldered and lean-hipped. And prudence suggested she should keep her distance.

'But I think there is.' Somehow, he had repossessed her

hand, and was leading her between the tables towards the exit.

'Will you let go of me, please?' Kate tried to tug her fingers from his grasp. 'I can look after myself.'

'You are deluding yourself, *thespinis*, especially when you keep company like that,' he added with a touch of grimness.

She lifted her chin. 'It's not for you, *kyrie*, to criticise my friends.'

'They are old and dear acquaintances perhaps?' The sardonic note in his voice was not lost on her.

She bit her lip. 'Not—exactly.'

'I thought not.' He walked her across the hotel foyer to the row of lifts and pressed a button.

'Where are we going?' she asked in alarm, as the lift doors opened.

'To my suite.' He steered her inexorably inside. 'My housekeeper will join us there.'

'Take me back to the ground floor, please.' Kate was shaking suddenly. 'I want to go home—now.'

'It will be safer for you to remain at the hotel tonight.' He paused. 'I have a confession to make to you, *thespinis*. I sent Takis to spill your drink deliberately.'

'You must be crazy.' Kate felt dizzy suddenly. 'You can't hope to get away with this—even if you do own the place.'

'Ah,' he said softly. 'So you know who I am.'

'Your fame goes before you. But I'm not interested in being added to your list of conquests.'

He laughed. 'You flatter yourself, my red-headed vixen. My motives, for once, are purely altruistic.'

The lift doors opened, and Kate found herself being marched along a wide corridor towards a pair of double doors at the end.

'No.' There was real panic in her voice. 'I want to go home.'

'So you shall,' he said. 'In the morning when I am sure you have suffered no lasting ill effects.'

'Ill effects?' Kate echoed, as another wave of dizziness assailed her. 'What are you talking about.'

He said flatly, 'Your drink was spiked, *thespinis*. I saw your companion do it.'

'Spiked,' Kate repeated. 'You mean—drugged? But—why?'

He shrugged. 'To make you more amenable, perhaps.' He opened the door, and guided her into the room beyond. 'There is something called the date-rape drug. You may have heard of it.'

She said numbly, 'Heard of it—yes. But you must be mistaken. It can't be true…'

His mouth twisted. 'If the man you were with had asked you to sleep with him tonight, would you have agreed?'

She gasped. 'God—no. He's repulsive.'

'But might not take rejection well, all the same,' he said drily. 'Which is why you must not return to your apartment tonight.'

'But I have to.' Kate was shaking. She put a hand to her forehead, trying to steady herself. Collect her thoughts. 'My—my things are there. I'm going back to England tomorrow. Besides, they may have drugged Lisa too.'

His mouth curled. 'I doubt they would need to.'

She said hotly, 'You have no right to say that. You don't know her.'

He smiled faintly, 'I admire your loyalty, *thespinis*, if not your judgement. Now, I think you should lie down before you fall down,' he added with a slight frown.

'I'm—fine,' Kate said thickly.

'I don't think so,' he said, and picked her up in his arms.

She knew she should protest—that she should kick and fight, but it was so much easier to rest her head against his shoulder and close her eyes, and let him carry her.

She could feel the warmth of his body through his clothing. Could smell the faint muskiness of some cologne he wore.

She sensed a blur of shaded light, and felt the softness of a mattress beneath her. Dimly she was aware of her zip being unfastened and her dress removed, and tried to struggle—to utter some panicked negation.

A woman's voice spoke soothingly. 'Rest easily, little one. All will be well.'

Kate felt the caress of clean, crisp linen against her bare skin, and then the last vestiges of reality slid away, and she slept.

She dreamed fitfully, in brief wild snatches, her body twisting away from the image of Dimitris bending towards her with hot eyes and greedy hands, her voice crying out in soundless horror.

Once, there seemed to be a man's voice speaking right above her in Greek. 'She could solve your immediate problem.'

And heard a cool drawl that she seemed to recognise in the wry response, 'And create a hundred more…'

She wondered who they were—what they were talking about? But it was all too much effort when she was tired—so tired.

And, as she drifted away again, she felt a hand gently touch her hair, and stroke her cheek.

And smiled in her sleep.

CHAPTER THREE

SHE was on fire, burning endlessly in feverish, impossible excitement. Because a man's hands were touching her, arousing her to feverish, rapturous delight. His mouth was exploring her, his body moving against her as she lay beneath him, making her moan and writhe in helpless pleasure. In a need she had not known existed—until then.

And she forced open her heavy lids and looked at the dark face, fierce and intense above her, and saw that it was Michael Theodakis.

Kate awoke, gasping. For a moment she lay still, totally disorientated, then she propped herself up on an unsteady elbow, and looked around her.

Her first shocked realisation was that she was naked in this wide, luxurious bed, her sole covering a sheet tangled round her sweat-slicked body.

In fact, the entire bed looked as if it had been hit by an earthquake, the blue and ivory embroidered coverlet kicked to an untidy heap at its foot, and pillows on the floor.

It was a very large room, she thought, staring round her, with a cream tiled floor, and walls washed in a blue that reflected the azure of the sea and sky. The tall shutters had been opened, and the glass doors beyond stood slightly ajar, allowing a faint breeze from the sea to infiltrate the room and stir the pale voile drapes in the brilliant sunlight.

She shook the sheet loose, restoring it to a more decorous level, as she began slowly to remember the events of the previous night.

She didn't know which was the most extraordinary—the danger she'd been in, or the fact that Michael Theodakis had come to her rescue.

He must, she thought, have been watching very closely to have noticed her drink being spiked. But his attention would have been attracted by Stavros whom he'd clearly identified as trouble.

And he'd naturally be anxious to avoid any whiff of scandal being attached to his hotel, however marginal that might be. But whatever his motivation, she couldn't deny she'd had a lucky escape.

Shuddering, Kate sat up, shaking the tangle of red hair back from her face in an effort to dispel the faint muzziness which still plagued her—and paused, her attention suddenly, alarmingly arrested.

Because this room bore signs of occupation which had nothing to do with her, she realised, her heart thumping. Like a brush and comb and toiletries on the mirrored dressing table, a leather travel bag standing on a trestle in one corner, and a man's jacket tossed on to one of the blue armchairs by the window. And she could have no doubt about the identity of their owner.

She whispered, 'Oh God,' and sank back against the pillows, her mouth dry, and her mind working overtime.

Just exactly what had happened during the night? she asked herself desperately. And to be precise, what had happened after Michael Theodakis had carried her up here in his arms? Carried her to his room. His bed.

Because that she did most certainly recall, even if the rest was just a jumble of confused impressions.

But that was the effect of the date-rape drug, she reminded herself. It rendered you insensible. And it was only some time afterwards, if at all, that you remembered what had been done to you. And while she'd been unconscious, any kind of advantage could have been taken of her, she thought, swallowing painfully against her tight throat muscles.

Was it possible that during the hours of darkness, her rescuer could have turned predator?

Slowly, reluctantly, she made herself remember her

dream—that shivering, frenzied erotic ravishment that had tormented her unconscious mind.

But had it really been a dream, she wondered, staring, horrified, at the disordered bed—or stark reality?

Surely she would know—there would be some physical sign—if her body had been subjected to that level of sensual possession.

Or would she? Was this deep, unfamiliar ache inside her induced by physical frustration—or a passionate satisfaction that was entirely new to her?

Kate realised with shock that she could not be sure. And that maybe she never would be, which was, somehow, infinitely worse.

Oh, dear God, she thought, in panic. I've got to get out of here.

But where were her clothes? she wondered, staring fruitlessly round the room. Apart from her shoes, left by the bed, they seemed to have vanished completely.

And, as she absorbed this, a door opened and Michael Theodakis walked in.

Kate grabbed frantically at the slipping sheet holding it against her breasts, as her shocked brain registered that he himself was wearing nothing more than a towel draped round his hips. The rest of him was smooth olive skin, and rippling muscles, and in spite of herself, she found the breath catching in her throat.

He halted, looking her over slowly, brows lifted and eyes brilliant with amusement. He said '*Kalimera.* So you're awake at last.'

She stared at him, her pulse rate growing crazy. A sick certainty welling up inside her.

She said hoarsely, 'What—what are you doing here?'

'Shaving,' he said. 'A habit I acquired in adolescence.' He nodded towards the room he'd just left. 'I am sorry that we have to share a bathroom, but now you have it to yourself.'

'Share?' she said. 'A bathroom?'

'This suite only has one.' He seemed totally at ease with the situation, and with his lack of clothing too. But undoubtedly he was used to displaying himself in front of women in a towel, or even without one.

Whereas she—she was strangling in this bloody sheet.

'Which does not matter when I am here alone, as I usually am,' he went on.

'But last night,' Kate said, her voice shaking. 'Was different.'

'Of course,' he said softly. 'Because you were here.' He paused. 'I have ordered breakfast to be served to us on the terrace. Would you like me to run a bath for you?'

'No,' she said. 'I think I've had enough personal services for one lifetime. Like being undressed and put to bed last night.'

'You could not do it for yourself.' He made it all sound so reasonable, she thought in helpless outrage. 'You were barely conscious, *pedhi mou.*'

'I'm aware of that,' Kate said between her teeth. 'And I am not your little one.'

He frowned slightly. 'You have had a shock,' he said. 'But it is over now, and you have come to no harm.'

'Perhaps I don't see it like that.' The sheet was slipping, and she hitched it up, anchoring it with her arms. A gesture that was not lost on him.

There was still laughter in his eyes, but that had been joined by another element. Something darker—more disturbing. Something she had glimpsed in those dark, heated hours in the night, but did not want to recognise again.

Yet, at the same time, she realised that she had to confront him—had to know. Had to…

'Then how do you see it?' The dark eyes moved over her in frank assessment. He was enjoying this, she thought, her anger mounting. 'Maybe we can reach a compromise.'

Kate drew a shaky breath. 'I'd prefer the truth. Did you come to this room during the night.'

'Yes. I came to check that you were all right. So did the housekeeper, and also the hotel doctor. It was quite a procession,' he added drily.

She swallowed. 'But you were also here alone.'

He frowned. 'I have said so.'

She touched her dry lips with her tongue.

'Did you—touch me?'

There was a silence. Then, 'Yes,' he said quietly. 'I did not mean you to know, but I could not resist. Your hair looked so beautiful spread across my pillow. I had this irresistible desire to feel it under my hand.'

She stared at him. 'And was that all—your only irresistible desire, Kyrios Theodakis?'

He sighed. 'There was a tear on your cheek. I brushed it away.'

'And then you left,' she said. 'Is that what I'm supposed to believe?'

The dark eyes narrowed. He said softly, 'What are you trying to say?'

Kate bit her lip. 'Where exactly did you spend the night, Mr Theodakis?'

'This is a suite, Kyria Dennison. There are two bedrooms. I slept in the second. And I slept well. I hope you did too,' he added courteously.

'No,' she said. 'I didn't. I had the strangest dreams.'

The dark eyes narrowed. 'The effect of the drug, perhaps.'

'Perhaps,' she said. 'But this was such a vivid dream. So realistic.'

'You are fortunate,' he drawled. 'I rarely remember mine.'

'I'd give a hell of a lot,' Kate said stormily, 'not to remember this one.'

'You interest me.' He was frowning again, his eyes fixed watchfully on her flushed face. 'You can describe it to me over breakfast.'

'I don't want any breakfast,' she hurled at him. 'And I certainly don't want to eat with you. Because I don't believe it was a dream at all—you unspeakable bastard. Any more than I believe you spent the night in another room.'

His brows lifted. 'You're saying this dream involved me in some way?'

He sounded politely interested, no more. But there was a new tension in the tall figure. A sudden electricity in the room.

'Yes, I am. I'm saying you—used me last night.'

'"Used",' Michael Theodakis said musingly. 'An interesting choice of word. Do you mean that we made love?'

Kate's voice shook. 'I said exactly what I meant. And you took a filthy advantage of me. Oh, you're so damned sure of yourself,' she went on recklessly. 'So convinced that you're the answer to any woman's prayer. I expect you thought I'd be honoured—if I ever remembered.'

'So let us test this memory of yours,' he said softly. 'Tell me, *agapi mou*, exactly what I did to you.'

She said defensively, 'I can't recall the actual details.'

'But was it good for you?' He sounded almost casual. 'You must remember that. For instance, did you come?'

Kate gasped, colour flooding her face. 'How dare you.'

'But I need to know. I would hate to think I had disappointed you in any way.' He walked slowly towards her. 'Perhaps I should—jog your memory a little.'

'Keep away from me.' Kate shrank back.

'But why?' There was danger in his voice. He bent lithely, retrieving one of the pillows from the floor. Tossing it on to the bed beside her. His smile did not reach his eyes as he looked at her. 'When we have already been so close—so intimate? And this time, my beautiful one, I will make sure that you do not forget—anything.'

His hand snaked out, hooking into the folds of linen tucked above her breasts, and tugging them free, uncovering her completely.

Kate gave a small wounded cry, and turned instinctively on to her side, curling into a ball, and sheltering her body with her hands from the arrogance of his gaze, as humiliated tears burned in her throat.

'Why so modest?' His tone lashed her. 'According to you, there is nothing that I have not already seen and enjoyed.'

'Please,' she managed, chokingly. 'Please—don't…'

'But I am an unspeakable bastard, *agapi mou*,' he said softly. 'So why should I listen?'

She couldn't think of a single reason, huddled there on his bed, her breath catching on a sob.

For a moment there was silence and a heart-stopping stillness, then he sighed harshly, and turned away. He picked up a towelling robe from a chair and tossed it down to her.

'Put this on,' he directed curtly. 'You will find it safer than a sheet.'

As she obeyed hurriedly, clumsily, he went on, 'As you have just discovered, I have a temper, *thespinis*, so do not provoke me again. I have never taken a woman in anger in my life,' he added grimly. 'I do not wish you to be the first.'

She wrapped herself in the robe, tying the sash with shaking fingers.

He came to the side of the bed and took her chin in his hands, forcing her to look up at him.

He said quietly, 'The mind can play strange tricks, *pedhi mou*. But I swear I did not share your bed last night. Because if I had done so, you would have remembered, believe me.'

For a fleeting moment, his hands cupped her breasts through the thickness of the robe, his touch burning against her skin, making her nipples harden in sudden, painful need.

She heard herself gasp, then she was free, and he had stepped back from her.

He said, 'I am going to dress. Then you will join me for breakfast.'

She found the remains of her voice. 'My—clothes…?'

'My housekeeper took them to be laundered—after she undressed you last night.' He allowed her to absorb that.

'They will be returned to you after you have eaten.' He paused. 'Shall we say half an hour?'

And left her, staring after him, her bottom lip caught painfully in her teeth.

As she slid down into the scented bubbles of the bath, Kate was almost tempted to go one stage further, and drown herself.

Since the moment she'd opened her eyes that morning, she'd behaved like a crazy woman. But now she was sane again, and hideously embarrassed to go with it.

Oh, God, what had possessed her to hurl those accusations at Michael Theodakis? she asked herself despairingly.

Well, she supposed it had been triggered by him strolling in, next door to naked, and behaving as if it was an ordinary occurrence. As it probably was to him, but not to her…

She stopped right there, her brows snapping together.

What on earth was she talking about? Working as a holiday rep she encountered men far more skimpily clad every day, and had never found it any kind of problem.

So, why had she over-reacted so ludicrously? It made no sense. She bit her lip, as the realisation dawned that it was nothing to do with the way he'd been dressed—or undressed, and never had been.

It was Michael Theodakis himself who'd rattled her—sent her spinning out of control.

From the moment she'd seen him, she'd been on edge, aware of him in a way that was totally outside her limited experience. She'd been on the defensive even before he'd addressed one word to her.

And the dream, she guessed miserably, had simply been a spin-off from being carried upstairs in his arms. Maybe some humiliating form of wish-fulfilment.

So, she'd behaved like an hysterical fool and, in turn, been treated pretty much with the contempt she deserved, she thought, wincing.

She should have stuck to Plan A and just left quietly. After all, she could always have rung the apartment and got Lisa to bring her a change of clothes.

Lisa…

Kate groaned aloud. Until that moment, she hadn't spared her flatmate a thought. And anything could have happened to her.

This, she thought forcefully, is not like me.

Overnight she seemed to have turned into a stranger—and a stranger she didn't like very much.

In spite of her red hair, she'd always been cool, level-headed Kate, and she wanted her old self back. Michael Theodakis might be a devastatingly attractive man with a powerful sexual charisma, but that did not mean she had to go to pieces when she was around him.

Polite, grateful and unreachable. That was the way to handle the next half hour. The only way.

And then she would be gone, not just from this hotel, but from Greece too, and she would never have to set eyes on him again.

She dried herself and reluctantly donned the towelling robe again, knotting the sash for extra insurance. It masked her from throat to ankle, but it didn't inspire the confidence her own clothes would have done, and she needed all the assurance she could get, she thought wretchedly.

She combed her hair with her fingers, and emerged reluctantly into the bedroom, steeling herself to walk to the windows.

Outside, a table had been laid, overlooking the sea. And here Michael Theodakis was waiting, leaning against the balustrade in the sunlight.

Kate drew a deep breath, stuck her hands in the pockets of the robe to hide the fact that they were trembling, and went out to join him.

He was wearing shorts, which showed off those endless legs, she observed waspishly, and a short-sleeved polo shirt, open at the throat and affording a glimpse of the shadowing of body hair she'd already had plenty of opportunity to observe.

He said quietly, '*Kalimera*—for the second time. Or shall we erase the events of the past hour, which do credit to neither of us, and pretend it is the first?'

'Yes.' Kate looked down at the tiled floor, aware that she was blushing. 'Maybe we should—do that.'

'At last,' he said. 'We agree on something.'

She hastily transferred her attention to the table, set with a jug of chilled fruit juice, a basket of crisp rolls, dishes of honey and dark cherry jam, a bowl of thick, creamy yoghurt, a platter of grapes, apricots and peaches, and a tall pot of coffee.

She forced a smile. 'It all looks—delicious.'

'Yes,' he said softly, a quiver of amusement in his voice. 'It does.'

She found she was trembling suddenly, hotly aware that he was still looking at her, and not the food.

'Please sit down,' he went on, and Kate moved round the table, choosing a chair that would be as far away from him as it was possible to get, without actually jumping off the terrace. And she might even try that if all else failed.

'I hope you found your bath soothing,' he said silkily, as he poured the juice into glasses, and handed her one.

'Yes,' Kate said. 'Thank you.'

'But perhaps a body massage might be even more relaxing,' he went on. 'If you would like one, you have only to ask.'

Kate thumped an inoffensive bread roll on to her plate.

'How kind of you,' she said grittily. 'But I'll pass.'

He smiled at her. 'It was not a personal offer, *thespinis*. We have an excellent masseuse at the health spa, who comes highly recommended. But it's your decision.'

Wrong-footed again, thought Kate, taking a gulp of fruit juice and wishing dispassionately that it was hemlock.

'Honey?' Michael Theodakis proffered the dish. 'It might sweeten your disposition,' he added casually.

'My disposition is fine.' Kate spooned some on to her plate. 'Perhaps you just bring out the worst in me, Kyrios Theodakis.'

'My name is Michael,' he said. 'Or Mick, if you prefer. Just as you are Kate, rather than Katharina.'

She put down her knife. 'How do you know my name?' she demanded huskily.

He shrugged. 'Your papers were in the purse you left in the club last night. I did not think your identity was a secret. Besides, the police needed to know.'

'The police.' She stared at him, lips parted in shock, eyes widening.

'Of course.' He sounded matter of fact. 'Your friend Stavros also had ecstasy tablets in his possession when he was searched. Both he and his cousin spent the night in jail. The first of many, I suspect.'

'And Lisa?' Kate asked, with distress. 'Oh, God, they didn't lock her up too, surely.'

'No,' he said. 'I arranged for her to have her freedom. But it is as well she is leaving Zycos today, and I doubt she will ever be permitted to return. She keeps bad company.'

'You—arranged?' Kate said with disbelief. She shook her head. 'How gratifying to have such power.'

'No,' he said, and gave her a cool smile. 'Merely useful sometimes.'

Kate ate some bread and honey, forcing it past her dry throat.

At last she said stiltedly, 'I must sound very ungracious, *kyrie*.' She took a breath. 'I—I have to be grateful, to you, naturally. You saved me from potential disaster, but, for the rest of it, I'm totally out of my depth here.' She shook her head. 'Drug dealers—jail—I've never experienced these things before. I don't know how to handle them.'

He said quite gently, 'You don't have to, *thespinis*. They

have been dealt with for you. Please do not allow them to cloud your memories of Zycos.' He picked up the silver pot. 'Coffee?'

But, as she took the cup from him with a subdued murmur of thanks, Kate knew that it would not be her brush with the horror of Dimitris that would return to haunt her in the days to come, but the thought of this man, and the smile in his dark eyes. The warmth of his body, and the remembered scent of his skin as she'd been carried in his arms.

And, even more disturbingly, that there wasn't a thing she could do about it.

It was not the easiest meal Kate had ever eaten.

The necessity to appear untroubled—to make light, social conversation without revealing her inner turmoil—was an unlooked-for struggle.

'The weather's still wonderful,' she said over-brightly, after a pause. 'But I suppose it can't last forever.'

'Very little does.' He was preparing a peach, his long fingers deft, but he looked across at her and smiled. 'Did you know that the sun turns your hair to fire?'

'I'm aware it's red,' Kate said, with something of a snap. 'You don't need to labour the point.'

'And you should learn to accept a compliment with more grace, *matia mou*,' he said drily. 'Make the most of the sun,' he added. 'Because it will rain soon.'

She looked up at the cloudless sky. 'How do you know?'

He shrugged. 'These are my islands. It is my business to know. And our autumns tend to be damp.'

'Are you from Zycos originally?'

'No.' There was a sudden curtness in his voice. 'I was born on Kefalonia, and my real home was always there.'

'But no longer?' She remembered Stavros mentioning a family dispute.

He was silent for a moment. Then, 'I travel a great deal.

I have no permanent base just now.' He paused again. 'And you?'

'I share a flat in London.'

He frowned. 'With this Lisa?' There was a sudden austerity in his voice.

'Oh, no,' Kate said hastily. 'We were colleagues here for the season, and it just seemed—convenient. My flatmate in London is called Sandy, and she's very different. She works as a researcher on a national newspaper.' She hesitated. 'I shall—miss her when I move.'

'You are planning to do so?' He sounded politely interested.

'Yes,' she said. She took a deep breath. 'Actually—I'm going to be married. Quite soon. So—you see—I have every reason to be grateful for what you did for me. And I do—thank you. Very much indeed.'

There was silence—a slow tingling silence that threatened to stretch into eternity. Expressionlessly, Michael Theodakis looked down at her ringless hands. Studied them. Returned to her face.

He said, 'You are very much in love?'

'Naturally.' Kate stiffened defensively.

'And is it also natural to enjoy erotic fantasies about another man—a stranger?'

Her mouth was suddenly very dry. 'My fiancé is the one who matters. I'm not interested in anyone else.'

'Truly?' he asked softly. 'I wonder.' He pushed back his chair and came round the table to her, pulling her up out of her seat. His arms went round her, pulling her close to his body. Then he bent his head and kissed her, slowly and very thoroughly, his enjoyment of her mouth unashamedly sensuous.

Time stilled. His tongue was slow fire against hers, the practised mouth teaching her things she'd never known she needed to learn. Suddenly, she couldn't breathe—or think.

When he released her at last, he was smiling.

He said, 'I think, *pedhi mou*, that you are fooling yourself.'

Kate took a step backwards. She brushed a shaky hand across her burning lips, her eyes sparking anger at him. Anger she could shelter behind. 'You're despicable,' she flung at him. 'You had no right to do that—no right at all.'

He shrugged an unperturbed shoulder. 'Why not? I am a single man. You are a single woman.'

'But I told you. I'm going to be married.'

'Yes,' he said. 'You did. Be sure to send me an invitation to the wedding. If it ever happens. Because if I was going to marry you, Katharina *mou*, I would make sure you only dreamed of me.'

He lifted her hand, and dropped a brief kiss on to its palm, then turned and walked away into the suite, and out of her life.

Leaving her standing there in the sunlight, looking after him, white-faced and totally defenceless.

CHAPTER FOUR

SHE had a lot to think about on the flight back to Britain.

But her priority was the deliberate, systematic banishment of Mick Theodakis from her mind. Because there was nothing to be gained from remembering the glinting amusement in his dark eyes, or the incredible feel of his mouth on hers. Nothing at all.

So, she made herself contemplate her immediate future instead, which, to her dismay, proved just as tricky.

Because she knew with total and shattering certainty that she couldn't marry Grant. Not any more.

Clearly, he would want to know why she'd changed her mind, she thought wretchedly, and she didn't have a single reason to give that made any real sense, even to herself.

And whatever she said would be bound to hurt him, she thought wincing, and she didn't want to do that. Perhaps she could say that her time in Greece had changed her in some basic way. That she wasn't the same person any longer.

After all, it was no more than the truth.

But she had to recognise that she hadn't harboured a single doubt about her future with Grant until Michael Theodakis had crossed her path. Which was crazy, because you didn't overturn your entire life because of a casual kiss from a seasoned womaniser.

She needed to remember that, for Mick Theodakis, the kiss had been little more than a reflex action, she thought, plus an element of punishment for misjudging him.

All this she knew. So, why didn't it make any real difference?

She was still wondering when she walked into Arrivals

and saw Grant waiting for her, smiling, with a bouquet of flowers.

Kate's heart sank. She'd been counting on a slight breathing space before they met.

'Darling.' His arms hugged her close. 'God, I've missed you. From now on, I don't let you out of my sight. We have a wedding to plan, and I can't wait.'

She walked beside him in silence to the car, wondering how to begin.

'So, where's the crazy Lisa?' Grant asked cheerfully, as he stowed her bags in the boot. 'I thought she'd be with you.'

Kate bit her lip, remembering how she'd returned to the apartment to find it bare and empty, with Lisa's keys discarded on the living room table.

She said quietly, 'She decided to take another flight.' She took a deep breath, knowing she couldn't pretend—or hedge any more. 'Grant—I have something to tell you.'

His reaction was every bit as bad as she'd feared. He started with frank disbelief, moved to bewilderment, then to resentment and real anger.

On the whole, she thought, standing outside her flat, watching him drive away, the anger had been the easiest to cope with.

And now she had to deal with Sandy.

'Where's Grant?' was her flatmate's first inevitable question, after a welcoming hug. 'I was going to open a bottle of wine, then tactfully vanish.'

'No need.' Kate squared her shoulders. 'Grant and I are no longer an item.'

Sandy stared at her. 'When did this happen?'

'At the airport. He was making plans. I realised I couldn't let him.'

'Fair enough,' Sandy said equably. 'So—who's the new man?'

'Grant asked that too,' Kate said, aware that she was flushing. 'Why should my breaking up with him imply there's someone else?'

'Because that's the way it generally works.' Sandy poured the wine. 'So don't tell me he doesn't exist.'

Kate paused. 'It was nothing.'

'Then you did meet someone,' Sandy said triumphantly. 'I knew it.'

'No,' Kate shook her head. 'I *encountered* someone. Very briefly. Big difference.'

'Details please?'

'His name was Theodakis,' Kate said reluctantly. 'His family owns the Regina hotel chain, plus the Odyssey cruise fleet, and the Helicon airline. Does that tell you enough?'

'Absolutely.' Sandy gave her a narrow-eyed look. 'And that's a hell of a lot of info for just a brief encounter.'

'He didn't tell me all of it.' Kate's flush deepened. 'I—looked him up on the office computer before I went to the airport.'

'Good move.' Sandy approved. 'When's the wedding, and please may I be bridesmaid? I'd like to meet his friends.'

'I doubt he has any,' Kate said with a snap. 'He's arrogant and totally impossible.'

'Yet he's made you think twice about Grant, who's always been the soul of sweet reason.' Sandy clicked her tongue. 'I spy muddled thinking here, babe.'

'Not at all,' Kate retorted with dignity. 'I simply found out that absence—hadn't made my heart grow fonder.'

'Ah,' said Sandy. 'In that case, you should have no problem getting over Mr Theodakis either.' She raised her glass. 'Good luck,' she added cheerfully. 'You're going to need it.'

When Kate reported for duty at Halcyon's head offices a couple of days later, she was aware of an atmosphere, and sideways looks from other members of staff.

It didn't take her long to discover that Lisa had been fired, and had openly blamed Kate for getting her into trouble with the Greek police.

When the other girl came in to collect some paperwork, Kate confronted her, but Lisa remained obdurate.

'You dropped us all in it,' she accused. 'Now the lads are in jail, and I've got a police record. I'll probably never work in Greece again.'

'Lisa,' Kate said quietly. 'Stavros and Dimitris spiked my drink. They were seen doing it.'

'Rubbish,' Lisa said defiantly. 'It was just a giggle—something to relax you, and take the starch out of your knickers. You—over-reacted.'

'They were also carrying ecstasy tablets.' Kate spread her hands. 'They were drug dealers, Lisa. They could have caused us more trouble than we've ever dreamed of.'

Lisa shrugged, her face hard. She said, 'A word of advice. Whatever you may think of Stavros and Dimitris, they aren't even in the same league as Mick Theodakis. When it comes to ruthless, he invented the word. I don't know why he chose to meddle, but he probably had his own devious reasons. Because Sir Galahad he ain't.'

Kate bit her lip. 'Thanks—but I never thought he was.'

The next two weeks were difficult ones, especially when Grant decided to launch a charm offensive to win her back, turning up at the flat in the evening with flowers, bottles of wine, theatre tickets and invitations to dinner, all of which she steadfastly refused.

Work helped. Halcyon's winter City Breaks programme took her away a lot and, when she was at home, she let the answering machine field Grant's increasingly plaintive calls.

And eventually, her life steadied and found a new rhythm. A new purpose. One which did not include any lingering memories of Michael Theodakis, she told herself determinedly. And certainly no regrets.

After a weekend trip to Rome which had thrown up more than its fair share of problems, she was spending a wet

November afternoon at the office, working on a detailed report, when reception buzzed to say she had a visitor.

Kate groaned inwardly. Surely not Grant, again, she thought glumly as she rode down in the lift. He was beginning to be a nuisance, and she'd have to instruct Debbie to say she wasn't there in future.

She was already rehearsing the words, 'This has got to stop,' when the lift doors opened, and she stepped out into the foyer, to be brought up short, the blood draining from her face as she saw exactly who awaited her.

'Katharina,' Michael Theodakis said softly. 'It is good to see you again.'

Goodness, Kate thought breathlessly, has nothing to do with it.

He was lounging against the desk, immaculate in a formal suit and dark overcoat. Dressed for the City, for meetings and high-powered business deals. Smooth, she thought. Civilised. But she wasn't fooled for a moment.

She felt as if she'd strayed into a pet shop, and found a tiger on the loose.

Her mouth was suddenly dry. 'Mr Theodakis—what are you doing here?'

'I came to find you *matia mou*. What else?' He smiled at her, totally at his ease, the dark eyes making an unhurried assessment of her.

Making her feel, in spite of her neat grey flannel skirt and matching wool shirt, curiously undressed.

She said, her voice barely a whisper. 'I don't understand…'

'Then I will explain.' He straightened. The tiger, she thought, about to leap.

'Get your coat,' he directed. 'I have a car waiting.'

'But I'm working,' Kate said, desperately searching for a lifeline. 'I can't just—leave.'

'Mr Harris says you can, Miss Dennison.' Debbie, who'd been devouring him shamelessly with her gaze, broke in eagerly. 'Mr Theodakis spoke to him just now. I put him through,' she added proudly.

'Oh,' Kate said in a hollow voice. 'I see.'

One mention of the Theodakis name, she knew, would be enough to get the Halcyon boss jumping through hoops. He would dearly love to get exclusive rights at the Regina hotels for his holidays. And, quite suddenly, Kate had become the possible means to that end. Or so he would think.

In the cloakroom, Kate thrust her arms clumsily into the sleeves of her raincoat, but did not attempt to fasten it because her hands were shaking too much. When she tried to renew her lipstick, she ended up dropping the tube into the washbasin. Better not try again, she thought as she retrieved it, or she'd end up looking like a clown.

And she felt quite stupid enough already.

She found herself avoiding Debbie's envious glance as Michael Theodakis took her arm and walked her through the glass doors to the street.

The car was at the kerb, with a chauffeur waiting deferentially to open the door.

What else? Kate thought, as she sank into the luxury of the leather seating. And either I've gone crazy, or this is a dream, and presently I'll be awake again.

But there was nothing remotely dream-like about the man sitting beside her in the back of this limousine. He was living, breathing flesh and blood, and her every nerve-ending was tingling in acknowledgement of this. In terrifying awareness.

As the car drew away, he said, 'You are trembling. Why?'

No point in denial, she realised. He saw too much.

She said, 'I think I'm in shock.' She made herself look at him, meet the lurking laughter in his dark eyes. 'You're the last person in the world I ever expected to see again.'

He grinned at her, the lean body relaxed and graceful. 'Truly? Or did you just hope that I was out of your life?'

Kate lifted her chin. 'That too.'

'Then I am sorry to disappoint you,' he said without any

sign of contrition. 'But it was inevitable. The world is such a small place, Katharina *mou*. I always knew we would meet again. And I decided it should be sooner rather than later.'

Kate sat bolt upright. 'I can't think why.'

'Naturally, I wished to make sure you had recovered from your traumatic experience on Zycos,' he said silkily. 'Have you?'

'I never give it a thought,' Kate said shortly, resisting the urge to ask which particular trauma he was referring to.

'You are blessed with a convenient memory, *matia mou*.' His tone was dry. He looked her over, his glance lingering on the thrust of her breasts under the thin wool. 'You have lost weight a little. Why?'

'I lead a busy life.' His scrutiny brought a faint flush to her cheeks.

'Then you should make time to relax,' he said. 'Taste the wine. Feel the sun on your face.'

Kate sent a dry look towards the drenched streets. 'Not much chance of that today.'

'There is always sun somewhere, *agapi mou*.' He spoke softly. 'You must learn to follow it.'

'Then why aren't you doing so?'

'Because I am here—with you.' He paused. 'It is too early for dinner, so I thought we would go somewhere for tea. I told my driver the Ritz, but perhaps you'd prefer somewhere else.'

'That would be fine, although I can't imagine you'll find afternoon tea very exciting.' Kate tried to speak lightly.

He said gently, 'But you have yet to learn what excites me, Katharina.'

Kate's throat tightened. She felt herself blushing again, and bent her head slightly. A strand of hair fell across her cheek and she lifted a hand to brush it back.

He said, 'Leave it. You should not wear your hair scraped back from your face.'

'It's neat,' she said. 'And tidy. For work.'

'But you are not working now. And I like to see your hair loose on your shoulders. Or across a pillow,' he added softly.

Her face burned. 'But I don't style it to please you, Kyrios Theodakis.'

He smiled at her. 'Not yet, anyway.'

Kate tucked the errant tress behind her ear with a certain stony emphasis.

Immediately, she felt the focus of his attention shift. He moved sharply, his fingers closing round her wrists, capturing her hands while he studied them.

Kate tried to pull away. 'What are you doing?'

'Still no ring, *agapi mou*?' There was an odd note in his voice. 'Your lover cannot be very ardent. He should tell the whole world that you belong to him.'

Kate looked down at her lap. 'I—we decided to wait a little longer. That's all.'

His tone hardened. 'Katharina—look at me.'

Reluctantly, she obeyed, almost flinching at the sudden intensity of his gaze.

'Now,' he said. 'Tell me the truth. Are you engaged to this man? Do you plan to be married?'

She knew what she should do. She should tell him it was none of his damned business, and request him to stop the car and let her out.

The silence seemed to close round them. The air was suddenly heavy. Charged.

Kate swallowed helplessly. She heard herself say, 'I—I'm not seeing him. It's over.'

'Ah,' he said softly. 'Then that changes everything. Does it not, *agapi mou*?' Still watching the bewildered play of colour in her face, he lifted one hand, and then the other to his lips.

At the brush of his mouth, she found herself pierced by such an agony of need that she had to bite down on her lip to stop herself crying out.

Her voice shook. 'No. *Kyrie*—please...'

He made no attempt to release her. The dark eyes glittered at her. 'Say my name.'

'Mr Theodakis…'

'No.' His voice was urgent. 'Say my name as I wish to hear it. As you, in your heart, want to speak it. Say it now.'

Her mouth trembled. 'Michalis—*mou*.'

'At last you admit it.' There was a note of shaken laughter under the words. 'And now I will tell you why I am here. Because there is still unfinished business between us. I know it, and so do you.' He paused. 'Is it not so?'

'Yes.' Her voice was barely audible.

He made a slight, unsmiling inclination of his head, then leaned across and tapped imperatively on the driver's glass partition.

He said. 'The Royal Empress Hotel. And hurry.'

They stood together in the lift as it sped upwards. They were silent, but Kate could hear the sound of her own breathing, harsh, even erratic.

They did not touch, but every inch of her was quivering as if it already knew the caress of his hand.

Her heart was thudding painfully, as he unlocked the door, and ushered her into the large sitting room beyond.

Mutely, Kate allowed herself to be divested of her raincoat, then stood, trying to compose herself as she took stock of her surroundings.

It was a beautiful room, she saw, with elegant, highly polished furniture and large pastel sofas, complementing an exquisite washed Chinese carpet.

One wall seemed to be all glass, giving a panoramic view of the Thames.

And a door standing ajar allowed a glimpse of the bedroom with its king-size bed draped in oyster satin. Bringing her suddenly, joltingly back to a reality.

Dry-mouthed, she thought, 'What am I doing here?'

She knew she was being ridiculous. She was a grown

woman, and she was here of her own free will, but she was still as nervous as a teenager on her first date.

Because the truth was that she didn't really know what to expect. Not this time.

She'd been alone with Grant often, she reminded herself with a kind of desperation, either at her place or his, but she'd never felt like this. Never been so much at a loss, or in this kind of emotional turmoil.

But then her relationship with Grant had been quite different. They'd been finding out slowly and cautiously whether they might have a future together.

But, if she was honest, she'd never burned for him. Craved the touch of his mouth—the caress of his hands on her body. Never been so conscious of his sheer physical presence. She'd assumed that going to bed with Grant would be the final confirmation of their commitment to each other. Settled, even comfortable.

But with Michael Theodakis she could make none of those assumptions.

He would demand total surrender, and the thought of losing control of her body—and her emotions—so completely frankly terrified her.

But that wasn't all.

The brutal reality of the situation was that she'd come here to go to bed with a man she hardly knew. Someone infinitely more experienced than she was, who might well make demands she could not fulfil.

Biting her lip, she took a quick look over her shoulder.

He'd discarded his overcoat and jacket and was on the phone, waistcoat unbuttoned, tugging at his tie with impatient fingers as he talked.

She wandered across to the rainwashed window, and stared out, her thoughts going crazy.

If she told him she'd changed her mind, how would he react? she wondered apprehensively. He'd warned her that he had a temper. Could she risk provoking him again?

He replaced the receiver and came over to her, sliding his arms round her waist and drawing her back to lean against him. He bent his head, putting his lips against the side of her neck where the tiny pulse thundered.

He said softly, 'I hope you like champagne. I've asked them to send some up.'

'Yes,' she said breathlessly. 'That would be—lovely.' She glanced back at the window. 'On a fine day, this view should be spectacular.'

Oh, God, she thought. She was actually making conversation about the weather.

'Then it's fortunate it is raining.' He sounded amused. 'So we do not have to waste time admiring it.'

He turned her to face him, his hand sliding under the edge of her shirt to find the delicate ridge of her spine. Making her shiver in nervous anticipation as his fingers splayed across the sensitive skin.

He pulled her intimately, dangerously close to him, forcing her to the awareness that he was already strongly, powerfully aroused.

She stood awkwardly in the circle of his arms, her heart thudding. She thought, 'I don't know what to do…'

He cupped her face in his hands, making her look up at him.

He said. 'You are shaking. What is there to frighten you?'

She tried to smile. 'There's—you.'

His mouth twisted wryly. 'I am only a man, Katharina *mou*, not a monster. And I ask nothing that you have not given before.'

She said huskily, 'That's just the problem.'

He frowned slightly. 'I don't understand.'

She swallowed. 'Michael—I just don't—do things like this.'

His face was solemn, but his eyes were dancing. 'Is that a matter of principle, *agapi mou*, or do you simply not want to do them with me?'

She said baldly, 'I mean I never have.'

There was a pause. 'But you were seeing a man,' he said quietly. 'A man you planned to marry.'

'Yes,' she said. 'But we weren't—living together. We decided to—wait until I came back from Greece.'

He was very still. 'And before that?'

'There was no one I cared about sufficiently.' She stared rigidly at the pattern on his loosened tie. 'I—I always swore to myself that I'd avoid casual sex. That I'd only ever go to bed with a man if I couldn't help myself. If the alternative was altogether more than I could bear. I—I suppose I felt it should actually mean something…'

Her voice tailed off into silence.

'And now?' he asked.

She shook her head. 'I just don't—know any more.' She looked at him. 'I'm sorry. I should never have come here. I don't know what I was thinking of.' Her voice rose a little. 'I mean, we're strangers, for God's sake.'

'Hardly strangers,' he reminded her, a note of laughter in his voice. 'After all, you have spent one night in my bed already.'

'Yes,' she said huskily. 'But that time I was alone. Now it would be—different.'

'Yes,' he said. 'It would.'

There was another silence, as he looked down at her, his eyes meditative. His thumb stroked her cheek, and moved rhythmically along the line of her jaw, and the curve of her throat above her collar. She caught her breath, her heart juddering frantically.

'You don't want me to touch you?' he asked gently.

'I—didn't say that.'

'Then you think I will be unkind—uncaring in bed? That I will not give you pleasure?'

He sounded completely matter of fact—as if he was asking whether she preferred classical music to jazz, she thought wildly.

She said shakily, 'It's—not that. I'm scared I won't know how to please you. That you'll be disappointed.' She paused. 'You've had so many other women.'

'But never you, *matia mou*,' he said. 'Never until this moment. And while I have been seen with a great many women, I have actually slept with very few of them. Perhaps I think it should mean something too,' he added drily.

'Then—why me?'

He swung her round, so that she could see herself reflected in the window. He pulled the clip from her hair, letting it tumble in a shining mass on her shoulders.

'Look at yourself.' His voice was oddly harsh. 'This is the picture of you that I have carried in my mind—in my heart all these weeks. That has tormented me by day and kept me from sleep at night. And now I want the reality of you, naked in my arms. But, if necessary, I am prepared to wait. Until you are ready.'

She said unevenly, 'And if you have to wait a long time?'

He shrugged. 'I can be patient. But, ultimately, I expect my patience to be rewarded.'

He turned her round to face him, his hands framing her face.

'Do you accept that, Katharina?' His eyes seemed to pierce her soul. 'Do you agree that one day—one night—when you cannot help yourself—you will come to me?'

'Yes.' Her voice was a thread of sound.

He smiled, and released her, stepping back.

He said quietly, 'Then it begins.'

CHAPTER FIVE

AND that was where it should also have ended, Kate told herself bitterly.

She should have taken advantage of the brief respite he'd offered, and vanished. After all, Halcyon owed her leave, and she could have gone anywhere. Stayed away until he'd tired of waiting, and gone back to Greece. And found someone else to act as his smokescreen.

Her hair was dry, so, wearily, she began to make preparations for the night, turning off the fire, extinguishing lights, rinsing her beaker in the kitchen.

She was tired, but her mind would not let her relax from this emotional treadmill.

Oh, she'd been so easy to deceive, she thought, staring into the darkness. So eager to believe anything that he told her—to accept all that he seemed to be offering.

And he'd been clever too, making her think that she was in control—that she was making the choice. When really he'd been playing her like some little fish on his line.

Starting with that first afternoon…

The champagne had arrived with a bowl of strawberries, and a plate of small almond biscuits.

Michael had beckoned to her. 'Come and drink some wine with me,' he invited. 'And let us talk.'

Kate walked reluctantly across the room and seated herself on one corner of the sofa he indicated while he occupied the other.

'Is this a safe distance?' he asked mockingly, as he handed her a flute of champagne. 'I am not sure of the rules in this situation.'

'I expect you usually write your own.' The champagne was exquisitely cool and refreshing in her dry mouth.

'In business, certainly.' His tone was silky. 'But not usually in pleasure.' He let her digest that, then picked a strawberry from the dish, dipped it in champagne, and held it out to her. 'Try this.'

Kate bit delicately at the fruit, feeling self-conscious. 'That's—delicious.'

'Yes.' He was watching her mouth, as he took the next bite himself. 'It is.'

Kate crossed her feet at the ankles, nervously smoothing her skirt over her knees. 'So what do you want to talk about?'

'It occurred to me that we might get to know each other a little better.' He drank some champagne. 'What do you think?'

She shrugged nervously. 'If you wish. What do you want to know?'

'Everything.' He offered her another champagne-soaked strawberry. 'Are your parents living?'

'No,' she said. 'They died five years ago. Their car—skidded on black ice, and hit a wall.'

His brows snapped together. He said quietly, 'I am sorry, *pedhi mou*. Does it still hurt you?'

'Not like it once did.' She shook her head. 'But it meant I had to grow up fast, and make my own life, which I've done. And now I have a job I like which allows me to travel.' She paused. 'Are you an only child too?'

'I was for twelve years, and then my sister Ismene was born. She was only six when our mother died.'

'Oh,' Kate put down her glass. 'That must have been terrible.'

'It wasn't easy, especially for Ismene, although my aunt Linda did her best to take my mother's place.' He paused. 'The Regina hotels were named after her.'

Kate was silent for a moment. Then, 'What's your sister like?'

He considered. 'Pretty—a little crazy—and talks too much.' He shrugged, his mouth slanting wickedly. 'A typical woman.'

'Oh.' Kate's hands clenched into fists of mock outrage, and he captured them deftly, laughing as he raised them to his lips, then turned them so that he could brush her soft palms with his mouth, swiftly and sensuously.

'And she falls in love all the time with the wrong men,' he added softly. 'Something you would never do, I'm sure, *matia mou*.'

No, Kate thought, her heart pounding. But I could come dangerously close…

She removed her hands from his grasp, and picked up her glass again. A fragile defence, but all that was available.

'What—kind of men.'

'While she was at school in Switzerland last year, we had to buy off her art master, and a ski instructor.'

Kate choked back a giggle. 'She sounds quite a girl.'

'You could say that,' Michael agreed drily. 'In the end, my father decided it would be safer to keep her at home on Kefalonia.'

She waited for him to say something more about his father, but instead he took the champagne from the ice bucket and refilled her glass.

'I wasn't going to have any more,' she protested. 'I'm going to be drunk.'

'I don't think so.' He smiled as he replaced the bottle. 'A little less uptight, perhaps,' he added, proffering another strawberry.

She had plenty to be uptight about, Kate thought, taking a distracted bite and watching him transfer the rest to his own mouth.

Somehow, imperceptibly, as they talked, he'd been moving closer to her. Now, his knee was almost brushing hers, and his arm was along the back of the sofa behind her. She could even catch the faint, expensive fragrance of the cologne he used, reminding her, all too potently, of the brief giddy moments she'd spent in his arms.

She felt his hand on her shoulder, gently stroking its curve, and jumped, splashing champagne on to her skirt.

Michael clicked his tongue reprovingly, and leaned forward, brushing the drops from the fabric, his fingers lingering on her stockinged knee.

He said softly, 'I do not think the mark will be permanent.'

But he was so wrong, Kate thought, her pulses leaping frantically. Because she could be scarred for life.

He kissed her cheek, his lips exploring the hollow beneath the high bone, then dropped a fugitive caress at the very corner of her mouth. He traced the line of her jaw with tiny kisses, before allowing his tongue to tease the delicate whorls inside her ear.

As her head sank, helpless, on to his shoulder, his lips brushed her temples, her forehead, her half-closed eyes.

Everywhere he touched her, her skin bloomed, irradiated with a delight—an urgency she had never known before. Her whole body was melting, liquid with desire.

But he didn't kiss her mouth, as she needed him to do so badly, and his hand only caressed her shoulder and arm through the thin wool, and not her eager breasts.

And she was longing to feel his hands—his mouth on her body. To know him naked against her.

How was it possible, she wondered dazedly, for him to touch her so little, yet make her want him so much?

'Michael.' Her voice was husky suddenly, pleading. 'This—isn't fair.'

She felt him smile against her hair. 'Are you speaking of love—or war, *matia mou*?'

'But you said you wouldn't…'

'I came a long way to see you, *agapi mou*. Do you grudge me this small taste of you?' He tugged at her earlobe gently with his teeth. 'After all, I am torturing no one but myself.'

'You know,' she whispered. 'You know that isn't true.'

She turned, pressing her mouth almost frantically to his, begging him wordlessly for the response she craved.

But he moved back a little, framing her face between his hands.

He said, 'I think, Katharina, it would be wise if I took you somewhere for dinner now. We need other people round us.'

'Why?' She stared at him.

'Because if we stay here, you may have too much champagne and I—I may succumb to temptation.' He got to his feet in one swift lithe movement, pulling her up with him.

His voice sank to a whisper, 'So let us behave well, *pedhi mou*—for tonight at least.'

As they rode down in the lift, she said, 'I'm not really dressed for going out to dinner. Can it be somewhere not too smart?'

'Of course. No problem.'

'Oh,' Kate said. 'You've just reminded me of something.'

'What is it.'

She frowned, trying to remember. 'That night on Zycos, you were in my room talking to another man. Something about problems—solving them or causing them. I can't quite recall…'

There was an odd silence, then he shrugged. 'You must have been dreaming again, *pedhi mou*.'

'But it seemed so real,' she protested.

'So did the other dreams you had that night,' he reminded her drily, sending warm colour into her face. He paused, his mouth hardening and his eyes suddenly remote. 'But always reality is waiting.'

She felt as if a cold hand had touched her. She said his name questioningly, and he looked back at her, his face relaxing.

'Come, my beautiful one.' He took her hand. 'Let us enjoy our own dream a little longer.'

He was warning me, Kate thought, tears running down her face in the darkness. Because that's all it ever was—all it ever could be—a dream, and I was a fool to believe in it. To believe in him.

But I did, and now I have to live with the consequences. And the memories. And I don't know if I can bear it…

Lack of sleep left her feeling jaded, and aware of a slight headache the following morning. Although that was probably the least of her troubles, she reminded herself wearily.

And her day proved just as tricky as she'd expected. The French youngsters hadn't the slightest interest in the Tower of London and, clearly, would have preferred playing computer games in some arcade. But, in a way, Kate was glad of the challenge. Because it stopped her from thinking.

But when she'd bidden a final '*au revoir*' to her reluctant charges and their harassed supervisors, she was once again alone, with a decision to make, and nowhere to hide.

She would have to agree, she thought wearily, as she let herself into the flat. Let him see that no sacrifice was too great in her determination to end their marriage.

But first a hot shower, to remove the kinks of the day, she thought, peeling off her clothes and reaching for her gingham robe. And also to give her time to think how to phrase her acceptance of his outrageous terms in a way that would leave her a modicum of dignity.

Not easy, she told herself wryly, as she adjusted the temperature control of the water.

She was just unfastening her robe when her front door buzzer sounded. For a moment she stood still, staring into space, her mouth drying as she realised the probable identity of her visitor.

Michael couldn't wait for her answer, of course. Oh, no, he had to apply the pressure, she thought bitterly.

She could always pretend to be out, she told herself, then remembered that her living room light was on and clearly visible from the street. On the other hand, she didn't have to let him in.

She tightened the sash round her waist, then walked to the intercom panel by the door.

'Yes?' Her tone was curt.

'Darling,' Grant said. 'I need to see you. Please let me in.'

It was almost, but not quite, a relief to hear him.

She said, 'It's not really convenient…'

'Katie,' he interrupted firmly. 'This is important. We have to talk.'

Sighing, Kate released the front entrance button, and walked to her own door.

'I've been worried about you,' he said, as he came in. 'You haven't returned any of my calls.'

She sighed again, under her breath. 'Grant, when I came back from Greece you were very kind, and I'll always appreciate it, but we can't live in each other's pockets. But as I've tried to tell you, we both need to move on.'

'Darling, you need time. I understand that. But as for moving on…' He handed her the newspaper he was carrying. 'Have you seen this?'

It was a picture of Michael, leaving the airport, smiling, and a caption.

Millionaire tycoon Michael Theodakis flew in yesterday to finalise the acquisition of the ailing Royal Empress group for his Regina Hotel chain. He is also planning a romantic reunion with his English bride of eight months, Katharine, who has been spending a few weeks in London.

'Oh, God.' Kate's throat tightened uncontrollably, as she threw the paper to the floor. 'I don't believe this.'

'Talk to your lawyer,' Grant advised authoritatively. 'Get an injunction.'

She wrapped her arms round her shaking body. 'It's a little late for that. I've already seen him.'

Grant stared at her. 'But when you came back, you said it was over. That you were never going to see him again.'

'Mick has other ideas.' Kate drew a steadying breath. 'In fact, he's asked me to go back to Kefalonia with him for a family wedding. But it's no romantic reunion,' she added wearily, as Grant's mouth opened in protest. 'It's a *quid pro quo* arrangement. I do him this favour. He gives me a quick divorce.'

'Kate, for God's sake.' Grant's voice rose. 'Don't tell me you're actually considering this preposterous deal.'

'Oh, but she is,' Mick said softly from the doorway. 'If it is any concern of yours.'

He was leaning against the doorframe, apparently at his ease, but his eyes were like obsidian, and there was a small, cold smile playing about his mouth.

Kate swallowed. 'How—how did you get in?'

'Your obliging neighbour again.' His icy gaze scanned the gingham robe, then turned inimically on Grant. 'She did not realise you were already—entertaining.'

'I'm not,' Kate said angrily aware that her face had warmed. But what the hell did she have to feel guilty about? Mick was the one who'd betrayed her. Who'd destroyed their marriage.

She bent and retrieved the newspaper. 'Grant just came to bring me a message. He's—just leaving.'

'Kate,' Grant gasped.

She didn't look at him. 'Just go—please.'

'Very well.' He gave Mick a fulminating look as he stalked past him. 'But I shall be back.'

'No,' Mick said, his eyes flicking him with cool disdain. 'You will not.'

For a moment they faced each other, then Grant, his face working, turned away, and Kate heard him going down the stairs.

Mick walked forward into the room, and kicked the door

shut behind him. He said, 'Your guard dog lacks teeth, *pedhi mou*.'

'Grant is a friend, nothing more.' Kate faced him defiantly.

'You once thought you were in love with him,' he said. 'And now I find you here with him, half-naked.'

'I'm perfectly decent,' she flung at him. 'I was about to have a shower when he arrived.'

Mick took off his jacket and flung it across a chair. 'Did you plan to share it with him, as you used to do with me?' His voice was low and dangerous.

'And what if I did?' Her voice shook, not just with anger but pain. 'You have no right to question me—not with your track record, you—appalling hypocrite.'

'You think not? Maybe it is time I reminded you, *agapi mou*, that you are still my wife.'

He reached her in one stride. His hands grasped her arms, pulling her forward, and his mouth descended crushingly on hers. At first she fought him in sheer outrage, but he was too strong, and too determined, his fingers tangling in her hair, as his lips forced hers apart.

She couldn't breathe—she couldn't think. She could only—endure, as his hand swept her from breast to thigh in one stark act of possession. Reminding her with terrifying emphasis that her body's needs had only been suppressed. Not extinguished.

When at last he let her go, she took a shaky step backwards, stumbling over the hem of her robe in her haste, and pressing a hand to her reddened mouth.

'You bastard,' she choked. 'You bloody barbarian.'

'I am what I always was,' Mick retorted curtly. 'And I have warned you before not to make me angry.'

'You have no right to be angry. Or to accuse me when you—you…'

The words stuck in her throat. She couldn't speak them. Couldn't face him with his betrayal. Not then. Not now. It hurt too much, and always had. Besides, she might cry in front of him—the great agonised sobs which had torn her apart night after night when she'd first fled from Kefalonia. And she couldn't let him see what he had done to her—how close he'd brought her to the edge of despair and heartbreak.

By remaining silent, she could perhaps hang on to some element of her pride.

He shrugged. 'I'm a man, Katharina, not some plaster saint on an altar. I made no secret of it, yet you still married me.' His tone was dry.

'And very soon lived to regret it,' she flashed.

'Even with all that money to sweeten my barbaric ways,' he mocked her. 'You are hard to please, my Kate.'

She said in a low voice, 'I am not—your Kate.'

'The law says otherwise.'

'Until I get my decree.'

'For which you need my goodwill,' he said softly.

'I think the price may be too high.' She steadied herself, and looked back at him. 'I want it understood that my return to Kefalonia does not give you the right to—maul me whenever the whim takes you.'

'Not a touch, *agapi mou*?' His drawl mocked her. 'Not a kiss?'

'Nothing,' she said. 'Otherwise the deal's off—however long it takes me to be rid of you.'

'I'll settle for a pretence of affection, and some common civility, *matia mou*.' There was a harsh note in his voice. 'I'm told when you worked on Zycos, you were a model of diplomacy. Bring some of your professional skills to bear.'

Kate bit her lip. 'When exactly am I expected to begin this—charade?'

'At once.' He pointed to the crumpled newspaper she was still clutching. 'As you see, your tabloids have discovered that we are both in London, but not together. That must be remedied at once. I do not choose to have my private life examined by the gutter press.'

Kate stiffened. 'In what way—remedied?'

'By packing what you need, and coming with me to the hotel tonight. Making the resumption of our marriage public.'

'But we're getting a divorce,' she objected. 'You can hardly keep that a secret.'

'Let us deal with one problem at a time. Tonight, I require you to accompany me to the Royal Empress.'

'The Royal Empress.' The breath caught in her throat. 'No—I won't do it. I agreed to attend Ismene's wedding, but nothing was said about—cohabiting with you here in London.'

He said coldly, 'That is not for you to choose. Nor is it what I intended, or wished,' he added with cutting emphasis. 'However, it is—necessary, and that must be enough.' He paused. 'But I am using the penthouse suite—one that holds no memories for either of us.'

She looked down at the floor, swift colour rising in her face, angry that he should have read her thoughts so accurately. Angry, too, that she'd let him see she was still vulnerable to the past.

'It is larger too,' he went on. 'With luck, *matia mou*, we may never be obliged to meet. And certainly not—cohabit.'

Kate bit her lip. 'Very well,' she agreed, her voice constricted. She hesitated. 'I—I'll get my stuff together. Perhaps you'd send the car for me—in an hour.'

Mick sat down in her armchair, stretching long legs in front of him. He said, 'I can wait.'

'But I've got things to do,' she protested. 'I told you—I was going to have a shower.'

'Then do so.'

'There's no need to stay on guard,' she said. 'You surely don't think I'm going to do a runner?'

His mouth curled slightly. 'It would not be the first time, my dear wife. I am not prepared to take the risk again. Now, go and take your shower.'

Kate gave him a mutinous look, then went into her bedroom, and closed the door. She looked over the small stock of clothing in her wardrobe, most of it cheap casual stuff bearing no resemblance to the collection of expensive designer wear that she'd abandoned on Kefalonia.

But, then, she was no longer the same girl, she reminded herself.

She put underwear, a couple of cotton nightdresses and some simple pants and tops in to her travel bag. After her bath, her housecoat and toiletries would join them.

She collected fresh briefs and bra, and picked a knee-length denim skirt and a plain white shirt from her remaining selection of garments. Practical, she thought, but the opposite end of the spectrum from glamorous.

Carrying them over her arm, she trailed self-consciously from the bedroom to the bathroom.

Mick was reading her discarded newspaper.

'I hope you've forgotten nothing,' he said courteously, without raising his eyes.

'I hope so too.' Damn him, she thought. He never missed a trick.

And she didn't need him to point out, however obliquely, the contrast between the warm joyous intimacy of their early married life where no doors were ever closed, and the embarrassed bitter awkwardness of their present relationship. She was already well aware—and hurting.

'Would you like me to wash your back?' His voice followed her. It held faint amusement, and another intonation that sent a ripple of awareness shivering down her spine.

'No,' she said curtly and slammed the door on him, and the memories the question had evoked. She shot the bolt for good measure, although it was too flimsy to debar anyone who really wanted to come in.

She swallowed, firmly closing her mind against that possibility.

The warm water was comforting but she was not disposed to linger. Besides, commonsense told her that it would not be wise to keep Mick waiting too long, she thought wryly, as she dried herself swiftly and put on her clothes.

Armouring herself, she realised, as she brushed back her hair, and confined it at the nape of her neck with a silver clip. And if Mick didn't like it, he could lump it, because she was going to need every scrap of defence she could conjure up.

Drawing a deep breath, she slid back the bolt and emerged.

She said, 'I'm ready.'

He was shrugging on his jacket, but he paused, looking her over with narrowed eyes in a lengthening silence.

'Are you making some kind of statement, Katharina?' His voice was gentle, but cold.

'I dress to please myself now.' Kate straightened her shoulders. 'I'm sorry if I don't meet your exacting standards.'

Mick sighed. 'Tomorrow, *pedhi mou*, I think you must pay a visit to Bond Street.'

She lifted her chin. 'No. And you can't make me.'

He gave her a thoughtful glance. 'Is this what you wear at your work?'

'Of course not. The company supplies a uniform.'

'But now you are working for me,' he said softly. 'In a different capacity. Which also requires a uniform. So, tomorrow you will go shopping. You understand?'

Looking down at the floor, she gave a reluctant nod.

'And you will also wear this.' He walked across to her, reaching into an inside pocket, and produced her wedding ring.

'Oh, no.' Instinctively, she put both hands behind her back. His name was engraved inside it, she thought wildly, and the words 'For ever.' She couldn't wear it. It was too cruel. Too potent a reminder of all her pitiful hopes and dreams.

She said, 'I—I can't. Please…'

'But you must.' He paused, his gaze absorbing her flushed cheeks and strained eyes, then moving down to the sudden hurry of her breasts under the thin shirt, his dark eyes narrowed, and oddly intent.

He lifted his hand and ran his thumb gently along the swell of her lower lip. He said in a low voice, 'I could always—persuade you, *agapi mou*. Is that what you want?'

A shiver tingled its way through her body. 'No.'

'Then give me your hand.'

Reluctantly, she yielded it. Watched, as he touched the gold circlet to his lips, then placed it on her finger. Just as he had done on their wedding day, she thought, as pain slashed at her. And if he smiled down into her eyes—reached for her to kiss her, she might well be lost.

But he stepped back, and there was the reassurance of space between them.

And, building inside her, anger at his hypocrisy—his betrayal.

She whispered, 'I hate you.'

There was a sudden stillness, then he gave a short laugh.

'Hate as much as you want, Katharina *mou*,' he said harshly. 'But you are still my wife, and will remain so until I choose to let you go. Perhaps you should remember that.'

As if, Kate thought, turning blindly away, as if I could ever forget.

CHAPTER SIX

THE journey to the hotel was a silent one. Kate sat huddled in her corner of the limousine, staring rigidly through the window, feigning an interest in the shop-lined streets, the busy bars and restaurants they were passing.

Anything, she thought shakily, that would reduce her awareness of the man beside her. And the unbridgeable gulf between them.

As the driver pulled up in front of the Royal Empress, she heard Mick swear softly under his breath.

He said quietly, 'Not a word, *matia mou*—do you hear me?'

Then, suddenly, shockingly, she was being jerked towards him. She felt the silver clip snapped from her hair, found herself crushed against him, breast to breast, held helplessly in his arms while his mouth took hers, hard, experienced and terrifyingly thorough.

Then the car door was open, and she was free, emerging dazedly on to the pavement, standing for a moment as cameras flashed, then walking pinned to Mick's side, his hand on her hip, to the hotel entrance.

'Quietly, my red-haired angel.' She heard the thread of laughter in the voice that whispered against her ear. 'Scream at me when we're alone.'

People were greeting her. She saw welcoming, deferential smiles, and heard herself respond, her voice husky and breathless.

The manager rode up in the lift with them, clearly anxious that his arrangements should be approved by his new employer.

It was a beautiful suite. Even anger and outrage couldn't

blind Kate to that. There was the usual big, luxuriously furnished sitting room, flanked on either side by two bedrooms, each with its own bathroom.

There were flowers everywhere, she saw, plus bowls of fruit, dishes of handmade chocolates, and the inevitable champagne on ice. By the window was a table, covered in an immaculate white cloth, and set with silverware and candles for a dinner *à deux*.

All the trappings, Kate thought, her heart missing a beat, of a second honeymoon…

Someone was carrying her single bag into one of the bedrooms with as much care as if it was a matching set of Louis Vuitton, and she followed, hands clenched in the pockets of her navy linen jacket.

One of the walls was almost all mirror and she caught a glimpse of herself, her hair loose and tousled on her shoulders, her mouth pink and swollen from kissing, even a couple of buttons open on her shirt.

She looked like a woman, she thought dazedly, whose man couldn't keep his hands off her.

'We are alone.' Mick was standing in the doorway behind her, his dark face challenging. 'So, you may shout as much as you wish, *pedhi mou.*

She took a deep, breath. 'What the *hell* was all that about?' Her voice shook.

He shrugged. 'I saw the cameras waiting for us. They wanted proof that our marriage was solid. It seemed wise to give it to them. I have my reasons,' he added coolly.

'Reasons?' she echoed incredulously. 'What possible reason could there be?' She tried to thrust her buttons back into their holes with trembling fingers. 'You made it look as if we'd been having sex in the back of the car.'

'No,' he said. 'The prelude to sex perhaps.'

'There's such a big difference.' Her voice radiated scorn.

He had the nerve to grin at her. 'Why, yes, *matia mou.* If

you remember, I prefer comfort—and privacy. I find the presence of a third person—inhibiting.'

But there was always someone else there, she thought in sudden agony, although I didn't realise it then. Every time we touched—made love, Victorine was there—Victorine…

She lifted her chin. 'I hope you haven't arranged any more—photo opportunities. Because I won't guarantee to co-operate.'

'Is that what you were doing in the car—co-operating?' Mick asked sardonically. 'I would never have guessed.'

She glared at him. 'I never pretended I could act.'

He said courteously, 'You do yourself less than justice, *pedhi mou*.' He glanced at his watch. 'At what time do you wish them to serve dinner?'

'I'm not hungry.'

Mick sighed. 'Would your appetite improve if I said that you were dining alone?' he asked wearily.

'Oh.' She was taken aback. 'You're going out?'

He shrugged. 'Why not?'

She bit her lip. 'I'll order something later—a club sandwich maybe.'

'The chef will be disappointed—but the choice is yours.'

She unfastened her travel bag. 'I think we both know that isn't true,' she said tautly. 'Or I wouldn't be here.'

She extracted her uniform dress and jacket, and moved towards the fitted wardrobes.

'What are those?' His tone sharpened.

'My work clothes.' Kate paused, hanger in hand.

'Why have you brought them?'

'Because I have a job to go to in the morning,' she said. 'But perhaps it's a trick question.'

'You had a job,' Mick corrected, the dark brows drawing together haughtily. 'If you write out your resignation, I will see it is delivered.'

Kate gasped. 'I can't do that. And I won't,' she added

stormily. 'When this—farce is over, I'm going to need a career.'

'But the farce has still a long time to run,' Mick said with steely softness. 'And in the meantime, Katharina *mou*, my wife does not work.'

'And how long does this embargo last?' Her voice shook. 'Until after the divorce?'

'Forever,' he said curtly. 'Married or divorced, I shall continue to support you financially. As I am sure your lawyer has made clear,' he added with a certain grimness.

'Yes,' Kate said raggedly. 'And I want nothing from you—except my freedom. You don't have to buy me off, *kyrie*, or pay for my silence, either.' She took a deep breath. 'Our marriage—should never have happened, but I won't dish the dirt on it—sell the unhappy details to the newspapers. And I'll sign any confidentiality clause that your legal team can dream up.'

He was very still. He said slowly, '"Unhappy details" *matia mou*? Is that—truly—all you remember?'

For a moment, her mind was a kaleidoscope throwing up image after image. Mick walking hand in hand with her through the snow in Central Park—teaching her to skate, both of them helpless with laughter—fetching paracetamol and rubbing her back when she had curse pains.

And holding her as she slept each night.

That above all, she thought with agony. The closeness of it. The feeling of total safety. Of what I thought was love…

She looked stonily back at him. She said, 'What else was there?'

He said with immense weariness, 'Then there is nothing more to be said.'

As he turned away, she said swiftly, 'Before you go—may I have my hairclip, please.'

'I'm sorry.' Face expressionless, he gave a brief shrug. 'I must have dropped it in the car—or in the street, perhaps. Is it important?'

'No,' she said slowly. 'It doesn't really matter.'

And watched him walk out, closing the door behind him.

'Nothing matters,' she whispered, when she was alone. 'Nor ever will again.' And felt tears, hot and thick in her throat.

She walked over to the wide bed, and sat down on its edge, burying her face in her hands.

Who was the first person, she wondered, to state that love was blind?

Because she'd realised that she'd fallen in love with Michael Theodakis before they'd even sat down to their first dinner together, loved him, and longed for him during the weeks that followed.

Every night that he'd been in London, and he seemed to be there a great deal, his car was waiting for her when she left work.

He took her to wonderful restaurants, to cinemas, theatres and to concerts. He took her for drives in the country, and walks in the park.

He did not, however, take her to bed.

His lovemaking was gentle, almost decorous. There were kisses and caresses, but the cool, clever hands that explored her body aroused, but never satisfied. He always drew back before the brink was reached, courteously, even ruefully, but with finality.

Leaving her stranded in some limbo of need and frustration, her senses screaming for fulfilment.

She was on wires, her eyes as big as a cat's, her face all cheekbones.

Only Sandy knew her well enough to be concerned—and to probe.

'Do you know what you're doing?' she asked abruptly one day, when Kate was trying on the little black dress she was planning to borrow from her.

'What do you mean?' Kate's tone was defensive.

Sandy sighed. 'You're swimming with a shark, love.' She sat down on the edge of the bed.

'I thought you liked Mick.' Kate stared at her distressed.

'I do like him. He's seriously good-looking, too charming for his own good, and filthy rich. What's not to like?'

Kate forced a smile. 'And I'm none of those things, so why is he bothering with me? Is that it?'

Sandy spread her hands. 'Kate, I'm in love with Gavin, and going to be married, but when Mick Theodakis does that smiling-with-his-eyes thing, I become a melted blob on the carpet. I can understand why you're seeing him.'

She paused. 'But honey, he's seen a lot of women. He's been on some "eligible bachelors of the world" list since he was in his teens."

She shook her head. 'You know who he used to date? That supermodel who became an actress—Victorine. One of the girls on the social page told me that they were a real item. He was supposed to be crazy about her—talking marriage—the whole bit. Now, he's back on the market, and she's gone to ground somewhere, and no one's heard of her for over a year.'

She got to her feet. 'The thing is, he may not believe in long-term commitment, Katie, and I don't want you to break your heart.'

I think, Kate told herself wryly, that it may be a little late for that.

The following day Mick flew to New York and was there for about a week. He called several times, but, just the same, she missed him almost desperately.

On the day of his return, she flew out of the office, only to find a complete stranger waiting for her.

'Kyria Dennison?' He was a stocky man, with dark shrewd eyes, and a heavy black moustache, and she recognised him as one of the men sitting with Mick in the nightclub the night they met. 'I am Iorgos Vasso. Kyrios Michalis sends his apologies, and asks me to escort you to the hotel.'

'Is he ill?' Kate questioned anxiously.

The dark eyes twinkled. 'He is jet lagged, *kyria.* Sometimes it affects him more badly than others.'

'Oh,' Kate said slowly. 'Well—maybe I should leave him to rest.'

'Jet lag is bad,' Iorgos Vasso said solemnly. 'But disappointment would be far worse. Let me take you to him.'

'Your voice sounds familiar,' Kate said, frowning a little, as the car inched its way through the traffic. She paused. 'Didn't I hear you talking with Mr Theodakis in my room that night on Zycos—about solving a problem?'

He shrugged, his smile polite and regretful. 'Perhaps, *kyria.* I really don't remember.'

She sighed. 'It doesn't matter.'

Mick was waiting for her impatiently in the suite. He looked rough, but his smile made her heart sing. He pulled her into his arms and held her for a long time.

'This week has been hell,' he told her quietly. 'Next time, I take you with me.'

They dined quietly in the sitting room, but he only toyed with his food.

'I'm, exhausted, *pedhi mou,*' he told her frankly, when the meal had been cleared away. 'Would you mind if I took a nap for half an hour? I will try to be better company afterwards.'

'You're sure you don't want me to go—give you some peace?'

'No.' He kissed her. 'Wait for me—please.'

He went into the bedroom, and shut the door. When he still hadn't reappeared nearly two hours later, Kate went across and tapped on the door.

There was no reply, so, she turned the handle gently and peeped in. One shaded lamp burned in the room and Mick was lying on top of the bed, sound asleep, his shoes and jacket discarded.

Kate walked to the bed, and stood looking down at him.

She had never seen him sleeping before and, with his long eyelashes curling on his cheek, he looked much younger. Almost vulnerable.

He's not going to wake up, she thought. I could simply kiss him goodnight, and leave.

Instead, she found herself kicking off her own shoes, and lying down beside him on the satin coverlet.

She wasn't planning on sleeping herself. She just wanted to lie quietly for a while, and watch him, and listen to his soft, regular breathing.

But the room was warm, and the bed soft and comfortable, its crisp linen faintly scented with lavender and, in spite of herself, Kate found her eyelids drooping.

She thought, 'I ought to go home…' And then she stopped thinking altogether.

She awoke suddenly with a start, and looked around, momentarily disorientated, wondering where she was. Then she saw Mick, propped on one elbow, studying her, his face grave, his dark eyes hooded.

She said, a little breathlessly, 'I must have—fallen asleep. What time is it?'

'The middle of the night.' His brows lifted. 'You should be more careful, *matia mou*. Has no one told you it is dangerous to tempt a hungry man with crumbs?'

She said, with a catch in her voice, 'Perhaps I'm starving too.'

He smiled into her eyes, as he smoothed the dishevelled hair back from her face, and ran his finger gently across her parted lips.

He said softly, 'I hope it is true, yet you may still change your mind—if you wish.' He paused. 'But if you allow me to touch you, it will be too late.'

'I'm here because I want to be,' she whispered. 'Because I can't help myself.'

She sat up, and pulled off her black sweater, tossing it to the floor.

Mick drew a sharp breath, then took her into his arms, kissing her slowly and very deeply.

His hands were unhurried, too, as they removed the rest of her clothes, his lips paying sensuous homage to every curve and hollow that he uncovered.

When she was naked, he looked at her for a long moment. He said huskily. 'How beautiful you are.'

Shy colour burned in her face, but she met his gaze. 'You've seen me before.'

'But then you were angry.' His hand cupped her breast, his fingers teasing her nipple, making it stand proudly erect. 'You were not like this. So sweet—so willing.'

But when she tried to unbutton his shirt, to undress him in turn, he stopped her, his hands closing over hers.

'Not yet.' He kissed her again, his mouth warm and beguiling, then bent his head to her breast, his tongue flickering against the taut rosy peak. 'First, *agapi mou*,' he murmured, 'I need to pleasure you.'

It was a long, languorous journey into arousal. Kate found herself drifting almost mindlessly, aware only of the message of her senses in response to the whisper of his hands and mouth on her body. Conscious of the slow, irresistible heat building within her that demanded to be assuaged. Somehow.

When his hand parted her thighs, she heard herself make a small sound in her throat, pleading, almost animal.

'Yes.' His low voice seemed to reach her from some vast distance. 'Soon—my dove, my angel, I promise.'

His fingers explored her gently, making her gasp and writhe against his touch. Almost immediately it changed, his fingers still stroking her delicately, but creating a new, insistent rhythm as they did so. Gliding on her. Circling. Focusing on one small, exquisite point of pleasure.

Her body moved restlessly, searching, seeking, as her awakened senses whispered of a goal to be attained.

As his fingers strummed the tiny moist pinnacle of heated

flesh, his mouth enclosed her breast, caressing the sensitised peak with his tongue.

Delight lanced through her as she arched towards him in wordless demand.

It was difficult to breathe. Impossible to think. She could only—feel.

Then, deep inside her, she experienced the first sweet burning tremors that signalled her release. Felt them ripple outwards. Intensify. Heard herself sob aloud as the last vestiges of control fell away, and her entire being was consumed—ravished by pulsations so strong she thought she would be torn apart.

The storm of feeling lifted her, held her in a scalding limbo, then let her drift in a dizzying spiral back to earth.

She lay, dazed, trying to regulate her ragged breathing.

She was vaguely aware that Mick had moved slightly, shifting away from her, and she tried to murmur a protest from her dry throat.

He said softly, 'Rest a little, *pedhi mou*.' And she felt him draw the sheet over her damp body.

She floated, rocked by some deep and tideless sea, her body still tingling from the force of its enrapturement.

She realised that Mick had returned to lie beside her. She reached out a drowsy hand and encountered bare skin.

Her eyes opened. 'Oh.'

'Oh?' There was a smile in his voice, but his face was serious and very intent. He took the welcoming hand and guided it down his body. 'Touch me,' he whispered. 'Hold me.'

At first her compliance was tentative, but she gradually became more confident, encouraged by his small groans of pleasure as she caressed him.

He kissed her hotly, his tongue gliding against hers. His fingers stroked her breasts, moulding them, coaxing them to renewed delight.

His hands strayed the length of her body, delineating the

long supple back, the slender curves of her hips, and thighs. Where they lingered.

Kate was trembling suddenly, aware that the same delicious excitement was overtaking her again. Beginning, incredibly, to build inside her.

She was lying facing him, and Mick's hands slid under her flanks, raising her slightly towards him. He kissed her mouth gently.

He said, 'Take me—please, my dove. My beautiful girl.'

She brought him into her slowly, the breath catching in her throat as she realised how simple it really was—how right. And just how much she had wanted to feel all that silken strength and potency inside her. To possess, and be possessed.

'Do I hurt you?' His whisper was urgent.

'No.' Her answer was a sigh. 'Ah, no.'

His movements were gentle at first, and smoothly, rhythmically controlled. And all the time he was watching her, she realised. Looking into her eyes. Observing the play of colour in her face. Listening for any change in her breathing.

And she smiled at him, her eyes luminous.

He hesitated, then moved away from her.

'What's the matter?' She stared at him in shocked bewilderment. 'Did—did I do something wrong?'

'No, *matia mou.*' He stroked her cheek reassuringly. 'I need to protect you, that is all.'

When he turned back, he lifted himself over her, entering her in one strong, fluid movement. She wound her arms round his neck, and, instinctively, lifted her legs to clasp him closer.

The rhythm he was imposing was more powerful now, and she joined it, moving with him in breathless unison.

She could feel the first, elusive blossoming of pleasure, and clung to him, striving for it. Demanding it.

The next moment, her whole being was convulsed in a fierce and scalding rapture. She cried out in ecstatic surprise, and heard Michael answer her as his own body shuddered into climax.

When she could speak, she said, 'Is it always like that?'

'Always with you, *agapi mou.*' He smoothed the hair back from her damp forehead, then wrapped her in his arms. She curled against him, sated and languid, and felt his cheek rest against her hair.

There was a silence, then he spoke, his voice barely a whisper. 'Marry me.'

She turned her head, and stared at him, her eyes wide, and her lips parted. 'You don't mean that.'

'I am perfectly serious,' he told her. 'I am asking you to be my wife, Katharina *mou.*'

'But you can't,' she said, almost wildly. 'It's ridiculous. I—I don't belong to your world.'

'We have just made our own world, *agapi mou*. I want no other.'

'But your family,' she protested. 'They'll expect you to marry some heiress.'

'My father lives his life.' His voice was oddly harsh. 'And I live mine. I wish to spend it with you.' He paused. 'But perhaps you don't want me?'

She said, 'I think I've wanted you since that first night on Zycos. And, yes, I'll marry you, Kyrios Michalis.'

He framed her face in his hands, and kissed her deeply, almost reverently.

He said, 'We should celebrate. I'll call room service and tell them to bring champagne.'

She smiled up at him. 'And strawberries?'

'You remember that, hmm?' He threw the covering sheet aside and got out of bed, stretching unselfconsciously.

Watching him, Kate felt her mouth go dry, and her throat tighten.

She said, 'Of course. But I couldn't understand why you didn't just—seduce me, there and then.'

Mick picked up a red silk robe from a chair and slipped it

on. He said softly, 'But I have been seducing you, *agapi mou*, every moment we have spent together since I first saw you. Don't you know that.'

He blew her a teasing kiss and walked away into the sitting room.

Two weeks later they were married in a quiet registry office ceremony with Sandy and Iorgos Vasso as witnesses.

They spent a brief honeymoon on Bali, then flew back to New York where Mick was supervising the completion of the latest Regina hotel.

'Does he usually take so personal an interest?' Kate asked Iorgos, who had soon become a friend.

'This is particularly important to him,' Iorgos admitted. 'There are elements on the board who have always been opposed to any expansion outside the Mediterranean, or indeed to any kind of change,' he added drily. 'It is no longer a foregone conclusion that he will succeed his father as chairman of the board when Ari eventually retires. So, Michalis needs a proven success to overcome the doubters.'

'I see.' Kate paused. 'Is his father one of the doubters?'

'That is something you should ask your husband, *kyria*.'

'I have.' Kate sighed. 'I asked him, too, when we'd be going to Greece so that I could meet his family, and he just changed the subject.'

She shook her head. 'He never talks about family things. Why, I didn't even know his mother had been a native New Yorker until I discovered we were living in her old home.'

'Does it make a difference?'

'No, but I'd like to have been told. And I wish he'd discuss this estrangement with his father, because I know it exists.'

He said gently, 'You are a very new wife, *kyria*. Maybe Mick feels you have enough adjustments to make for now. Enjoy the happiness you find in each other, and leave any problems for another day.'

And with that, she had to be content.

The apartment, in an exclusive district, was a sumptuous,

gracious place, all high ceilings, and rich wood panelling, and Kate had loved it on sight.

Mick gave her *carte blanche* to change anything she wanted but, in the end, she altered very little, replacing some carpets and curtains, and introducing a lighter colour scheme for their bedroom.

'I'm saving my energies for the nursery,' she told him happily.

'Well, there is no hurry for that.' He kissed her. 'Unless I am not enough for you,' he added softly.

The hotel was completed by Easter, and Kate, smiling confidently to conceal her inner trepidation, cut the ribbon which declared the New York Regina open for business.

It was barely a week later when she returned from a shopping trip to find a full-scale row in progress, with Mick pacing the drawing room, his face set and thunderous, while Iorgos tried unavailingly to calm him.

'What's happened?' Kate put down her packages, alarmed.

'We have been sent for,' Mick flung at her.

'Mr Theodakis has requested Michael to bring you to Kefalonia,' Iorgos explained more temperately.

'Is that such a bad thing?' Kate felt her way cautiously, keeping a wary eye on her husband's angry face. 'After all, we were bound to pay a visit eventually—weren't we?'

Mick snorted in exasperation, and stalked over to the window.

'It would not be wise to refuse,' Iorgos said quietly. 'Consider that, Michalis.'

'I have,' Mick said curtly, without looking round. 'And I know it must be done.'

For the first time in their marriage, he did not come to bed that night. Kate, disturbed, found him in the drawing room, slumped on a sofa with a decanter of whisky for company.

She had never seen him like this, she thought, as she knelt beside him. 'Darling, what's wrong? Talk to me, please.'

He looked at her, his eyes weary, and frighteningly distant.

'The reality I once spoke of, *pedhi mou.* It has found us. Now leave me. I need to be on my own—to think.'

And she had turned and gone back to their room, alone and suddenly scared.

CHAPTER SEVEN

KATE'S first glimpse of Kefalonia had been from the company private jet.

In spite of the uneasiness of the previous week, she couldn't repress a tingle of anticipation as she looked down on the rocky landscape beneath her.

Maybe, she thought, things will change now we're here. Go back to the way they were.

Because, ever since his father's summons, there'd been a strange new tension between Mick and herself which she seemed powerless to dispel, however much she tried.

Now, when he made love to her, he seemed remote, almost clinical in the ways in which he gave her pleasure. The warmth, the teasing, the laughter that had made their intimacy so precious was suddenly missing.

For the first time it was almost a relief that Mick still insisted on using protection during lovemaking, because she didn't want their baby to be conceived in an atmosphere like this.

She'd been surprised too when Mick told her to pack summer clothes and swimwear.

'But it's only April.' She stared at him. 'How long will we be staying on Kefalonia?'

'I am Greek, Katharina.' His voice was cold. 'The Villa Dionysius is my home.'

She said quietly, 'I'm sorry. I thought your home was with me. But I'll pack for an indefinite stay if that's what you want.'

His smile was brief and wintry. 'Thank you.'

She'd read as much as she could about the island and its history, prior to setting out, and knew that, because of the devastation caused by the earthquake which had struck in 1953, most of its buildings were comparatively modern.

But the Theodakis family home, the Villa Dionysius, had somehow survived. And soon she would be there.

Again she was aware of an odd prickle of nervousness, but told herself she was being ridiculous. Mick and his father might have been at odds in the past, but now a reconciliation was clearly indicated, and maybe her marriage was going to be the means of bringing that about. Which had to be a good thing—didn't it?

When they reached the villa, her spirits rose. It was a large rambling single-storied house, white-walled, with a faded terracotta roof. Flowering vines and climbing shrubs hung in festoons over the door and windows, and the garden was already bright with colour.

The whole place, she thought, had an air of timelessness about it, as if it had grown out of the headland on which it stood amid its encircling pine trees.

As she got out of the car, Kate could smell the resin, and hear the rasp of cicadas in the sunlit, windy air. Through the trees, she could see the turquoise sea far below, dancing with foam-capped waves.

She thought, 'I was crazy to worry. This is paradise.'

As she turned to look at the villa, the big door swung open, and a woman stood, dramatically framed in the doorway. She was tall and slim, with black hair that hung like a shining curtain down her back. Her skin was magnolia pale, and her almond-shaped eyes were tilted slightly at the corners. Her smiling mouth was painted a deep, sexy crimson, and in her figure-hugging white dress, she looked like some exotic, tropical flower.

Kate's throat tightened in instant, shocked recognition. She was aware of Mick standing rigidly beside her, his face like stone.

For a moment the newcomer stayed where she was, as if allowing them to fully appreciate the picture she made.

'Welcome home, *cher*.' Her voice was low-pitched and throaty. 'You shouldn't have stayed away so long.'

She walked to where Mick was standing, twining her arms round his neck, and kissing him on the lips.

'Mmm,' she murmured as she stood back. 'You taste so good—but then you always did.'

She looked at Kate. 'And this is your new wife.' Her eyes flickered over the suit in dark-green silk with a matching camisole that Kate had worn for the journey, and her smile widened. 'Won't you introduce me?'

'I already know who you are,' Kate said steadily. 'You're—Victorine.'

Not gone to ground, as Sandy had said, she thought, her heart pounding sickly, but here on Kefalonia, living in Mick's home…

But how? Why?

'I'm flattered.' Victorine laughed. 'On the other hand, you, *chère*, came as a complete surprise to—all of us.' She looked at Mick, pouting in reproof. 'Your father wasn't very pleased with you.'

Mick said harshly, 'When was he ever?' He paused. 'Where is he?'

Victorine shrugged. 'Waiting in the *saloni*. It's quite a family gathering. But you must promise me not to quarrel with him again. Though I'm sure you'll be on your best behaviour—now that you are married.'

Kate said, coolly and clearly, 'It was a long flight. I think I'd like to take a shower and change before any more introductions.'

'But of course.' Victorine turned to Mick. 'You have your usual suite in the West wing, *cher*.' She paused. 'Is there any particular room you would like Katherine to have?'

Mick said coldly, 'My wife sleeps with me.'

The slanting brows lifted. 'How sweet—and domestic.' She smiled at Katherine. 'You have managed to tame him, *chère*. I congratulate you.' She lowered her voice confidentially. 'Michael used to hate to share his bed for the whole night with anyone.'

Kate smiled back at her. 'Well,' she said lightly. 'That proves I'm not just—anyone.'

She walked sedately beside Mick through the wide passages, but under her calm exterior she was seething with a mixture of emotions. Anger was paramount, with bewilderment a close second.

At the end of one corridor were wide double doors, heavily carved. Mick opened them silently, and ushered her through. Kate found herself in an airy spacious sitting room, furnished in dramatic earth colours, with low sofas clustering round a table in heavy glass cut in the shape of a hexagon.

Beyond it was the bedroom, its vast bed draped in a coverlet the colour of green olives, which matched the long curtains at the windows.

Mick strode across the room, and opened another door. He said, 'The bathroom is here. You will find everything you need.'

'Including honesty?' Her voice shook. 'And some straight talking?'

Mick took off his jacket and tossed it across a chair.

He said shortly, 'Katharina—we are both jetlagged and out of temper, and I am shortly to have a difficult interview with my father. Oblige me by postponing this discussion.'

She said, 'No, I think I deserve an explanation now.' She began to wriggle out of her suit.

His mouth tightened. 'What do you wish to know?'

She stared at him. 'You and Victorine—you were lovers. You—you don't deny that.'

'No,' he said coldly. 'I do not. And isn't it a little late to start making my past an issue?'

'Yet now I find her—here—in your home.' She spread her hands. 'Why?'

'She is my father's mistress.' His tone was harsh. 'Does that satisfy your curiosity?'

Kate shook her head. 'You mean you passed her on—when you had finished with her?'

'No,' he said. 'I do not mean that. Victorine makes her own choices. And so does my father.'

'Did you—love her?'

His brows lifted mockingly. 'You have seen her, *agapi mou*,' he drawled. 'It must be clear what I felt for her.'

'And—now?'

'Now, I am with you, *pedhi mou*.'

She stared at him. Her voice was almost a whisper. 'Why did you marry me?'

He said, 'For a whole number of reasons.' He looked her over, standing in front of him, wearing only a few scraps of silk and lace, and his mouth twisted. 'And this is only one of them.'

Two strides brought him to her. Before she could resist, he picked her up in his arms and carried her to the bed.

She was beating at his chest with her fists. 'Put me down,' she ordered breathlessly. 'Do you hear.'

'Willingly.' Mick tossed her on to the mattress, following her down with total purpose, deftly unfastening his clothing.

'No.' Kate struggled, trying ineffectively to push him away. 'Don't you dare. I won't…'

'No, my Kate?' The dark eyes challenged her, laughter dancing outrageously in their depths. 'And how are you going to stop me?'

He bent to her, pushing the lacy cup away from her breast with his lips, and allowing his tongue to tease her uncovered nipple, while his hand slid under the silken rim of her briefs.

She said his name on a little sob, and her arms went round her neck, her body opening in heated, moist surrender as he entered her.

When the storm was over, Kate lay beneath him, drained and boneless.

'What happened?' Her voice was a shadow.

'My new cure for jet lag, *agapi mou.*' He kissed the tip of her nose. 'I may patent it.'

'You'll make another fortune,' she said weakly. 'I don't think I'll ever move again.'

'Unfortunately, you must. We have a shower to take, and my father to meet.' He sat up, raking the sweat-dampened hair back from his forehead. 'He will not appreciate waiting much longer,' he added with a touch of grimness.

'Yes,' she said. 'Of course.' She watched him disappear into the bathroom and gave a happy sigh, stretching languidly.

Then paused. Because, in reality, she thought frowning, she was no wiser about Victorine—or Mick's relationship with her, past or present.

Her concerns had been smothered by the most passionate lovemaking she'd experienced for days, but they hadn't been answered.

And I need answers, she thought, and shivered.

Aristotle Theodakis was standing by the window of the *saloni* as they came in, a dark figure against the sunlit vista of the sea outside. He turned to regard them frowningly, his whole stance radiating power and a certain aggression.

He was not as tall as his son, Kate saw, but more ruggedly built. His thick hair was silver, and his eyes were brilliant and piercing beneath their heavy brows.

He was undoubtedly a handsome, charismatic man, Kate thought, as she walked across the room towards him, her hand clasped firmly in Mick's. But she was still amazed that Victorine could have abandoned the son for the father.

She glanced around her, trying to assimilate something of her surroundings. The *saloni* was a vast room, but furnished with comfort rather than overt luxury. The colours were cool, and clear, and the walls and surfaces uncluttered. One of the few embellishments was a large portrait of a dark-haired woman with a serene face positioned above the huge, empty fireplace, which Kate assumed was the late Regina Theodakis.

She was aware of other people in the room too—a tall fair-haired woman standing quietly beside the fireplace, and, at her side, a much younger girl, with dark hair and eyes, her vibrantly pretty face spoiled by a sullen expression.

Mick halted a couple of yards from his father and inclined his head, coolly and unsmilingly. 'Papa.'

Aristotle Theodakis did not even glance at Kate. He said in his own language, 'I have spent months trying to prevent my daughter from making a fool of herself over some penniless nobody. Now, my son does the same thing. I had other plans for you, Michalis.'

Before Mick could reply, Kate said in her clear, careful Greek, 'Perhaps your children are old enough to decide their own fates, *kyrie*.'

His head turned abruptly towards her, and she waited to be blasted out of existence. Instead, he said slowly, '*Po, po po*. So, you speak our tongue?'

'Not very well. But Michael has been teaching me.'

'Hmm.' He looked her over, slowly, as if something puzzled him, taking in the simple cream dress she'd changed into. 'Perhaps he is not as stupid as I thought.'

He stepped forward, opening his arms imperatively and, after a brief hesitation, Mick returned his embrace.

'Sit down.' He waved Kate towards one of the wide, deeply cushioned sofas which flanked a low table. 'Ismene will pour you some iced tea. And for the sake of your wife and Linda, we will speak English, Michalis.'

He indicated the fair woman. 'Katharina—this is my late wife's cousin, Linda Howell. She used to be my daughter's companion.'

'And she still could be,' Ismene said petulantly, pouring the tea into tall glasses. 'Why can't I go and live in her house at Sami?'

'Because she would be too soft with you,' her father

growled. 'You would be running off to meet Petros Alessou all the time, and she would do nothing to stop you.'

'It's hard to object to Ismene meeting with a young man she's known since childhood.' Linda's voice was quiet, with a slight American drawl. She gave Kate a rueful look as she came to sit beside her. 'I'm afraid you've walked into an ongoing problem.'

'There is no problem,' Ari Theodakis scowled. 'Ismene does not see the Alessou boy, and that is final.' He snorted. 'A newly qualified doctor, with only his ideals in the bank. A fine match for my daughter. And the problems it has caused with his father.' He threw up his hands. 'I haven't had a decent game of backgammon in weeks.'

He looked at Kate. 'Do you play?'

'No,' lied Kate who had seen the speed and ferocity that the Greeks brought to the game, and didn't fancy her chances.

'Then Michalis can teach you that too—in the evenings while you are waiting for my grandson to be born.'

There was a sudden devastating silence. Kate gasped. 'Mr Theodakis—there isn't—I'm not…' She paused, aware her cheeks were burning, and turned to Mick whose expression was like stone.

'Of course not,' Linda said soothingly. 'Ari—you're impossible,' she added sternly. 'Why, the children are still on honeymoon.'

His shrug was unrepentant. 'Then why the hasty marriage?'

'Because there was no reason to wait.' Mick's tone was silky, but there was danger in it too. 'And I thought, Papa, that you wished me to be married—settled in life. You—and your supporters on the Theodakis board.'

'I did. I do.' Ari Theodakis frowned. 'But a man needs children to give him real stability.'

'Yes,' Mick said quietly. 'But in our own good time—not yours.'

'Well, it's just not fair,' Ismene burst out. 'I'm not allowed to see Petros, yet Michalis has married someone without money, and Papa did not interfere.'

Mick's face relaxed slightly. 'Only because I did not give him the opportunity, little sister.'

'So you can marry a penniless nobody, and I am expected to take Spiros Georgiou just because his family is rich. A man who wears glasses and has damp hands, besides being shorter than I am.'

There was real unhappiness mingled with the outrage in Ismene's voice and Kate bit back her involuntary smile.

'And you will mind your tongue, my girl,' her father cautioned sternly. 'Or go to your room.'

Ismene set down the jug with a crash. 'It will be a pleasure,' she retorted, and flounced from the room.

Kate heard Linda Howell sigh softly.

She said, 'Katherine, shall we take our tea out on the terrace and leave the men to talk?'

Kate forced a smile. 'That would be good.'

The terrace was wide and bordered by an elaborate balustrade. Kate leaned on the sun-warmed stone and took a deep breath, as she looked down through the clustering pines to the ripple of the sea. 'It's beautiful.'

Linda smiled. 'It's also a minefield,' she said wryly. 'As you must have noticed.'

'Yes.' Kate bit her lip. 'Has there—always been friction between Mick and his father.'

'Not when Regina was alive, although I know she could foresee problems when Mick became fully adult and challenged Ari's authority.

'Is that her portrait over the fireplace?'

'Yes.' Linda's mouth tightened. 'I'm surprised it's still there. Each time I visit, which isn't often these days, I expect to find it's been consigned to some cellar.'

'You and Regina were close?'

'We were raised together. My father was a career diplomat,

and always on the move, so I stayed in New York with my aunt and uncle. Regina and I were more like sisters than cousins. When she married Ari, the villa became a second home for me. After she died so suddenly, it seemed natural to stay on and care for Ismene.' Her blue eyes were sad. 'And apart from that Ari and I could help each other grieve.'

'How did she die?'

'She had this heart weakness. It was incredible because she was the strongest person I knew—she was a marvellous rider, and she sailed and played tennis like a champion. But she had a really hard time when Michael was born, and the doctors warned her against any more pregnancies. But she and Ari had always wanted a daughter, so she decided to take the risk.' She shook her head. 'She was never really well afterwards and one day—she just went.'

She pursed her lips ruefully. 'I wish, for her sake, I'd done a better job with Ismene, but each time I tried to impose rules, Ari would undermine them. He wanted Ismene to be a free spirit like her mother. What he didn't grasp was that Regina's freedom came from self-discipline. Now he's trying to close the dam, and it could be too late.'

'Because of this Petros?' Kate drank some of her tea. 'You think they should be allowed to marry?'

'He's a great guy, and she's known him for ever. I always guessed that one day she'd stop looking on him as just another big brother, and she could have made so many worse choices.' She sighed. 'But she approached it the wrong way. She should have let Ari think it was all his idea. Just before you arrived, she demanded that Petros come to tonight's family dinner as her future husband.' Linda pulled a wry face. 'I tried to talk her out of it. The Theodakis men do not respond well to ultimatums.'

'I'd noticed.' Kate set her glass down on the balustrade. 'Mick's been in an odd mood ever since his father sent for us.' She paused. 'Of course there could be another reason for that,' she added carefully.

'Ah,' Linda said. 'So you've met Ari's other house guest?'

'Yes.' Kate stared hard at the view.

Linda sighed. 'If you want me to give an explanation, I can't. She was with Mick, now she's with Ari. End of story.'

Kate caught a sudden glimpse of pain on the calm face, and realised she'd stumbled on a different story altogether.

'But whatever happened,' Linda went on after a pause. 'Mick married you, and not the dynastic heiress his father would have chosen.' She gave Kate a swift smile. 'Maybe we'd better check on them—see there's no blood on the floor.'

'Is there really that much friction?' Kate asked, troubled.

'It's natural.' Linda shrugged. 'Mick's the heir apparent, and he has a lot of support in the company, but Ari's still king, and he's not ready to abdicate—not by a mile. They'll work it out.' She paused. 'And if things get too heavy, you can always retreat to the beach house.'

She pointed downwards through the trees to a splash of terracotta. 'Ari had it built for when there was an extra influx of guests, but Regina really made it her own place. He was away a lot, and she found the villa big and lonely without him. It has its own pool, and this wonderful platform overlooking the sea where she used to sit and paint.'

She glanced at her watch, and uttered a faint exclamation. 'Hey, I must be off.'

'Aren't you staying for dinner?' Dismayed, Kate took the hand she was offered.

'No, I was asked to meet you, which I've done, and now I'm going home.' She smiled at Kate. 'I hope you'll come and visit at Sami. Get Ismene to bring you over. You didn't see her best side today, but she has a lot going for her. And she could do with a friend.'

'Perhaps,' Kate thought as she watched her go. 'Ismene isn't the only one.'

She turned back to look down at the beach house. It sounded as if it could become a sanctuary. Tomorrow, she decided, she would find her way down there. Ask Ismene to show her the way perhaps.

She heard the sound of voices, and Mick and his father emerged from the *saloni* and came to join her.

'Has Linda gone?' Mick put his arm round her, resting his hand casually on her hip.

'Yes, you've just missed her.'

'I asked her to stay for dinner.' There was a touch of defensiveness in Ari's tone. 'But she said she had plans.'

'Well, perhaps she did.' Mick shrugged. 'I hope so. She's a very beautiful woman.'

There was a silence, then Ari turned to Kate. 'Well, *pedhi mou*. Do you think you will be happy here?'

'I'm happy to be wherever Michael is,' she returned quietly.

'Good—good.' He smiled. 'I am glad my son is proving an attentive husband.'

The colour deepened in Kate's cheeks, but she returned his gaze without wavering. 'I have no major complaints, *kyrie*.'

Mick looked at her, his mouth relaxing into a faint smile. He said softly, 'You will suffer for that tonight, my girl.'

'Well restrain your ardour until after dinner,' Ari said with sudden joviality. 'Androula is preparing her special lemon chicken and she will not forgive if you are late.'

He clapped Mick on the shoulder. 'It will be like old times, *ne*?'

Mick looked at the sea, his face expressionless. 'As you say.'

They're like a pair of dogs, Kate thought uneasily, circling each other, getting in the odd nip. But the main event is still to come.

'I thought tomorrow I would ask your sister to show me around,' she said later, when she was alone with Mick in their bedroom, changing for dinner. 'Get to know her.'

'A word of advice,' Mick said, adjusting his black tie.

'Don't get drawn into Ismene's intrigues. They always end in tears.'

'I'm not,' Kate protested. She was sitting at the dressing table in bra and briefs putting the finishing touches to her makeup. 'But your father's choice of a husband for her doesn't sound very appealing.'

'Don't worry about it. There will be no enforced marriage.' He paused. 'Your hair looks beautiful.'

'Someone called Soula did it.' Kate touched the artfully careless topknot with a self-conscious hand. 'Apparently your father sent her to look after me. She did all our unpacking, too, and would have helped me dress if I'd let her.'

'Then I'm glad you sent her away,' Mick said softly. 'I wish to retain some privileges.' He went into the adjoining dressing room, and emerged a moment later with a length of black silk draped over his arm. 'Wear this tonight, *agapi mou*.'

'Really?' Kate's brows lifted doubtfully. It was an elegant bias-cut dress with a low neck and shoestring straps that he'd bought her in New York. 'Isn't that a little much for a family dinner. I—I can't wear a bra with it.'

'I know.' He undid the tiny clip, and slipped off the scrap of lace. 'So—have this in its place.'

It was a diamond, cut in a classic tear-drop shape, and glowing like captured fire against her skin. Kate gasped in disbelief, as Mick fastened the fine gold chain round her neck. Her voice shook. 'It's—beautiful.'

His eyes met hers in the mirror. 'But the setting,' he told her gently, 'is even more exquisite.' And for a tingling moment, his hands grazed the tips of her bare breasts. 'A jewel,' he whispered. 'For my jewel.'

He dropped a kiss on her shoulder and straightened. 'Stand up, *matia mou*.'

She obeyed, and he dropped the black dress deftly over her head, without disturbing a strand of hair, and zipped it up.

She said unsteadily, 'You are—almost too good at that.'

Laughing, he took her hand. 'You inspire me, my Kate.'

Then why don't you tell me you love me? she wondered fiercely. Because you never have. Not once in all these months.

When she entered the *saloni* on Mick's arm, she found it deserted apart from Ismene who was glancing through a fashion magazine beside the log fire which had been kindled to fight the evening chill. The younger girl looked up. 'Michalis, Papa wishes you to go to him in his study. There has been a fax you should see.'

'Very well,' Mick said. 'But look after Katharina for me. Get her a drink—and call her no names,' he added grimly.

Ismene came over to her with an ouzo, looking subdued.

'I wish to apologise, sister. I was rude when I called you a penniless nobody. Although Papa said it first,' she added, her brow darkening.

Kate laughed. 'Let's forget it and begin again, shall we?'

'I would like that. But I cannot help being jealous, because Michalis has married whom he wishes, and I may not.' She gave Kate a speculative look. 'You are not like his other women,' she offered.

Kate's smile held constraint. 'I've noticed.'

Ismene giggled. 'So you have met her. I wish I had been there. How she must hate you.'

Kate said slowly, 'But—that's all in the past now—surely?'

'Is it?' The pretty face was suddenly cynical. 'Maybe. Who knows?'

Kate struggled with herself and lost. 'How did Victorine come to be with your father?'

Ismene shrugged. 'It is a mystery. We thought at first that she had come to wait for Michalis—to be with him when he returned. We could not believe that Papa had invited her—and that she was his *eromeni* instead.'

She shook her head. 'And when Michalis did come, he was so angry—like a crazy man. We could hear him with Papa, shouting at each other.' She shuddered. 'Terrible things were said.'

'Did he care about her so much?' Kate concentrated fiercely on her drink.

Ismene shrugged. 'Naturally. She was the ultimate trophy woman, and Papa took her from him.

She brightened. 'But now you and Mick are married, he need not stay away any more. Because he cannot still be in love with Victorine, and Papa need not be jealous.'

'No.' Kate said quietly, her throat tightening. 'It's all—worked out very well.'

'I wish life could be as good for me. Do you know that Papa will not even allow my Petros to come to the house any more.' She tossed her head. 'But it makes no difference, because we are still engaged to each other.'

Kate picked her words carefully. 'Perhaps your father feels you're still young to be making such an important decision.'

Ismene snorted disrespectfully. 'I am the same age as Mama when Papa married her. And I would not be too young if I agreed to marry that horrid Spiro. Although I would rather die.'

Kate's face relaxed into a grin. 'I'd say you had a point,' she conceded.

Ismene looked at her hopefully. 'Perhaps Mick would speak to Papa for me. Talk him round?'

Kate gave a constrained smile, but did not answer because at that moment Victorine entered the *saloni*. She was wearing another clinging dress in fuchsia pink, its low-cut bodice glittering with crystals.

She helped herself to a drink, then came across to Kate, her eyes fixed on the diamond pendant.

'A new necklace, *chère*?' She ignored Ismene. Her mouth smiled, but her eyes were venomous. 'Men usually buy their wives expensive gifts because they feel guilty about something. I wonder what Mick has on his conscience?'

'Bitch,' Ismene whispered succinctly as Victorine moved off towards the fire, using the distinctive swaying walk which had graced so many catwalks. 'Don't let her wind you up.'

Easier said than done, Kate thought wryly.

Ari gave her the place of honour beside him at dinner, and talked to her kindly, but she had the feeling she was being screened, so it wasn't the most comfortable meal she'd ever had.

It was undoubtedly one of the most delicious though, and she said so as she finished the famous chicken, fragrant with lemon.

'I'm glad you liked it.' He gave her an approving smile. 'From tomorrow, it will be for you to order the meals, *pedhi mou*, and run the household. I have instructed Androula, and Yannis my majordomo, to come to you for your orders each day.'

Kate stared at him. 'But I've never…'

'Then you must begin.' His tone demolished further protest, and alerted the attention of everyone round the table to Kate's embarrassment. 'You are the wife of my son, and you take your rightful place in his home.'

He gave Mick a fierce look, and received an unsmiling nod in reply.

'And don't keep me waiting too long for my grandson,' he added, more jovially, turning back to Kate, who looked down at her plate, blushing furiously, aware that Victorine was watching her.

It was a long meal and, afterwards, there was coffee in the *saloni*, and another hissed diatribe from Ismene about her father's injustice, and the general misery of her life.

In fact, meeting Linda had probably been the highlight of a rather fraught day, Kate thought, as she prepared for bed that night.

When she emerged from the bathroom, Mick was standing

by the window in his dressing gown, staring into the darkness.

She slid her arms round his waist. 'Coming to bed?'

'Presently.'

She rested her cheek against his chest. She said softly, a smile in her voice, 'Well, we have our instructions. Your father wants a grandchild.'

He detached himself from her embrace. He said coldly, 'Understand this, Katharina. I give orders. I do not take them. And now I intend to sleep.'

He took off his robe and tossed it over a chair, then walked, naked, to the bed, and got in, turning on his side so that his back was towards her for the first time in the marriage.

Leaving her standing there, shocked, bewildered and suddenly totally isolated. With Mick's diamond burning like ice between her breasts.

CHAPTER EIGHT

I BELIEVED, Kate thought flatly, that it wasn't possible to be more unhappy—more alone than I was that night. But what did I know?

She looked round the impersonal luxury of the hotel room she now occupied alone, and shivered.

She should have realised, she thought. Made the connection there and then. Seen that her brief marriage had begun to collapse—and faced the reason.

Yet, on that following morning, when she'd woken to find herself in his arms, and heard him whisper, 'I'm sorry, *agapi mou*. Forgive me…' she'd been able to tell herself it was just a temporary glitch. That he'd had a difficult day too.

And she'd drawn him down to her, her lips parting willingly under his kiss.

Of course, Kate thought flatly, as the memories stung at her mind, I didn't realise just how much there was to forgive.

Because I was never a real wife—just a red herring, intended to draw his father away from the truth about his relationship with Victorine. The solution to a problem, just as I heard him discussing with Iorgos that night on Zycos.

And Mick didn't want us to have a child because he knew the marriage wasn't going to last. At least he didn't pretend about that.

And that, too, is why he never said he loved me. It was as near as he could get to honesty.

She heard herself moan, softly and painfully. She got up from the bed and began to pace restlessly round the room, then paused, and took a deep breath.

She shouldn't be doing this to herself, and she knew it. It was all still too new. Too raw.

After all, less than two months ago, she'd still been living in her fool's paradise.

And soon now she would be back on Kefalonia, and all the old wounds would be open and bleeding again.

She would have to stand in the village church, and watch Ismene make her marriage vows to the man she loved, and see Petros' rather serious face alight with tenderness as he looked at her.

And she would have to see Mick and Victorine together, exchanging their secret lovers' glances. Become part of the betrayal she had run from. Until Mick chose to let her go.

I can't do it, she thought, nausea acrid in her throat. No one should be expected to play a part like that. Pretend…

But no matter how battered she felt—how emotionally bruised—she couldn't deny the magic of those first weeks she'd spent on Kefalonia.

Beginning at breakfast that first morning when Ismene, eyes dancing, told her that Victorine was no longer at the villa.

'She's on her way to Paris to do some shopping,' she confided. 'To buy a bigger diamond than yours, Katharina *mou*,' she added naughtily.

Kate tried to look reproving. 'Has your father gone with her?'

'No, no.' Ismene looked shocked. 'Because there will be meetings soon with some of the other directors of our companies. Last time Victorine was *so* bored.' She rolled her eyes. 'She likes the money, you understand, but she is not interested in how it is made. Maybe this is why Papa encouraged her to go,' she went on. 'Or perhaps he is still not quite sure…' She stopped, guiltily, her eyes flying to Kate's suddenly frozen face. 'But no—that is silly.'

'Yes,' Kate agreed quietly. 'Very silly.'

'And, of course, you will be Papa's hostess—to prove to everyone that he and Mick are friends again.' Ismene went on eagerly. 'There has been much anxiety, you understand,

and people have taken sides, which is not good. But everything will be better now.'

'I hope so.' Kate forced a smile. 'Perhaps Victorine won't come back.'

'But she will.' Ismene pulled a face. 'Unless she finds a richer man than Papa.'

Whatever the reasons for it, Kate couldn't be sorry about Victorine's absence, especially when days lengthened into weeks with no sign of her return.

Not that she had time to brood about anything. Her new responsibilities had not been exaggerated, she discovered from the moment Yannis and Androula took her on the promised tour of the house.

The Villa Dionysius was much larger than even her first impression had suggested—a positive labyrinth of passages, courtyards and rooms, and Kate saw all of it, down to the cellars, the food stores and the linen cupboards.

'Each generation has added to the house,' Yannis told her proudly. 'And you and Kyrios Michalis will do the same—when the children come.'

Kate bit back a smile. It was ridiculous, she thought, the way everyone was trying to prompt them into parenthood. And what a pity she couldn't share the joke with Mick.

She couldn't help being nervous as the first of the promised guests began to arrive, but was able to draw on her training as a courier to give each of them a composed and smiling welcome, and make sure their comfort was catered for in every way.

It was not an easy time. Not all the meetings went smoothly, and she was aware of tensions and undercurrents as people came and went. Both Mick and his father were grim and thoughtful at times.

But at last, all the visitors departed, and Kate, their compliments still ringing in her ears, was able to draw breath.

'You have done well, *pedhi mou*,' Ari told her. He gave a satisfied smile. 'In fact, it has all been most successful.' He darted a glance at Mick. 'And I am not quite ready for Yeronitsia, *ne*?'

'Yeronitsia?' Kate repeated puzzled.

'A high rock near Ayios Thomas,' Mick supplied unsmilingly. 'From which, legend says, the old and useless used to be thrown. My father,' he added, 'likes to joke.'

But Kate couldn't feel it had been a joke. And a few days later, when Linda took her on a tour of the island, she mentioned it, while they were sitting drinking coffee on the waterfront at Fiscardo.

Linda sighed. 'You're right, it's not funny, but I guess it was inevitable. Ari was so pleased and proud when Mick joined the company, but less so as he began to find his own voice—formulate his own ideas.'

She shrugged. 'You can understand it. Ari was proud of what he'd achieved, and was wary of change—especially the kind of expansion Mick was advocating. Also,' her smile was wry, 'he was beginning to feel his age, and he resented this. He began to say that Mick was too young—too wild to step into his shoes. That the Theodakis corporation should not go to someone with such a high-profile social life. And for a time there, Mick supplied him with all the ammunition he needed,' she added ruefully.

'And, Ari likes to play games—to hint at his retirement in private, then deny it in public. But there've been signs that the board is getting restive—that support for Michael is growing. I—I hope Ari goes with dignity before he's forced out. It would have broken Regina's heart to know how far things had deteriorated between them,' she added huskily.

She didn't speak Victorine's name, but then she didn't have to, Kate thought with a sudden chill.

And one day soon the beautiful Creole would return.

But, in the meantime, Kate could relax and enjoy herself. Already the Villa Dionysius was beginning to feel like home. The staff were so well-trained that the house almost ran itself, and this gave her the opportunity to explore the rest of the island, sometimes with Linda, but usually and joyfully in Mick's company, making the most of its many beauties before the influx of tourists arrived.

She loved hearing him talk about Kefalonia's sometimes stormy history, and share his knowledge of the archaeological discoveries that had taken place over the years.

She was thrilled by the various underground caves with their dark and secret lakes that he showed her, but shivered away from the village of Markopoulo after Mick told her that the Church of Our Lady there was visited each August by crowds of small snakes.

'They crawl up to her icon,' Mick said, amused at her horrified expression. 'We look on them as good luck, especially as they stayed away during the last war, and in the earthquake year.'

'I prefer miracles that don't wriggle,' Kate said with dignity. 'I think I shall arrange to be somewhere else in August.'

Remembering those lightly spoken words now, Kate bit her lip until she tasted blood. Perhaps she shouldn't have been so flippant about the island's luck. Because hers had begun to run out not long afterwards.

Ismene's feud with her father over her wish to marry Petros had shown no signs of abating. Although she had been forbidden to see him, she continued to meet him in secret and, on several occasions, Kate had been her unwilling accomplice, driving her into Argostoli, the island's capital, on vague shopping expeditions.

Ismene had insisted on introducing them, and Kate had to admit that, apart from his lack of worldly goods, she couldn't fault him. He was more serious in his manner than Ismene, but blessed with a quiet sense of humour. He was also good looking, and intelligent.

'Papa says he is not good for me,' Ismene said soberly as they drove home. 'But, in truth, Katharina, he is much too good, and I know it. All the same, I will be a good and loving wife to him.'

Kate found herself unexpectedly touched to the heart by this little speech. But when she mentioned it to Mick, he was angry.

'I told you not to get involved,' he reminded her coldly. 'Now you are joining her in her deceit.'

They almost had a row about it, and matters did not improve when Ismene mounted another tearful and highly vocal campaign to get her father to approve her engagement.

Kate had not been altogether sorry when Mick had insisted on the move down to the peace of the beach house. It had already become one of her favourite places, and she had taken to swimming in the pool there every day anyway, now that the real summer heat had begun, but the sea was still cold.

It was much smaller than the villa, with just two bedrooms, a large living room, as well as a kitchen and bathroom, but it was furnished with exquisite comfort, and it had the great advantage of seclusion. And the big platform at the front that Linda had mentioned was perfect for sunbathing.

'A second honeymoon,' Kate said dreamily on their first evening alone there.

Mick raised his eyebrows. 'And less chance for you to become embroiled in Ismene's mischief, *matia mou*,' he told her, pulling her into his arms.

She was disappointed when she discovered that he was about to depart on visits to the Regina hotels on Corfu, Crete and Rhodes, and that she would not be going with him.

'It's pure routine. You'd be bored.' He'd kissed her swiftly as he left for the airport. 'Try not to let Ismene and Papa kill each other, and I'll be back before you know it.'

But she felt restless, edgy without him. The days were long, but the nights were longer, and his daily phone calls were only part consolation.

She had to put up with sulks from Ismene too, when the younger girl discovered that Kate was not going to drive her to any more secret rendezvous.

She began to spend more time at the beach house. Quite often she was joined there by Linda, and Ismene too when she regained her good humour, and Kate enjoyed preparing poolside lunches for them.

Regina Theodakis had clearly been keen on reading as well as painting, and a large, crammed bookcase was one of the features of the living room. Kate found herself making new discoveries every day, as well as renewing her acquaintance with some old favourites.

Mick had been gone almost two weeks, when Victorine returned. As soon as Kate walked into the villa she was aware of a subtle shift in the atmosphere. She didn't really need Ismene's whispered, 'She's back,' to know what had happened.

'And she's in a really good mood—all smiles,' Ismene went on disparagingly. 'You should see the luggage she's brought back. She must have bought the world. And she's given me a present.'

She extracted a silky top with shoestring straps and exquisite beading from a bag emblazoned with the name of a boutique from the exclusive Kolonaki Square in Athens, and held it up. 'See?'

Kate's brows rose. 'Very nice,' she commented drily. 'Perhaps she's going on a charm offensive.'

But her optimism was short-lived.

'The sun has given you some colour, *chère*.' Victorine was stretched out on a lounger on the terrace, wearing a miniscule string bikini, the expression in her eyes concealed behind designer sunglasses. 'That shade of hair can make a woman look so washed out,' she added disparagingly.

'And good morning to you, too,' Kate said coolly, pouring herself some fruit juice.

'So you are not pregnant yet.' Victorine began to apply a fresh layer of sun lotion to her arms. 'Ari is very disappointed. It might be wise not to keep him waiting too long, or he might begin to wonder about this marriage of yours.

Especially as Michalis has apparently become—restless again, and left you all alone here.'

'Mick's on a business trip,' Kate said, resisting the urge to throw the fruit juice over her antagonist. 'We don't have to be joined at the hip every moment of the day.'

'Or the night either.' Smilingly, Victorine recapped the bottle. 'You are very understanding to allow him these little diversions, *chère*. I hope your trust is rewarded. Michalis can be so wicked when he gets bored.'

'Well, you should know,' Kate said blandly, returning her glass to the tray, and walking off.

But even the pleasure of having the last word couldn't sweeten the little exchange for her.

'I'll keep out of the way,' she thought, thanking her stars that she had a sanctuary, but, to her dismay, Ari made it clear that he expected her to be present at dinner that evening, and perform her usual duties, so she reluctantly obeyed.

Victorine was in her element at dinner, her behaviour to Ari seductively possessive, as she regaled them with the latest film-world gossip, hinting at the lucrative contracts that were still being offered her.

'But how could I be away for months at a time, *cher*, when even a few weeks is too much.' Lips pouting, she put a caressing hand on Ari's arm.

Kate was just wondering what excuse she could make to avoid coffee in the *saloni* when the door of the dining room opened, and Mick walked in.

Amid the exclamations of astonishment and welcome, Kate got shakily to her feet.

'Why didn't you tell me?' she whispered, as he reached her.

'I wanted to surprise you, *agapi mou*.' His arms went round her, drawing her to him. His mouth was warm on hers. 'Have I succeeded?'

'Shall I tell Androula to bring you some food, boy?' Ari barked.

'I had an early dinner in Athens with Iorgos. Now I just want to wash off the city grime, and relax a little.' He smiled at Kate. 'Come and run a bath for me, *matia mou*,' he invited softly.

As Kate went with him, blushing, to the door, she was suddenly aware of Victorine watching her, her eyes cold with derision, and something oddly like pity…

'Was it a successful trip?' Kate lay in the circle of Mick's arms, as the scented water lapped round them.

'The homecoming is better.' He wound a long strand of her damp hair round his fingers and kissed it. 'Maybe, I should go away more often.'

'I disagree.' She touched his face gently with her hand, then paused. 'I didn't know you were going to Athens.'

'Nor did I, but it was unavoidable. A last-minute thing.' He picked up the sponge and squeezed warm water over her shoulders. 'So, what has been happening here? Has Ismene been behaving herself?'

'I try not to ask.' She bit her lip. 'Victorine came back this morning.'

'Leaving a trail of devastation in every design salon in Europe, no doubt.'

Had she imagined the fractional hesitation before his dismissive reply.

'She was shopping in Athens too,' she ventured.

'It's a big city, *agapi mou*.' He kissed the side of her neck. 'Now, let's dry ourselves. Our bed is waiting, and you can show me all over again how glad you are to see me.'

And Kate forgot everything—even that strange, niggling doubt—in the passionate bliss of their reunion.

But, with hindsight, she could have no doubt that Mick had been with Victorine in Athens. He'd brushed aside her tentative query, but he hadn't denied it.

And, however much she'd longed for his return, she

couldn't pretend it was all honey and roses in the days that followed.

Within twenty-four hours, it was evident that relations between Ari and himself were strained, and Mick seemed to retire into a tight-lipped, preoccupied world of his own.

More visiting executives came and went, and there was another endless stream of meetings. Kate struggled to fulfil her role as hostess, but found her smile beginning to crack after a while. She felt as if she was living on the edge of a volcano, but, when she tried to question Mick about what was going on, she found herself blocked.

'But I want to help,' she protested.

'You are helping.' He kissed the top of her head. 'Be content.'

But that was easier said than done.

Even when they made love, Kate had the feeling that he'd retreated emotionally behind some barrier, and she had to search for him, reach out to him, in the joining of their bodies.

But at least in the early afternoons she had him all to herself. They had gone down to the cove to swim at first, but then had found Victorine there, sunbathing in nothing but a thong. Mick ignored her stonily, but, when he found Ismene emulating her, he gave his sister a telling-off in cold, fierce Greek which reduced her to tears.

After that, they had stayed up at the beach house, and Mick had given strict orders that their privacy there was not to be disturbed by anyone. Even Ismene did not dare to intrude on them.

One hot and windless day, lying in the shelter of a poolside umbrella, Kate put down her book, and said, 'When are we going to have a baby?'

He was glancing frowningly through some papers. 'Has my father been asking again?'

'No,' she said. 'This time it's all my own idea. Michael—can we at least talk about it—please?'

His mouth tightened. 'This is not a good time for me, *pedhi mou.*' His voice was gentle but inflexible.

She swallowed. 'Then when can we have a discussion about our marriage—our future?'

He was silent for a moment. 'When I get back from America. We'll talk then.'

She sat up, staring at him. 'You're going to New York? When?'

'Next week. I shall be gone about ten days—perhaps less.'

She said breathlessly, 'Take me with you.'

'It's a business trip, Katharina,' he said. 'I shall be in meetings twelve hours a day. We would never see each other.'

'Mick—please. This is important to me.'

'And you are important here,' he said drily. 'I gather the household can't function without you.'

'That's nonsense, and you know it.' Her voice rose. 'The house runs like clockwork.'

'But you, *agapi mou*, wind the clock. My father is pleased with you.'

She said huskily, 'Is that why you're abandoning me here—to keep him sweet? He already has someone to fill that role.'

His tone was curt. 'Be careful what you say.'

'Michael.' Her voice appealed. 'I'm your wife. I want to be with you. Can't you understand that?'

'But you would not be with me,' he said. 'Because I should always be with other people.' He picked up his papers again. 'And I will soon be back.'

She said raggedly, 'This is why your mother used to stay here, isn't it? Not because it had wonderful views she could paint, but because the villa was too big and too lonely, and your father was always away on business as well. Maybe she even persuaded herself she didn't mind. But I do mind, Michael. I mind like hell.'

'Is it really such a penance to stay here?' He got to his

feet angrily. 'You live in comfort. The servants adore you. Ismene loves you as a sister in blood.'

'And your ex-mistress thinks I'm a bad joke.'

'Ah, Victorine,' he said softly. 'Somehow I knew the conversation would come round to her.'

'You can't pretend it's a normal situation.'

'But one we have to accept—for now, at least.' There was finality in his tone.

'Can you accept it?' She was frightened now, but she pushed herself on. Letting her darkest thoughts out into the harsh sunlight. 'Is that why we live down here, Michael—because you can't bear to see her—to think of her with your father? Tell me—tell me the truth.'

In spite of the intense heat, his glance chilled her. Silenced her. Made her heart flutter in panic.

'You are being absurd, Katharina. Unless you wish to make me angry, do not speak of this again.' He picked up his watch, and fastened it on to his wrist. 'I am going to shower, and drive into Argostoli. At the risk of being accused of abandonment,' he added cuttingly, 'I am not going to invite you to come with me.'

When he'd gone, she retrieved her book, and tried to read, but the words blurred and danced in front of her eyes. Her throat tightened painfully, and she thought, 'Oh, God, what have I said? What have I done.'

He returned while she was dressing for dinner—several scared, aching hours later. She'd put on the black dress he liked, and hung his diamond at her throat.

'Mick.' Her voice shook. 'I'm sorry. I didn't know what I was saying.'

He put his hands on her shoulders. In the mirror, she met his gaze, hooded, enigmatic.

He said, 'Perhaps we both have some thinking to do, Katharina. And my trip will give us the necessary space, *ne*?'

No, she thought. We don't need that. There's too much space between us already. I can't reach you any more.

But she smiled steadily, and said, 'I expect you're right.' And knew she was weeping inside.

Kate put her hands up to her face, wiping away the tears she did not have to hide any more.

Why did she have this total recall, she asked herself desperately, when amnesia would have been so much more merciful?

She thought I can't go on—torturing myself like this. I can't…

She went into the bathroom and washed her face, trying to conceal the signs of distress.

Then she went out into the sitting room. She would have to confront Michael once and for all. Tell him she'd changed her mind. That even if their divorce took for ever, she would not go back to Kefalonia and be made to relive any more of her humiliation and betrayal.

She was halfway across the room when his bedroom door opened and he came out. He was wearing dark, close-fitting pants, and a white shirt, with a silk tie knotted loosely round his throat. He was carrying a light cashmere jacket in a fine check over one arm, and fastening his cuff-links with his free hand as he walked.

He halted, his brows lifting. 'You should have stayed in your sanctuary a little longer, *matia mou*.' His tone was sardonic. 'Then you would have been spared the sight of me.'

'You're going out?'

'Evidently.'

'Where are you going?'

'Be careful. Katharina *mou*,' he said softly. 'You are beginning to sound like a wife. Although I am sure you do not wish to be treated as one.'

She flushed, biting her lip. 'It's just that—I need to talk to you.'

'But I am not in the mood for conversation. I am going

out to find some congenial company.' His eyes raked her dismissively. 'God knows it will not be difficult.'

She flinched inwardly. 'Please listen to me.'

'No, Katharina. We have already said everything that is necessary to each other.'

She lifted her chin. 'I've changed my mind.'

He was very still. 'In what way?'

'I can't go back with you,' she said rapidly. 'I won't.'

'Your rebellion is too late, *matia mou*. I shall not permit you to back out now.'

'You can't make me.' The words were uttered before she had time to think. And they were a mistake. She knew that even before she saw him smile.

'You don't think so? I say you are wrong, my wife.' He tossed his jacket on to a sofa. Took a step towards her.

'Perhaps I shall stay here after all, and show you that I can—persuade you to do anything I want. That I can take from you anything I desire, and you will let me. Because—still—you cannot help yourself. And you know it.'

He paused, letting the words sink in. 'Or would you prefer to stick to the bargain we have made after all—and spend your nights alone?'

'Yes,' she said. She kept her voice level, even though she was shaking inside. 'Yes, I would—prefer that.'

'You are wise.' His voice was mocking, as he retrieved his coat and shrugged it on. The dark eyes were hard. 'It has been a long time since I touched you, *agapi mou*, and almost certainly I would not have been gentle.'

He watched the colour drain from her face and nodded. He added courteously, 'I wish you a pleasant evening,' and went.

CHAPTER NINE

As THE plane began its descent to Kefalonia airport, Kate broke the silence she'd maintained throughout the flight.

'The divorce.' Her voice was constricted. 'Have you really told—no one? Not even Iorgos Vasso?'

He would not have to tell Victorine, she thought. Because she already knew…

'No one.' Mick's tone was uncompromising, his eyes cold as he turned to look at her. 'And I intend it to remain a private matter between us, for the present, anyway. I do not wish to spoil a happy time for my sister.'

She bit her lip. 'You're all heart.'

He sighed. 'However if that is your attitude, we will deceive no one. And you will have reneged on our bargain.'

'God forbid,' Kate said bitterly. 'Don't worry, *kyrie*, I'll play the dutiful wife—in public at least.'

He said, 'It will also be necessary for us to exchange a few remarks from time to time—in public at least,' he added drily.

She lifted her chin. 'I'll do that too—if I must.'

'A small price to pay for freedom, surely?'

Oh, no, she thought, pain closing her throat. It's going to cost me everything.

The days they'd spent together in London had been almost more than she could bear. Not that they'd been together in any real sense, she reminded herself. Mick had been scrupulous about keeping his distance. During the daytime, he'd been in meetings, and she tried not to think where he could be spending his evenings and the greater part of each night. Clearly fidelity, even to Victorine, had never been on his agenda.

They deserve each other, she thought wrenchingly.

Yet, at the same time, all she knew was that she lay alone in the darkness, unable to sleep, straining her ears for the sound of his return.

And that, of course, was madness.

She had little to fill her days either. Iorgos Vasso had dealt with her employers, agreeing an extended and unpaid leave of absence, rather than the notice that Mick had advocated. He'd also arranged with an astonished Mrs Thursgood to have Kate's flat kept an eye on, and her mail forwarded.

The life she'd begun laboriously to assemble was being smoothly erased, she realised helplessly, and when she came back from Kefalonia, finally alone, she would have to rebuild it all over again.

Although that, at least, would give her something to think about, which she suspected she might need.

In accordance with Mick's instructions, she'd trawled reluctantly round Bond Street and Knightsbridge and bought some new clothes, more in keeping with her role as Mrs Theodakis, but she'd kept her expenditure to an absolute minimum.

And she would bring none of them back with her when she left. Her Kate Dennison gear was safely stowed in the bottom of one of her cases, waiting for this nightmare to be over.

The drive to the villa seemed to take no time at all. She had wanted time to compose herself for the ordeal ahead—to resist the ache of familiarity in the landmarks they were passing. To fight to the death the sense of homecoming that had assailed her as soon as the plane touched down.

The staff were clearly delighted to have her back. She was greeted with beaming smiles on all sides, and conducted ceremoniously indoors.

I feel a traitor, she thought angrily.

Her father-in-law was in the *saloni* glancing through some

papers, but he rose as Kate walked in and welcomed her with a swift, formal embrace.

'It is good to see you.' He stepped back, and looked at her critically. 'But you are thinner. This will not do.' He glanced at Mick. 'You will have to take better care of her, my son.'

'I intend to,' Mick returned, unsmilingly.

'I was worried when you went without saying goodbye.' Ari indicated that Kate should sit beside him. 'But Michalis told me it was an emergency. That you had been called away urgently.' He paused, eyeing her shrewdly. 'I hope it is all resolved now.'

She mustered a taut smile. 'Well—nearly, I think.'

'Perhaps we could have helped,' Ari suggested. 'We have teams of lawyers—accountants—business advisers—all with too little to do. Did Michalis not explain this?'

Kate bit her lip. 'It was a—private matter. I didn't want to trouble anyone else.'

'You are a Theodakis now, Katharina.' Ari patted her hand. 'Your problems are ours. But, you will be tired after the flight. Michalis, take her down to the beach house, and see that she rests.'

Kate's heart was thumping as she walked beside Mick down the track through the pine woods. How many times had she taken this same path with him, she wondered, knowing their bed and his arms awaited her?

And now she was on her way to pain, betrayal and deception. Just as she had been only a few short weeks before.

She stumbled on a loose stone, and he caught her arm, steadying her.

She wrenched herself free, glaring at him. 'Don't touch me. Don't dare.'

There was a shocked pause, then he said bleakly, 'You would rather fall than have me catch you. I understand.'

For a moment there was an odd expression on his face—bewildered. Almost—lost.

He still can't believe he isn't irresistible, Kate thought, lashing herself into fresh anger.

The house was just as she remembered it, with its faded terracotta tiles, and white walls festooned with flowering plants.

There were flowers inside, too, she discovered dazedly. In the master bedroom, every surface was covered by bowls full of blossoms. Like some bridal bower, she thought, checking in the doorway, faint nausea rising within her, as she looked across at the bed and remembered…

Saw her luggage standing in the corner.

She turned on Mick, standing silently behind her, her voice was harsh, strained. 'No—not this room. I won't stay here. Please have my things put in the other bedroom.'

His brows snapped together. 'I have been using that myself.'

'Then you'll have to change,' she flung at him.

You sleep in here. You live with the memories. Because I won't. I can't.

'If not, I'm leaving,' she went on recklessly. 'Going back to England, and to hell with our deal. To hell with everything. And if it blows your whole scheme out of the water—tough. But there's no way I'm going to sleep in that bed ever again.'

His face looked grey. He said hoarsely, 'Katharina—how in the name of God did we come to this?'

'Ask yourself that, *kyrie*.' Her voice was like stone. 'I'm just passing through.'

She went past him and walked the few yards down the passage to the second bedroom. The queen-size bed had clearly been freshly made up with clean sheets, and she sank down on its edge aware that her legs were shaking.

Mick followed. He said quietly, 'I have left a few things in the closet. I'll take them.'

'Yes,' she said. 'Then I can do my own unpacking.'

'Soula will do that, as usual.' He paused. 'And your clothes will stay in the other room—with me.'

'No.' Kate got to her feet. 'You can't do that.'

'You came here to preserve the illusion that we still have a marriage.' His voice bit. 'Most couples share a room—a bed. I ask you only to share a wardrobe. You may sleep where you please, *pedhi mou*. The night brings its own privacy.'

She bit her lip. 'Very well. Then I'll try and choose everything I need for the day each morning. At other times, I—I'll keep out of your way.'

There was silence, then he said very softly, 'I do not know if I can bear this.' And went.

Kate stood in the middle of the room, her arms wrapped round her body, until she stopped shaking. She felt bone-weary, but she knew that if she lay down, she would not be able to relax.

But it was still very warm for late September, so perhaps she would sit by the pool—or even go for a swim.

Her bathing suits were all in the master bedroom, she realised without pleasure. She went quietly along the passage, and knocked on the half-open door, but Mick was nowhere to be seen, so she went in.

The scent of the flowers was almost overwhelming as she searched for her black bikini.

As she retrieved it, and the pretty black and white overshirt that accompanied it, she heard swift footsteps approaching, and, a moment later, Ismene flung herself at her.

'Kate *mou*, at last. Oh, I am so happy you have come. I was so afraid you would not.' She pulled a face. 'Michalis made me send you the invitation. He said only when you saw it in black and white would you believe Papa had agreed.'

'What made him change his mind?' Kate shook her head. 'He seemed so adamant.'

Ismene shrugged, her expression puzzled. 'I do not know. He talked very strangely to me. Said how few people found the one person in the world who could make them happy, and what right had he to deny me when Michalis had you, and he himself had loved Mama so much.'

She lowered her voice confidentially. 'Do you think he is growing tired of Victorine, perhaps? Wouldn't it be wonderful if he sent her away?'

Kate forced a smile. 'I—wouldn't count on it.'

'Anyway, what of you, sister?' Ismene went on, after a pause. 'Why did you leave like that—without even saying goodbye, *po, po, po*?'

'It was an emergency,' Kate said steadily, falling back on the agreed story. 'A family thing. I—I can't really discuss it.'

'But all is well now, and you will be staying here?'

Kate forced a smile. 'Nothing is certain in this uncertain world,' she said. 'But I'll definitely be here to see you married.'

'My dress is wonderful,' Ismene confided. 'Silk organza, and the veil my mother wore. Petros and I will marry in the morning at our village church, and then there will be a celebration in the square. And at night there will be a party here with dancing.' She sighed. 'But I shall miss most of that because I shall be on my honeymoon.'

Kate laughed in spite of herself. 'A honeymoon is far better than any party, believe me.'

Ismene eyed her speculatively. 'You and Michalis—did you do it *every* night?'

Kate gasped, feeling a wave of heat swamp her face, as she searched vainly for a reply.

Mick said from the doorway, 'That is none of your business, Ismene *mou*.' He strolled into the room, his face expressionless as he surveyed his wife's embarrassment. 'And if you make my Kate blush again, I shall tell Petros to beat you.'

She sent him a mischievous look. 'Perhaps I should enjoy that. But I can tell when I am no longer wanted,' she added with a giggle. 'I will see you later, Katharina.'

And she flew off again, leaving husband and wife facing each other.

Kate's face was still burning. She said, 'I—I thought I'd sit by the pool.'

He glanced at the bikini, dangling from her hand, and his mouth curled. 'Then I will use the beach.'

She looked at the floor. 'Isn't that rather going to extremes?' she asked in a low voice. 'Surely we don't have to avoid each other to that extent.'

'Ah, but we do,' he said. 'I promise you, *agapi mou*. You see, I still find the sight of you wearing next to nothing too disturbing to risk.' He began casually to unbutton his shirt. 'I am sure you understand.'

Kate sank her teeth into her lower lip. 'Yes,' she said. 'Yes, of course.' She remembered suddenly that the beach was Victorine's favourite haunt. 'But I'm sure you'll find an even more appealing view,' she added hastily, regretting it at once.

Mick tossed his shirt on the bed, and gave her a narrow-eyed look. 'What is that supposed to mean?'

She shrugged. 'Nothing. After all, you were the one who told me Kefalonia was a beautiful island.'

'But clearly not beautiful enough to tempt you to stay in our marriage.'

She stared at him in disbelief. 'You dare say that to me?' Her voice shook. 'When it was you—you…'

'You knew what I was when you met me.' Mick unbuckled his belt and unzipped his trousers. 'I never pretended that I could give you my undivided attention.'

'Am I supposed to admire your honesty?' Kate asked bitterly.

'I would have settled for acceptance.' He slipped his discarded trousers on to a hanger, put them in the closet, then walked over to her. 'Have you forgotten all the happy hours we spent in this room, *matia mou*.' His voice sank huskily. 'Is my sin really so impossible to forgive?'

It occurred to her suddenly that he was wearing nothing but a pair of his favourite silk shorts. Her throat tightened, and, flurried, she took a step backwards.

'Don't run away, Katharina *mou*.' He spoke softly, seductively. 'And don't you fight me any more. Stay with me now. Let me make amends to you. Show you how much I need you.'

His hands were gentle on her shoulders, drawing her close.

For a crazy moment, she found herself remembering how long it was since she'd really touched him. Since she'd let her fingers stray over his naked skin, tracing the steel of bone and muscle. Since her lips had adored the planes and angles of his lean, responsive body.

She wanted to run her fingers along the line of his shoulder, and kiss the heated pulse in his throat. She was hungry—frantic to feel the maleness of him lifting gloriously to her caress.

And then as if a light clicked on in her head, she remembered, and pulled herself free.

'Don't touch me,' she said between her teeth. 'Oh God, I should have known I couldn't trust you.'

Something flickered momentarily in his eyes, then he laughed curtly. 'You have a short memory, dear wife. This is my room—you were quite insistent about it. And I did not invite you here. You came of your own free will. You watched me undress.' He shrugged, his mouth twisting. 'It could be thought you were sending me a signal.'

'Then think again,' Kate flashed stormily. 'Do you seriously think that an—afternoon romp with you could repair the damage between us? And in this of all places.' She drew a harsh shuddering breath. 'Oh, God, I despise you. I hate you.'

He said quietly, 'I am beginning to understand that. I confess that I thought a—romp could be a start for us. A new beginning. But I see now that there is no hope.'

He paused. 'I will tell Soula to take all your clothing and

belongings to your own room after all. Then you need never set foot in here again.' He turned away. 'Now go.'

All Kate really wanted to do was crawl into her room, and hide in some dark corner while she licked her wounds.

But that was impossible. Even though she was dying inside, she had to salvage her pride—to pretend she didn't care. That Michael no longer had the power to hurt her.

She'd said she was going to spend some time by the pool, and that she would do, she resolved, straightening shoulders that ached with tension. Even if it killed her.

She stripped, and put on her bikini. The golden tan which she'd acquired earlier in the summer still lingered, she thought, subjecting herself to a critical scrutiny in the long wall mirror.

But, she was still losing weight. When she'd married Michael; her figure had been nicely rounded in all the right places. Now she could count the bones in her ribcage.

But, even at her best, she'd never come near Victorine's sinuously voluptuous quality, she thought, biting into her lower lip.

And her performance in bed would never match the sultry Creole's either.

That was a painful truth she could not avoid.

She was married to a passionate, experienced man, who had taken her for his own reasons. And, for him, the gift of her loving heart would never have been enough.

He wanted more, she thought. The kind of sophisticated playmate he'd been accustomed to in the past. Something she could never be.

Of course, he'd been endlessly patient with her in those first months, but, however willing the pupil, it was probably inevitable that he'd become bored with being the teacher. And the novelty had worn off for him long ago.

But that didn't mean she would ever accede to his cynical suggestion that she go along with this smokescreen marriage she'd been tricked into. Turn a blind eye to his amours for the prestige of being Mrs Michael Theodakis.

She felt tears prick at her eyelids, and fought them back.

This might be the norm for marriage in the circles Michael Theodakis moved in, but it would never do for her. She cared too much, which no doubt rendered her doubly unfashionable. And no amount of money or luxury was going to change a thing.

Sighing, she trailed out into the sunshine.

It might be the day from hell, she thought, unhappily, as she adjusted the umbrella over her lounger and stretched out on the cushions, but there was still the evening, with the inevitable family dinner to endure somehow.

And Victorine…

There hadn't been a glimpse of her so far, or a mention, but Kate knew the other woman would simply be biding her time, waiting for the most destructive moment. She shivered. The sun was still warm, but the memory of that other hot, golden day hung over her like a shadow, impossible to dispel.

She'd run down through the pines that day with wings on her feet, on fire to see Mick—to throw herself into his arms and resolve the differences that had caused them to part in anger.

She'd been stupid to make the matter of her travelling with him into an issue. She should have been persuasive rather than confrontational. But when she realised that he meant what he said, and she was not going with him to New York, she'd simply lost her temper.

'I'm not some submissive wife,' she'd hurled at him. 'You can't just dump me in any convenient backwater while you go off roaming the world.'

'My work involves travel,' Mick snapped back. 'You know this. You have always known it, so why the fuss?'

'Because we're married, and I want to be with you—not spending my life alone in some different part of the universe.

I'm your partner, Mick, not your housekeeper. Or your mother,' she added recklessly.

And because we were happy in New York, she thought. Because we were by ourselves with no family around—or memories of the past…

His face closed. 'We will leave my mother out of the discussion, if you please. She was content with her life.'

'Was she?' Kate asked bitterly. 'I'd like to have her ruling on that. Just because she knew her place, it doesn't follow she was happy with it.'

The dark brows drew together. 'You go too far, my girl. And you would be alone anyway on this trip. I have already told you I would have no time to give you, or your reproaches, when you tell me that you're bored,' he added bitingly.

'I presume you'd be coming home to sleep at some point?' Kate glared at him. 'I'd be with you then. Or is that the problem?' she went on recklessly. 'Are you not planning to spend all your nights in the same bed, *kyrie*? Is that why you don't want me with you—because I might cramp your style?'

His face was like stone. 'Now you are being ridiculous,' he said harshly. 'And insulting. I have given you my reasons. Let that be the end of it.'

She said shakily, 'Don't tempt me…'

Her words dropped like stones into the taut silence.

Mick sighed. 'Katharina *mou*, I swear I will be back before you know it.'

'Oh, please.' Her voice radiated scorn. 'Don't hurry back on my account.'

That night, when he tried to take her in his arms, she'd turned away from him. 'I have a headache.'

There was a silence, then he said coldly, 'That is a lie, and we both know it. But let it be as you wish. I will not plead.'

And when she'd woken the next morning, he'd gone.

'Kyrios Michalis told us that you were unwell, *kyria*,'

Soula said, her forehead wrinkled with concern. 'And that we were to let you sleep.'

She said quietly, 'That was—considerate of him.'

But she couldn't fool herself. Not for a minute. For the first time, she and Mick had parted in anger and silence, and it hurt.

Nor was it any consolation to remind herself that it wasn't just a tiff, but a matter of principle.

I didn't handle it well, she told herself ruefully. And the headache thing was just stupid. All I've done is deprive myself of some beautiful memories to help me through his absence.

She sighed.

She'd have to make sure his welcome home was just perfect, which shouldn't be too difficult—especially if he was missing her as much as she was already longing for him.

As soon as he calls, she thought, I'll tell him so. Put things right between us.

But the first time he telephoned, she was visiting Linda.

'He was sorry to have missed you, *pedhi mou*,' Ari told her, and Kate made a secret resolve to stay round the villa and await his next call, however long it took.

But this plan misfired too, for, a few evenings later, her father-in-law informed her that Mick had telephoned during the afternoon.

'Why did no one ring me at the beach house?' she protested. 'I've been there all day.'

'It was only a brief call,' Ari said soothingly. 'And I thought also you had gone to Argostoli.'

She caught a glimpse of Victorine's catlike smile, and knew exactly who had sown that little piece of misinformation.

She managed a casual, smiling shrug. 'Ah well, better luck next time.'

But she wouldn't trust to luck, she decided grimly. Not with a joker like Victorine in the pack. She would phone their New York apartment herself. But her calls were fruitless, because, as he'd predicted, he was never there.

And in spite of herself, she could not help wondering where he was—and who he might be with…

'You're looking a little ragged round the edges, honey,' Linda told her critically one day.

'Is that all?' Kate forced a smile. 'According to Victorine, I've lost what few looks I ever possessed. Not a day goes by without some snide remark,' she added smoulderingly.

Linda sighed. 'The woman is poison. Men can be so damned blind sometimes…' She paused. 'Anyway, Mick wouldn't want you to mope.'

Kate sighed. 'I'm not sure I know what Mick wants any more.'

'Theodakis men are never predictable.' Linda's tone was wry. 'It's part of their charm.'

She was silent for a moment. 'I'm going across to Ithaca tomorrow to collect some pots a friend of mine has made for me. Come with me.' Her eyes twinkled suddenly. 'After all, Ithaca's the island where Penelope waited all those years for Odysseus to come back. Maybe it'll put things in perspective for you.'

Kate smiled reluctantly. 'Not if I remember correctly some of the things Odysseus got up to on his travels. But I'd love to come.'

It would be good to get right away from the villa for a few hours, she thought. Ismene had relapsed into a slough of simmering discontent which made the atmosphere disagreeable enough without the addition of Victorine's softly-spoken jibes.

Much as she liked her father-in-law, he was no judge of women, she thought. Then paused, her heart thudding, as she remembered that Mick had been equally culpable in that particular respect.

After all, he chose her first, she thought, biting her lip.

'Come to the beach with me?' Ismene pleaded in an undertone at breakfast the next day. 'I need to talk to you, sister. To ask your advice.'

'I can't, Ismene. I'm going to Ithaca with Linda.' Kate said. She was faintly ashamed of her relief that she had a get-out. Besides, she reminded herself, she had already given Ismene the best possible advice many times—to be patient, and to try not to antagonise her father any more.

She turned to Ari. 'I hope that's all right. I'll be back for dinner.'

He waved an expansive hand. 'Enjoy your day, *pedhi mou*. I shall not be here either. An old friend of mine is staying near Skala, and we are going fishing together.' He looked at Victorine who was crumbling a bread roll and looking exquisitely bored. 'Are you sure you will not come with us, *chrisaphi mou*.'

Victorine shuddered elaborately. 'I'm sorry, *cher*, but I can think of nothing worse. Except, perhaps, a trip to Ithaca,' she added, flicking a derisive glance at Kate.

'Then it's fortunate we didn't invite you,' Kate said sweetly, as she rose to her feet.

But, in the hallway, she was waylaid by Yannis. 'The telephone for you, *kyria*.'

Could it be Mick? Kate wondered, her heart lurching in sudden excitement. She glanced at her watch, trying to work out the time difference as she lifted the receiver, but it was Linda's voice that reached her.

'Kate, honey, we're going to have to take a rain check on the Ithaca thing. I'm starting a migraine, so I'll be out of things for at least two days.'

'Oh, Linda, I'm so sorry. Is there anything I can do?'

'Not a thing.' Linda gave a weak chuckle. 'I just need to lie down in the usual darkened room, and take my medication. I'll be in touch when I'm better.'

Kate replaced the receiver and stood irresolute for a moment. She could always stay at home, she supposed, but then she was bound to be buttonholed by Ismene with another list of complaints about her father's tyranny, and she wasn't sure she could cope.

I have my own problems, she thought sighing.

And it might also be difficult to avoid Victorine, and the constant pinpricks she liked to inflict on Kate's already sensitised skin.

So she would use her day of freedom to go for a drive, she decided. To revisit some of the places Mick had shown her in happier times. And, to try and get her head together.

The holiday season was in full swing now, so she avoided the usual tourist spots, and drove up into the Mount Enos national park. She left her car near the tourist pavilion, and walked up through the dark firs to the summit. There was no mist today, and she could see the neighbouring island of Zakynthos rising majestically out of the turquoise and azure sea, and, further to the east, the mountains of the Peleponnese.

The air was like spring water from a crystal glass. It was very still. No voices—just the faint sigh of the breeze in the clustering trees, and the distant drone of an aircraft making its descent.

She looked, up, shading her eyes, to track its progress, and suddenly Mick was there with her, his image so strong that she could have put out a hand and touched him.

The clustering islands blurred, and the iridescent glitter of the sea broke into tiny fragments as the tears came.

She whispered brokenly, 'Michalis *mou*.'

She knew in that moment that whatever their differences, however great the apparent difficulties, she would do anything to make her marriage work.

Mick would never fit some Identikit New Man pattern of the ideal husband. In spite of his cosmopolitan background, he was too fiercely Greek for that. But, if he beckoned, she would walk through fire for him, and that was all that really mattered.

There would have to be adjustments, and these would need to be mutual, because she was no doormat, but she felt more at peace, and more hopeful than she had done for weeks.

She drove down with care to the main road, and turned north. She had a leisurely stroll along the beautiful Myrtos beach, then drove on to Assos for a seafood lunch.

When she got back to the villa, she decided as she drank her coffee, she would get on the phone to New York, and stay on it until she'd spoken to Mick, and told him she loved him. She'd call the apartment, the office—even his favourite restaurant if she had to, but she'd find him.

Or, she would take the first flight she could get to America and tell him in person.

I'll get Yannis to call the airline, she thought in sudden excitement. He can make me a reservation. And I'll do it now.

There was a telephone in the taverna, but, before she could tell Yannis what she was planning, he had burst into excited speech. 'Kyria Katharina, it is so good that you have rung. Because Kyrios Michalis is here. He returned two hours ago. He asked for you, and I told him you had gone to Ithaca.'

'That didn't happen, Yannis. I'm at Assos instead, and I'm coming straight back. But please don't tell him. I want to surprise him.'

'You are coming back from Assos, and you wish to make it a surprise, *kyria*,' he repeated, and she knew he was smiling. 'I understand. I will say nothing.'

As she drove back, she remembered the aircraft she'd heard on the mountain—the certainty that Mick was with her.

I must have sensed that was his plane, she thought wonderingly.

She'd been in such a hurry to see Mick, she'd left the keys in the car, hurtling recklessly down the track to the beach house.

She was breathless, laughing as she'd opened the bedroom door. And seen, in one frozen, devastating moment, the end of her marriage, and the ruin of her happiness. The death of faith and trust. The total destruction of every cherished hope and dream she'd ever had.

Or ever would have.

Because until she could stop loving Mick, cut him out of her heart and mind forever, she would be unable to move on.

And she knew now, with a terrible certainty, that, in spite of what he'd done, it wasn't over yet.

Because nothing had changed, she thought despairingly. This was the truth she had to face.

That, God help her, she was doomed to love him for all eternity.

CHAPTER TEN

KATE wrapped her arms round her body, stifling the involuntary moan of pain forcing its way to her lips as she remembered Victorine's mocking smile, and the way she'd allowed the encircling towel to slip down from her bare breasts.

How she'd glanced at the bed, where Mick lay face down, his naked body totally relaxed in sexual exhaustion, as if to silently emphasise the totality of the betrayal.

Of course, I was supposed to be on Ithaca, Kate thought. And Ari was out on his friend's boat. They must have thought they were safe—that it was the perfect opportunity.

But how many times before that? How many snatched hours had there been?

There was Athens, of course. Victorine had practically flaunted that red flag in front of her.

So many signs. So many signals that she'd been too naïve—too trusting—too damned stupid to pick up.

She bit into her lip. The earthquake of realisation might be over, but the aftershock still lingered. The agony of accepting that her marriage had only ever been a cynical charade to conceal Mick's secret passion for his father's woman—the flamboyant, sensual beauty he had never ceased to want.

There was no one she thought bitterly, whom he would not betray in his pursuit of Victorine.

But he would not consider that he'd short-changed his convenient wife in any way. After all, she'd had his name, his money, and sex on demand—she would no longer call it love-making—so what more could she possibly want?

I wanted love, she thought achingly. The one thing he never offered.

Had it never occurred to either of them that she might carry her pain and shock to Aristotle Theodakis? That this reckless, forbidden passion might have robbed Mick of his other major ambition—to rule the Theodakis empire?

Or had he counted on Kate's innate sense of decency to keep him safe? The knowledge that she would not willingly involve anyone else in her suffering—especially the father-in-law who had treated her with such unfailing kindness?

But then Mick liked to take chances—in his business as well as his personal life. For him, that would have been just one more justified risk.

Like bringing her back here…

Her throat was dry and aching. She got up from the lounger, and trailed wearily into the house. She needed a cool drink.

In the kitchen refrigerator she found a tall jug of fresh lemonade, and she filled a tumbler, and added ice cubes.

She'd just taken a long, grateful swallow, when she heard footsteps approaching quickly along the tiled hallway and Victorine appeared in the doorway. She was wearing a brief white skirt, and a low-cut silk top in her favourite deep pink.

'So.' Her voice had a metallic ring. 'You came back. I did not think it possible.'

'Well, don't worry.' Kate replaced her glass with care on the counter top, aware that her hand was shaking. But she kept her voice steady, and her glance level. 'It's only a short visit. I'll be gone soon—permanently.'

Victorine hunched a shoulder, her gaze inimical. 'What have I to worry me? I am merely astonished you have so little pride that you return here.'

'I came for Ismene's sake, and at her invitation. No other reason.' Kate lifted her chin. 'But there is one thing. While I am here, you will not set foot in this house again. You and Michael must find some other corner to pursue your sordid little affair. Do I make myself clear?'

Victorine shrugged gracefully. 'As crystal, *chère*. But it

makes little difference.' She gave Kate a cat-like smile. 'We can wait. Anticipation can be—most exciting, don't you find?'

'Why yes,' Kate said calmly. 'For instance, I can hardly wait to get out of here, and leave this whole squalid situation behind me.'

Victorine laughed, her eyes hard. 'You are being very sensible. No scenes. No whining. Be sure that Michalis will pay generously for your discretion.'

No, thought Kate. I'm the one who'll pay. For the rest of my life.

Her voice was cool and clipped. 'Kindly go now, Victorine, and stay away from me. Or I might change my mind, and blow the whole thing out of the water.'

She retrieved her glass, and moved towards the window, deliberately turning her back on her adversary and, after a moment, she heard the receding click of her heels as the other woman retreated.

She leaned against the wall, her shoulders sagging wearily, sudden tears thick in her throat. She'd won the encounter, but it was a hollow victory.

But, if self-interest prompted the Creole girl to keep her distance, it might make Kate's enforced stay on Kefalonia marginally more bearable.

Certainly, it was the best she could hope for.

She glimpsed her reflection in the window, the white strained face, the over-bright eyes, and trembling mouth.

And thought, 'You fool. Oh, God, you pathetic fool.'

She took a long, warm bath, then lay on her bed, with the shutters closed, and tried to sleep. To stop her brain treading the same unhappy paths all over again.

Selective amnesia, she thought, staring into the shadows. That was what she needed. The events of the past year painlessly removed from the memory banks.

And if she'd only obeyed her instincts and not gone to the

Zycos Regina with Lisa that night, she would never have met Mick, and none of this would have happened.

When she eventually dozed, she was assailed by brief troublous dreams, which left her tense and unrefreshed.

But she had no real reason to feel relaxed, she reminded herself ironically. She had the evening's family dinner to get through.

She pulled a straight skirt in sapphire-blue silk jersey from the wardrobe, and found the matching top, long-sleeved, and scooped neck.

She was brushing her hair, and trying to decide whether to sweep it up into a loose knot, or leave it unconfined on her shoulders, when there was a swift tap on the door and Mick walked in.

She swung round defensively. 'I didn't say ''Come in.'''

His smile did not reach his eyes. 'But I'm sure the words were hovering on your lips, *agapi mou*,' he drawled.

He placed a velvet covered case on the dressing table, and put a small Tiffany's box beside it.

'Your pendant,' he said. 'I would like you to wear it tonight.'

'And your orders naturally must be obeyed.'

He said quietly, 'I'd hoped you would look on it as a request, Katharina—but, so be it.'

She touched the other box. 'And this?'

'Some earrings to match it.' He paused. 'I brought them back from New York some weeks ago, but you were not here to receive them.'

Kate stiffened. 'Another attempt to salve your guilty conscience?' Her voice bit.

He was silent for a moment. 'What do you wish to hear? That I am not particularly proud of myself? I admit it.'

'Big of you to say so,' she said huskily. 'Only, it doesn't matter any more.'

'It matters to me.' He pushed the little box towards her. 'Please open your gift.'

'I prefer to regard it as an unwanted loan.' She had to stifle a gasp when the blue fire of the exquisite drops flared up at her from their velvet bed.

'Put them on,' Mick directed softly. Standing behind her, he buried both hands in the silky mass of her hair, and lifted it away from her ears, watching as Kate, summoning every scrap of self-control she possessed, fastened the tiny gold clips into her lobes.

'Beautiful.' He bent his head, letting his lips graze the smooth curve between throat and shoulder, his hand gently stroking the nape of her neck.

She felt a shiver run through her nerve-endings at his touch. Experienced the shock of need deep within her.

She looked down at her hands, clenched together in her lap, refusing to meet the compulsion of his dark gaze in the mirror.

She said in a stifled voice. 'Don't—touch me.'

There was a silence, then he straightened, moving unhurriedly, away from her.

He said mockingly, 'You have a saying, *matia mou*—that old habits die hard. I suspect it may be true for us both.'

A moment later, she heard the door close.

But when she emerged from her room, he was waiting for her.

'I regret the necessity.' He spoke curtly. 'But it will look better if we arrive together.'

'And we must never forget appearances.' She fiddled with the thin wool wrap she was wearing round her shoulders.

'But, of course not. Isn't that why you're here?'

And there was no answer to that, she reflected bitterly, as she walked up through the tall sighing pines, at his side.

The evening was not, however, as bad as she'd expected. Petros was there, with his parents whom she had never met before. Dr Alessou was a squarely built, grizzled man, and his wife was tall with a shy smile, and Kate liked them both immediately. It was a pleasure to stand and talk to them, as well as a lifeline.

Linda was also present.

'Hi, stranger.' She gave Kate a swift hug. 'It's good to have you back.'

'Thank you.' Kate's smile was constrained, and Linda's brows drew together as she studied her.

'Come to lunch tomorrow,' she said. 'If Mick can bear to let you out of his sight.'

Kate straightened her shoulders determinedly. 'That's—not a problem.'

'Really?' Linda queried drily. 'I'll expect you at twelve.'

The only awkward moment came halfway through the meal, when Ismene, who was on bubbling form, spotted Kate's earrings.

'Are they to welcome you back?' she demanded breathlessly. 'How much he must have missed you, *po, po, po*.' She sent a laughing look at her silent brother. 'If I were Katharina, I would go away again and again. What will you bribe her home with next time, Michalis—a ring, perhaps, with a stone like a quail's egg?'

He was leaning back in his chair, out of the candlelight, so Kate could not see his expression. But his voice was cool even with a note of faint amusement. 'I am saving that, *pedhi mou*, until our first child is born.'

'What is this?' Ari barked jovially from the head of the table. 'Have you some news for us, my girl?'

'No.' Kate was burning from head to foot. Suddenly she was the focus of everyone's attention—genial, interested, excited—and, in one case, poisonous. She just wanted to get up from the table and run. 'No, of course not.'

'They are both young.' Dr Alessou looked at her kindly. 'There is plenty of time. Ari, my friend.'

'But times are changing.' Ari Theodakis looked round the table commandingly. 'I have reached a decision. At the next full meeting of the board, I shall officially announce my retirement as chairman of the International Corporation. It is time I made way for new blood.'

He inclined his head towards Mick. 'I leave my companies in your safe hands, my son.'

There was an astonished silence.

'But what are you going to do, Papa?' Ismene was wide-eyed.

He smiled benignly. 'I have my plans. My friend Basilis Ionides has just completed the purchase of his property, which as you know includes the old Gianoli vineyard. We are going to restore its fortunes—make wine together. And I shall tend my olives, go fishing, and sit in the sunlight. And play with my grandchildren.' He grinned at Dr Alessou. 'I may also find time for the occasional game of *tavli*, eh, my friend?'

Kate still struggling to regain her composure saw Victorine's face turn to stone, indicating that Ari's announcement was news to her. She saw, too, the lightning glance that the other woman darted at Mick.

He's got what he wanted, she thought. And now he can have her too. Once he's officially chairman, there'll be nothing to stop him.

And Victorine likes the high life. She wants a millionaire not a Kefalonian farmer. Vines and olive groves will never be enough for her. Surely Ari must realise that.

But there won't be a thing he can do about it, once he's given up the reins. So, there'll be a ghastly scandal, the press will have a field day, and the family feud will break out all over again.

She looked down at the golden gleam of her wedding ring. And she would be bound to be dragged into it too—splashed across the newspapers as the wronged wife. Made to relive every bitter moment all over again. A far cry from the quiet divorce she'd planned.

But no one could hope to escape unscathed from this kind of situation, she reminded herself wretchedly. It was only astonishing that no enterprising journalist had managed to dig out the facts about this sordid little love triangle a long time ago.

Or was it just proof of the influence the Theodakis family were able to wield, and the privacy their money had always succeeded in buying for them?

But it wasn't her problem. Not any longer. And in a few months she'd be free of it all, she told herself, sinking her teeth into her bottom lip. And her transient encounter with the rich and mighty would be eventually forgotten.

Although, not by her. That was too much to hope for.

She was sitting in her own little cocoon of silence amid the welter of laughter and surprised comment around the rest of the table when a slight prickle of awareness made her look up.

Mick was watching her across the table. He was frowning faintly, his face taut, the dark eyes concerned, and questioning.

Oh, please don't worry, she assured him silently, and bitterly. I won't rock the boat. Not at this juncture.

I'll run away again, as soon as Ismene's wedding is over, and you can tell your father I couldn't cope with the prospect of being the chairman's lady. That I simply wasn't up to it. The truth can wait for a more convenient moment—after the official announcement that you're the new chairman.

She drank some wine from her glass, then turned determinedly to Dr Alessou, an authority on island history, to ask a bread and butter question about St Gerassimos, who was Kefalonia's patron, and to whom the village church was dedicated.

He launched himself into his subject with enthusiasm, and when Kate next dared steal a glance under her lashes at Mick, she found he was talking with smiling courtesy to the doctor's wife.

* * *

The evening seemed endless, and wore the air of an occasion, thwarting any hopes Kate might have had of making an unobtrusive exit.

Especially when Yannis entered ceremoniously with champagne.

'A double celebration,' Ari explained. 'My retirement, and your return to us, *pedhi mou.*'

Kate smiled, and felt like Judas.

But at last the Alessous took their leave, and Kate felt free to escape too.

She said a general 'Goodnight,' but she had only gone a few yards down the moonlit track to the beach house, when Mick caught up with her.

'What do you want?' She faced him defensively.

'It's our first night here together,' he said. 'It would be thought odd if I did not accompany you.'

'It must be a relief to know that you won't have to keep up appearances for much longer.'

'So it seems.' His tone was wry. 'It came as quite a bombshell.'

'The first of many, I'm sure,' Kate said crisply, and set off down the track, shoulders rigid.

'And for that very reason, we need to talk, my Kate.'

She said unevenly, 'Don't call me that. And there's nothing more to discuss. We established the terms for my return in London. Nothing has changed.'

'You were very angry in London. I have been waiting—hoping that, perhaps, your temper had begun to cool.'

'I'm not angry, *kyrie*. I'd just like to get on with the rest of my life.' She paused, wrapping her arms defensively round her body, not looking at him. 'After all, you've just achieved your heart's desire.'

He said slowly, 'If you think that, *agapi mou*, then our marriage has taught you nothing.'

'Then it's as well it's over,' Kate returned curtly, and walked on.

He caught her arm, and spun her round, making her face

him in the moonlight. He said quietly, 'I do not—cannot believe you mean that, Kate. Not in your heart.'

'Fortunately I've started using my brain instead, *kyrie*. Something our marriage *has* taught me.' She tried to tug herself free. 'Now let go of me.'

'How easy you make that sound.' Mick's voice was bitter. 'But perhaps I am not ready to give up on us so easily, *matia mou*.'

She took a step backwards. 'You can say that.' Her voice shook. 'You *dare* to say that.'

'Katharina.' He sounded almost pleading. 'I know what I did was wrong, but is my fault really so unforgivable? Could we not—negotiate some new terms?'

What do you want from me? she cried silently. To go on with this charade—pretend we have a marriage? Enjoy the money and the prestige and turn a blind eye to your other pleasures? Because I can't. I can't…

She said tautly, 'That's impossible, and you know it.'

'I know nothing any more.' Mick's voice was harsh. 'Except that, for one stupid act, my life with you has been destroyed.'

'I was the stupid one,' Kate said bleakly. 'Thinking I could ever be content with the kind of half-life you had to offer.'

'*Agapi mou*.' There was real anguish in his tone. 'Believe me, I never meant to hurt you like this.'

No, she thought. Because I was never meant to find out. I was expected to stay the naïve innocent until you decided otherwise.

'Oh, my Kate.' His voice sank to a whisper. 'Even now, couldn't you find it in your heart to forgive me? Offer me another chance? We could be happy again…'

'No.' She began to walk down the track again. 'I'm not the same person. Not the blind idiot you married.'

She knew that note in his voice. It had always been the prelude to lovemaking. And she had always responded to it.

He was still holding her arm, as he walked beside her, and

she felt his touch through the silky sleeve, scorching her flesh, burning her to the bone. She was falling to pieces, suddenly, blind and shaking. Her reason fragmenting.

And soon—all too soon—they would reach the house where the lamps would have been lit in their absence, and the wide bed in the main bedroom turned down in readiness, just as always.

That room, where the pale drapes shimmered in the breeze through the shutters, and the moonlight dappled the floor.

Where she heard her name whispered in the darkness and opened her arms to him in joy and welcome.

That was how it had been only a few short weeks before.

And how it could never be again.

That was the truth—the rock she had to cling to as emotion and stark need threatened to overwhelm her.

'I've changed too, *agapi mou.*' His voice reached her softly, pleadingly. 'Surely—surely that could be a start—a way for us to find each other again.'

'You said you wouldn't do this,' Kate accused raggedly. 'Oh, why the hell did I come back here? Why did I ever trust you?'

'Did you really believe I would just let you walk away?' Mick followed her into the dimly lit hallway. 'And I said I would allow you to sleep alone—not that I wouldn't fight to get you back.'

'Well the battle's over, *kyrie.*' She wrenched herself free from his detaining hand. 'And you lost.'

'Are you so sure?' he asked quietly. His eyes went over her, registering the widening eyes, the tremulous parted lips, and the uncontrollable hurry of her breathing.

He moved towards her, and she took a swift step backwards only to find further retreat blocked by the wall behind her.

Slowly and deliberately, he rested his hands against the wall on either side of her, holding himself at arm's length, not touching her in any way, but keeping her trapped there just the same.

Over his shoulder, she could see the half open door of his bedroom. All the flowers had been removed, but their scent still seemed to hang in the air, sweet and evocative.

'Shall I show you that there are no certainties between a man and a woman, *matia mou*—just an infinite range of possibilities?' There was a note of shaken laughter in his voice. 'Won't you let me make amends for the past?'

Kate lifted her chin, making herself meet the power—the unconcealed hunger of his dark gaze with white-faced defiance.

'What are you suggesting, *kyrie*—that we should solve everything by having sex?'

His brows lifted 'It might at least provide a beginning—a way back. And I had hoped that we would make love to each other,' he added with cool emphasis.

Kate shrugged. 'Dress it up however you want. It comes to the same thing in the end.'

'No,' he said with sudden bitterness. 'It does not, my innocent wife.' He looked down at her, his mouth tightening harshly. 'Do you wish me to demonstrate.'

'No.' Her voice was a thread.

He sighed. 'Don't fight me any more, Kate *mou*.' His voice gentled. 'Because I could—make you want me, and you know that.'

'Not any more.' She crossed her arms defensively over her breasts—a gesture that was not lost on him. 'Understand this, Michael. Whatever you did to me, whatever you called it, it would be nothing more than rape. And I'm sure you don't want that on what passes for your conscience.'

His head went back as if she had struck him across the face.

He said hoarsely, 'Kate—you do not—you cannot mean this. In the name of God, you are my wife.'

'Only in the eyes of the law,' Kate said. 'And even that will change soon.' She swallowed. 'Now let me go.'

There was a long, tingling silence. She saw the incredulity in his eyes fade and become replaced by something infinitely more disturbing—even calculating. A look that sent a shiver curling through her body.

Then Mick straightened slowly, almost insolently, his arms dropping to his sides.

So that technically she was free. And all she had to do was turn and walk away. Only she couldn't seem to move—leave the support of the wall, or the ice-cold compulsion of his gaze.

He said too softly, 'So—what are you waiting for. To be wished a restful night, or, perhaps—this?'

There was not even time for a heartbeat. Suddenly, Kate was in his arms, crushed without gentleness against his lean body, her parted trembling lips being plundered by his.

There was no tenderness in the kiss he subjected her to. Just a ruthless, almost cold-blooded sensuality that bordered on punishment.

Her first faint moan of protest was smothered by the bruising pressure of his mouth. After that, she was incapable of speech or even thought. Even to breathe was a difficulty. But there was no mercy in the arms that held her, or the hard lips that moved on hers with almost brutal insistence.

Behind her closed eyelids, fireflies swirled in a frantic, mocking dance.

In spite of herself, her starved body was awakening to stinging, passionate life under the searing shock of his kiss. The scent, the taste of him filled her nose and mouth with a frightening familiarity. The awareness that he was strongly starkly aroused sent swift heat coursing through her veins, and awoke memories as potent as they were unwelcome.

Her head was reeling. Her legs were shaking under her. She was going to faint. She might even die. But nothing mattered except the urgent, agonised necessity of feeling the burning strength of him inside her, filling her.

She pressed herself against him, letting the wild current of feeling carry her away to recklessness.

Later, she would be ashamed. Would hate herself.

But tonight, for a few brief hours, he would belong to her alone. An encounter to treasure in the loneliness ahead.

And in that instant she found herself free, her release as sudden and startling as a blow. Mick stepped backwards, away from her, studying her through narrowed eyes, as he fought his own ragged breathing.

Kate sagged back against the wall, staring back at him, her wide eyes clouded with desire, a hand pressed to her swollen mouth as she waited.

Waited for him to lift her into his arms, and carry her to bed. Waited to feel his mouth on hers again, demanding the response she longed to give.

He was close enough to touch, yet the distance between them had suddenly become a vast and echoing space, impossible to bridge.

And his smile, she saw, was cold, and faintly mocking.

Swift dread invaded her, like a sliver of ice penetrating her heart.

'Kalinichta, matia mou,' he drawled. 'Goodnight—and I wish you sweet dreams. As sweet as that night on Zycos, perhaps.'

She watched him walk away from her across the passage, and heard the finality of his door closing.

Shutting her out. Leaving her in a limbo of her own making, composed of shame and regret.

CHAPTER ELEVEN

IT WAS a long time before Kate could move. Before she could find the strength to walk, stumbling a little, the few yards to her own room.

She closed the door with infinite care, then trod across the room to the bed. She sat on its edge, hands clenched in her lap in a vain attempt to stop them shaking.

She'd made him angry. That was the only logical explanation for the last shattering minutes. She'd refused to be manipulated. To allow herself to be used.

Because that was all it was, she told herself. He couldn't risk a rendezvous with his mistress, and he needed a woman. So, why not amuse himself by seducing his gullible wife all over again?

Kate winced as her teeth grazed the tender fullness of her lower lip.

Perhaps he'd thought again about the public resumption of his liaison with Victorine, recognising it as the kind of conduct the Theodakis board would condemn.

Or maybe he'd decided he needed the surface respectability of his current marriage after all, no matter what might happen in private.

The cynicism of it nauseated her.

But, that being the case, why hadn't she walked away from him, while she had the chance? What had induced her to stay, and provoke him into that storm of devastation that he'd unleashed on her.

It was madness—and, bitter as the acknowledgment might be, she only had herself to blame.

And why hadn't she fought him? she asked herself wildly.

She could have struggled—kicked—bitten. But she'd done none of those things.

She slipped off her shoes, and lay back on the bed in a small, defensive curve.

Because she hadn't wanted to, she thought. That was the next unpalatable truth she had to deal with.

However much her reason might condemn Mick, and affirm that she could not go on living with him after such a betrayal, her physical responses were operating on a different planet.

At his lightest touch, her body seemed to open, like a flower, creating that deep, molten ache which only he could heal. Even the thought of him could make her whole body clench in hunger and need.

None of the hurt, the anger and bitterness had managed to cure her of wanting him, and she was going to have to live with that.

But, which was far worse, Mick was totally aware of the war going on between her mind, and her too-eager senses, because he knew her better than she knew herself.

He'd pinpointed her weakness with mind-numbing brutality, leaving her without a hiding place, or even an excuse. And he'd done it quite deliberately.

He was also the one who had, in the end, walked away.

And, somehow, she had to survive the despair and humiliation of that knowledge, and go on.

When all she really wanted to was run ignominiously away.

Except that would be pointless, Kate thought, burying her face in the pillow. There could be no escape, because Mick had her on the end of some invisible chain, and all he had to do was tug, and she would be drawn back inexorably. And no amount of time or distance would change a thing.

And how was she going to live with that?

She cried for a while, then, silently, achingly. When there

were no more tears left, she sat up wearily, pushing back her hair from her face.

She took the diamonds from her ears and around her throat, and put them back in their cases, then undressed, and donned her simple white cotton nightshirt.

She had known from the beginning, she thought, as she lay in the darkness listening to the whisper of the sea, that she and Mick came from two different worlds. Yet in truth they were light years apart.

How could he regard such a transgression, such a complete betrayal, so lightly? she asked herself wretchedly. Unless he felt he was powerful enough to ignore the normal rules of morality.

He'd clearly expected her to shrug and smile, and take him back when he asked for forgiveness. Presumably that was how other wives of his acquaintance reacted to their husbands' passing adulteries.

But this was no trivial, transient affair, she reminded herself unhappily. No moment of weakness to be instantly regretted.

Because Victorine had clearly got into his blood. A habit he was unable to break. Maybe even a necessity…

Her mind closed at the thought.

Perhaps he even hoped that I'd be docile—besotted enough to accept some kind of *ménage à trois*, she thought bitterly.

She shivered, and turned over, trying to compose herself for sleep, but it would not come. Her mind was wide awake, endlessly turning on the treadmill of their last encounter.

Or perhaps she was just scared to sleep. Frightened in case the dreams that Mick had ironically wished for her might indeed be waiting to enclose her in their dark thrall, and draw her down to her own private hell.

It was nearly dawn when she at last closed her eyes, and only a few hours later when the sun woke her again, pouring through the slats in the shutters.

For a moment, she was tempted to stay where she was. To

pull the sheet over her head, and lie still, like a hunted animal gone to ground. Or even to feign illness.

But Ismene wanted her to talk about the wedding arrangements, she remembered, and she was also having lunch with Linda. Life was waiting for her, and could not be avoided.

It won't be for much longer, she told herself, as she bathed and dressed in her denim skirt and a simple white vest top. She hung small gold hoops in her ears, and used concealer to cover the shadows under her eyes, and blusher to soften her pallor.

She could hear the clash of crockery in the kitchen, and a woman's voice singing softly in Greek as she went through the living room, and out on to the terrace by the pool.

A table had been laid there, now littered with the remains of breakfast, and Mick was seated beside it, engrossed in some papers.

He was wearing shorts and a thin cotton shirt, open to the waist, and his hair was damp, indicating that he'd been swimming.

Kate paused, slipping her hands into the pockets of her skirt, and feeling them ball nervously into fists.

He glanced up at her hesitant approach, his gaze cool, almost dispassionate, with none of the mockery she'd feared.

He said, '*Kalimera*,' and pushed a small silver bell across the table towards her, as she took her seat. 'If you ring, Maria will bring you some fresh coffee and hot rolls.'

'Is that who was in the kitchen?' Kate frowned. 'Why is she here?'

'I decided it would be better if one of the servants was here to look after us.' His tone was expressionless.

'But I've always done that.' The words were out before she could stop herself.

'Ah, yes,' he said. 'But that was then. This is now.' His brief smile did not reach his eyes. 'And I have resolved, *matia mou*, to spare you *all* your wifely duties.'

She was aware that warm colour was staining her face, but kept her voice steady. 'I see.'

'But, of course, there are also the nights,' he went on. 'When Maria will not be here.' He paused. 'So, a man is coming from Argostoli this afternoon to put a lock on your bedroom door—in case my animal instincts should suddenly overwhelm me, you understand.'

'Please—don't…' Her voice was husky.

'Why not?' Mick shrugged. 'I am merely trying to simplify matters. To make your final days here as trouble free—and as safe—as I can. I thought you would be grateful.'

'Yes,' she said. 'You're—very considerate.'

'Thank you.' His mouth twisted. 'Perhaps we can maintain the normal courtesies, if nothing else.' He rose, stretching casually, causing Kate to avert her gaze rapidly from the long, tanned legs and the silken ripple of muscles across his bare chest and diaphragm.

'Now ring for your breakfast,' he added, putting his papers together. He offered her a quick, taut smile. 'I will not stay here to spoil your appetite.'

She wasn't hungry, but she made herself eat some of the rolls, honey and fresh fruit that Maria brought.

She might be sick at heart, she thought, but there was no point in making herself physically ill as well.

After all, the last thing she wanted was to look as if she was fading away under Victorine's gloating gaze.

'You do not look as if Michalis allowed you much sleep last night, sister,' was Ismene's exuberant greeting, when Kate joined her up at the villa. She gave her a wide smile. 'Life is good, *ne*?'

'Very good,' Kate returned, mentally crossing her fingers for the lie. And so much for cosmetic cover-ups, she added silently.

It was a relief to escape from her own problems into Ismene's joyful plans for her marriage.

Rather to Kate's surprise, the wedding was not to be some

glittering international event packed with the rich and famous.

The Theodakis clan was a vast one, and Petros also came from a large and widespread family. After that the guest list seemed restricted to old friends.

Most of the arrangements were already in place, largely thanks to Linda, Kate gathered. Her own task was largely one of room allocation at the villa, and booking accommodation in local hotels for the overflow.

As she'd suspected, Victorine's sole contribution had been a series of snide remarks about Ismene's marrying beneath her.

'But I told her that would never be her problem,' Ismene said with undisguised satisfaction. 'As there is no way down from the gutter.'

Kate choked back a laugh. 'Ismene—you could get into real trouble.'

'I thought so too,' Ismene admitted. 'But although she told Papa and he was stern with me, I do not believe he was really angry.' She gave Kate a hopeful look. 'Do you think he is becoming tired of her, Katharina? I could not bear it if she became my step-mother. And nor could Michalis.'

'No.' Kate's throat tightened. 'I—I'm sure he couldn't.' She hesitated. 'I think maybe we need to leave them to—work things out for themselves.'

But, perhaps, in the end, everyone would get what they wanted without scandal or an explosive rupture between Mick and his father, she thought later, as she drove down to Sami.

If Ari no longer wanted Victorine, he might not care too much if she was ultimately reunited with Mick. Father and son seemed to share a cynical view of women as commodities to be traded.

If only she herself could have been excluded from this sexual merry-go-round.

Yet, she knew in her heart that, in spite of betrayal and

heartbreak, she would not have missed the heady delights of those first months with Mick for anything in the world.

Although that was small consolation when she contemplated the empty desolation that awaited her.

'I thought we'd have lunch in the garden,' Linda said briskly, leading the way to her sheltered courtyard. 'While we still can. The weather's going to change,' she added, directing a critical look at the sky.

'How do you know?' Kate asked baffled.

'Live here for long enough, and you get the feeling for it.' Linda smiled at her. 'I bet Mick would tell you the same.'

'Yes.' Kate returned the smile with determination. 'Can you forecast whether we'll have a fine day for the wedding?'

'I can guarantee it.' Linda poured wine. 'The sun always shines on the Theodakis family. Haven't you noticed?' She paused as her maid brought bread and salad, and a platter of *crasato*—pork simmered in wine. So Kate was not forced to reply.

'Well,' Linda said when they were alone, and eating. 'What's the problem?'

Kate dabbed at her lips with the linen napkin. 'I don't know what you mean.'

Linda sighed. 'Honey—who are you kidding? You do not have the look of a girl in the throes of a blissful reunion with her man. And Mick looks as if he's strung up on wires, too. So, what's happening.'

Kate stabbed at her pork. 'I can't tell you. Not yet.'

Linda whistled, her face concerned. 'That bad, huh?' She was silent for a moment. 'I admit I wondered when you just disappeared like that. I planned to talk to Mick about it, if he'd let me, but he was never around long enough. Always working like a demon, rarely touching base. Which should have told me something, too,' she added thoughtfully.

'But when I heard he was bringing you back, I hoped that meant you'd managed to resolve your differences. God knows, there were bound to be plenty. You're both strong characters. But so were Ari and Regina, and they rode out their storms. In fact, they thrived on them. I thought you'd be the same.'

Kate smiled over-brightly. 'I think that would rather depend on the storm.' She took some more salad. 'This food is delicious. And what herb has Hara used in the potatoes?'

Linda picked up the cue, and the conversation turned to food, and, from there, to the wedding.

'Have you decided what you're going to wear?' Linda asked.

Kate wrinkled her nose. 'Not really. I have this pale-green dress that Mi…that I bought back in New York. That's a possibility. But Ismene is talking of going to Athens shopping for a couple of days with Mrs Alessou,' she added. 'I could always go with them and find something there.'

They were just drinking their coffee, when they heard footsteps and Ari came round the corner of the house. He halted, brows lifting when he saw Kate.

'*Me sinhorite*. I beg your pardon, Linda. I did not realise you had a visitor. I should have knocked at your door and not taken it for granted that you could receive me.'

'Old friends never intrude,' Linda assured him, her face faintly flushed. 'Sit down, Ari, and have some coffee with us.'

'No, no, I was just passing, and I thought…' He sounded awkward. 'The vineyard I mentioned last night. I am going there now, and I wondered if you would care to come with me. But I see it is not possible. Another time, perhaps.'

'It's perfectly possible,' Kate said firmly, concealing her surprise. She pushed back her chair, and stood up. 'I was about to go, anyway. I have an ocean of things to do this afternoon.'

'You could always come with us, *pedhi mou*,' Ari suggested, with what Kate felt was real nobility.

She smiled and shook her head. 'Not today. Three's a

crowd, and always will be.' As I know only too well, she added under her breath, wincing.

'So,' she said mischievously, as Linda accompanied her out to her car. 'How long has this been going on?'

Linda's flush deepened. 'There's nothing "going on",' she responded with dignity. 'Just as I said, we are old friends. And he dropped by a couple of times while you were away to ask my advice about Ismene. That's all.'

Kate kissed her lightly. 'And now he wants to consult your expertise on winemaking. Fine.'

She was smiling to herself as she drove away. Maybe one good thing was going to emerge out of this unholy mess after all, she thought wistfully.

Although it would also mean that Mick was totally free to reclaim Victorine for himself. His trophy woman, she thought, as an aching sigh escaped her.

Within a few days, the countdown to the wedding had begun in earnest, leaving Kate little time for unhappy introspection. But, though her days might be full, her nights were another matter. Behind her locked door, she tossed and turned, searching vainly for peace and tranquillity.

Sharing the beach house with Mick was not easy, although she couldn't fault his behaviour. He was working hard, constantly away on short trips. But, when he was at home, he kept out of her way as much as possible, and, when they did meet, treated her with cool civility. Which, she supposed, was as much as she could hope for.

The weather had changed as prophesied, and rain fell from grey skies accompanied by a swirling wind. Without her usual escape routes through the pine woods, and to the beach, Kate began to feel almost claustrophobic, especially as nervous pressure began to build up at the villa with Ismene complaining that the village party would be ruined.

Even when money was no object, weddings were still tricky to arrange, Kate realised, as she dealt with temperamental caterers, and found a replacement for the folk-dance troupe whose leading male dancer had broken his leg.

The shopping trip to Athens was a welcome break, with Ismene making heroic and endearing efforts to keep her spending within bounds, so as not to shock her future mother-in-law.

Kate had no need to set herself any such limits. She had been stunned to discover how much money was waiting in her personal account. It seemed that Mick had continued to pay her allowance during their separation. She couldn't fault his generosity in that regard, she thought, biting her lip.

And yet, in the end, she spent hardly anything. She trawled the boutiques and designer salons around Kolonaki Square with almost feverish energy, and tried on an astonishing array of garments to try and find an outfit for the wedding, but there was nothing that aroused more than a lukewarm interest in her.

In the past, when she'd gone clothes shopping, Mick had usually accompanied her. It had been fun to emerge from the changing room and parade breathlessly in front of him, waiting for him to signal approval or negation as he lounged in one of those spindly gilt chairs.

A nod was generally enough but, sometimes, she saw his attention sharpen, brows lifting, and mouth slanting in a smile as his eyes met hers, making her dizzyingly aware that he was anticipating the pleasure of taking off whatever expensive piece of nonsense she was wearing.

Now, it no longer mattered what she wore, she thought.

And she had the pale-green dress in reserve, she reminded herself. It was simple and elegant, and not overtly sexy, so it was suitable for a wedding, and, hopefully, would enable her to fade into the background during the day-long celebration.

But her restraint had not passed unnoticed.

'She tried on every dress in Athens,' Ismene reported teasingly on the evening of their return, when the family had assembled in the *saloni* before dinner. 'And bought none of them. What do you think of that, Michalis?'

'Only that, for once, my prayers have been answered,' he returned wryly. Above the laughter, he added, 'And, anyway, I have my own ideas about what Kate should wear to your wedding, *pedhi mou*.'

'*Po, po, po.*' Ismene turned to Kate. 'What is he planning, do you suppose?'

'Who knows.' Kate made herself speak lightly. 'Your brother is good at surprises—and secrets.'

Her glance met his in unspoken challenge.

He said softly, 'And for that, *matia mou*, I shall make you wait until the day itself.'

As they went into the dining room, Kate found Victorine beside her.

'Your thrift is admirable, *chère*, and also wise.' The crimson mouth was smiling, as she whispered in Kate's ear. 'After all, one's financial circumstances can change so quickly, *n'est ce pas*? It is good to be prepared.'

Kate drew a sharp breath. 'I am more than ready, believe me,' she said icily, and turned away.

In spite of Ismene's gloomy forebodings, the clouds rolled away the day before the wedding, and a mellow sun appeared, bringing the island to life in shades of green and gold.

In twenty-four hours it will all be over, Kate thought bleakly. Ismene will be a wife—and I shall cease to be one.

A top hair stylist had come from Athens to attend to the bride, on the morning of the wedding, but Kate had declined his services. She already planned to wear her hair loose, with a small spray of cream roses instead of a hat.

But she still hadn't the least idea what dress Mick wished her to wear. The subject had not been referred to during any of their fleeting encounters, and she was damned if she was going to ask.

Let him be mysterious, she told herself, lifting her chin.

What difference does it make? It's just one more thing to endure on one more day from the rest of my life.

She had a leisurely bath, applied her favourite body lotion, and put on bra and briefs in ivory silk and lace, smoothing gossamer tights over her slim legs.

Holding her robe round her, she walked back into her bedroom, and checked, her lips parting in a little cry of shocked negation.

Lying across her bed was a slender slip of a dress in cream silk, cut on the bias so it would swirl around her as she moved, and beside it, its matching collarless jacket, the front panels embroidered with a delicate tracery of gold and silver flowers.

Her own wedding dress—worn only once before on that December day in London when all the happiness she'd ever dreamed of seemed to be within her grasp.

The last time she'd seen the dress, it had been hanging in her closet in the New York apartment.

He'd brought it back with him specially, she realised numbly. But why?

How could he hurt her like this? Why provide such a potent reminder of how things had once been between them, when they both knew their marriage was over? And that he was about to discard her forever?

She snatched up the folds of silk from the bed, and stormed down the passage to his room, rapping sharply at the closed door.

He called, '*Peraste*,' and Kate opened the door and marched in.

He was standing at the dressing table fastening his tie, but turned, brows raised, his gaze flicking her robed figure, and the dress hanging over her arm.

He said coolly, 'Is there a problem? Do you need help with your zipper perhaps?'

'No problem. I simply came to return this.' Kate confronted him, chin lifted, allowing anger to mask her hurt and bewilderment. 'I won't wear it. You can't expect me to.'

He turned back to the mirror, making minute adjustments to the elegant knot at his throat.

'But I do expect it, Katharina *mou*,' he told her quietly. 'None of my family were at our wedding, so they have never seen you in that dress, or known how beautiful you looked. An omission I intend to rectify today.'

He paused. 'Besides, I told them last night what I was planning, so you cannot disappoint them. Such a romantic gesture to convince them all that we are the picture of marital harmony,' he added icily. 'Remember our bargain, and that you still have your part to play in it.' His smile was hard. 'Look on it as your costume for the last act, if you prefer. That might make it easier to bear.'

She said unevenly, 'I never thought you could be so cruel. Don't my feelings matter in all this?'

'Did you consider mine when you ran back to England?' he shot back at her. 'Without giving me a chance to explain—to apologise? Forcing me to invent stories to explain your absence.'

She said shakily, 'What you did was beyond apology. It would have been more honourable to have accepted responsibility and told the truth. But of course that might have jeopardised your ultimate ambition.'

'We are preparing for my sister's wedding,' Mick said flatly. 'Shall we discuss my ambitions at a more convenient moment?' He turned and confronted her, hands on lean hips, long legs sheathed in elegant charcoal pants, his crisp white shirt dazzling against his olive skin.

'Now go, and change,' he directed. 'Unless you wish me to dress you with my own hands,' he added significantly.

She took a step backwards. 'You wouldn't dare.'

'Don't tempt me, *agapi mou*.' His voice slowed to a drawl, blatantly sexy, almost amused. 'Or we might miss the wedding altogether. Now go.'

She gave him a fulminating glance, then turned and went out of his room back to her own, trying not to run.

She closed her door and leaned against it. Her reflection in the mirror opposite showed spots of colour burning in her pale face, and an almost feral glitter in her eyes.

Further protest was futile, and she knew it. Even if she locked herself in, and refused to go to the wedding, she couldn't win. Because no lock would be strong enough to keep him out, if he decided to impose his will on her, and she knew it.

'Damn him,' she said raggedly. 'Oh—damn him…'

CHAPTER TWELVE

KATE learned to smile that day. To smile at the aunts, uncles and cousins who embraced her and welcomed her so warmly to the family.

To smile at Ari when he said slowly, 'But what a vision, *pedhi mou*. A bride again yourself. Your husband is indeed a fortunate man.'

To smile as she stood beside Mick in the small incense-filled church, brilliant with candlelight and glittering with icons, and he took her hand in his. And the female members of both families sighed sentimentally, because they thought it was a gesture of love and he was remembering his own wedding day. Because they didn't know the truth—that it was all a pretence.

And to smile, at last, with genuine mistiness at Ismene, as she appeared, amid gasps and sighs from the onlookers, in her shimmering gown, her veil floating around her, to join her bridegroom.

It was a beautiful ceremony full of symbolism and ritual, and Ismene's voice was tremulous as she took her vows in front of the tall bearded priest. Petros was looking at her as if she was some goddess come to earth, and Kate felt tears prick her eyelids as she scattered handfuls of rice over the newly married pair at the conclusion of the marriage.

Afterwards musicians conducted Ismene and Petros to the square outside. It was festive in the sunlight, draped with bunting, and wreaths of flowers. Long tables had been set up, with platters of fish and chicken, bowls of salad and hummous, and still-warm loaves of bread. There was lamb roasting on spits, and tall jugs of local wine. The whole village seemed to be in attendance, and there was a carnival atmosphere as they jostled for seats.

Kate realised that Mick was taking her to the top table, where the bride and groom were already ensconced. Victorine had not attended the church ceremony, but she was there now in a vivid yellow dress and a matching picture hat, fussing over where to sit.

Kate hung back. 'Please, I—I'd rather sit somewhere else.'

He said quietly, 'Kate, you are my wife, and you will take your proper place.'

'Well, my son,' Ari came up to them. 'Are you asking Katharina's forgiveness for having cheated her?'

There was a sudden roaring in her ears. She said faintly, 'What—did you say?'

But he'd turned back to Mick. 'Your wedding should have been like this. Not in some cold London office,' he chided jovially. 'But I was thinking, as I watched the children just now, that we should ask the good father to perform a blessing on your marriage, in the church with all of us to see. Kate would like that, *ne*?'

Kate murmured something faintly, and let Mick lead her away. She stole a glance at him, and saw that his face was grim, his mouth hard and set.

She said, with a catch in her voice, 'We can't go on like this. You must—say something.'

He said brusquely, 'I intend to.'

She saw an empty chair and took it, finding herself wedged between Dr Alessou and an elderly aunt, with a fierce stare and a diamond brooch like a sunburst.

She applauded as Petros and Ismene walked round the square, handing out sugared almonds from decorated baskets, and pretended to eat when the food was served. And she did not once look at Mick who was sitting further down the table, with Victorine beside him.

Was it intended as some kind of public declaration? she wondered. Had it begun?

It was good when the dancing started, and she had something she could focus on. The dancers wore traditional costume, the men in waistcoats and baggy breeches, with broad sashes and striped stockings, and the girls, their heads covered by scarves, in long skirts under flowered aprons, but there was no doubting the sheer athleticism of their performance.

And when they'd finished their exhibition, it was everyone else's turn. The dancers began to weave their way round the square, between the tables, pulling people up to join them in a long chain.

Kate saw Linda seized, laughing a protest as she went.

Then they reached her, and a plump woman in a red dress grabbed her hand, tugging her up in turn.

At first Kate felt clumsy—a fish out of water—as she tried to copy the intricate pattern of steps they were repeating over and over again, but the women holding her hands on either side were loud in their encouragement, and gradually the rhythm took over, and she was able to follow them with mounting confidence.

I used to do this kind of thing all the time when I was a rep, she thought. I'm just out of practice.

As the chain twisted and wove past the top table again, she saw Ari clapping enthusiastically, and Ismene and Petros beaming at her. And she saw Mick, his expression unreadable. And his companion, her beautiful face a mask of contempt.

To hell with her, Kate thought with sudden passion. To hell with both of them.

The sun was on her face, and the throb of the music had found an echo in her veins. In spite of herself, she was caught up in the sheer exuberance of the moment. The unexpected pleasure of belonging.

The rhythm changed, and she found herself dancing with a man from the village, linked to him by the coloured handkerchief he ceremoniously offered her.

She was breathless when the music eventually paused, and excused herself smilingly, amid protests.

She sank into her seat, grateful for the water that Dr Alessou poured for her.

'Why did he do that?' she asked, as she put down the empty glass. 'With the handkerchief, I mean? The other men are holding the women's hands.'

The doctor smiled at her. 'Because you are still a new wife, *kyria*, and it is believed that your hand should touch no other man's but your husband's.'

'Oh,' Kate said, and hastily poured herself some wine.

At sunset, the cars arrived to take the guests back to the villa, and the private evening party, but the celebrations in the village would clearly go on well into the night.

The *saloni* had been cleared for dancing, and there was more food laid out in the dining room.

Petros and Ismene opened the dancing, moving slowly to the music in each other's arms. Champagne was drunk, then Ari made a speech formally welcoming Petros to his family, and then the bride and groom were free to get changed and leave on their honeymoon.

Kate was at the back of the laughing throng that watched them depart, and she turned back with a sigh, wondering if it would be noticed if she too slipped away.

The music had resumed in the *saloni*, the small band playing something soft and dreamy, and people were heading back there. Kate went along with them, ostensibly part of the group, but separate, making her private plans.

She'd go out on the terrace as if she needed air, then take the steps at the end to get to the beach house. Where she would pack. She wouldn't be able to get off the island tonight, but she would leave first thing in the morning, and Mick would be free to do whatever he wanted. And she would not have to watch.

She began to move round the edge of the room, looking

down to avoid eye contact. Trying to be as unobtrusive as possible.

Only someone was barring the way. She raised unwilling eyes and saw Mick regarding her gravely.

He said quietly, 'Dance with me, *matia mou*.'

'In order to keep up appearances?' Kate lifted her chin. 'I think I'll sit this one out.'

'No,' he said. 'You will not. You have danced with everyone else today. Now it is my turn.' He took her hand and drew her on to the floor.

His arms enfolded her, holding her intimately against him, as they began to move to the music.

For a moment, Kate was rigid in his embrace. Her reason, the sudden clamour of her outraged senses were all telling her that this was a pretence too far. That she should not permit him to take this advantage.

Then, almost imperceptibly, she began to relax. To move with the flow, and go where the music and her husband's arms took her.

She felt the touch of his cheek against her hair. The swift brush of his mouth on her temple.

Even with that briefest of contacts, she felt her heartbeat hurry into madness. She felt the warm blood mantling her face. Was aware that her nipples had hardened in sweet, excruciating need against the silk that covered them.

And as if in response to some secret signal, Mick's arms tightened around her, his hand feathering across her spine, and his lips grazing the curve of her cheek, the corner of her trembling mouth.

With a little sigh of capitulation, Kate slid her arms up around his neck and buried her face in his shoulder.

She was no longer a separate entity, she realised, but part of him. Indivisibly. Unequivocally. Bound to him in some mysterious region of the senses where logic, commonsense—even decency—counted for nothing.

Where the only truth was that he was her man, and she

was his woman, and she would burn for him until the end of eternity.

She could count every day, every moment, every second that they had been apart. Recall every night when her imagination had brought him hauntingly back to her.

She could think of nothing—remember nothing—anticipate nothing but the glide of his hands on her naked skin delighting every pulse, every nerve. The lingering arousal of his mouth. The moment when her starved body would open to receive him.

She was dimly aware that the music had stopped—had been replaced by another sound.

As she raised her head uncertainly she realised with shock that she and Mick now had the floor to themselves, and the sound she could hear was applause from the other guests, clustering round to watch them in laughing, vociferous approval.

Bringing her back with a bump to sudden, stark reality.

Kate's face flamed in horrified embarrassment, and she tried to tug free, bent on flight, but Mick was holding her too firmly.

'Smile, *agapi mou*,' he murmured, acknowledging the plaudits with mocking self-deprecation.

She said between her teeth, as she obeyed, 'You'll stop at nothing, will you?'

'At very little, certainly.' He spun her round, away from him, then pulled her close, his lips taking hers in a brief hard kiss. 'And before tonight is over, you will be glad of it, my wife,' he added softly. 'This nonsense between us is over, and you are coming back to my bed where you belong.'

He released her, and she walked away from him, trying not to run. At the edge of the floor, she nearly collided with someone. She glanced up, her lips shaping an apology, and saw it was Victorine, her eyes glittering with malice and derision.

She held Kate's arms above the elbow, and leaned forward as if to embrace her.

'That was good, *chère*,' she breathed in her ear. 'What a pity Michalis has to run the Theodakis corporation. He would have made such a wonderful actor.'

Kate shook her off, uncaring who might see, and pushed past. She had to fight her way out of the room. Everyone wanted to speak to her, it seemed, and shake hands. But, at last, she won free, and found a quiet corner where she could recover her equilibrium a little.

She asked a passing waiter to bring her some fruit juice, and stood, sipping it, relishing its coolness against her parched throat, as Mick's parting words ran mad circles in her brain.

It was some new game he was playing. It had to be. He wasn't serious. He couldn't be. Because they had a deal. A bargain.

But all the same, she wouldn't waste any time getting away. Not the airport this time, but one of the ferries. It didn't matter which. Nothing mattered very much. Not any more.

And because of that, she could go back into the *saloni* this one last time, and act as the hostess. She could talk to people, and dance with anyone who asked her. And she would not—*not* let herself think of Mick's arms, and the familiar strength and urgency of his body.

No, she thought. She would never think of that again. And one day, her mind would have ground the image of him into such tiny particles that she would actually be able to forget him, and start to live again.

It was dawn before the party ended, and the last stalwarts made their way to their rooms, or were driven to the nearby hotels.

She saw Mick go into the study with his father, laughing, their arms round each other's shoulders, and drew a deep breath. She would never have a better opportunity.

She slid out of the house, and went down through the quiet pines to the beach house.

There was a chill in the air, heralding an autumn she would never see. And a chill in her heart that no sun could ever warm.

Once in her room, she drew a steadying breath. It was time to go.

She took Mick's diamonds from her ears and throat, and replaced them in their cases, then removed her wedding dress, and hung it back in the closet.

She would take with her only what she had brought, she decided, slipping on her robe, and fastening its sash.

She found her smallest travel bag, and began to fill it with underwear and shoes. She still had money left over from the Athens trip, and her car keys.

But not her passport, she realised with sudden dismay. Mick had that. She could remember him slipping it into the inside pocket of the jacket he'd been wearing.

Oh, let it still be there, she thought with panic. Don't let him have locked it in the desk up at the villa.

She trod barefoot down the passage, and went into his room, trying unsuccessfully to remember which coat it had been. Well, she would simply have to look in all of them, she thought sighing. Starting with the one hanging on the back of the chair.

'Tidying up for me, *agapi mou*?' His voice from the doorway behind her made her jump, and she whirled, holding his jacket against her like a shield. 'Maria will complain.'

He came further into the room, and kicked the door shut behind him. He was in his shirt sleeves, his tie hanging loose, his coat slung over one shoulder. And he was smiling.

He said softly, 'So you are here at last.'

'No,' she said. 'You—you're mistaken. I came to look for something.'

'And so did I.' He tossed his jacket and tie on to the empty chair, and began to unbutton his shirt, his eyes never leaving hers.

'What are you doing?' Her voice sounded high, unnatural.

'Taking off my clothes. I usually do before I go to bed. And then, *matia mou*, I shall undress you.'

Kate backed away. 'Don't come near me,' she said hoarsely.

'But that wouldn't work.' He dropped his shirt to the floor, and unzipped his pants. 'For what I intend, my Kate, we need to be gloriously, intimately close. As we used to be, such a short time ago. Before I made you angry and you decided you hated me.'

She said passionately, 'But I do hate you. And I am not—*not* going to allow you to do this.'

He sighed. 'Kate, I was your lover for six exquisite months. I know your body as well as I know my own. I can feel your response when I touch you, and while we were dancing tonight, you wanted me.'

'No.' She wanted the denial to be fierce, but instead it sounded as if she was pleading. 'You can't do this.'

'I must,' he said almost gently. 'Because without you, *agapi mou*, I am dying inside. I need you to heal me. To make me whole again.'

He took her in his arms, the naked heat of his body permeating her thin robe.

He said softly, 'Don't fight me, Kate. I am so very tired of fighting.' And then he kissed her.

His lips were a seduction in themselves, moving warmly and persuasively on hers, coaxing them apart, while his hands untied her sash, and pushed the concealing robe from her shoulders. Her eyes closed and she surrendered, allowing him the access he desired to the sweet moisture of her mouth.

Then he lifted her, and carried her to the bed, lying beside her as his long supple fingers began to rediscover her. And the scraps of silk and lace she was wearing were no barrier at all.

When he kissed her again, she responded swiftly, ardently, making her own feverish demands.

The tips of her bared breasts grazed his chest. Her hands sought him. Enclosed him.

And she felt, in her turn, the shiver of his touch on her thighs, and heard herself moan softly in need.

He whispered, 'No, *agapi mou*. You take me.'

And he turned on to his back, lifting her above him. Over him.

Her possession of him was slow and sweet, her body closing round him like the petals of a flower as she filled herself with him deeply, gloriously.

And he lay watching her, the breath catching in his throat as he caressed her, his fingertips brushing subtly across her flesh, making the pink nipples pucker and lift.

His hands stroked the length of her body from her shoulders to her flanks, and back again, tracing the vulnerable curve of her spine so that her body arched in sudden delight.

She began to move on him slowly, savouring every distinct, separate sensation, then increased the rhythm, hearing his breathing change as she did so.

She controlled him like a moon with a tidal sea, using her body like an instrument to bring him pleasure.

And then, before she was even prepared for it, all control was gone, and their locked bodies were straining frantically together seeking a consummation.

She heard him gasp her name, and answered him wordlessly as they took each other over the edge, and down into the abyss.

Afterwards, he slept in her arms, and she held him, as the slow tears edged out from under her lashes, and scalded her face.

Then quietly, inch by inch, she eased herself away from him, towards the edge of the bed. She found her robe, and put it on, then retrieved her underwear.

Moving gingerly, she opened the closet door, and began to search through his clothes for her passport.

It was nearly ten minutes before she found it. Ten precious moments of early morning turning into broad daylight, and increasing the risk of discovery.

She took one last look at Mick's sleeping figure.

She thought, 'Goodbye, my love' and knew that her heart was weeping. Then she slipped quietly out of the door, and back to her room.

She collected fresh undies, and a straight cream skirt with a black short-sleeved top, then went into the bathroom to shower and dress, and collect her toiletries.

The house was still quiet, and there was no sign of Maria. Maybe everyone was sleeping late today. So far, so good, thought Kate and went quickly and cautiously across the passage and into her room.

Mick was standing by the window. He'd dressed in denim pants and a polo shirt, and his arms were folded across his chest.

She halted, her throat closing in panic. She said huskily, 'I thought you were asleep.'

'I missed you beside me,' he said. 'And it woke me.'

He looked from her to the hastily packed travel bag, his mouth curling.

He said quietly, 'Were you planning to leave me another note, Katharina? What would this one have said, I wonder?'

'The same as the last one.' She flung back her head. 'That our marriage was a mistake, and I can't stay with you.'

'Nor can you leave,' he said. 'Not now. Because a little while ago, we may have given our child life.'

She stared at him. 'No.' Her voice shook. 'That's—not possible.'

He sighed. 'You cannot be that naïve. But the point is this. I want to make a baby with you, if not now, then in the future. And I intend our child to grow up with both parents.'

She said slowly, 'You want a child? But why now—of all

times? You've always refused to consider it before.' She paused. 'Oh, I understand. I suppose my replacement doesn't want to be pregnant. Doesn't want to spoil her wonderful figure. So, you'll just use me instead.' She gave a small, hysterical laugh. 'My God, I should have seen that coming.'

He said impatiently, 'You're talking like a crazy woman. What replacement in the name of God?' He didn't wait for an answer. 'But if you want to know why I hesitated over a baby, it was because I was scared.'

'You—scared?' Kate stared up at him in patent unbelief. 'Oh what, pray?'

He said roughly, 'Of losing you, *pedhi mou*, as I lost my mother. If she had not given birth to Ismene and myself, she could have been alive today. But the strain of it weakened her heart.'

'And you thought that might happen to me? That's absurd.' She lifted her chin. 'I prefer my own version. That you want a child, and you know Victorine won't give you one.'

'Victorine?' he repeated. 'What does she have to do with all this.'

'She's your mistress.' At last she'd made herself say the word. 'And she's going to be your wife, once you've got rid of me and taken over the company. So there's no room for me. And if I am having a baby, I'm damned if I'll surrender it to you to bring up—with her. The stepmother from hell.'

Mick said slowly, 'Why, in the name of God, should I marry Victorine? Yes, we were involved—once. You knew that. But it is long over. And will never be resumed.'

She said, 'That isn't true. Because you were here with her—on the day you came back from the States. When you thought I was in Ithaca. I *found* you together, both of you naked. In—that other room. In that bed—where we…' She couldn't finish the sentence.

He stared at her. 'You—found us having sex?'

'No,' Kate said. 'It was just the aftermath, but it had the same kind of punch. You were asleep on the bed, and she'd been having a shower. Neither of you were wearing any clothes.' Her voice shook. 'She—suggested I should—knock in future.'

He was very still. 'So, possessing this indisputable evidence, maybe you would prefer it if I left, and took Victorine with me.'

'I don't think she'd go.'

'No?' His smile chilled her. 'Well, let us see.'

He took Kate by the wrist, and marched her to the door. She struggled a little.

'Let me go. Where are you taking me?'

'We're going up to the villa,' he said. 'To ask her.'

CHAPTER THIRTEEN

'MICK, you can't do this.' Kate stumbled in his wake as he strode up the track towards the villa. 'You'll ruin everything for yourself. Lose everything you've worked for.'

'You speak as if that matters,' he threw over his shoulder at her. 'There are worse losses.'

'But think what it will do to your father,' she panted. 'Even if he did take her away from you, he doesn't deserve that kind of humiliation.'

'Now there we differ. A man who does that deserves everything he gets.' He walked into the villa's hallway, pulling Kate behind him, and paused. 'I presume they will still be in their suite at this time.'

'Yes,' she said. 'But please stop and think before you go in there.'

'What is there to think about?' Mick swung round, his eyes blazing. 'According to you, my passion for Victorine has corrupted my mind—my sense of honour. Therefore, I no longer have to consider the consequences of my actions.'

Kate said shakily, 'In that case, I'd rather stay here.'

'But you cannot,' he said. 'Because this is the moment when all your reasons for leaving me will be totally confirmed. When your condemnation of me for a liar and an adulterer will be completely justified.

'So, you should be there, *agapi mou*. It is not something you can afford to miss. Come.'

Kate went with him because she had no choice. She was trembling as he knocked imperatively at his father's door, and heard him call, 'Enter.'

They found Ari lying on the sofa, in dressing gown and

pyjamas, reading a newspaper, with a pot of coffee beside him.

He put down his book and studied them frowning slightly. 'Is this not a little early for social calls? All our guests are still asleep.'

'I am aware of that,' Mick said brusquely. 'But I have a matter to deal with which will not wait. I need to speak to Victorine urgently.'

Ari's frown deepened. 'She is also sleeping. Perhaps I can give her a message for you—at some more reasonable time?'

'No,' Mick said. 'I need to talk to her. We have been having a passionate affair behind your back, you understand, and I have decided to ask her to go away with me.'

Kate folded her arms across her body, feeling suddenly sick. She waited for the explosion, but it didn't come.

Instead, Ari said composedly, 'I see now why this cannot wait. I will fetch her.'

He rose and went into the bedroom and, a few minutes later, Victorine emerged. She was wearing a black lace night-gown with a matching peignoir clutched round her.

Her hair was a mess and Kate noticed with pleasure that her eyes were puffy.

'What is this, *cher*?' She seated herself on the sofa, disposing her draperies with conscious elegance. She was smiling, but her eyes were wary. 'Ari says you want me.'

'More than life itself, it seems,' Mick said. 'So much so, that I have wrecked my marriage for you. And now I am here to put an end to all this hidden passion and deceit, and admit our love openly.'

Victorine stiffened. She said. 'What are you talking about? Have you gone mad?'

'I have simply decided that nothing matters more than our love.' Mick shrugged. 'Naturally, I shall have to resign from the Theodakis Corporation, when the press learn the truth. But that will simply give me more time to devote to you, my dear Victorine, and your career. It is fortunate that you have an alternative source of income. I have become used to certain standards.'

He smiled blandly at her. 'So, if you will pack your things, we can be leaving.'

She said hoarsely, '*Tu es fou.* You are crazy—or drunk. What nonsense is this?'

'No nonsense, my sweet. Have you forgotten that Kate found us enjoying an illicit afternoon of love together? I think—I really think you should have mentioned to me that she saw us. It explains so much.'

Victorine looked at Kate, her face ugly. 'She is lying,' she said. 'She is trying to make trouble for me.' She turned to Ari, who was standing beside her, his face expressionless. '*Cher*, you do not believe this ridiculous story?'

'You were in our bedroom,' Kate said steadily. 'Mick was asleep, and you were combing your hair. You had a towel on, and nothing else. And you told me to knock in future.'

'No.' Victorine's voice rose. 'None of this is true. You are making it up—to blacken me in Ari's eyes. But it will not work.'

'Are you telling me you have forgotten it all?' Mick asked reproachfully. 'The passion we shared? The promises we made to each other?'

Victorine transferred her glare to him. 'I am saying it did not happen,' she returned shrilly.

'It was the day Mick came back from New York,' Kate continued. An immense calm seemed to have settled on her. 'I was supposed to go to Ithaca, and Mick's father had gone fishing with a friend. But my trip was cancelled, and when I rang home, Yannis told me that Mick was here. So, I came rushing back to the beach house to see him. Only, I found you as well.' For the first time there was a break in her voice.

'A terrible betrayal.' Ari's tone was meditative. 'We have both been deceived, Katharina.' He paused. 'Is this why you went back to England so suddenly, *pedhi mou*?'

'Yes.' Kate bit her lip.

'Without speaking of what you had seen—or demanding an explanation from my son?'

'I couldn't say anything. It was too painful. And there was no reason for anyone else to be hurt,' she added with difficulty. 'Besides, the evidence was there. I know what I saw.'

'So, you decided to spare my feelings at the expense of your own.' Ari nodded thoughtfully. 'That was kind, my child, but unnecessary. I have long known the truth.'

He looked at Mick. 'What happened that afternoon, my son?'

'I wish I knew.' Mick shrugged. 'I returned from New York earlier than planned, but when I arrived Yannis told me Kate had gone out for the day.

He frowned. 'I went down to the house to change. The jet lag had hit me hard, so I tried taking a shower. In the end, I decided to have a brief nap. I remember nothing more.'

He looked at Kate. 'Except that at some point you touched me, and said my name. I suppose you were trying to wake me. And I said "I love you."'

Kate's eyes widened, and her hand went to her throat.

'But when I eventually awoke,' he went on almost conversationally. 'It was to find you had left me—with a note simply stating our marriage was over.'

His mouth twisted. 'I assumed that you were still angry about my refusal to take you to New York—and that other disagreement we'd had.

'But I couldn't believe you'd gone without giving me a chance to put things right between us, and so I got angry too.

'But, of course, I didn't realise you'd discovered my flagrant infidelity,' he added reflectively. 'Little wonder that you did not wish to remain with me.'

'Ari,' Victorine spoke desperately. 'Don't listen to them. This is all nonsense. You heard—their marriage is in deep trouble, and because of that they are trying to destroy our relationship too.'

'What I see,' Ari said, 'Is that something happened that afternoon that was sufficient to put Katharina to flight. To make her wish to end her marriage to my son. And that is serious.

'Or perhaps not,' he added meditatively. 'Maybe it was intended as a joke—only it misfired a little.' He looked at Victorine. 'Is that how it was, *kougla mou*?'

His voice was gentle, but there was a note in it that sent a shiver down Kate's spine.

There was a long taut silence, then Victorine said sullenly, 'A joke, yes. But she was too stupid to realise she was being teased,' she added with a venomous look at Kate.

'I see.' Ari nodded. 'But why did you not explain this good joke as soon as you saw that it had gone wrong? That it had caused real hurt? Because you must have realised this very quickly.'

There was another silence, then Victorine shrugged defensively. 'They were—neither of them here. Michalis was working, and the girl was in London.'

'The girl?' Mick's voice bit. 'You will speak of my wife with respect.'

'What is there to respect?' Victorine spat back at him, her face twisted, ugly with dislike. 'She has nothing—is nothing—that pale-faced English bitch. What has she to offer any man? And you—you could have had me.'

There was another telling silence, then Mick said gently, 'There was never any question of marriage between us, Victorine, and I made that clear to you from the first. If you believed that might change, I am sorry.'

'Sorry.' She threw back her head and laughed harshly, the creamy skin tinged with an unhealthy flush. 'Yes, you have been sorry, Kyrios Theodakis, as you deserve. Because no man ever finishes with me. I am the one who leaves—always. Always—do you hear me?'

'Is that what this was all about?' Mick closed his eyes for a second. 'Dear God, it is unbelievable.'

'And then your wife left you,' Victorine went on gloatingly. 'So you found out what it was like. Oh, that made me happy.' And she laughed again.

'Please.' Kate's voice was barely audible. 'I don't think I can bear any more of this.'

'You do not have to, *pedhi mou*. None of us do.' There was a cold harshness in Ari's voice. He looked at Mick, 'Go with your wife, my son. Make things right between you.'

He paused. 'But first be good enough to ask Iorgos Vasso to come here. There are arrangements to be made. And send Androula also,' he added. 'Victorine will need help with her packing.'

'You are telling me to go?' Victorine's voice cracked.

'*Ne*,' he said. 'As I should have done long ago.' He gave a bitter sigh. 'I was wrong to bring you here, and I knew it. It was an act of stupidity and vindictiveness by a man who had quarrelled with his son.' He looked at Mick. 'You made me feel old, Michalis, and I did not wish that. I wanted my youth back again—my strength. But I have learned my lesson.'

'You can send me away—after all we have been to each other?' Victorine's tone was pleading.

'You are a beautiful woman, Victorine. And I am a rich fool. It is not a very admirable combination. But, let us not waste time in recrimination,' he added more briskly. 'Iorgos will arrange to have you flown anywhere you wish to go.'

She stumbled to her feet. 'Yes,' she said thickly. 'You are a fool—to think that I could ever want you. It was Michalis—always. Can't you see that? I thought if I came here, I could make him want me again.'

'Yes,' Ari said quietly. 'He saw that, but I would not, and we quarrelled again. But now it is all over. And you, *kougla mou*, will have to find another rich fool.'

'But then he brought *her*,' Victorine went on as if he had not spoken. 'And I saw the way he looked at her, and spoke. I knew that he loved her, and I wished to destroy that. I was there when Yannis took her call, so I went down to the beach house and found Michalis asleep.' She gave a throaty giggle. 'It was perfect. All I had to do was undress also—and wait.'

Kate pressed her knuckles against her mouth. 'Oh, God.'

Mick's arm was round her, holding her as she swayed. 'Come, *agapi mou*. You don't need to hear any more. Let us go back to the house.'

'Look after her,' Ari called after them. 'But do not forget that we have guests. I need Katharina to preside at the breakfast table.'

'Then you will be disappointed, Papa,' Michael tossed back at him. 'Do not expect either of us until dinner.'

In the hallway, he said, 'I must find Iorgos, and Androula. Will you wait for me?'

'Yes,' she said. 'I'll wait.'

He framed her face with his hands, looking into her eyes. 'And you won't run away from me again?'

Her lips trembled into a smile. 'Not this time. I'll be on the terrace.'

Outside, the wind was fresh and clean. Kate leaned on the balustrade, looking down at the foam-capped waves through the trees.

He came to stand beside her. 'What are you thinking?'

She said, with a shiver, 'That was—horrible.'

'Perhaps.' He shrugged. 'But also effective.'

'I almost feel sorry for her.'

'Save your compassion, my Kate. She showed no pity for you.'

Kate hesitated. 'Whatever she's done, she *is* very beautiful. Were you ever in love with her?'

'No,' he said quietly. 'I found her amusing at first, but I soon realised that her loveliness was only skin deep. I ended the relationship without regret.'

'How on earth did your father get involved with her?'

'To spite me,' he said wryly. 'You heard what he said, *matia mou*. They met at a party, not by chance, I am sure, and somehow she convinced him that she had ditched me, not the other way around, and that she found younger men boring.'

He grimaced. 'At the time, it was what he wanted to hear. He was very lonely when my mother died, and Linda had become, perhaps, too much part of the household. A companion for Ismene rather than himself.'

He sighed. 'I knew what she was, and tried to warn him. But that was a disaster. He said that I was jealous because she'd found him the better man. I could have dealt with that, but then Victorine started to make him jealous by coming on to me.' He shook his head. 'It was a nightmare.'

She said neutrally, 'So—you needed a wife. An answer to your problem.'

'If you remember,' he said softly. 'I said you would create more problems than you would solve. And how right I was.' He tutted reprovingly. 'Fighting with me. Refusing to be demure and obedient like a good Greek wife.'

'Is that what you wanted?'

'I wanted you, *agapi mou.*' He put his arm round her, as they walked down the steps to the track. 'From that first moment. Did you think it was a coincidence I turned up in London?' He shook his head. 'It was not. I came to find you.'

He gave her a swift, sidelong glance. 'If I am honest, I am not sure I intended marriage, not at first. But long before we made love, I knew that I could not live without you.'

'And yet you went to New York on your own.'

'Yes,' he said. 'And missed you like hell at every moment. Is that what you wanted to hear? That's why I came back early—to tell you that I was all kinds of a fool, and ask you to forgive me. And promise that I would never go anywhere without you again.'

He was silent for a moment. 'I also knew that I had to tell you why I'd been reluctant for us to have a baby. That it wasn't fair to hide my fears from you. Only, I wasn't used to having to explain myself—or to being married.'

'You will have to make allowances for me, *agapi mou,*' he added ruefully.

'When I awoke and found you gone, I felt as if someone had ripped out my heart. I wanted to come after you right away, but I told myself I should give you a chance to cool down—to miss me a little.'

'And instead, I asked for a divorce.'

'That,' he said quietly, 'was the worst day of my life. I kept asking myself how this could have happened? How I could have lost you. And began to come up with answers I did not want.'

'What sort of answers?'

He sighed. 'A friend of mine on Corfu met a girl on holiday,' he said reluctantly. 'The marriage lasted a year, then she went back to England, and took their child. She told him she had never loved him, and never wished to live in Greece. It was only his money she wanted. The divorce settlement.'

Kate gasped. 'And you thought that I—I was the same?' She tried to pull away from him. 'Oh, how could you?'

But he held her firmly. 'When you are hurt and angry, anything seems possible,' he told her levelly. 'And after all, my Kate, you had never once told me you loved me.'

She said breathlessly, 'But you knew how I felt. You must have done.'

'I knew you liked being in bed with me.' His tone was wry. 'But I needed more. I wanted you to speak the words.'

'Well, you didn't say them either,' Kate pointed out. 'Or not until that dreadful afternoon—and even then I thought you'd mistaken me for Victorine.'

'However deeply asleep I was, I would always hear your voice, *agapi mou*. Know your touch, and no other. Every soul in this world could see that I was crazy for you—even Victorine,' he added soberly.

She shivered. 'And she nearly destroyed us. Oh, Mick, happiness is such a fragile thing.'

'Together, we will make it strong.' He lifted her up into his arms and carried her over the threshold of the beach house.

'Our marriage begins again here,' he told her softly. 'I love you so much, my Kate.'

'Yes.' She smiled up at him, her eyes luminous. 'And I love you, Michalis *mou*. Now and for ever.'

'For ever,' he whispered. And kissed her.

THE MEDITERRANEAN TYCOON

by

Margaret Mayo

Born in the industrial heart of England, **Margaret Mayo** now lives in a Staffordshire countryside village. She became a writer by accident, after attempting to write a short story when she was almost forty, and now writing is one of the most enjoyable parts of her life. She combines her hobby of photography with her research.

Margaret Mayo has a new novel, *Bought for Marriage*, available in Mills & Boon Modern Romance® in November 2006.

CHAPTER ONE

PETA'S chin had a determined thrust as she knocked on the door. Many tales had travelled around the company about the dynamic new owner. He was the literal clean-sweeping new broom.

Already, in the space of a few weeks, many employees had left; no one wanted to work for the Tyrant, as he'd promptly been nicknamed. And now she had been promoted to his personal assistant. His third one in as many weeks! He hadn't asked whether she would like the job, oh, no. A directive had been sent to her. It implicated that she either take the job or leave the company.

It had put Peta's back up. She had disliked him immediately and intensely, but the fact was that she needed the job and couldn't afford to turn it down.

'Come!'

The voice was deep and resonant. She'd seen Andreas Papadakis when he'd stalked the corridors of Linam Shipping, when he'd swept through the offices, dark eyes seeing all. They'd rested on each employee in turn, reading and assessing, causing several of her female associates to swoon.

Peta had seen only a tall, arrogant man, who would have been handsome if his face wasn't creased into a permanent scowl. He'd projected a tough, invincible image, and she hadn't been impressed. She liked men with humanity and warmth. This man certainly hadn't the right disposition to warm himself to his employees. He was simply here to turn an already profitable company into a much bigger money-spinner.

She took a steadying breath before opening the door, her back ramrod-straight as she walked across the oatmeal carpet towards the huge, dominating desk. It was the first time she'd been in this holy sanctum and the oak panelling, the original oil paintings and the antique furniture were very impressive, though she somehow guessed they weren't what this man would have chosen for himself. He'd already installed a whole bank of computers and other high-tech office equipment, and they sat uneasily in what had once been old Mr Brown's office.

Andreas Papadakis stood to one side of the fine desk, his hair brushed uncompromisingly back, black brows beetled together, brown eyes narrowed and assessing. He looked the very picture of intimidation and Peta squared her shoulders. 'Good morning, Mr Papadakis,' she said evenly.

'Miss James.' He inclined his head. 'Sit down—please.' The please seemed to be an afterthought as he indicated the chair in front of his desk.

Peta sat, then wished she hadn't when he remained standing. He had to be at least six foot four, broad-shouldered and powerfully muscled, and those rich chestnut eyes watched every movement she made, making her feel distinctly uncomfortable.

Not that she let it show. She lifted her chin and fixed a bright smile to her lips, pencil poised above her notebook.

The rest of the day passed in a whirlwind of note-taking and meetings, of barked orders, of booking appointments and sending dozens of e-mails. Peta's opinion of Andreas Papadakis didn't change one iota; if anything she thought him even more arrogant and overbearing. But she nevertheless felt quite pleased with the way she had handled herself, sure that she'd passed her induction with flying colours, and was on the verge of putting on her jacket when her new employer flung open the connecting door between their two offices.

'Not so fast, Miss James. There's still work to be done.'

Peta glanced at the clock on the wall. 'I thought my hours were nine till five,' she said, her wide blue eyes fixed challengingly on his. 'It's already two minutes past.' Adding beneath her breath, And if you think I'm going to work late you have another think coming. I have a home life even if you don't.

'I couldn't care less if it's twenty past,' he lashed out. 'I need you.'

If this was the way he'd spoken to his previous secretaries then it was no wonder they'd walked out, decided Peta. What was wrong with asking politely instead of yelling and demanding? Unfortunately, if she wanted to keep the job, it looked as though it was a case of holding the candle to the devil.

'Very well,' she answered calmly, while seething inside as she hung up her jacket again. 'What is it you want me to do? I've finished all the work.'

He threw a tape down on her desk. 'I want this report by six. Make sure you type the figures correctly; it's very important.'

I bet it is, Peta said to herself, as soon as he'd closed the dividing door between them. Everything is important, according to you. She'd tied her thick auburn hair back this morning, but during the course of the day it had come loose and she tossed it back angrily now.

Picking up the phone, she called her neighbour. 'Marnie, I have to work late. Do you think you could look after Ben a while longer?' She hated having to leave her son a minute more than was necessary, felt guilty about it, even, but there was no way round it. Ben was very special to her. She wanted him to have the best possible start in life, and if that meant going out to work then that was what she had to do.

'Of course I will, love,' came the immediate reply. 'Don't worry about him. I'll give him his supper, shall I?'

Marnie loved looking after Ben. Her grandchildren were now teenagers and she missed having a small child around the house. She was a treasure. Peta didn't know what she'd do without her.

It was almost seven by the time she finally left the office. Andreas Papadakis was a workaholic and expected everyone else to be the same, heaping work on her that would surely have waited until the next day. She'd heard that some mornings he was at his desk by six.

She had no idea whether he was married or not. He didn't wear a ring and he protected his privacy fiercely, although all sorts of rumours floated around the company. Rumours of strings of attractive girlfriends, of a wife in Greece and a mistress in England, of properties in New York and the Bahamas, as well as in Europe and his homeland. How he had time for all this Peta wasn't sure.

When she arrived for work at ten minutes to nine the next morning he was waiting for her. 'I wondered when you were going to show up,' he muttered tersely, brown eyes glaring. His tie was hanging loose, top button undone, and his thick, straight hair looked as though he'd constantly raked agitated fingers through it. In fact he looked as though he'd spent the night in the office wrestling with insurmountable problems.

'I need coffee, strong and black, and half a dozen muffins. Blueberry. See to it, will you?'

The day had begun! Peta nodded. 'I could order you a proper breakfast if you'd—'

'Just do as I ask,' he cut in impatiently. 'And bring in your notebook. There's lots of work to get through.'

He was in a foul mood for the whole day but Peta stubbornly refused to give in, remaining pleasant, polite and helpful, no matter what harsh thoughts she entertained beneath the surface, and there were plenty of those.

By the end of the week she began to feel complacent; she felt that she now totally understood her employer and hopefully he was happy with her. His moods were legendary but Peta chose to ignore them—and on the whole it worked. It was not until he once more asked her to work late that it all began to go wrong.

'I'm sorry, I can't,' she said firmly. Why did he have to choose today of all days?

The famous frown dragged his brows together, beetling them over glittering chestnut eyes. 'I beg your pardon?'

'It's impossible for me to stay on today.'

'I presume you have a good reason?' he barked.

'Yes, I do as a matter of fact,' she announced, her chin just that little bit higher. 'It's my son's birthday.'

He looked thunderstruck. 'You have a son? Why the hell wasn't I told? You're no good to me if you're constantly taking time off.'

Peta's eyes flashed a deep, defensive blue. 'What do you mean, constantly? This is a special occasion, Mr Papadakis. Ben's eight today and he's having a party at McDonald's; I refuse to let him down. The only other occasion I couldn't work was when he had appendicitis. And even then I counted it as my holiday.'

She saw the flicker in his eyes, the faint doubt, then the grim nod. 'Very well. Can you manage a few hours in the morning?'

He was asking, not telling! A faint victory! It was Saturday tomorrow, and Ben's football practice. But under the circumstances Peta felt that it would be unwise to refuse him again. Marnie would take Ben; she'd love it. 'Yes, I can do that.'

'Good.' With a nod he dismissed her.

It never ceased to amaze Peta how good Andreas Papadakis's English was. He had scarcely the trace of an accent. If it hadn't been for his dark Hellenic looks she would have taken him for an Englishman any day. She could see why most girls in the office fancied him. What they hadn't experienced were his flashes of temper, his holier-than-thou attitude. It made you instantly forget how good-looking he was, how sexily he moved.

He was without a doubt a lethally attractive man—she had felt his physical presence many times; she'd have had to be made of ice not to—but in the main all she ever saw was the face of a tyrant. And she disliked him as much now as she had in the beginning. She found it hard to believe that he'd backed down over her working this evening.

'Mum, this is the best party ever,' Ben announced, munching his way through his second burger.

Peta grinned. The noise was deafening, every one of his eight friends talking at once, all happy and excited. To them this was a million times better than having a party at home with jelly and ice cream.

'And which one of you lucky young fellows is Ben?' asked a deep voice behind her. A familiar voice! Peta twisted in her chair, gasping in amazement when she saw Andreas Papadakis just a couple of feet away, a huge parcel tucked under one arm and an amazing twinkle in his eyes. He looked a very different man from the one she had left a couple of short hours ago.

'Mr Papadakis,' she gasped. 'What are you doing here?' She stood up then, felt her heart hammering a thousand beats a minute.

'I've brought a present for the birthday boy. Which one is he?'

By this time all eyes were on Ben, whose face had flushed with embarrassment. 'Who are you?' he asked, his chin jutting in the same way as his mother's. There was no mistaking their relationship. Although his hair was darker, he had the same wide-spaced blue eyes and an identical jawline.

'I'm your mother's employer. She told me it was your birthday. I thought you might like this.' And he handed Ben the giant parcel.

Peta was too shocked for words. This wasn't the same man. The Andreas Papadakis she worked for would never have thought about buying a birthday present for an employee's child, let alone personally delivering it.

'You're—very kind,' she murmured. 'You didn't have to do that.' There came the faint notion that perhaps he was checking on her, finding out for himself whether she'd been telling the truth when she said it was Ben's birthday, but no sooner had the thought flitted into her mind than she dismissed it as disloyal. She really didn't know the first thing about this man—except that he was the devil incarnate to work with.

'I can't stay,' he said now, 'I have other things to do.

Enjoy the party. I'll expect you at nine in the morning, Miss James.'

'Yes,' said Peta faintly. 'And thank you again.'

No one else noticed him leave, everyone was watching Ben open his parcel, and there was a collective 'Oooh!' when the colourful wrapping fell to the floor revealing a magnificent Scalextric set. And when the lid came off the box there was so much track and so many cars that Peta felt sure it would take up the whole floor area of Ben's bedroom and spill out onto the landing as well. It was every boy's dream.

Her first instinct was to say that he couldn't accept such an expensive gift and that he must give it back, but seeing the look of sheer pleasure and amazement on Ben's face made her think again. It wasn't as if Andreas Papadakis couldn't afford it.

Maybe it was a thank-you for all the hard work she'd put in. Or—her mouth twisted wryly—maybe it was a sweetener so that she wouldn't say no to him again when he asked her to work late! She couldn't really believe that her boss had a big enough heart to buy her son a present when he hadn't even met him. She wasn't even sure he had a heart. But whatever his reasons it had pleased Ben, and he was her main concern.

When she went in to work on Saturday morning she fully intended thanking Mr Papadakis again, but gone was the man of yesterday evening. He was in his head-of-the-firm mode and it brooked no personal conversation. Nevertheless when he stood over her, one hand on the back of her chair, one on the desk, watching the screen as she typed a letter he was waiting for, she was aware now that a warm human being existed behind that harsh exterior. And because of that she began to feel his primal sexuality, the sheer physical dynamics of the man.

'You've missed out a word.'

Peta silently groaned. She'd do more than that if he didn't move. He was wearing a musky sandalwood cologne that was essentially male and would remind her of him for evermore. It took a supreme amount of willpower to carry on typing the letter and she made more mistakes in that one page than she normally did in a whole day.

'What's wrong?' he asked sharply. 'Not got it together yet? Did the party tire you out?'

Hardly, when it had been finished by eight. Had he no idea that he was the one making her nervous? 'I'm all right,' she answered. 'And by the way, thank you again for buying Ben that Scalextric. It was much too expensive a present, but he's absolutely delighted with it. He had me up at six this morning helping him put it together.'

'Good, I'm glad he liked it. Bring the letter in to me when you've printed it. And I'd like Griff's report next.'

He strode away, clearly not interested in discussing Ben's party or his gift. And she'd thought he had a heart after all. How wrong could she have been?

The morning fled. No mention had been made of how long he wanted her to work, though Peta had assumed she'd finish about one. But one o'clock came and went and there was no sign of him letting up.

His voice came through the open doorway. 'Miss James, get some lunch sent in.'

Peta groaned inwardly; surely he wasn't expecting her to remain here all day?

Then he strode into her office. 'After that you'd better go home and spend some time with your boy.'

'Thank you,' she said, wondering at his sudden generosity. 'And if you don't mind me saying so, you work far too hard yourself. Mr Brown didn't used to do the hours you do.'

'That's why the company was running downhill fast,' he retorted.

'What do you mean, downhill?' Peta asked quickly. 'It was extremely successful.' She'd always counted herself lucky to be working for such a flourishing firm.

Andreas Papadakis shook his head. 'That's the impression he wanted you to have. He didn't want unhappy employees, but a few more months and you'd have all been out of work.'

She looked at him with a disbelieving frown. 'Is that true?'

'Of course it's damn well true. I bought a sinking ship, Miss James, it's what I do. But I sure as hell make sure they never capsize.'

Peta supposed she ought to have known from the content of his correspondence that there were problems, except that she'd thought he was simply sweeping clean all the old methods and installing new ones of his own. He'd drummed up an awful lot of new business as well. She had privately accused him of rubbing his hands at all the extra money he was generating, not realising for one second that if he hadn't she'd have lost her job. It looked as if she'd wrong-footed him every step of the way.

Only once in the days that followed did he ask her to work late. 'I appreciate that you want to spend time with your son,' he said, 'but this really is important.'

How could she refuse when he asked her like that? But when on Friday afternoon he said that he wanted her to attend a conference with him on the following Monday and that it would mean a very late night she looked at him sharply. 'I don't think I can do that.'

She had never in the whole of Ben's life let anyone else bath him and put him to bed. It was a pleasure she looked forward to. It was their special time of day; it eased the guilt of her leaving him while she went to work. Marnie would be in her element, and Ben would probably enjoy it too if the truth were know because he adored her as much as the older woman adored him, but Peta knew that she would feel truly awful.

In any case, what conference went on into the early hours? He had to be joking. 'I can't promise anything,' she said.

'Can't or won't?' he demanded, mouth grim all of a sudden. 'I can easily find someone to step into your job, Miss James.'

This was the first time in ages that she had seen a flash of his old self. She ought to have known that his understanding behaviour was too good to last. 'I doubt it,' she replied, adding with great daring, 'No one else has been able to put up with your impossible demands.'

Fierce black brows jutted over narrowed eyes. 'Is that why you think my other PAs left?'

She nodded. 'It's what everyone believes.'

He perched himself on the edge of her desk, too near for comfort, causing an alarming flurry of her senses. They were becoming too frequent for her own good. She was joining the others, seeing him as a sexually exciting male instead of an impossible boss.

'Then I think I should put the matter straight,' he announced. 'They didn't leave because they couldn't work with me. I fired them because of their inadequacies.'

Peta shot him a flashing blue glance. 'Maybe what

you call inadequacies and what we girls consider to be unfair requests are two different things.'

His eyes narrowed still further until they were no more than two glittering slits. 'I think I've been more than reasonable, but if you think it unfair that I occasionally ask you to work extra hours, for which I might add you are handsomely paid, then I suggest you put your coat on and walk, too.'

Peta couldn't believe she had landed herself in this situation. She really oughtn't to have spoken to him like that. He was her employer after all. 'It's all right, I'll do it,' she said hastily.

'Good,' he clipped, and returned to his office.

She was walking out through the door at the end of the day, her thoughts already running ahead to her darling son and how she could make it up to him, when Andreas Papadakis's voice arrested her.

'The conference starts at two on Monday. Wear your smartest suit, Miss James, and it might be advisable to pack a cocktail dress for the evening.'

Warning bells rang in her head. She lurched round and stared at him. 'A cocktail dress?'

'That's right.'

Something was seriously wrong here, she decided as she headed towards her car. It sounded as though he needed a partner, not a personal assistant. And she wasn't sure that she wanted to be that person. The trouble was she had already promised.

CHAPTER TWO

ON SUNDAY afternoon Peta took Ben to the park to feed the ducks. She'd wound down from her hard week at work and was feeling happy and relaxed, enjoying Ben's company—until, on their return, she saw Andreas Papadakis's sleek black Mercedes parked outside her cottage. Her heart-rate increased a thousandfold and she couldn't even begin to think why he was here.

'Wow!' exclaimed her son. 'Whose is that?'

There was no time to answer because, as they approached, her employer levered his long frame out of the car and leaned nonchalantly against it, arms folded, legs crossed, a faint smile softening his all-too-often austere features. His casual pose emphasised his dynamic sexuality and Peta felt a tightening of her muscles. Her smile in response was little more than a grimace.

It was the first time she'd seen him in anything other than a collar and tie. In a blue thin-knit half-sleeved shirt, grey chinos and loafers he looked far less formidable. But infinitely more dangerous! She was scared of the sensations he managed to arouse in her these days.

Ben broke the awkward silence. 'You're my mummy's boss, aren't you? Thank you for my Scalextric; I love it. Me and Mummy put it together. Would you like to come and play?'

Andreas Papadakis smiled briefly. 'Some other time, perhaps. I need to talk to your mother.'

Somehow Peta couldn't see this indomitable man getting down on his knees and playing racing cars with an eight-year-old boy. 'Mr Papadakis is here on business, Ben. He hasn't time to play,' she consoled him, at the same time wondering exactly why he had come calling.

She unlocked the door and Ben ran straight up to his room, and as her boss was standing right behind her she had no alternative but to invite him in, even though she would have preferred to talk outside.

It wasn't really a cottage, although it went under that name. It was a small, old town house on the outskirts of Southampton. She would have liked something grander but it was all she could afford, and it was home. It was clean and tidy and the furniture she'd renovated suited the house. She was happy here.

In her sitting room she turned to face him. 'This is quite a surprise, Mr Papadakis. Is the conference off tomorrow? Is that what you've come to tell me?'

'No, indeed,' he stated emphatically. 'I simply wanted to make sure that you'd come prepared. You looked somewhat shocked when I suggested a cocktail dress.'

'I was,' she claimed. 'I still am. You make it sound as though we're going to a party. And I—'

'It's no party, I assure you,' he interjected swiftly.

'Then why the cocktail dress?' She wondered whether she ought to suggest he sit down. But no, he might stay too long, and that was the last thing she wanted.

'Because after the conference we're having dinner,' he explained with exaggerated patience. 'Naturally we'll go on talking business, but it's not the sort of place where you can underdress.'

Peta narrowed her eyes speculatively, her head tilted to one side. 'And in what exact capacity would I be going?' It was something she needed to get very clear in her mind right from the beginning.

Eyebrows rose. 'Why, as my very able assistant. I

thought you understood that. I shall rely on you to take notes, make sure I didn't miss anything. You can familiarise yourself with the agenda in the morning. As I said, the conference begins at two. We'll have a sandwich lunch in the office.' He paused and studied her face intently. 'You still don't look as though you're sure about coming.'

'I somehow don't think I have a choice.'

'Correct. It's all part of the job. Is it your son you're worried about? Have you no one to look after him?'

'I have, yes, but he's my whole life, I hate leaving him. I feel I'm letting him down.'

He nodded as if he understood, but she couldn't see how, and when he turned towards the door she gave a sigh of relief. 'I'll see you at nine sharp in the morning,' he said. 'Say goodbye to your son for me.'

'His name's Ben.'

'Say goodbye to Ben for me, then.'

'Why don't you do it yourself? He's dying for you to see his Scalextric in action.' Now, why had she said that when she was anxious to be rid of him? Peta gave a mental shake of her head. She was out of her mind.

Andreas shot a look at his watch. 'I really should be getting back, but—maybe a couple of minutes.'

Back to whom? wondered Peta as she led him up the stairs. His current girlfriend? His mistress? Or back to the office? Did he work on a Sunday?

She felt his eyes boring into her back, maybe assessing her figure, her bottom in her tight denim jeans, checking her out to see whether she could be added to his list of conquests. Some chance!

But Ben had spotted them. 'Hello, have you come to play?' he asked brightly.

'Only to look,' explained Andreas. 'It's a very fine

layout you have there, but maybe if you…' In no time at all he was on his knees making adjustments, much to Peta's amazement, and it was another half-hour before he finally left.

Ben couldn't stop talking about him. 'Is that man going to come again?' he kept asking. 'Look what he did, Mummy. It's so much better. Come and play with me.'

But Peta had other more important things on her mind. 'Not now, darling, we have to go and see Auntie Susan.' Sue wasn't really Ben's aunt; she was a friend from her schooldays, divorced and happy, leading a full social life.

'Peta, how lovely to see you. And hello, Ben. How are you, little man? Come in, come in. I'll put the kettle on. Unless you'd like wine, Peta? You look worried. Is everything OK?'

'I've come to ask a favour. I need a cocktail dress for tomorrow night.'

Sue's brown eyes widened and her mouth broke into a smile. 'You've got a new boyfriend? Wonderful! Tell me about him. What's his name? How did you meet? Where—?'

'Shut up, Sue,' laughed Peta. 'It's nothing like that. It's a business do. I'm going with my boss.'

'The one you told me about? The Tyrant? Goodness, I bet you're not looking forward to that!'

Peta grimaced. 'It's either go or lose my job.'

Sue's eyes flashed. 'The man's a pig. Come on; let's have a look. We need to knock that man dead. Make him realise how irresistible you are. Hey, Ben, do you want the telly on while we go upstairs?'

'I don't want to be irresistible,' retorted Peta.

'Indispensable, then; you know what I mean,' said Sue airily. 'What sort of a do is it?'

'I don't altogether know,' said Peta, following her friend. 'A conference, followed by a black-tie dinner, but the meeting goes on while we eat, apparently.'

'Sounds fishy to me,' snorted Susan. 'Are you sure he hasn't got his eye on you?'

Peta laughed. Andreas Papadakis certainly had no designs on her, of that she was very sure.

At work the next morning her employer gave her no time to think about what lay ahead. It was head down and get on with it. They hardly had time to eat the smoked-salmon sandwiches he had sent in.

'You can use my private bathroom to freshen up,' he said when it was almost time for them to go. 'You've brought something along for tonight?'

Peta nodded, thinking uneasily about the dress that hung in a garment carrier on the back of her office door. She ought never to have let Sue persuade her to wear it. The black one would have been so much more suitable.

In the close intimacy of his car Peta felt his presence as if she never had before. She could feel every one of her nerve-ends skittering simply because she was sitting close to him, the skin on her bones tightening, and the most damning heat invading her body.

'What's wrong?'

My heart's thumping so loud it hurts, that's what's wrong, she thought. And it was complete and utter madness. She lifted her chin and dared to look at him. In profile, he was the essence of autocratic arrogance. A high forehead, a Roman nose, full lips, a firm chin. And, what she hadn't noticed before, long, thick eyelashes.

He turned to look at her. 'Well?'

'Nothing.'

'You're uptight about nothing?' he demanded crisply.

'Maybe because I don't think I'll live up to your expectations, Mr Papadakis.' Dammit, she hadn't meant to say that. She wanted him to think that she was Miss Efficiency. But something had made her say it; probably a need to point him away from the real reason that she was on edge.

'All you need to do is make notes. We talked about it earlier; I thought you understood. You haven't let me down so far. I have every faith in you.' Adding after a slight pause, 'I'd prefer it if you called me Andreas when we're alone.'

Peta only just stopped her mouth from falling open. Progress indeed! Not many people on the company, she was sure, called him Andreas. It was always Mr Papadakis, even from his most senior staff. His attitude didn't invite familiarity. 'Very well,' she agreed, but somehow she couldn't see herself doing it.

'That's good, Peta.'

She rather liked the way her name rolled off his tongue. He made it sound beautiful and exotic.

'So no more nerves, hey?' he asked as they pulled up on the hotel forecourt. And his smile did the most nerve-chilling things to her body. This wasn't the Andreas Papadakis she knew, and she didn't want him turning into anything else. She had grown used to his harshness. She could handle it. If he turned all soft on her she would end up a mushy mess.

But once the conference got under way she need not have worried. This was her employer at his most efficient. He was chairing the meeting, and every now and then when some pertinent point was made his eyes darted in her direction to make sure she had made a note of it. He need not have worried either. She was writing *everything* down.

Each delegate wore a name badge, so she knew exactly who was saying what, and she soon found herself either agreeing or disagreeing with the various statements. Once she almost jumped up to argue with a guy who said that the reason the shipping industry was going into decline was due to apathy on behalf of the ship owners.

It was Andreas himself who slapped him down. Peta found him fascinating to watch. In a dark grey cashmere suit, white silk shirt and a discreet red and grey tie, he was the epitome of a successful businessman. He was clearly respected and his points of view always carefully listened to. She saw several heads nod whenever he made a point; rarely did anyone disagree with him.

But she also saw Andreas the man, the incredibly sexy man. She was able to look at him without fear. She was able to look at those liquid brown eyes with their long curling lashes, at the sensuality of firm, full lips, and she even allowed herself to wonder what it would be like to be kissed by him.

With horror she realised that she had let her mind drift, that she hadn't heard what had just been said, and Andreas Papadakis's eyes were shooting daggers. The man never missed a thing! But thankfully he asked Peter Miller to repeat what he had said, as though he himself hadn't fully heard. And after that Peta was careful not to let her mind wander.

So much was said, so much discussed, that Peta knew it would take her hours to type up the notes. Hours she didn't have. Unless, of course, she could wangle a laptop out of him and take it home. It would solve the problem of asking Marnie to look after Ben and she would be able to spend precious hours with her son.

The afternoon fled and it was soon time for dinner; time to change into the dress that filled her with horror whenever she thought about it. Andreas had booked her a room and she was able to shower and take a short rest before making up her face and doing her hair.

Peta rarely wore much make-up but this evening she felt that she needed some protective armour, something to make her feel good in the dark green dress. And so on went the foundation and the blusher, the eye shadow and mascara, and a much deeper-pink lipstick than she normally used.

Finally she was ready, and at almost the same time her employer tapped on the door. Peta awaited his reaction, dreading it, not surprised when he slowly and carefully eyed her up and down. It sent a whole gamut of emotions rushing through her as she stood there and suffered his appraisal, notwithstanding the fact that he looked totally devastating in his dinner suit.

He missed nothing. Not the way the satin material defined the curve of her hips, the flatness of her stomach, or the soft roundness of her breasts. It had been horrendously expensive, according to Sue, and made Peta look taller and extremely elegant. And yet all she was aware of was how low the neckline dipped and the way Andreas Papadakis's eyes had lingered there.

She even caught a glimpse of desire, gone in an instant, and she might have imagined it because all he did was slowly nod his head in approval. 'Let's join the others,' he said crisply.

The more she thought about it the surer Peta was that she'd been mistaken. He didn't even compliment her, which was the least he could have done, considering the way she'd put herself out for him.

Nevertheless she drew admiring glances from the other delegates, which went some way to appeasing her, and although conversation over the meal still rested on business it was far less formal and there was no need for her to take any notes.

She was extremely conscious of sitting by Andreas's side and wished he had placed her somewhere else. She was the only female present—obviously the other men had seen no reason to bring their secretaries—and it was only sheer stubbornness that made her get through the evening without feeling uncomfortable.

Andreas, to give him his due, didn't ignore her. He included her in all conversations, surprising her sometimes by asking her opinion, listening attentively when she spoke. Peta had worked for the company long enough to have formed her own ideas, and was able to contribute successfully.

The only problem was sitting close to Andreas. He had an indefinable charisma, which she was sure even the men must feel, although not in the same way as she did. He was capable of controlling a room full of people with a word and a look, but she couldn't control the tingle of her senses. It had begun faintly and grown with every passing minute until her veins fairly sizzled.

It was idiotic of her to feel such a response, and yet there was nothing she could do to stop it. She had never for one moment expected, when she was summoned to work for him, that he would evoke such feelings in her. They were contrary to every thought she had, contrary and undesirable. Sex had never played an important part in her life, not after Joe, and she couldn't understand why this man aroused her baser instincts now.

By the end of the evening she wished that she'd never come, and when he offered to take her home Peta shook her head. 'It's all right, I'll get a taxi.' In the confines of his car her torture would be even worse.

'No, you won't,' he stated firmly, 'and if your refusal

is because I've had a few drinks, there's no need to worry because my driver is waiting for us.'

There was no way out.

Peta took her time collecting her coat and bag, willing her hormones to settle down and ignore this magnificently sexy male who just happened to be her boss. Lord, if only he knew! She'd be out of a job like a shot, or—an even more terrifying thought—he'd take advantage. He'd use her!

Her face was serious when she finally joined him in the hotel foyer. This last thought had scared her, made her realise how stupid she was being. 'I'm ready,' she said abruptly.

He gave her a strange look but said nothing, slipping into the car beside her and giving his driver her address. He sank back into the soft leather seat and closed his eyes. Peta huddled into her corner and closed her eyes, too, hoping to ignore him. Impossible! She could still smell his distinctive cologne, sense his powerful body so near to hers. There was enough space between them for another person but it made no difference. He was still far too close for comfort.

'You've done a good job today, Peta.'

His voice made her eyes snap open. He was looking at her from beneath half-closed lids. A lazy, sensual look that set her nerves on edge again.

'I appreciate it. And good work needs rewarding.' He leaned towards her and Peta panicked. What sort of reward was he talking about? A kiss? More than that? She shrank even further into the seat.

'You'll see a handsome bonus in your pay cheque at the end of the month.'

Peta breathed a sigh of relief. 'I've not typed my notes out yet,' she pointed out. 'You might be disappointed.'

'I don't think so. You're by far the best assistant I've had in a long time.'

'In that case,' she said, taking advantage of one of his rare moments of companionship, 'could I take a laptop home to do the notes? I really won't have time at the office and I don't want to work late and leave Ben again.'

'Consider it done,' he said. 'He needs you as much as I do.'

Peta must have shown her surprise because he added, 'Believe me, Peta, I do appreciate that you have a home life. I press people hard, I know—it's the only way to get anything done—but I too have a life outside work.'

'You do? I thought there was nothing more important than turning around ailing businesses.'

'I know I give that impression. I've always worked hard.'

'So what do you do outside work hours?' she asked, amazing herself by her temerity.

'I too have a son,' he admitted. 'A son who complains that he never sees enough of me.'

His confession stunned Peta. Of all the rumours that had spread through the company, this wasn't one of them.

'You look surprised.'

'I am. I didn't know; I didn't realise; I thought…' Her voice tailed off in confusion.

'You thought I was a workaholic, maybe even a bit of a playboy in my spare time? I do know what's being said about me, Peta.'

'But you don't care to correct it?'

'My private life is just that—private. I prefer it to remain that way.'

'You can rest assured I'll say nothing,' she said, and at that moment they drew up outside her house.

'Wait!' He leaned forward and put a hand over hers when she made to open the door. 'Gareth will let you out.'

His touch meant nothing and yet it took her breath away. She turned her head to look at him and his brown eyes darkened and his lips brushed her cheek. Just that, nothing more, yet it felt as though he was making love to her.

'Thank you, Peta, for brightening up my evening. You look truly beautiful.'

Peta was saved answering by his driver opening her door. She climbed out speedily, turning only at the last minute to smile weakly at her boss. The compliment was late, yet it made more of an impact because of it. Her fingers trembled as she put the key in the lock, and the car didn't move until she had safely closed the door behind her.

CHAPTER THREE

ANDREAS pondered his problem. He could, of course, get another girl from the agency, but how many was that now? And Nikos had liked none of them. There had to be another answer. He drank cup after cup of black coffee until finally a solution came to him. It put a smile on his face as he showered and got ready for work, and he was impatient for Peta to arrive.

When she did he called her straight into his office. Andreas Papadakis didn't believe in beating around the bush. If he had something to say he came straight out with it. In his opinion it was the only way.

'Miss James…Peta, I need your help.'

He saw the way she frowned, pulling her delicately shaped brows together. He saw the way she bit her lower lip, which she always did when she wasn't sure what to expect of him. Gone was the sexy dress of last night, replaced by one of her smart suits. The dress had amazed him. He had never imagined her wearing anything so revealing. Amazed and pleased him. He'd heard a few whispered comments about what a lucky so-and-so he was to have an assistant like that. And it had certainly made him look at her in a new light.

Not that he hadn't already realised her potential. She was an exceedingly attractive girl who never made the most of her assets. That gorgeous auburn hair, for instance, was always tied uncompromisingly back, and those lovely dark blue eyes were never shown off to their advantage. Last night, when she'd carefully made them up, he had felt their full impact for the first time. The things they'd done to him were best forgotten. She was such an ice-cold maiden that if she'd read the ignoble thoughts in his mind she would have very likely walked out of her job. And now he needed her more than ever.

'Can you think of anyone in the secretarial pool who'd do your job as well as you?'

'You're sacking me?' The colour faded from her cheeks, her eyes widening in dismay.

'Of course not,' he assured her quickly. 'I have something else in mind.'

Her chin lifted in another of her delightful habits and she looked at him warily.

'I need someone to look after Nikos.'

'Your son?'

'Yes.'

'And you're asking me. Why?'

'Because his current nanny's handed in her notice.'

Her incredibly blue eyes flashed her indignance and he wondered why the hell he hadn't noticed long before now how gorgeous they were. They were enough to send any man crazy.

'I'm a qualified secretary, not a child-minder,' she retorted. 'I don't want to spend my life looking after someone else's children.'

Andreas hadn't expected her to say yes straight away, he had known she would need a lot of persuading, but she sounded so adamant that he feared she would never agree. Perhaps he ought to give her no choice, either she take the job or… No, if he did that he'd risk losing out both ways. 'You hate having to leave Ben every day, don't you?' he asked quietly.

She nodded. 'More than you'll ever know.'

'Oh, I do; you underestimate me. This is the perfect

solution. It will solve your dilemma as well as mine. You and Ben would move into my house, you'd be there for him whenever he needed you, and you could also do some work for me from home.' To him it was the simplest solution, the obvious one.

The look on her face spoke a thousand words. 'Mr Papadakis, living with you is the last thing I want. Ben and I are happy as we are. I love my little house. Why should I give it up? And, for that matter, where's your wife? Why can't she bring up her own child?'

Andreas's eyes shadowed as his thoughts raced back to the blackest days of his life. 'My wife's dead,' he told her bluntly, 'and you wouldn't need to give up your house; you could let it.' He saw the uncertainty in her eyes and pressed home his faint advantage. 'Sit down. Think again about the benefits.'

Reluctantly she perched herself on the edge of a chair, crossing her legs so that her skirt rode up. Not for the first time he felt a stirring in his loins. But that sort of thing had to be put to one side. He needed her to feel safe, not threatened. He hadn't failed to notice in the car last night how she had drawn back from him when he kissed her cheek. Someone, somewhere along the line, had destroyed her trust in men, and he had no intention of adding to it.

'I desperately need someone to look after Nikos. You know how much time I put in here—the poor little guy hardly sees me.'

'So why don't *you* work from home?'

It was a logical question and he grimaced. 'I'd love to, but if I'm to turn this company around I need to keep my finger on the pulse.'

'How long would you expect me to do the job?'

'I don't know. Until I find someone else, perhaps,

maybe even indefinitely if it works as well as I hope it will. You won't lose out, I assure you.'

'What if Nikos doesn't like me?'

'He will.' How could he not? Peta James was good with children, he'd seen that for himself. She was also exciting and provocative. He'd noticed at the conference how easily she talked to other people. In fact she had seemed far more at ease with some of them than with him. He hadn't liked it. He'd fancied her that night more than he'd ever expected.

'In fact,' he went on, 'it might be a good idea to take you to see him before we finally sign the deal.'

'Sign the deal?' she repeated with a frown.

'Figuratively speaking, of course,' he said with what he hoped was a reassuring smile. Smiling didn't come easy to him these days. There were too many pressures, too much to do, too many sad memories, and Nikos was the one who suffered. If he could persuade Peta to take this job it would be the best thing that had happened to his son in a long time. It might not be so good for him, here, because she was incredibly efficient, but his son's well-being meant more to him than anything else.

'We'll finish work early tonight and I'll take you to meet him,' he said decisively.

'I can't,' Peta said with the now familiar toss of her head. 'Ben's playing football. I try never to miss a match.'

It was Andreas's turn to frown. 'Bronwen leaves at the end of the week. I need to have everything sorted well before then. How about after the football match? Bring Ben with you. It will be good for the boys to meet.'

'How old is Nikos?' she asked, and he could see her mind turning over the situation.

'Seven,' he answered, 'though he's very grown-up for his age.'

'Does he have a Scalextric?'

'You bet.'

'Then I'm sure Ben will get on with him,' she said with a faint smile.

And the way she said it reassured him that her answer would ultimately be yes.

Peta's mind was in a whirl. Her first instinct had been to turn Andreas down. She still might, because would it be wise, feeling as she did about him? It was scary the way he'd managed to set her feelings alight last night. Scary and undesirable. She'd been hurt too much in the past to want to get involved. It was far better to keep things on a purely professional level. But would she be able to do that living in the same house?

She placed the last lot of post on his desk for signing. 'How do I get to your house?' She had no idea where he lived. Again the rumour machine had him living in a fantastic mansion overlooking Southampton Water with a whole host of servants at his beck and call.

'No need to drive; I'll pick you up. What time does the match finish?'

About to say he didn't have to put himself out, Peta decided against it. She was the one doing the favour so why should she do the running?

Peta clapped and yelled enthusiastically every time Ben's team scored a goal. And when Ben himself scored she went wild with delight. 'Well done, Ben!' she shouted, jumping up and down, clapping her hands. 'Go for it!'

Another much louder voice echoed her words from behind. 'Well done, Ben!'

She turned and there was an instant's sizzling reaction as she met the eyes of Andreas Papadakis. She was the first to look away, praying fervently that he wasn't able to read her mind. It was all so wrong, this physical attraction. Despite her telling her body to behave itself, it had gone into involuntary spasm and there was nothing she could do about it.

At his side was a boy roughly Ben's height, dark-haired and dark-eyed, but with a much rounder face than his father's and a thinner mouth. 'How did you find us?' she asked. They'd arranged for him to pick her up at her house, which was a five-minute walk away.

'I followed the noise. It sounds an exciting match.'

'It is,' she agreed. 'And this is Nikos, I take it?'

'It is, indeed. Nikos, this is the lady I told you about, the one who's going to look after you when Bronwen leaves.'

Nikos looked up at her with serious brown eyes. 'I don't like Bronwen. She shouts a lot.'

Peta wondered whether he deserved it, whether he played her up when his father was absent. 'Ben's dying to meet you,' she said with a warm smile.

When she'd told Ben they might be moving he'd been at first upset and then excited, especially when he learned that there'd be someone his own age to play with, and they'd probably be living in a much bigger house.

'It will be good to have some company,' said Nikos. 'I get bored on my own. Which one is Ben? I like football. I'd like to play with them.'

Peta's eyes met Andreas's and she smiled, remembering him telling her how grown-up Nikos was for his age. And she was amazed at how good his English was, too. Ben hadn't even started to learn a foreign language yet.

'Doesn't your school have a football team?'

'Yes, but I am never allowed to take part. Dad is always too busy, and none of my nannies has liked football.'

Again Peta looked at Andreas. His lips turned down at the corners and he shook his head, suggesting that he knew nothing about it. Which was about par for the course, she decided. Andreas spent far too much time working, relying heavily on other people to look after his son. It was no wonder he didn't know the thoughts that went through Nikos's head.

'Well, I like it,' she said. 'So go ahead and join your team; I'll always come and cheer you on.'

'You will?' His eyes shone with delight. 'Thank you. Thank you very much. Did you hear that, Dad? I think I am going to like my new nanny.'

Peta only hoped that his matches wouldn't clash with Ben's. She would hate to let Nikos down now that she'd made her promise.

When the match was over Peta wanted to take Ben home to shower and change, but Andreas insisted that it didn't matter, and in the back of the car the two boys soon got to know one another.

'They're getting on well,' murmured Andreas.

Peta nodded. 'Ben's a good mixer. What made you come so early?'

He gave a guilty grimace. 'When I explained to Nikos where we were going it was his idea. I hadn't realised he was so interested in football.'

'Most small boys are.'

'Am I being chastised?'

She looked at him then, and it was a big mistake.

There was a hint of wry humour on his face, something she had never seen before. He was no longer the Tyrant but a father, with a son he loved but didn't know much about. And he was sharing that knowledge with her.

It felt oddly like a bond, and she could so easily fall into the trap of revealing her feelings. But that wasn't what he wanted, and neither did she, for that matter. Andreas needed someone to care for his son when he was unable to. And he had placed that trust in her. She dared not let him down by showing a marked preference for his body.

For once the rumour machine was right. He did live in a big house, though it wasn't overlooking Southampton Water. It was set in its own grounds, hidden from the road, suddenly emerging as they rounded a bend in the drive. It was a red-brick and timber building, several hundred years old, by the look of it, with ivy clambering over some of the walls, tall chimneys reaching for the sky, every window gleaming in the late-evening sun.

'I don't own, I rent,' he told her, seeing the look of awe and amazement on her face. 'I took it while I looked around for somewhere suitable, but to tell you the truth I haven't had time, and actually I like it here. I'm considering making the owner an offer.'

Nikos and Ben were already out of the car and running towards the house. Andreas and Peta followed. She felt uncomfortable walking beside him; it felt wrong to be going to her employer's house, to even consider living with him. She wasn't a nanny; how could he expect her to do a nanny's job? Her only qualification was bringing up her own son. The tempting part was that she would see more of Ben. No more leaving him with Marnie while she worked late, or even when he came home from school. She would be there for him always. The thought brought a smile to her lips.

Andreas wasn't looking at her, and yet he must have sensed her smiling because he turned and spoke. 'You're happy about the situation?'

'I guess so. I was thinking about being able to spend more time with Ben.' What she didn't dare think about was spending time with Andreas. Not that she expected to see very much of him. With her safely ensconced in his house looking after his precious son, he would be able to stay at the office for as long as he liked.

And if he brought work home for her to do that would be even better, because there would be hours in the day while the boys were at school when she would have nothing to do. Unless he expected her to look after the house as well? She didn't mind cooking for Nikos but what else would he expect of her? Exactly what were a nanny's duties?

The boys had raced upstairs, where, presumably, Nikos had his Scalextric laid out. Peta stood in the entrance hall and looked around her. Impressive wasn't the word. A carved oak staircase curved its way up to a galleried landing. Stained-glass windows cast coloured reflections, and oil paintings, presumably of owners past, decorated the walls. It was like something she'd seen in a film but never first-hand.

He led the way along a lengthy corridor to a huge, comfortable kitchen, where a buxom middle-aged woman stood making pastry. 'I wasn't expecting you yet, Mr Papadakis,' she said, looking flustered. 'Nor was Bronwen. She's gone out to meet her boyfriend.'

A harsh frown creased his brow. 'Perhaps it's as well she's leaving,' he said tersely. 'Bess, I'd like you to meet

Bronwen's replacement, Peta James. Peta, this is Bess Middleton, my housekeeper.'

The woman's thin brows rose into untidy grey hair. I wonder how long you'll last? she seemed to be saying.

'Hello, Bess.' Peta held out her hand, then laughed when she realised the other woman's was covered in flour. 'I'm not starting until next week. Andreas thought I ought to have a look over the place.'

'You've met Nikos, I take it?' the woman asked.

Peta nodded. 'I have a son about Nikos's age. They'll be good company for each other. They're upstairs now.'

'I see. Good luck, then. I hope you'll last longer than the others.'

Peta looked at Andreas. She hadn't realised he was watching her and her face flushed at his intense scrutiny. It was faintly disapproving. Was it because she'd called him Andreas in front of his housekeeper?

'Come,' he said abruptly, 'I'll show you the rest of the house.' It was a whistle-stop tour and entirely unnecessary in her opinion, because she'd need a map to find her way around. On the ground floor there were five different reception rooms and a study, while upstairs there were six bedrooms, each with an *ensuite* bathroom, as well as a spacious room in the attic. It was here that they found Nikos and Ben happily playing with the Scalextric. There was so much of it that it must have cost a small fortune.

'Mummy,' said Ben excitedly, 'look at all this.'

'It's wonderful, darling, but I think we ought to be going.'

'No!' came the disgruntled response. 'Not yet—we've only just got here.'

'And you're going to live here soon,' she reminded him, 'so come on, you'll have plenty of time to play.'

Andreas had hardly spoken on their tour. He'd pointed out which would be her room and which one Ben's, and she'd seen his bedroom, in shades of burgundy and dark green—an entirely impersonal room with not even a pair of slippers on view. He probably didn't have time to wear slippers, she'd thought bitterly. He was too manic about work.

'Leave them,' he said now. 'We'll go to my study and discuss your duties.'

'Very well.' She kept her tone crisp and her eyes directly on his, and as soon as they were seated in the oak-panelled room she asked, 'What have I said that's made you angry?'

He shook his head. 'I'm not annoyed with you; it's Bronwen. She had no idea that I wouldn't need her tonight. She might be working her notice but she has no right to take liberties. I've half a mind to tell her to go now.'

'Except that I can't start straight away,' declared Peta. 'There's too much to sort out.'

'Like what?' he demanded.

'I have to pack, for one thing. Finalise bills, see about letting, tell everyone where I've gone, especially my parents…a hundred and one things.' Her parents lived in Cornwall, where she herself had been brought up. She'd stayed in Southampton after finishing university, and now only went home on the occasional weekend and during holiday periods. But her mother rang often, wanting to know how she was coping, how Ben was, and why didn't she come home to live? What would she say when she heard that her precious daughter was moving in with the boss?

'I can organise most things for you,' he informed.

'I'm sure you can, but I'd prefer to do it myself,' she

said tightly. 'You can see to the letting, if you wish, but everything else I'll do.'

'One of the new era of independent females.' He leaned back in his leather chair and studied her. 'I'm not sure whether I like it. I think I prefer the chivalrous days when a woman depended on a man, when he cosseted and protected her, when he made her feel feminine and beautiful and very, very much wanted.'

His eyes smouldered, his voice growled, and he looked at her with far more intent than he ever had before. Peta felt her nerve ends quiver. Was he trying to tell her something or was it her imagination? Was she reading what she wanted to read? Or was he interested? Would it be wise to move in with him? Had he manufactured this job especially so that he could get her into his bed?

'Now what are you thinking?'

'Why?'

'You look as though you believe I have designs on you.'

Oh, Lord, was she that transparent? Peta felt her cheeks flame. 'You couldn't be further from the truth,' she said distantly.

'You have a very expressive face, Peta. Didn't you know?'

'And you are jumping to entirely the wrong conclusions. I'm not interested in any man, Mr Papadakis.'

'Andreas.'

She grimaced. 'Very well, Andreas, although I don't think it's a good idea. Did you see the way your housekeeper looked at me when I called you Andreas?'

'She was probably wondering how you'd managed to get past the formality stage. Not many people do, I assure you. I find it doesn't pay.'

Peta wasn't sure she agreed with that. The senior staff at Linam Shipping would almost certainly feel much happier if they were on first-name terms with him. 'So I'm honoured?' she asked.

A faint smile quirked the corners of his mouth. 'You could say that.'

'Why?'

He thought for a long moment. 'Let's say I felt it would improve our relationship.'

'You mean you thought you'd get more work out of me?' she asked smartly, but she couldn't stop a faint smile.

'I don't always think about work, Peta. Ninety-nine per cent of the time, perhaps, but I do have red blood in my veins. I'm not entirely without feelings.'

Peta gave an inward groan. Was she jumping into a situation she would quickly regret? Ought she to tell him to stuff his job? Except that she would be upsetting both boys if she did. Ben would never forgive her; he was so looking forward to living here and having a friend to play with. To say nothing of the extra time she'd be able to spend with him. It was by far the best thing that had happened to her.

'So,' she said, pushing these thoughts to the back of her mind, 'tell me exactly what my duties are going to be.'

It was arranged that she take Nikos to and from school, plan his meals, cook them if Bess wasn't there, supervise his homework and make sure he always had a supply of clean clothes. All housework would be done by Bess Middleton and a local girl who came in twice a week.

'Is there anything else you want to ask me?'

Peta shook her head. 'Nothing that I can think of at the moment.'

'So it's settled. You'll start on Sunday?'

'I'll move in late on Sunday,' she corrected. 'I'll need the weekend to tie everything up.'

He nodded, looking well-pleased, and when they stood he shook her hand. 'Thank you, Peta. I do appreciate all that you're giving up.'

The scorching heat that ran through her at his touch told her that she was giving up far more than a little cottage and a certain lifestyle. She was in grave danger of giving up her freedom.

CHAPTER FOUR

AS PETA locked the door and walked to her car, where Ben was already wriggling excitedly on his seat, she wondered for the thousandth time whether she was doing the right thing. She'd thought about it a lot since she'd given her word, and several times had considered backing out. The one thing that had stopped her was the thought that she'd see more of her precious son.

She really had hated having to go out to work, leaving Marnie to pick him up from school. She'd missed seeing the excitement on his face when he told the older woman all that he'd been doing. Obviously he'd told her, too, when she got home, but the initial enthusiasm had gone. And especially in school holidays—there had been so much she could be doing with him, so many places they could have gone. Instead she'd had to rely on her neighbour to keep him entertained while she earned the money to clothe and feed them and run her house.

There was also Nikos to consider. She couldn't get out of her mind his cheerful face when she'd mentioned watching him play football. She could imagine how her own son would feel if she never went to see him play. To Ben, having his mother watch and encourage him was the most important thing in the world. It was a pity Andreas didn't see things that way. Poor Nikos was missing out on such a lot—and so too was Andreas, if only he knew it.

When they arrived Andreas was outside waiting for them.

Smiling.

The smile stunned her. It was unlike any other smile he had given her. It was a predatory smile. It heated her blood and sent a violent reaction through her body. This was definitely a big mistake. She hadn't agreed to do the job because she'd thought the move would be good for Ben, or because it would help Nikos, but because of this man. This lean, sensual man with the devastating good looks and compelling dark eyes. It was a disturbing discovery.

And it was suddenly clear that he was equally hungry for her! She was now his victim. And yet, even as she stared at him in chilling horror, the smile changed. It became a warmly welcoming one, a friendly one, nothing in it to suggest that he had designs on her. Had she imagined it? Was she becoming neurotic because of her own unstoppable, unwanted emotions?

'I was beginning to think you'd changed your mind.' He came hurriedly down the steps as she climbed out of the car, damningly attractive in an open-necked shirt that revealed a scattering of dark curly hairs on his hard-muscled chest. 'Let me help you unload.'

'Where's Nikos?' asked Ben eagerly as he too scrambled out.

'Already in bed,' Andreas answered. 'He tried to wait up but sleep got the better of him.'

'I'm not tired,' said Ben bravely, at the same time fighting back a yawn.

'In that case you can carry some stuff up to your room,' snapped Peta when she saw that he was going to dash indoors empty-handed.

Her tone was sharper than she'd intended and she saw Andreas frown. She oughtn't to have rounded on her son; it wasn't Ben she was annoyed with—it was herself for imagining something that wasn't there. Andreas couldn't care less about her; he was interested only in Nikos's well-being. That was what she was here for, nothing else, and she'd do well to remember it.

Once all the stuff was piled into their rooms he offered Mrs Middleton's help to unpack but Peta declined. 'I can manage,' she said tensely.

'As you wish,' he agreed with a laconic shrug. 'When you've put Ben to bed come and join me. I'll be in my study.'

There was a lot to unpack and it took her ages; Ben was asleep before she'd finished, but even then she was reluctant to go downstairs.

She remembered the room, quite a big room, oak-panelled with an immense desk across one corner. In front of the window, with excellent views of the landscaped gardens, were two easy chairs, and it was in one of these that she found him.

He'd left his door wide for her to walk in, though she tapped on it first to alert him to her presence. 'Welcome to your new home,' he said to her now. 'I think this calls for a celebratory drink. What would you like?'

Peta didn't much care for alcohol; it held too many bad memories. She'd had wine on the day of the conference, but only because she hadn't wanted to cause a fuss, and even then she'd taken only a few sips. 'A soft drink, I think. Coke or lemonade, I don't mind which.'

She sat down on the chair next to him, stifling the tingle of electricity that alerted her senses to the very real danger he posed.

'Are you sure that's all you want?'

Peta nodded and turned her head to watch Andreas as he walked to a cunningly concealed bar and flipped the top off a bottle before pouring Coke into a glass.

'I really do appreciate what you're doing for me,' he said when he returned to his seat, handing the drink to her.

Their fingers touched and Peta jumped, some of the Coke going down her clean white skirt. She swore beneath her breath.

'How clumsy of me,' said Andreas swiftly.

'It wasn't your fault,' she assured him, conscious of the sudden heat in her cheeks. 'I'd best go and change; rinse it out before it stains.'

'You *are* coming back?' he asked, and for the first time Peta noticed lines of strain on his face. He was probably apprehensive about how things would work out with her and Nikos, and all the problems at work wouldn't help either, and here she was worrying over her own stupid reactions.

'Of course,' she agreed with a faint smile, even though she'd actually planned on staying upstairs, where it was safer. At the office she could ignore his sexuality and concentrate on the work in hand. Here it was a different story. The trouble was, if she didn't go back down he'd more than likely come charging up to see where she was.

She had not realised when she'd agreed to take the job as Nikos's nanny that she would spend any time with Andreas. It was too intimate, too disturbing, too everything. The blood fairly sizzled through her veins, and the thought of them sitting close together watching the sky darken as the sun went down was enough to send her frantic with fear.

Peta deliberately took her time rinsing the skirt, and when she finally plucked up the courage to rejoin Andreas it was to find him fast asleep in his chair, legs outstretched, his head resting on a cushion. The perfect excuse to creep upstairs, she thought, but somehow her legs wouldn't carry her away. She stood there looking at him, drinking in the beautiful, sculpted lines of his face, the way his hair curled crisply around his ears, the fullness of his lips, curved upwards at the corners as though he was having a pleasant dream.

It wasn't long before her eyes wandered down to the rise and fall of his chest. The dark hairs, some of which she could see at the V of his shirt, were visible through the fine silk. Her fingers itched to touch. He had a tremendous body, finely honed, with not an ounce of superfluous fat anywhere.

His narrow hips next, and the hard flatness of his stomach. She quickly skimmed over the next bit, feeling a tightening of her stomach muscles as she did so, before considering the long length of his powerful legs. He really was a tremendously exciting male animal. The first man in a long, long time who had aroused any feelings in her.

Suddenly, without warning, his hand shot out and caught her wrist, pulling her down onto his lap. 'Like what you see, do you?' he growled in her ear.

Peta's cheeks flamed as she felt the hardness of his arousal. Thank goodness he couldn't tell what was going on inside her own body. 'What the hell do you think you're doing?' she demanded, struggling to free herself. 'If this is the reason you've got me here then—'

Her words were cut off by an angry snarl. 'Pardon me, lady, you were the one doing the looking, and judging by your expression you were highly interested—and, if my judgement isn't wrong, highly aroused as well.'

Peta's eyes blazed. 'Pardon me also, but you couldn't be further from the truth. If you want to know what I was thinking, it was how I'd managed to allow myself to be sucked into this arrangement. If I'd wanted to be a nanny I'd have trained as one.' And with that she managed to wrench free.

He laughed. A deep belly laugh that didn't amuse her.

'I'm glad you find it funny; I don't,' she said caustically and loudly.

'It's your indignation I find amusing,' he said, proceeding to push himself up. 'You really were caught in the act. But never mind, consider it forgotten. I value you too much to spend time arguing.'

How could she forget such an embarrassing moment? Especially as he'd read her thoughts and feelings so accurately—it didn't bear thinking about.

Not until Peta had gone to her room did Andreas allow himself to mull over that telling moment. It wasn't the first time he'd been eyed up so thoroughly, and it probably wouldn't be the last. He was a reluctant target for sex-hungry females. But he hadn't expected it of Peta James.

She'd always given the impression of being completely uninterested in him. In any man, for that matter. She lived for her son alone. Everything she did was for Ben. He admired her for her devotion. Meanwhile he had discovered another dimension in her make-up. An interesting one.

And one day he might do something about it. But not yet. He didn't want to frighten her away before she'd even begun the job, even though his own hormones were having a field-day and he felt a shocking need to take her to bed. He wanted to lose himself in her body; he wanted to touch, to taste, to get to know intimately every single inch of her.

She was an exciting woman, was Peta James, a

woman of many layers. At work she was the perfect PA. The most efficient he'd ever had. More often than not she anticipated his needs. He was going to miss her a great deal in that respect.

Then there was Peta the siren. That was how she had looked in that green satin dress. And yet still she had retained her cool demeanour. She'd seemed not to notice the admiring glances certainly hadn't played on it, but he'd have liked to bet that there wasn't a man in the room who hadn't fancied her. As he had himself.

And now, a few minutes ago, she was a hot-blooded woman ripe for making love. He had seen the depth of hunger in her eyes when she'd thought him asleep. How long since Ben's father had disappeared out of her life? How long since she'd had a man?

Her house was small but carefully and thoughtfully furnished. It was a home, not just a house. She had lovingly made it into a comfortable home. Not the way Maria had, or his mother—both of their houses had been showplaces. Peta's was so comfortable, so lived-in, that he'd felt completely relaxed there.

And he had taken her away from it!

The thought was not a pleasant one. And yet if she hadn't agreed to come he'd have probably threatened to sack her. He'd been prepared to go to any lengths to get what he wanted. A deep frown gouged his brow. Was that really the type of guy he was? He'd had to be ruthless to get where he was, but to put someone out of a job when they had a child to clothe and feed and a house to run wasn't quite playing the game. He'd done it in the past, though, without a second thought. He put his fingers to his temples and rubbed at the nagging pain. What was this woman doing to him?

* * *

Peta woke from a troubled sleep. She'd been dreaming but she couldn't remember what the dream was about, only that it had left her feeling deeply disturbed. And when she opened her eyes she thought that she must still be asleep, because this wasn't her room. This was a spacious bedroom decorated in cool greens and cream. Hers was tiny and cosy in pink and lavender.

It was a few seconds before the reality of the situation hit her and her first thoughts were of Ben. How would he feel, waking in a strange room? Last night he'd been too tired even to notice his surroundings, but this morning he might be afraid.

She leapt out of bed and without even bothering to pull on her dressing gown dashed out of her room—and catapulted straight into Andreas Papadakis.

His strong arms steadied her. 'Whoa, there; what's the rush?' he asked in amusement.

'I must go to Ben.' Her voice came out strange and breathless. The heat of his body flamed her senses. She felt as though she was spinning out of control. It was an instant thing, one she could do without and one she needed to fight. 'He might be frightened waking up in a strange place.'

Andreas smiled calmly, but it did nothing to steady her racing pulses. His hands still held her, his hard body grazing her own through the thin material of her nightdress, and his velvet-brown eyes looked down into hers.

He was enjoying it, she realised. Enjoying making her feel uncomfortable.

'Ben and Nikos are having breakfast,' he informed. 'Bess is looking after them.'

'What time is it?' she demanded, finally wrestling herself free, conscious now that with space between them he could look at the way her breasts had peaked against the soft cotton.

'Just turned eight.'

'What?' She was horrified. She was always up by seven on days she had to go to work. 'He'll be late for school. I'll be late for work. And you're usually at the office by this time.' He hadn't shaved yet, she noticed; he must have risen late as well. She liked the dark stubble on his strong square jaw. It made him less severe, more of an action man than a dark-suited tycoon.

'I think you're forgetting, Peta, that your job now is here. There's plenty of time for you to get Ben to school. I'll take Nikos today; I want a word with his teacher.'

She had forgotten. In the panic of waking up in a strange place she'd completely lost it. She was no longer his PA but Nikos's nanny. And she'd already failed in her breakfast duty. Not that Andreas seemed to mind, which was a surprise. He was a different man here. More dangerous. More threatening to her sanity. And her body!

With a tiny cry of distress she swung away and returned to her bedroom.

The day went surprisingly quickly. Karen, her replacement, phoned a couple of times with queries about work, and Andreas himself phoned her once. Other than that she spent the day typing up notes from the conference. At Andreas's suggestion she set herself up in his study, using the laptop that he had put at her disposal. It wasn't an ideal arrangement as far as Peta was concerned because it was too easy to imagine him there. The room was eternally filled with his presence and the lingering smell of his cologne, so much so that she began to doubt her sanity in agreeing to his suggestion.

It was a relief when she left the house to pick up Nikos from his private school and then Ben from Marnie's. Marnie had been sad to see her leave, but delighted that she still had the privilege of meeting Ben out of school and taking him to her house, if only for a short time, to await his mother's arrival.

In the car on the way home the two boys chatted incessantly, making Peta realise how lonely Ben had been before. She'd always envisaged having two or three children quite close together—until fate had decreed otherwise.

Andreas didn't get home until after the boys were in bed and Peta had already eaten. She was passing through the hall when he arrived. He was still in work mode; she could tell by the distant look in his eyes, the intense frown on his forehead. How had his day gone without her? she wondered. How had he got on with Karen? And how had Karen coped with his often unrealistic demands?

But it was not something she dared to ask. Theirs wasn't the sort of relationship where they could sit and discuss the day's events. She was still his employee. She had her own sitting room, and it was to this that she took herself now.

She flicked through the channels on the TV, but found nothing much there, so she curled into a corner of the sofa with a book. It was number one in the best-seller lists and she was lost in a world of espionage and double-dealing when Andreas came to find her.

At first she didn't see him; it was not until he cleared his throat that she looked up and realised that he was standing watching her.

'Must be a good book.'

'It is.' He had showered and shaved and changed into

navy cotton trousers and a pale blue shirt. The worry lines had gone and in his hand was a tot of whisky. She felt her insides sear and shrivel as those chestnut eyes penetrated hers. Not with intent—there was nothing in his expression to suggest that he fancied her—but it was as though he was trying to look deep into her soul. To find out what made her tick, what her innermost secrets were.

She straightened her legs and put down the book.

'Won't you join me?' he asked, raising his glass.

Peta shook her head. 'I don't drink.'

'Not ever?'

'Maybe occasionally,' she said with a shrug. 'A toast for a wedding, something like that, but in the main, no.'

'Why's that? I don't think I've ever met anyone who doesn't drink. May I?' He indicated the chair opposite.

Peta couldn't really say no when it was his own house, even if he had given her this room for her own private use, so she nodded, at the same time drawing in a deeply troubled breath. Her past history wasn't something she wanted to share. It wasn't something she was proud of. But at some time or another he would insist on knowing, so perhaps now was as good a time as any.

'I used to,' she confessed. 'Like the rest of my student friends I used to hang around in pubs, but one day I had too much. So much that I didn't know what I was doing.' She paused as memories of that night vividly reclaimed her mind. 'Ben is the result. I'm deeply ashamed of it, but I wouldn't be without him for the world.' She stuck her chin in the air as she spoke, challenging him to say something derogatory.

But he didn't. He looked at her thoughtfully instead. 'So what happened to Ben's father? Does he know about him?'

Peta nodded. 'He was my boyfriend at the time, my first love. We were inseparable. I thought I would spend the rest of my life with him. But as soon as I told him I was pregnant he didn't want to know me. In fact he refused to believe the baby was his.'

She clamped her lips. Joe had totally destroyed her trust in men. He'd even started going out with her best friend immediately afterwards, proving that he'd never really loved her, not the way she had loved him. And in the dark weeks that had followed she'd heard dozens of similar tales from sympathetic student friends, convincing her that she'd be far better off without a man in her life.

'So you've not seen him since?'

'No. Nor do I want to.'

'Don't you think that one day your son might want to know exactly who his father is?'

It was a logical question, one she had asked herself many times. 'I'll cross that bridge when I come to it,' she declared, and, with a desperate need to change the subject, 'I've finished the conference notes. They're on your desk.'

'Good girl. I could have done with you at the office today. Karen's a quick typist but she goes to pieces in an emergency.'

All of his requests were emergencies, remembered Peta. 'It could be that you make her nervous,' she said with great daring, remembering how she had felt that first day.

Dark brows rode smoothly upwards. 'If the girl can't do the job, then—'

'She gets her marching orders,' finished Peta crisply. 'You think that solves everything, don't you?'

To her amazement he smiled, a warm lazy smile that

sent her pulses into spasm. 'Do you know, Peta, no other woman has ever tried to put me in my place?'

'I hardly think I've done that,' she said, taking a deep breath to try and regulate the uneven beating of her heart. That smile had done things to her which she'd rather not happen. 'But I do believe in sticking up for myself. In my opinion, most men in official capacities think they can walk all over any woman who works for them. Lord knows why. It has to be an inbred thing.'

She watched the way his nostrils flared as she spoke and wondered whether she had gone too far, but then the white smile flashed again. 'You're probably right. Should I give her another chance?'

'I think you should give her at least a month's trial.'

'A month?' he queried sharply. 'You were fully efficient in less than a week.'

'I had a strong motive,' she said.

He frowned.

'Ben. I couldn't afford to be thrown out on my ear. I had to learn quickly.'

'And was I a hard taskmaster?' He leaned back comfortably in his chair, legs outstretched, looking as though he was in for a long stay.

'The worst,' she admitted. 'But the more difficult you were the more determined I was to stay the course.'

He suddenly leaned forward, elbows on his knees. 'You're some girl, Peta James.'

Her eyes were drawn to his and she could feel herself beginning to drown in their sensual, velvety depths. Her heart rate increased, her skin overheated, and without her realising it she inched closer to him. Any second now he was going to kiss her. She could sense it; was ready for it. The tip of her tongue moistened dry lips and her breathing grew shallow.

Then with a swift change of expression he rocked back in his seat. 'I had a kidnap threat today,' he said tensely. 'My son's life is in danger.'

Andreas was still reeling. The tersely worded note had shocked and horrified him, sent his senses spiralling endlessly in space. It had jolted him into the realisation of how very much Nikos meant to him. He had been too busy working to… No, he wouldn't go down that path. His son was his entire universe. Without him life would have no meaning.

Be warned, the note had said, *I'm going to kidnap your son. You will never see him again unless you pay me one million pounds.*

It took Andreas's mind back to another place, another time, when his younger brother, Christos, had been kidnapped and his own parents had nearly gone out of their minds with worry. After Nikos was born he had harboured the vague fear that the same thing might happen, but never really believed that it would. Until now…

Peta's eyes were wide as she looked at him, her own shock mirrored in their amethyst depths. 'Have you been to the police?'

His lips twisted in bitter irony. 'They politely suggested it's a practical joke. They said that if someone was going to kidnap Nikos they wouldn't give me any warning; they'd simply snatch him.'

'But you don't believe them?'

'Would you, if it were Ben?'

'I'd be scared to let him out of my sight,' she agreed, looking as worried as he felt. 'Do you know who's making the threat? And why?'

He silently thanked her for her concern. He needed someone at a time like this. 'Money, of course,' he admitted grimly, adding after a moment's silence, 'My main reason for telling you is because you'll need to be extra-vigilant.'

Peta shook her head, both fear and distress in her eyes. 'I'm not trained for this sort of thing; I don't know how to cope; I can't—'

'I know it's asking a lot of you,' he interrupted gently, almost afraid that he would scare her away, 'but I'm sure you'll look after Nikos as much as you do your own son. Your dedication to Ben, the way you put him before yourself at all times, is what made me think you'd be the ideal person to replace Bronwen. And now I'm even surer of it. Besides, Nikos adores you already. He'll do whatever you say. He doesn't know about this, of course, and I'd prefer it to remain that way. He's had all the usual warnings about going off with strangers, but nevertheless I still want you to be on your guard.'

For a moment he thought that Peta was going to refuse, that she was going to walk away; he could see by her scared expression that she felt her life would be in danger, too, and he saw the faint shudder that ran through her. 'I'm trusting you, Peta,' he said quietly but determinedly. 'Don't let me down.' To his disgust there was a break in his voice.

'It's a huge responsibility,' she whispered, 'I'm not sure I'm prepared to handle it, not even sure that I'm capable.'

He leaned forward again and took her hands into his. 'Let's hope it all comes to nothing,' he said gruffly, and, pulling her gently to her feet, he held her close.

Sensation ricocheted through Peta's body with the force of a speeding missile. Even the shock of hearing that Nikos was in danger had done nothing to diminish the feelings Andreas managed to arouse. It took every ounce of will-power and several deep breaths to calm herself and hide her catapulting emotions.

For a while he held her still, appearing to draw comfort, but then one hand began to slowly stroke the back of her head while the other, low on her back, urged her closer. His arousal was sudden and shocking.

She seemed to be living life on a seesaw. One moment believing herself safe, convinced that Andreas had no ulterior motives. The next fearful that he wanted her for only one thing. She couldn't let it happen.

'Let me go!' she muttered through her teeth. 'If you're after a lover as well as a child-minder and protector then you've made a grave mistake.'

'But you want me,' he murmured, his voice a low, sensual growl. 'Deny it if you can.'

How could she when he'd read her body signals so accurately? Not only today but last night as well. 'You're the sort of man most women would willingly go to bed with,' she admitted. 'You must be aware of that. But it doesn't mean that I will. I'm not in the market for an affair. I've vowed never to give my body freely again. The next time will be to the man I'm going to marry.'

'Honourable sentiments,' he said with a faint smile, 'but are you sure you can stick to them?'

In other words he was asking whether she was capable of ignoring her needs. Whether she was capable of ignoring *him*. Peta stiffened and pushed her hands against his chest, desperately trying to break free. But Andreas had other ideas.

His arm tightened; his hand slid from her hair to the side of her face to gently stroke, to send even deeper shivers of sensation through her. And then he tilted her chin and made her look up at him. Her first thought was that she must hide her emotions, make out that she was unaffected by his touch, until she saw the raw need mirrored in his eyes.

Quite how it happened she didn't know, but the next moment his mouth was on hers.

What had started off as a need to reassure Peta, to bolster his own spirits, was quickly snowballing out of control. The kiss was truly exciting, even more exciting than Andreas had imagined kissing Peta would be, yet he wasn't sure that he was doing the right thing. Peta James wasn't your average girl. She was as likely to slap him across the face as she was to kiss him back.

It was a risk he was prepared to take. For the last twenty-four hours she'd been driving him crazy. There was still the problem with Nikos, but this little minx even had the power to take his mind off that.

From the moment he'd caught her looking at him he had not stopped thinking about what it would be like to make love to her. And the fact that she had instantly denied her feelings had intrigued him even further. Despite the image she portrayed of being coolly in control of her life there burned beneath that outer shell a woman with a very real need.

Her mouth was as soft and sensual as he had imagined it would be. She tasted like the sweetest nectar, engaging every one of his senses, sending his mind whirling into orbit. He moved his lips gently at first, slowly increasing the pressure until he felt the early stirring of response.

Even heard it! Very softly, from somewhere deep in her throat, he heard a slight sound, a satisfied sound! Encouraged, he touched her sensitive lips with his tongue, felt the ripple that ran through her, and when her mouth moved restlessly beneath his he urged it open.

It was his turn to groan this time. He wanted to rush, he wanted to plunder her mouth and take everything she had to offer. He wanted to crush her to him; feel the shape of her, explore, incite, demand. But even as these urges burnt into him he knew that to do so would lose him the one woman he trusted with his son's life.

He forced himself to slow down, to lessen the urgency, to reluctantly end the kiss. And when he put her from him he sensed that she was disappointed, too, though none of it showed on her face.

Instead her beautiful sapphire eyes shot daggers across the divide which a few minutes ago had been non-existent and now felt a mile wide. She shivered and hugged her arms across her body. 'What did you do that for?' she asked crossly.

'Do what?' There was harshness in his voice also. She made him feel as though he'd ravaged her against her will and this didn't sit well on his shoulders.

'You know what,' she tossed. 'I need a promise from you, Andreas. If I'm to stay on there will be no more kisses. I don't want you to even touch me. It will completely ruin our working relationship—and that's all I'm here for. Please remember that.'

She looked so fired-up and beautiful that it was all he could do not to grab her and kiss her again. He hid his desire behind hard, narrowed eyes. 'You didn't put up much resistance.'

'Would it have done any good?' she questioned.

'I have never, in my life, taken anything from a woman that she didn't want to give,' he declared shortly. 'You enjoyed it, Peta. Deny it if you like, but the proof was there. I don't take kindly to being accused of using force. If I were you I'd choose my words very carefully the next time you feel like flinging accusations.'

He saw the way she gritted her teeth, the way her fingers curled into her palms. But to give her credit her voice was quietly calm as she spoke. 'I'd like to be alone.'

When Andreas had gone Peta sank back into the chair and closed her eyes. What had she done? Allowing him to kiss her, not fighting back the instant he touched her, must have given him all sorts of wrong ideas. One moment they'd been talking about kidnappers, the next they'd been in a passionate clinch. How had that happened?

Hopefully, though, he was now convinced that she held him totally responsible, that she was as angry as hell and would walk out on the job if he dared try it again. But would she? Hadn't that kiss aroused every one of her senses? Didn't she want more?

The answer was painfully yes. And when Peta went to bed later that evening she was still burning from his touch. Her body felt as aroused now as it had when his lips met hers.

She would have liked to think that it was because she was hungry for a man, not this particular man, but any man. Her mind knew, though, that this wasn't true. She'd met plenty of men since Ben was born, and not a single one had a lit a spark inside her.

So what did Andreas Papadakis have that these other men hadn't? Was it because he was Greek? Because he was darkly handsome? Because he was wealthy? Because of the authority that sat so well on his shoulders? She didn't think it was any of these. It was an indefinable something that would continue to puzzle her for the rest of her life.

Surprisingly sleep claimed her quickly, and this time, so that she wouldn't be late getting up, she set her alarm. The following morning she got Ben and Nikos ready and they ran downstairs to the warm kitchen, where Bess Middleton had breakfast ready. 'Mr Papadakis has already left,' she told Peta. 'Says to tell you that there's some work for you in his study. Any queries, you're to ring him.'

Peta nodded, but wondered why he hadn't told her himself last night. Except that they'd both had other things on their minds. Her skin went warm at the very thought of what had happened, but she was determined not to let it bother her. There would be no repeat, she had made that very clear. She would do the job she was getting paid for and ignore completely any foolish signs her body made.

When they left the house in the land-cruiser that Andreas insisted she use to ferry the boys around, she saw a black saloon parked a few yards from the entrance gates, the driver sitting reading a newspaper. It might be nothing, she reasoned—and yet again it could be extremely significant.

Fear prickled her skin and as she drove away Peta constantly checked her mirror. To her relief he didn't follow but she knew that it was imperative she constantly keep her wits about her, She wasn't happy until Nikos was safely within the school gates and she saw a teacher keeping a vigilant eye on all of the children.

The next few days followed a similar routine. Andreas always left her work to do, but he never came to her sitting room again. If he wanted to discuss anything he invited her into his study.

It didn't stop her being aware of his presence, however; she still felt a tingling awareness whenever he was close, and more than once she caught his eyes on her with such a hungry look that she needed to clench everything to stop giving herself away.

She saw the car a couple of times more and decided to tell Andreas. It might be nothing, it might be a rep having a five-minute break, killing time before his first appointment somewhere in the city, but better to be safe than sorry.

He nodded solemnly when she told him, his eyes narrowing. 'There could be a simple explanation—or it might be someone monitoring your movements. You got the registration number, I take it?'

'Yes.'

'Then I'll get it checked.' He looked at her gravely. 'You're not unduly worried? I don't want to stress you out, but Nikos's safety is, of course, my major concern.'

Peta nodded. 'I'm not frightened. I simply thought it odd seeing the car more than once.' In fact she thought he was taking this whole kidnap thing very calmly. If it were Ben in danger she'd be paranoid. She wouldn't let him out of her sight. She certainly wouldn't rely on someone else to look after him.

'If you're sure.' He closed the gap between them and put his arms around her. There was nothing sexual in the action this time; it was a simple, comforting gesture. Peta realised this as she buried her head in his shoulder. But it didn't stop the blood shooting hotly through her veins, or her pulses frantically leaping.

It was for only a brief moment. The next second she found herself free, and when she looked into his face there was nothing to suggest that he too had been affected. In fact his face was closed and hard and she guessed that he was worrying more about his son than he let on.

The next morning when she walked out to the land-cruiser she found a note tucked behind the wiper blade. Her fingers shook as she opened it. 'SOON!' was all it said in bold black lettering, but she knew very well what it meant.

Andreas had already left, so she tucked the note quickly into her pocket before the boys saw, but her heart was in her mouth as she drove past the gates and looked for the black car. She intended getting a good look at the driver this time. It was almost a sense of anticlimax to find he wasn't there. Relief also, but it set her mind working.

When she gave Andreas the note that evening his face darkened. Muscles tightened in his jaw as he screwed the piece of paper up and tossed it into his wastebin. Almost immediately he realised what he'd done and fished it out again. 'The police will have to take it seriously now.'

He was back within the hour, his face tight with determination. 'Pack your bags,' he said tersely. 'We're leaving.'

CHAPTER FIVE

PETA looked at Andreas in wide-eyed shock. 'Leaving? At this hour?' The note must have scared him more than she'd thought. 'What did the police say?'

'They're checking fingerprints. And they'll take those of the owner of the black saloon—even though he's apparently a perfectly ordinary businessman. But I'm not leaving anything to chance. They took mine as well, and they want yours, but to hell with that. Go and get the boys ready.'

'But they're in bed,' she protested. 'It's unrealistic. A few more hours won't hurt, surely?'

Andreas drew in a deep breath, his hard-muscled chest rising. And then slowly, as he released it, some of the tension drained out of him. 'You're right,' he said, dragging a heavy hand through his hair. 'But we'll leave early tomorrow.'

Peta shook her head, still bemused by this sudden turn of events. 'Have the police suggested you move?'

'Hell, no. They're doing all they can. But I'm not leaving my son in danger any longer.'

'How about Linam's—your work there? Are you going to leave it to flounder?'

'Goodness, Peta, why all the questions? No, I am not. Within a few minutes I shall be on the phone, organising someone to step into my shoes. My younger brother, actually. He's very capable. I trust him completely.'

'So where are we going?'

'To Greece, of course.' He said it as though she was supposed to know.

'Greece?' she echoed shrilly.

'Yes, Greece,' he responded impatiently. 'Is that a problem for you?'

'Yes, it is, as a matter of fact. Ben doesn't have a passport. I got mine last year, when my mother insisted I take a holiday, but—'

'Then you'll have to leave him behind until he gets one.'

Peta couldn't believe he'd said that. She stared at him in wide-eyed horror and anger. 'I'm going nowhere without Ben,' she told him coldly.

Andreas clapped a hand to his brow. 'Forgive me. I spoke without thinking. I'll organise his passport first thing. You'd better get some sleep.'

It was impossible. Peta's mind was in a whirl. She couldn't quite take in the situation. It was all happening too quickly. Not that Ben would mind; he'd see it as a great adventure, especially as he'd have Nikos for company. Already he adored the other boy and they spent every minute together.

The next day, true to his word, Andreas sorted out Ben's passport and their schools and his own replacement. If she'd tried to do it she'd have come up against all sorts of red tape, but Andreas seemed to walk over everyone and get exactly what he wanted. This was Andreas Papadakis, action man. Not the seducer, not even the Tyrant, his mind was channelled on one thing only—getting his son away from the dangers that threatened. By the end of the day they were ready to go. 'First light we'll be on the move,' he announced.

* * *

Ben was awake before she was. He came bounding into her room, full of excitement. 'Wake up, Mummy. I want to go. I want to go now.'

In no time at all they were ready. Andreas drove to the airport, where he had his own jet fuelled up and waiting, but it was not until they were in the air that she saw him visibly relax. The smile came back to his face and he looked at her with a warmth that set her toes curling and her insides aflame.

'Thank you,' he said.

Her carefully shaped brows rose. 'For what?'

'For understanding, for obliging, for everything. You'll never know how much I appreciate it.'

'So long as Ben's OK then I am,' she declared with a slight shrug.

'That's how I feel about Nikos,' he admitted. 'I know I'm guilty of sometimes neglecting him, but I love him more dearly than life itself. If anything happened…' A dark shadow settled across his face.

He would have lost both his son and his wife, thought Peta. She wondered whether now would be a good time to ask how she had died. But Nikos spoke and the moment was lost.

She couldn't help thinking as she watched the boys playing with their pocket computer games that they looked like a family. Ben's hair wasn't as dark as Nikos's, but dark enough for them to pass as brothers. And anyone seeing her and Andreas with them could easily mistake them for husband and wife. It was an unreal situation.

When they arrived at Athens a car was waiting to whisk them swiftly away from the airport. Everything had been planned down to the last tiny detail. And they didn't have far to travel before the driver turned in through some magnificent iron gates and along a curving drive to a sprawling house which was every bit as palatial as the one they had left a few hours earlier. It had a red roof and white walls, and was built on several levels.

'My family home,' announced Andreas. 'We're expected.'

Even as they approached the central door opened and a dark-haired woman, probably in her late forties, stood waiting for the car to stop. She was dressed immaculately in a scarlet, black and white dress. Her nails were polished a similar red, her lips a slash of the same colour. She stood tall and proud with a haughty lift to her chin which Peta failed to recognise as one of her own particular stances.

She saw a strong resemblance and decided it was her boss's sister, at the same time acknowledging how little she knew about his family. She judged Andreas to be in his mid-thirties, and she'd just discovered he had a younger brother, now here was another family member. How many more were there?

She scrambled out of the car, calling Ben to stand by her, leaving Nikos to run across to the woman, who bent low and gathered him into her arms, smiling fondly as she did so. She greeted Andreas next; another wide smile and a hug, and a stream of Greek.

Then it was Peta and Ben's turn to be introduced. The woman looked at them with speculative eyes as they approached. No sign of a smile now. 'Peta,' said Andreas, 'I'd like you to meet my mother. Mother, this is Peta James, the girl I told you about, and this is Ben, her son.'

If a breath of wind had blown it would have knocked her over. This glamorous woman was Andreas's mother! She couldn't be; she wasn't old enough. Either she'd been a child bride or she was very adept at hiding her real age. Peta smiled faintly and held out her hand. It was taken reluctantly and limply, reinforcing Peta's impression that she wasn't welcome.

'So you are Nikos's nanny?' Her Greek was heavily accented. Brown eyes, so like her son's, looked coldly into hers. 'I hardly think he will have use for one here, but I have no doubt that we will be able to find something to keep you occupied.'

Peta's eyes flickered towards Andreas but he was busy talking to his son and gave no sign of having heard. She drew in a deep, steadying breath and held back a tart response. If she'd known they were going to be living with his parents she would have refused to come. She had, stupidly as it turned out, thought they'd be living alone, in Andreas's house, thought she would still be needed to look after Nikos.

'Come, let's go indoors,' Andreas said now. 'Stavros will see to our luggage.'

Inside the house was cool and airy. Mrs Papadakis clapped her hands and a young girl appeared on silent feet. She stood humbly in front of the older woman. 'Anna, please show the *despinis* to—'

'It's all right,' interrupted Andreas, 'I will take Peta myself. I'll join you in a minute, Mother.'

They walked what seemed like endless miles of corridor before entering, much to Peta's relief, a completely self-contained apartment. There was a well-sized living area, an enormous dining room, and a kitchen to die for. 'Mother's organised lunch today,' informed Andreas, 'but if my instructions have been carried out—' he peeked into a cavernous fridge and freezer '—which they have, there's everything we need here to be completely independent.'

Thank goodness, breathed Peta silently. The thought of joining his mother each mealtime was not a happy one.

On an upper floor her bedroom and Ben's were connected by a bathroom; big rooms, plenty of space for him to play. Andreas had his own suite, and Nikos's bathroom was next door to his room.

'I need to go and find my mother now,' Andreas said. 'Come and join us when you've freshened up.'

'If I don't get lost,' she warned. 'This place is huge.'

'You'll soon get used to it,' he said with a smile.

Peta nodded, even though she wasn't really sure.

Stavros brought up their cases, and after she'd unpacked Peta eventually found Andreas on the terrace, talking to his parent; Nikos was already in the pool.

'Oh, Mummy!' exclaimed Ben, his eyes wide and impressed. 'Can I go in?'

Andreas answered for her. 'But of course.'

Ben stripped down to his pants and jumped laughingly into the water to join his new friend. Peta watched him with an indulgent smile on her face. What an experience this was for him. And for her, too. Her life had completely turned around since she'd begun working for Andreas Papadakis. Who'd have thought a few short weeks ago that she'd be living here in this sun-drenched place with the man who had earned the reputation of being a tyrant? She was discovering that he was nothing of the sort. That he was a hot-blooded male who excited her beyond measure.

Andreas patted the seat beside him. 'Sit down. My mother wants to hear all about you.'

Peta bet she did. She was probably wondering whether she had any designs on her son, why he had brought a nanny all the way over from England when he could quite easily have found one here. And did he even need one when he had a doting grandmother to look after Nikos? Or wasn't Andreas's mother the maternal kind? She certainly didn't look it in her designer clothes and elegant sandals. It struck Peta that Mrs Papadakis was more interested in her own appearance than anything else.

'My son tells me that you are an unmarried mother,' were the woman's first words, a shudder of distaste running right through her pencil-slim body.

Peta lifted her chin proudly; she wasn't ashamed of it. 'Ben's lacked nothing because of it.'

'What happened to his father?'

'Mother, is this really necessary?' asked Andreas. 'It's none of our business.'

'I believe in the holy sanctimony of marriage,' declared the woman haughtily.

'It wasn't Peta's fault,' declared Andreas, with a warm smile in Peta's direction. 'In fact I think we can admire her for bringing up her son alone. He does her credit. And it's good for Nikos to have a companion.'

Peta felt a rush of warmth. She hadn't expected him to champion her.

'You should get married again, Andreas, and have more children of your own,' announced his mother.

And get rid of this woman who isn't necessary in your life. They were the unspoken words, decided Peta. His mother had for some reason taken an instant dislike to her. It was a wonder she was allowing her to sit with them, and if it wasn't for Andreas she probably wouldn't even be speaking to her now.

A faint bell sounded from somewhere in the interior of the house. 'Lunch is ready,' announced Andreas with some satisfaction. 'Come, Peta, you must be starving. Nikos, Ben, time to eat.'

The boys hauled themselves out of the pool, catching the towels Andreas tossed to them. 'Slip on your shirts, boys.'

Mrs Papadakis had already walked into the house, her back straight with disapproval, and Peta wasn't surprised when she didn't join them.

'I don't think your mother likes me,' she said when they had seated themselves at an oval table in a cool extension of the main kitchen.

'Since my father died my mother has found life very difficult,' he excused. 'In one respect it's her own fault because she doesn't make friends easily. Once she gets to know you she'll see what a wonderfully warm person you are. No one can help but fall for your charm, Peta.'

His eyes met and held hers. Peta felt her stomach turn over. What was he saying? That he wanted something more from their relationship? That the kiss had meant a whole lot more than she'd ever imagined? Her toes wriggled in her sandals and she fought to suppress the heat that was stealing over her skin. She didn't want a relationship with Andreas, not with anyone; she was happy as she was.

If that's the case, why did you come here? asked an inner voice. *You must have known what would happen.*

No, I didn't, she protested. I was merely helping him out.

To the extent that you gave up your home? Doesn't that tell you anything?

I felt sorry for Nikos.

Nikos? Rubbish! It's Andreas you're interested in, and the sooner you accept it the better.

Was her conscience right? Was she secretly hoping

for an affair? Or even something more? No! No! It couldn't be. She wouldn't let it. She didn't want a man in her life, not ever.

'Thank you for the compliment,' she said faintly. 'Time will tell.' And she turned to Ben. 'What would you like, darling?' The table was almost groaning under the weight of a splendid buffet lunch and soon the boys were chattering too much for them to hold a decent conversation.

Nevertheless she still felt Andreas's unsettling eyes on her more often than she would have liked. She really had thought that they'd come here to get away from the kidnap threats, not so that Andreas could make a pass at her.

Unfortunately the thought was tremendously exciting, and if she wasn't careful it would be revealed in her eyes. Deliberately now she kept her gaze on the table, or the boys, trying not to look at Andreas even when he spoke to her.

As soon as they'd finished eating Nikos and Ben wanted to go back into the pool, but Andreas forbade them until their lunch had gone down. 'Go and play football, but mind Nana's prized plants or you'll be in trouble.'

Peta said, 'I think I'll go and supervise.' Anything to get away from Andreas and the sensual signals he was sending out.

But Andreas had other ideas. 'Leave them. I want to talk.'

About what? Nikos? His mother? Or their own relationship? Her heart skittered along at an amazing pace.

'I'm worried about Nikos's education while we're out here. I don't want to send him to school because he's an easy target if—'

'You don't think that whoever's threatened to kidnap your son knows you've moved here?' she asked in horror.

'Of course not, but I'm not giving anyone a chance. I could bring in a private tutor for both boys, but I was wondering what you'd think about doing the job?'

Peta burst out laughing. 'From PA to nanny, to tutor. You must think I'm a many-talented person.'

'I have every faith in you.'

'Then you're mistaken. I can't teach, I don't know the first thing about it.'

'You're good at English and maths. And I'm sure you know enough about history and geography to teach a seven- and eight-year-old. I think you're eminently qualified. And what you don't know I do. I'll get all the relevant books and together we'll make a good team.'

Together!

It was the way he said it that filled her with foreboding. They were not a team, she didn't want to be a team. All the time he was adding to her list of responsibilities and now he was including himself in her duties. It wasn't on. This wasn't part of the original score.

'You don't look happy about it.'

'I'm not,' she flashed. 'If I'd known what was in store I wouldn't have come. I thought you'd be busy all day and every day and that I'd look after Ben and Nikos. I didn't even expect to be living with your mother. I assumed you had your own villa.'

He gave a typically foreign shrug. 'I sold it. I saw no point in keeping it on when I'm here so infrequently. Besides, when I do come over I feel obliged to spend time with my mother. And to check up on my inheritance, of course,' he added with a wry grin. 'I'm sorry you feel that way.'

'The whole situation is growing out of all proportion,' she argued.

'I want you to have a good time,' he said softly.

She raised her brows then and looked at him. 'This isn't a holiday.'

'No, but I don't want it to be onerous, I want you to enjoy it. Naturally there are things I need to do, I have to keep up with my business interests, but I want to spend time with Nikos as well.'

He hadn't done very much of that so far, thought Peta. Had it taken a kidnap threat to make him realise how important Nikos was to him? She couldn't understand the man. Ben was everything to her, always had been, always would be. She would never have neglected him the way Andreas neglected Nikos.

He stood now and moved to stand behind her. He touched his hands to her shoulders and she went tense. Instead of moving he began to massage.

Peta felt a deep heat invade her body and she wanted to jump up and run away before it took hold, but to do so would reveal too much about her feelings. She sat as still as a fawn caught in a car's headlights, not even breathing, hoping that he'd get the message and go away.

What was it going to take, Andreas wondered, to get Peta to relax with him? She was driving him crazy. He'd thought that she'd enjoy new sights and sounds, forget her animosity towards men in general and allow him into her life.

Nothing seemed further from her mind.

'I'm serious about wanting you to enjoy your time here, Peta,' he said, continuing to massage slowly and surely until he felt the tension start to drain out of her.

'It's not supposed to be all work and no play. We'll go sightseeing, we'll do all sorts of things together—the four of us.' The last was added when he felt her stiffen again, when he knew she was thinking that he'd meant just the two of them. Which he had!

He increased the pressure, massaging deeper and deeper, feeling great pleasure as she gradually relaxed. Her closeness intoxicated him, sent a lightness to his head as though he'd drunk an expensive wine. He felt himself swaying closer towards her, inhaling the heady fragrance of her perfume, hearing her faint murmurs of satisfaction. He became so engrossed in what he was doing, in the feel and smell of this exciting girl who was becoming such an important part of his life, that he didn't hear his mother enter the room.

'Andreas!' she rapped.

He felt Peta jump, felt the tension return with a vengeance and cursed his parent for intruding at this particular moment. With one word she had undone all that he'd achieved.

With a slow smile and no sign of embarrassment Andreas turned to his mother. Peta, on the other hand, felt mortified. If the woman hadn't thought it before she must surely now be convinced that she was trying to latch on to her son.

'You want something, Mother?'

Dark eyes flashed contemptuously in Peta's direction, and then back to her son. 'A little of your time, *if* you can spare it.'

Peta pushed herself to her feet, standing tall and proud, not letting this objectionable woman see for one second that she was disturbed by her presence. 'I'll go and find the boys,' she said pleasantly.

But outside she stood and fumed. She could see now where Andreas's autocracy came from. Except that somewhere deep inside him lived a warm, generous, compassionate human being. She doubted many people saw it. Maybe that part came from his father. Or was she misjudging his elegant mother? Was there warmth inside her, too? If so it was well-hidden.

She found Ben and Nikos kicking a ball around on one of the terraces, but they soon tired of it and begged to be allowed in the pool again. Peta decided to join them. But on her way up to her room to change she bumped into Andreas's mother.

The woman looked at her down the length of her nose. 'A word with you, please.'

Peta smiled carefully, doing her best to hide her inner tension.

'Follow me.'

She was taken to what Peta presumed was her own private sitting room. The walls were a yellow-ochre colour, and the easy chairs and cream leather settee sat on a square of carpet patterned in the same yellow, with splashes of sage-green and ivory. The rest of the floor was tiled in cream. In her scarlet, black and white outfit, the older woman stood out like a blot of red wine on a white tablecloth.

Mrs Papadakis carefully shut the door behind them and whirled to confront Peta. 'Tell me exactly why you are here.' The red slash of her lips was tight and straight, her dark brown eyes filled with suspicion.

'I think you already know.' Peta tried to keep her tone pleasant as she boldly looked the older woman in the eye, but it was difficult keeping it up in the face of such animosity.

'You are posing as Nikos's nanny, I believe. It is actually my son you are interested in, is that not so?'

Peta shook her head vigorously. 'Andreas hired me to look after Nikos. It wasn't my idea.'

'You were previously his personal assistant?'

'Yes.'

'You have no training in looking after children?'

'Not exactly, no paper qualifications, but I have Ben. I understand children and I love them. I—'

'And you are also in love with my son. Is that not so?'

'No!' Peta's response was immediate. 'Most definitely not.'

'It does not look that way to me. Let us get this straight here and now, Miss Peta James, you are not good enough for my Andreas. He will marry no woman who has a child out of wedlock; I will see to that. Besides, he is still in love with Maria.'

Peta felt a slither of discomfort. Who the hell was Maria?

Fine black brows rose. 'He has not told you about her? Maria was his wife. He loved her deeply. He went completely to pieces when she died. I doubt anyone will ever take her place.'

'I see,' said Peta quietly. 'But it makes no difference. Ours is purely a business arrangement.'

'Then why was he touching you?' asked Mrs Papadakis fiercely. 'You—you had your eyes closed and such a look of pleasure on your face that it was positively sickening.'

Oh, Lord! It was true, she had enjoyed his touch, it had created sensations that she'd rather not remember, but for his mother to have witnessed it was excruciatingly embarrassing. 'The pleasure was in having the tension in my shoulders relieved,' she announced primly.

'And why were you tense, may I ask?'

'I was up early, it's been a long day, everything's new.' And your less-than-warm welcome didn't help, she added silently. 'I worry too whether Ben will like it here. There are a hundred and one reasons.'

'And not one of them concerns my son?'

'Why should it?' asked Peta boldly. 'You're very much mistaken, Mrs Papadakis, in thinking that I'm interested in Andreas for any other reason than that he's paying my wages.'

'You do not find him remotely attractive?'

What the devil was his mother trying to do? Did she want her to say that she was angling after an affair with him? That he was a good catch and his money would be useful? Would that satisfy her? The answer was undoubtedly yes. It was the very ammunition Mrs Papadakis needed to throw her out.

'I think any woman would find your son attractive,' she said with her head held high, her blue eyes looking directly into the other woman's. 'He's not the sort of man you can dismiss easily. But I can assure you there's nothing going on between us, nor is there likely to be. I have no intention of getting involved with a man again, ever.'

She crossed her fingers behind her back, because if there was one man who could make her change her mind it was Andreas Papadakis. He had lit fires inside her that had taken her completely by surprise and she was having to fight every one of her self-imposed rules.

'Good,' came the swift response. 'I am glad to hear it. You may go now.'

The woman's tone set Peta's hackles rising; she was

treating her like a servant, like one of her own employees. About to open her mouth and ask who the hell she thought she was talking to, Peta had second thoughts. This was Andreas's mother, and if she wanted to keep her job then she'd better respect her.

She swung on her heel without another word, but was fuming as she made her way to their apartment. Did Andreas's mother ever come here? she wondered as she closed the connecting door. Or were these rooms sacrosanct? Were they totally Andreas's domain? She hoped with all her heart that it was so.

After changing swiftly into a swimsuit with a matching overshirt, Peta hurried back out and flung herself into the pool. She did several punishing lengths before she began to calm down, ignoring the cries of the boys as they tried to attract her attention.

It was Andreas who eventually stopped her, cutting in front and forcing her to slow down. 'What's wrong?' he asked. 'You look as though you're ridding yourself of demons.'

He urged her to the side, where they hauled themselves up and sat on the edge with their feet dangling in the water. He had an incredible body, she discovered, all hard muscle and deeply tanned skin. It did nothing for her equilibrium. It sent all sorts of indecent thoughts rushing through her mind.

'Maybe I was,' she mumbled, then corrected herself. 'I was in need of some exercise.'

'I see,' he said quietly, but she could see that he didn't. It was there in the frown that creased his handsome forehead, in the puzzled look. 'Has my mother said something to upset you?'

'Why should she?' asked Peta, not looking at him, watching her toes instead as she swished them in the water. She didn't want him to say anything to his parent, she didn't want the woman to think she had been telling tales.

'I know what she's like.'

Peta shook her head. 'It's not your mother. Like I said, I've been sitting all day; I needed to wake up my body. Having a pool of your own is the height of luxury as far as I'm concerned. Ben loves it already.' The boys were racing up and down the pool now, each one trying to outdo the other.

'There are other ways I could wake up your body.'

He spoke softly, and Peta thought she must have misheard, but when she glanced at him she knew differently. There was a burning light in his eyes and it sent a shiver down her spine. She looked away again quickly, pretended she hadn't heard, hadn't seen. 'Isn't it good the way Ben and Nikos get on together?'

'Mmm.' It was an abstracted sound, as though he hadn't been listening. He continued to look at her in that mind-burning way.

Even though his mother was probably right and his heart did belong to Maria, thought Peta, it didn't stop him wanting, perhaps needing a woman in his bed. And maybe that was what she wanted, too. Would an affair with him be such a bad thing? At least she would know from the onset that at the end of it they would each walk away with their hearts intact. But it was a big decision to make. She needed to consider it.

'I think I might join them again,' she said huskily, in an effort to delay the moment.

'No, Peta, wait.' His hand touched her arm and Peta knew that if she dived into the pool now she'd be electrocuted. Such a jolt had shot through her at his touch that it was all she could do not to snatch away. 'Why is it that you're afraid of me?' he asked quietly.

She attempted a laugh, but it came out as a hollow sound with no semblance of laughter. 'What are you saying? Why should I be scared of you?'

'You tell me.' He touched her chin and turned her face to him. 'I think we're both aware of a mutual attraction, so why fight it?'

'Because it wouldn't be proper,' she burst out breathlessly. 'I'm in your employ. Are you forgetting that? There's a world of difference between our lifestyles.'

'I couldn't give a damn,' he exploded. 'Barriers don't exist where need is concerned. I know you've been hurt, I know that you've sheathed yourself in ice so that no man can touch you again, but something tells me that the time has come for the ice to melt. In fact I think it's already melted a little. Am I right?'

Peta closed her eyes, wincing inwardly. He was so very near the mark. And before she could say anything he said, 'The fact that you're not denying it tells me all I need to know.'

'You think you're so clever, don't you?' Sharp words were her only form of defence. 'You think every girl you come into contact with falls for your charm. I don't want an affair with you, Andreas. If and when I ever fall in love again it will be all or nothing. I have no time for casual sex.'

She flattened her feet against the side of the pool, ready to dive back into the water, but Andreas, guessing her intention, reached an arm out as a barrier—and then he kissed her. Right there in front of the boys.

CHAPTER SIX

THE kiss lasted no more than a few seconds, but it was enough to tell Peta that the dam had broken and feelings and sensations such as she had never experienced before were flooding in. She wanted to cling, she wanted to kiss him again; she wanted to take all he had to offer.

And Andreas saw it. He saw the colour that flushed her cheeks, he saw the passion that darkened her eyes, and he saw the battle she had with herself.

'It's all right,' he murmured. 'It's all right to let go.'

She searched his face, looking anywhere except into his eyes because she knew that if she did she would be lost. But it was just as bad looking at his mouth, at those beautifully moulded lips that seconds ago had claimed hers. Unconsciously the tip of her tongue came out to moisten her own lips and she heard his warning groan before he leaned forward and took her mouth again.

His arms didn't hold her, she was as free as a bird, but it felt as if she was his prisoner. It felt as if his mouth was shackling her to him and there was no escape. It was telling her that this was what she wanted, needed, had been looking for ever since Joe let her down.

'Mummy!'

The spell was broken, and as she moved her head Peta saw out of the corner of her eye Andreas's mother watching them from an upstairs window. The pleasure of the moment faded, unease taking its place. This woman had the power to make her life here very uncomfortable, and she had unfortunately just given her the ammunition.

The water was blessedly cool as she launched herself in, and for the next half an hour she and Andreas played with the boys. It felt good, it felt as if they were a real family, and if it hadn't been for his disapproving parent Peta would have felt happier than she had in her whole life.

Parents were always reluctant to let go, she realised, even when you were grown up and capable of making your own decisions. Andreas's mother didn't want to accept that he was getting on with his life after Maria. And her own mother, when she'd phoned to tell her first of all that she was moving in with her employer, and then actually going to live in Greece with him, had been totally against it.

The fact that Peta hadn't had time to go and see her mother and father before leaving England had put her even deeper into their bad books. Of course, Peta hadn't told them about the kidnap threats for fear of worrying them further, and so her mother had immediately drawn her own conclusions. 'You won't be happy with a man like that,' she'd warned. 'Money doesn't bring happiness. It'll be a five-minute wonder and then where will you be? Really, Peta, at your age you should have more sense.'

Peta and Andreas tired before the boys did, stepping out of the pool and throwing themselves down on a couple of sun loungers. Here, the umbrellas hid them from the house; not that Peta had any intention of letting Andreas kiss her again. She must remember at all times that this was a job, that she wasn't here to indulge in anything sexual; she was here to look after Nikos.

The thought had her springing to her feet. If that was

the case, why was she lying here at all? No wonder his mother had drawn erroneous conclusions. The signals they gave off told entirely the wrong story.

It was Andreas's fault. If he'd remained the difficult tyrant none of this would have happened; if he'd remained aloof, if he hadn't insisted she call him Andreas. Now she was in danger of making a fool of herself.

'Where are you going?'

Peta turned reluctantly at the sound of his voice. He had pushed himself up on one elbow, a sharp frown etching his brow.

'I shouldn't be doing this,' she told him shortly. 'I'm forgetting my position. I'm going to shower and get changed.' And before he could say anything else Peta hurried towards the house.

Andreas was sorry to see Peta go. For the first time he had felt she was beginning to relax with him, really relax, and when he'd kissed her he could have sworn that she was enjoying it. He had wanted the kiss to go on and on, he had wanted more of her, everything, all! But knew he still had to tread carefully. And now it looked as though even that brief kiss had frightened her off again.

He lay back and closed his eyes. He listened to the boys shouting and laughing, and then he heard the click of footsteps coming towards him. Peta? She had dressed already, was back into the nanny role he had created for her.

Little had he known when he'd asked her to look after Nikos that he would fall under her spell. She was so very different from Maria, who had used her sex appeal to its full. It was what had enchanted him about her. He had loved it when she'd turned other men's heads with her sultry looks and swaying hips, loved the fact that she'd wanted no one but him. He'd been devastated when she died.

Peta appealed to him in an entirely different way. She had no artifices. What you saw was what you got. He had thought he would never love again, would never find anyone to capture his heart. He wasn't even sure that Peta had done that. He wanted her physically, yes—she drove him crazy in that respect—but did he want more? Of that he wasn't sure.

'Andreas,' said a voice in Greek, 'I need to talk to you.'

Damn, it was his mother. His train of thought vanished as he sat up. 'Couldn't it have waited?'

'No, it couldn't,' she said with some asperity. 'It's about Peta James.'

His eyes sharpened. He had picked up on the fact that his mother didn't approve, and now she was here to voice her opinion. 'What about her?'

The older woman sat gingerly on the edge of the lounger Peta had vacated. 'She's far too familiar with you, for one thing.'

Andreas allowed his brows to slide upwards. 'Mother, you're living in the wrong era. She might be Nikos's nanny, but that's no excuse for me to treat her like a servant.'

'I saw you kissing her,' she snapped. 'She told me there was nothing between you. I knew she was lying.'

'You've spoken to her about me?' he barked, swift anger beginning to rise. Now he knew why Peta had looked worried, why she had suddenly run away. 'You had no right.'

'I have every right,' she thrust back. 'I have no desire

to see a son of mine make a fool of himself over a girl who is entirely unsuitable.'

'And you think that's what I'm doing?'

'Is it not?'

'If you'd get to know Peta better then you'd know differently,' he retorted. 'She has integrity, intelligence, is an excellent mother, and what's more is the first girl I've been interested in since Maria died.'

'Are you saying that you no longer are in love with Maria?'

'In my memories I'll always love her,' he admitted with a hint of sadness, 'but life has to go on.'

'For me there will never be anyone but your father.'

'You had a long time together,' he pointed out. 'Maria and I had a few years. I have my whole life in front of me, I don't intend spending it alone.'

'Then for pity's sake find someone more suitable than that English girl. You are Greek, Andreas, are you forgetting that? You should marry someone from your homeland.'

'I've not said I'm going to marry Peta,' he insisted. 'Although now you've put the idea in my head it might not be such a bad thing.'

His mother shook her head in despair. 'Don't do this to me, Andreas.'

'There are some things over which a mother has no control,' he said to her gently. 'And her son falling in love is one of them.'

'So you do love her?' she accused.

'I haven't said that. I find her immensely attractive, but so far it's gone no further. And I'd appreciate it if you didn't frighten her off by threats.'

His mother clamped her lips; it was obvious she was having difficulty in holding back a further tirade. In the end she simply shook her head and walked swiftly back to the house.

Andreas didn't see Peta again until he found her sitting with the boys while they ate the supper she had prepared.

He joined her in the window-seat, keeping his voice low so that Nikos and Ben couldn't hear. 'My mother had no right speaking to you as she did. Oh, yes, I know all about it,' he added when she looked at him in surprise. 'She tried to get to me, too.' He smiled indulgently. 'She still thinks she can tell me what to do. I think it's because she has too much time on her hands. She's lonely, and she'd love me to move back here permanently.'

'How about your brother? Does he live at home?'

'What do you think?' he asked with a devilish grin. 'Neither of us could wait to move out. We loved our parents dearly but there comes a time when a man needs his own space.'

'Is Christos married?'

'No.'

It was Peta's turn to give an impish smile. 'Perhaps he'll find a nice English girl to settle down with.'

'And upset my mother altogether?' he said with a laugh. 'Poor dear, she really does live in another age. But let's not talk about her any more; let's talk about us.' He saw the startled light in her eyes, knew she wanted to move away, so he reached out and took her hand. 'You can't ignore the spark that exists.' Even now it was sending an army of sensations through his loins.

'I can and I do,' she told him heatedly. 'There can be nothing between us, Andreas. It's crazy even thinking about it. I didn't take the job because I wanted an affair.

I took it because I felt sorry for Nikos. He is my main responsibility.'

So he meant nothing to her. Andreas felt personally affronted. It hadn't felt like nothing when he kissed her, he was sure she had been equally aroused. So why was she denying it?

Peta knew she was right in declaring that she was here to do a job and nothing else. No matter what thoughts, what emotions, what sensations ran through her, she had to ignore them.

Andreas wasn't in love with her; he simply lusted after her. She had read it in his eyes, seen it in the way he looked at her, felt it in his kiss. It had done all sorts of things to her that should never have been allowed, but what was the point in indulging in an affair? His world was a far cry from hers. For all she knew he could have had a string of girlfriends since he'd lost Maria.

'What are you thinking?'

She looked at him then, saw that he was watching her, that his eyes were as dark as a midnight sky.

'I was listening to the boys.' Ben and Nikos were squabbling, she suddenly realised. It gave her the perfect excuse.

'Liar.' It was a gentle reproval, there was even the hint of a smile. 'You were thinking about us. Deny it if you dare.'

Peta shrugged her slender shoulders. 'Maybe I was. Maybe I was realising what a big mistake I've made.'

The smile changed to a frown. 'In letting me kiss you?' There was a faint edge to his tone this time.

'It wasn't the right thing to do, especially with your mother watching. Rest assured, it won't happen again.'

'In that case,' he said with a wicked smile, 'we'll have to be more careful.'

'There won't be another time,' Peta assured him sharply.

The grin widened. 'What if you can't help yourself?'

'I shall make sure I don't put myself in such a position,' she announced haughtily. 'Ben, stop that, will you?'

'Are you making a point here? Reminding me that it's the boys you're here to supervise? That I am a no-go area?'

She nodded. 'Exactly.'

'I think you might find that very difficult.' He sat more comfortably in his seat, looking wholly amused by the whole conversation. 'I think maybe you don't realise the strength of your own feelings.'

'And I think maybe you are seeing things that aren't there,' she retorted sharply, and, turning her head, said, 'Boys, will you please stop arguing?'

When they realised they were being observed Ben and Nikos shut up and got on with their meal.

'We'll finish this conversation later,' said Andreas, finally accepting that he was getting nowhere while the boys were present. Lazily he pushed himself up, but his eyes never left her. They stroked intimately over her whole body—arousing, hurting, even, sending sensation after sensation sizzling through her veins.

Peta closed her eyes until he had left the room. She didn't want to see, didn't want to feel. It had been a mistake coming here to Greece with Andreas and his son. She had thought they would all get on together, that it would be a good experience for Ben, but Andreas was spoiling it. He was asking far more of her than she was prepared to give.

Had it been his intention all along? Was that the reason he'd insisted she change her job? He'd virtually given her no choice; she would have been out of work altogether if she hadn't gone along with his request. And now she was in the unenviable position of allowing herself to be seduced by him or being shipped back to England without a job or a home to go to. There was always her mother, of course, but…

An hour later, when the boys were in bed and Peta was sitting out on the living-room balcony, enjoying the last rays of the sun which had turned the sky above Athens into a glowing red furnace, she sensed rather than saw Andreas standing beside her.

She hadn't been aware of him approaching, miles away with her thoughts, and now she looked at him in surprise and not without a little trepidation. She had been thinking about their conversation, about the way her body reacted when he was near, and whether she was being foolish denying herself the pleasure she knew he could give her. He was aware, of course, exactly how she felt, and if he put the pressure on she would be lost. But where would it get them? It would surely be better to maintain a safe distance, to do the job she had been brought out here for, and to hell with anything else.

'Aren't you hungry?' The words meant one thing, his eyes another.

Peta felt a stinging sensation hit the very core of her. Damn him! 'I wasn't sure whether you were. I didn't know what you expected of me.' In truth food was the furthest thought from her mind.

'Actually, I'm starving,' he said 'You stay here and enjoy all these new sights and sounds. I'll rustle us both up something to eat.'

'You cook?' she enquired. This was a surprise, coming from a man who could afford an army of servants.

'You think I can't?'

Peta turned her lips down at the corners and shrugged. 'I've never really thought about it.'

'But you think I'm spoilt and pampered, unable to lift a finger for myself?' There was a twinkle in his eyes as he spoke.

'You said it,' she retorted with a grin.

'There are lots of things about me you don't know,' he told her. 'Be prepared for a culinary delight. Maybe madam would like a glass of wine while she's waiting?'

'Maybe madam doesn't drink.'

'Of course. I was forgetting. A fruit juice, then? Something long and cold and inviting?' His voice went down an octave, becoming suddenly seductive and exciting.

Peta gave a faint smile and nodded. 'That would be nice.' And her stomach did a somersault, which didn't bode well for an intimate evening spent together. Maybe there would have been something welcome about his mother being present after all.

It seemed that no time had elapsed before he announced that dinner was ready.

He'd laid the table with an ornately embroidered tablecloth and heavily engraved silver.

'It looks very formal for a simple supper,' she said doubtfully.

'The man wants to impress the lady.'

'I'll reserve judgement until I've eaten,' she answered.

He pulled out her chair, his hands dropping to her shoulders as she sat. Nothing more than a fleeting touch, but it was enough to send all her good intentions crashing to the floor.

The food was simple but superbly cooked: melon to start with, followed by chicken breasts in a delicious tomato sauce served with potatoes that had been braised in the same sauce. Peta wasn't sure how she got through it; she was aware of nothing but Andreas and the power he exerted over her. Power was a strange word to use, she thought. Andreas was a powerful man in the business world, he had a powerful body, too, but this was power of a different kind.

It was a silent, insidious power; power over her body. He was taking her over whether she wanted him to or not. It was a mind game. He was playing with her emotions, making her want him against her will.

They talked about all sorts of things while they ate—the state of the world, the state of the company back in England, the boys—anything and everything except themselves. But Peta thought that now might be a good time to ask him about Maria.

Here, in this apartment, she could feel her presence, feel an invisible third party. There was a portrait hanging on the upstairs landing of a beautiful young woman with jet-black hair and flashing dark eyes that followed her whenever she walked past. She guessed it was his wife because Nikos looked so very much like her.

'Yes, that's Maria,' Andreas admitted, when Peta dared to ask, and she saw the inevitable sadness in his eyes. It looked to her as though Maria's ghost would haunt him for ever.

'Did you live here when you were married?' she asked as she took a sip of her coffee, unable to think of any other reason for his wife's portrait to be here.

'Not until my father became ill and Mother couldn't manage. He was sick for a long time. And after he'd died my mother needed me more than ever.'

So that was the reason his parent was so possessive, thought Peta. 'Did it work?' she asked. 'Did Maria mind?'

'She loved it because she had company while I was out at work. I worked very long hours,' he admitted with a surprising touch of guilt. 'She and my mother got on well. Maria was the daughter of an old friend of my parents. I'd known her practically all my life. And when Nikos came along it was exactly what my mother needed to give her a new lease of life. There was no thought then of us moving out.'

'How long since Maria died?' Peta asked gently, feeling nothing but sympathy for this man who clearly still had very deep feelings for the woman who had borne him his son.

He drew in a slow, deep breath. 'Two years, almost. It was a tragic, tragic day.' His mind seemed to go back in time and it was several long seconds before he spoke again. 'It was a road accident. Nikos was with her. For some reason Maria didn't have her seat belt on; she stood no chance. Nikos was strapped in but he can remember nothing of it. I think the accident traumatised him to such an extent that he's blocked it out. If I ever catch the swine who drove her off the road I'll kill him,' he announced fiercely. 'It's a notorious bend, with a sheer drop, but Maria knew that road well, always took care.'

'So the police never traced the other car?'

'No. There was red paint on her car, so we know someone else was involved, but who it was will always remain a mystery. I sure hope whoever it was has it on his conscience for the rest of his life,' he finished bitterly.

'I'm so sorry,' said Peta. 'You must have been devastated.'

'To put it mildly,' he agreed. 'I blame myself entirely. I'd planned to take Maria and Nikos out that day, then something cropped up at work and as usual I refused to delegate. We had a row; she said I always put work before her.' He dropped his head, pressing his fingers to throbbing temples. 'And dammit she was right. I did. I do. I threw myself into my work more than ever after she died. And poor Nikos. I couldn't bear to have him around me. He's so like Maria that it was torture every time I looked at him. I didn't think the pain would ever go away.'

'It's all right,' said Peta softly. 'You don't have to tell me any more.' Because suddenly she understood. 'It's not an easy thing to get over.'

'I'm getting there,' he announced, finally lifting his head. 'And there's a certain beautiful young lady who's proving to me that there is life after Maria.' The look in his eyes said it all.

Peta tried to look away but couldn't. Their eyes locked in a heart-stopping moment that sent the blood screaming through her veins. 'We can't get involved,' she whispered.

'You tell me why not, when we both know it's what we want.'

The tension between them increased. 'You know why,' she managed to say.

'They're not valid reasons.'

'They are as far as I'm concerned,' she insisted.

'Then we need to do something about changing your mind. Let's get out of here; let's go for a walk.'

'But the boys…' It was a meek protest.

'They won't wake; you know that. You're looking for excuses.'

It was true. The next few minutes were going to be the turning point in their relationship. There would be no going back. Was she prepared for an affair that could lead nowhere? Would she be able to walk away at the end of it with her heart whole?

Night had fallen and mood lights were on in the pool and grounds, giving the whole place a magical air. Andreas put his arm about her shoulders as they walked, keeping her close to him, saying nothing, but his very silence sent its own message.

Peta knew deep down in her mind that she could fight him no longer, and when they were out of sight of the house, when he halted, when he turned her to face him, she gave a brief sigh of capitulation. The noise of cicadas filled the air, the heat of the day lingered, and the sky had become a canopy of shimmering stars.

Andreas stroked her cheek with the backs of his fingers and murmured something in Greek. He pulled down her lower lip and dropped a light kiss onto it; he urged her against him, and when she didn't demur, when she didn't back away, he gave a sigh of his own before claiming her lips.

Gently, experimentally—testing, waiting—wanting, needing. Peta's body grew hot, every nerve-end so sensitised that the briefest touch aroused her and evoked a need that shocked and thrilled at the same time. She returned his kiss with an amazed abandonment. It felt like release from a prison of her own making. A glorious release that had her soaring with the angels.

Andreas's groan of pleasure came from somewhere deep in his throat and his arms tightened, his kiss became deeper, his tongue touching hers now, exploring, inciting, taking everything that she offered. They suddenly couldn't get enough of each other. The floodgates had opened and their pent-up emotions were in full flow.

Only once did he hold back. 'You are sure?' he questioned, his voice deeper than she had ever heard it before.

Her response was a whimper of pleasure, her mouth reaching for his again.

Once more a flood of Greek. He was the most exciting man she had ever met. All the weeks she had known him she had been aware of his raw sensuality, but to feel it now, to taste him, to share the intimacy of mindless kisses when senses took over and the outer world was forgotten, was like nothing she had ever imagined or experienced.

How long the kiss went on Peta wasn't sure. Her mind had ceased to register anything except the thrill of kissing Andreas, the sheer headiness of having his body pressed close against hers. All barriers were down, they were existing on sensations alone, each drinking the sweet nectar of life from each other's mouths.

It was an extraordinary feeling. She had never, in her wildest imaginings, envisaged that she would kiss Andreas Papadakis, especially like this. He was the Tyrant. He was her boss. He was far beyond her reach.

'If I don't stop now—' his mouth edged away from hers, and his hoarse voice reached into her consciousness '—I won't be responsible for my actions.'

Nor would she, Peta realised, even as he kissed her again. She didn't want him to stop; she didn't want him to be responsible. She wanted everything he had to offer.

'You have no idea what you're doing to me,' he groaned.

Oh, yes, she had. If the kiss was affecting him half as

much as it was her then she knew exactly how he was feeling. His whole body would be on fire, his every instinct would be to make love to her, to drown in her body, to enjoy, to take everything that was willingly offered.

'Oh, Peta,' he muttered. 'I never dreamt that…'

He was robbed of the rest of his sentence by Peta's hungry mouth taking his. 'I know how you're feeling,' she whispered between passionate kisses, 'because I feel the same way.'

His answer was an even deeper groan, one hand moving to possessively capture an already swollen and tingling breast. A fresh surge of emotions coursed through her, an even greater need to be taken completely, and when Andreas let her go, when he stepped back a pace and looked at her with a mixture of sorrow and desire, she felt as though part of her had been snatched away.

'We need to take things slowly,' he said, shaking his head. He didn't sound as though he meant it. He sounded as though the words were being forced out of him by a hidden source.

That same hidden source had Peta agreeing with him. 'I don't know what came over me.' And as she thought about it a rich tide of colour stained her neck and face. To hide her embarrassment she turned from him and headed back towards the house.

'Peta!'

It was a command and she instinctively obeyed, halting but not turning, waiting but not wanting. This was all wrong. It could lead nowhere, could end only in disaster.

'Don't run away from me.' His voice got nearer. 'We both got carried away.' He was standing right behind her. She could feel his breath warm on her nape even though he was very carefully not touching her.

'It shouldn't have happened,' she whispered sadly.

'Oh, yes, it should,' he muttered thickly. 'It was a very natural, a very right thing to do. We both wanted it, we both needed it, and you can't walk away from me now.'

'But—'

'But nothing. You can't ignore your feelings, Peta.'

'I must,' she declared, finally turning to face him, and then wishing she hadn't when her eyes met his and she felt herself being drawn once more into their dark, disturbing depths. Why, oh, why had she agreed to come out here? she asked herself. For all these years she'd religiously kept men out of her life, and now, when she was least expecting it, she had fallen hook, line and sinker for a man who wanted nothing more from her than a brief affair.

'Why must you?' He put his hands on her shoulders and looked even more deeply into her eyes. 'Why not enjoy yourself while you can? I promise I won't hold you to anything. You'll be free to walk away whenever you like.'

The fact that he was saying what she already knew made Peta even more determined not to let herself get swept along on an unstoppable tide of passion. 'And you think I'd be happy doing that?' she tossed sharply. 'I'm not the type of girl to indulge in a passionate affair and then walk away. I can't even think why I let you kiss me.'

'Because you couldn't help yourself, the same as I couldn't. So why deny ourselves what we both want?'

'But I don't want it,' she flashed. 'I couldn't help kissing you, but I didn't want to do it.'

'You're not making sense, Peta.' His hands tightened on her shoulders, his eyes compelled her to look at him.

'Maybe not,' she agreed. 'But I don't want to start anything I can't finish. We both know that we're not into serious relationships. So for goodness' sake, Andreas, let this thing drop.'

His voice became a deep, throaty growl. 'You're driving me insane.'

'I'll take that as a compliment,' she said as another hot flush swept through her, 'but the way I see it any woman would suit your purpose. You don't strike me as the type to remain celibate for long. But don't expect me to satisfy your carnal desires because I won't do it.'

His hands fell from her shoulders and his mouth tightened. 'If that's really what you think then there's not much more I can say.'

She noticed that he didn't deny it. Besides, how could she get involved with a man whose attitude towards his son left a lot to be desired? Admittedly, he'd panicked when he had the kidnap threat, but prior to that he had put his work first, and probably would again. What sort of father was that?

If she ever married again—and it was a very big if—she would want a man who adored children, who would become the father Ben had never had. Andreas Papadakis certainly didn't fit the bill.

Peta went to bed, but not to sleep. She tried not to think of Andreas but that kiss insisted on resurrecting itself. She could feel his mouth on hers, feel the heat that rushed through every vein in her body, she even wriggled with excitement as though he were still touching her.

Damn the man! She had meant what she said. There would be no recurrences. She had to firmly fix it in her mind that he was her employer and she was to treat him as such—and that was the way she wanted him to treat her. But would he? Had she got through to him? Only time would tell.

CHAPTER SEVEN

ANDREAS threw himself into his work. His office in Athens was having staffing problems and he wanted to make some changes anyway. It was the perfect antidote. When finally he had thought he was getting his life back together Peta had declared she wanted nothing to do with him on a personal level.

He was finding it hard to handle. The woman drove him crazy. It would have been all right if he'd never kissed her—perhaps. If he hadn't felt the exciting heat of her body against his—maybe. If he hadn't been intoxicated by the sensual smell of her—possibly. But he had experienced all three, and there was no way that he was going to give up.

All he had to do was bide his time. She hadn't meant what she said, not deep down. It had been a heat-of-the-moment thing. He would show her. He would prove to her that she needed him as much as he needed her.

Neither of them wanted a permanent relationship. Peta didn't, she'd made that very clear, and he wasn't ready yet to put anyone into Maria's place. But why deny the extremely strong physical attraction they both felt? It could be termed as lust, he supposed, on his part anyway, but it felt something more than that. He didn't simply want to use her; she was too nice a person.

Even nice wasn't the right word to sum Peta up. It was a totally ineffective word. All he knew was that Peta entranced him.

But he showed her none of this. He'd decided that he would play it her way, for the time being.

Peta actually enjoyed giving lessons to the boys—except when Andreas's mother interrupted them. She seemed to think it was her given duty to supervise proceedings, and each day she would enter the playroom and silently watch. And as soon as she thought that Peta wasn't doing something correctly she would intervene.

'I'm no teacher,' flashed Peta on one occasion. 'I'm doing this because Andreas asked me to.'

'Andreas is a fool,' declared his mother. 'Quite easily I could employ a proper tutor.'

'Maybe Andreas thinks we won't be here that long.' Peta's blue eyes were hostile as she looked at the older woman. It was wishful thinking on her part, of course, she had no idea how long Andreas intended staying.

'He has said as much to you?' came the swift response.

Peta shrugged. 'Not in so many words.'

'Then I think it is you who does not want to stay. Believe me, my son is never happier than when he is with me here.'

Whether that was true or not Peta had no way of knowing. The fact that he *had* instinctively come here must mean something, though.

Most evenings when Andreas came home he was in a foul mood, and Peta kept well out of his way. Almost a week had passed since the kiss. A week in which she had relived it over and over again, had felt all the same sensations, but was still of the opinion that she had done the right thing.

On this particular evening, however, Andreas came home before she retired to her room. She'd just cleared away the toys the boys had used in the pool and was taking a moment to relax on the terrace when he rounded the corner of the house.

Her heart instantly stammered. He was wearing a lightweight business suit, the collar of his shirt undone, tie hanging loose. His eyes narrowed as he looked at her. 'Why have you been avoiding me?' he enquired sharply.

'What makes you think I have?' Peta's chin automatically rose in defence, and as she met the disturbing dark depths of his eyes she felt a slither of something suspiciously like desire. She had tried very hard to bury such feelings, had even thought she was succeeding, now she realised that they were still very much alive and in danger of giving her away.

'I haven't seen you for days.'

'That's your problem, not mine. I haven't left the house. If you're too busy to spend time with your son, don't take it out on me.' Now, why had she said that? It wasn't Nikos who was in question here. Although it was true he hardly ever saw the boy. He seemed content to leave him in her care.

'Let's leave Nikos out of this,' he rasped. 'It's you we're talking about. You hide away in your room as though you're afraid.'

Her eyes flashed a brilliant blue. 'I have no reason to be afraid, not of you.'

'That's right, no reason at all. So as soon as I've changed we're going out to dinner.'

Peta lifted her shoulders in a vague shrug. 'If that is your wish.'

'Be ready in half an hour.' And with a swift click of his heels he was gone.

Peta didn't move for a few seconds. She didn't want

to go out with him. She ought to have told him so, except that his tone had brooked no refusal. There had been a hardness in his eyes that she hadn't seen for a long time, so it definitely wasn't going to be a pleasurable evening.

Perhaps he wasn't happy with the way she was tutoring his son. His mother undoubtedly gave him running reports. Perhaps he was sending her back to England but softening the blow with an expensive meal. He didn't need her here, not when the child had a doting grandmother who gave him anything that he asked for.

She went up to her room and looked through her wardrobe. The fact that she owned only three summer dresses didn't make the decision hard. Mainly at home she wore tops and either skirts or trousers. Two of the dresses she'd originally bought for weddings; the third was a cornflower-blue sun-dress with shoelace-thin straps.

After showering she pulled on the blue dress and brushed her hair, twisting it up into a knot on the top of her head before applying the merest touch of mascara and lipstick. In less than half an hour she was back down.

'Good, you're ready. I hate a woman who keeps me waiting,' he announced crisply as she joined him on the terrace. 'Let's go.'

Andreas had changed into a pair of charcoal-grey trousers and a white linen shirt. His hair was still damp from the shower and he looked totally gorgeous. Peta hated to admit it but he did, and every sensitive point in her body absolutely refused to behave itself. It didn't augur well for the rest of the evening.

Sitting beside him in his car, even with the air-conditioning going full blast, she felt on fire. It had been a huge mistake agreeing to go out with him, except that he'd not given her much choice. Somehow she needed to control her errant emotions.

Their journey was made in silence. Stealing a glance at Andreas, Peta observed the grim set of his mouth and jaw, the way his long-fingered hands gripped the wheel so tightly that his knuckles shone white. Why he was so uptight she had no idea, and could only presume that she would soon find out.

The restaurant was a square white building almost in the middle of nowhere. Olive trees shaded it, a few distant houses offered some company, but there were no other cars parked outside. It didn't even look open.

She accompanied him inside and it took several long seconds for her eyes to become accustomed to the gloom. The windows were tiny and on every sill stood potted red geraniums, shutting out what little light there was. The tables had red gingham cloths and yet more geraniums in their centre.

Peta had been expecting something grander, and it must have reflected on her face because Andreas said, 'Don't judge by appearances. Mine host is a personal friend, the food is superb. In another hour or so there won't be an empty table in the place. There are tables out at the back or we can eat in here. Which would you prefer?'

'Indoors,' she said decisively. 'It's cooler.'

A short, stout, olive-skinned man emerged from a back room, and upon seeing Andreas he gave a shout of sheer pleasure. There was much back-slapping and hand-shaking and a volume of Greek. Finally the man turned to her, flashing a set of brilliant white teeth. 'And this is...?' he asked in broken English.

'Peta James,' introduced Andreas. 'Peta, this is Stellios, an old school-friend.'

Stellios made a great show of kissing her hand. 'You take her for your wife?'

Andreas shook his head. 'Peta looks after Nikos for me.'

'Ah, shame; she is very beautiful.' He clapped a hand to his heart. 'I marry you myself, except I already have wife.'

Peta dutifully laughed, though she felt somewhat embarrassed to be talked about like this.

'And Nikos?' went on the restaurant owner. 'You bring him to see me?'

'Soon,' promised Andreas. 'Soon.'

When the jovial man had gone they sat down and Peta picked up the menu. It was handwritten in Greek! She looked at it for perhaps half a minute, knowing she hadn't a cat in hell's chance of understanding it. 'I'll have what you have,' she said.

She looked up as she spoke and discovered to her dismay that Andreas was watching her. There was no expression on his face, nothing to tell her what he was thinking. His eyes were narrowed and calculating, and when they met hers it felt as though he had stabbed into her soul.

It was a swift, sharp pain and she almost winced because it felt so physical. And then it was gone. He dropped his gaze to the menu and she was left wondering what that look had meant.

'I think we'll let Stellios decide,' he said. 'What would you like to drink?'

'Water, please.'

'I can't tempt you with a glass of wine?'

Peta shook her head. And once the water had arrived,

and Stellios announced that he would bring to them a feast fit for a king, she asked the burning question. 'What am I doing here?'

There was the glimmer of a smile on his lips. 'You're having dinner with me, of course.'

'But why?'

'Because it doesn't look as though I'm going to see you any other way.'

'That's your fault; you're always out,' she declared hotly.

'There is much work to be done.'

Peta shook her head. 'Always work. Don't you ever stop to think that Nikos might want to spend some time with his father? You go out before he's up and come home after he's gone to bed.'

'Has he said anything?'

'Actually, no, but that's only because he has Ben to play with. You're failing in your duties, Mr Papadakis. I thought you were concerned about him.'

'I know he's safe here.'

'How do you know,' she argued, 'when you never see him?'

'My mother reports to me each evening.'

'I bet she does,' Peta flared. 'I bet she also tells you that I'm useless as a teacher. Exactly why have you brought me out here tonight? To give me my marching orders?'

A look of surprise crossed his face. 'Why would I want to do that?'

'Because I'm surplus to requirements. I don't fit in here, I never will.'

'You're talking nonsense, Peta. And as for your teaching abilities, I'll have a word with Nikos tomorrow, find out exactly what he has learned. My mother says you spend too long tutoring them; that is her only complaint.'

Peta wasn't sure that she believed him, and if she hadn't been hungry she would have suggested he take her home again. She didn't want this conversation. She didn't want to be sitting beside him in a little Greek restaurant where the owner kept popping his head round the door and smiling favourably on the two of them.

'Let's forget the whole thing,' said Andreas sharply. 'Let's concentrate on us.'

To what end? wondered Peta with a sharp stab of unease. 'What are you doing that's taking you away from the house for so many hours each day?' she asked, determined to steer the conversation away from anything personal.

One eyebrow lifted, as though he had guessed her tactics, nevertheless he answered evenly, 'I have an office in Athens—it's the main hub of my company. I'm restructuring it. If it wasn't for the fact that I need you to look after Nikos I'd whisk you away there to help me. Some of those girls don't know the first thing about efficiency.'

'I'm flattered,' she said. 'How long is this...restructuring going to take?'

'I have no idea.'

'So your son's going to see nothing of you for several more weeks?'

His lips tightened. 'You don't believe in pulling punches, do you?'

'I would never neglect Ben.'

'Nikos isn't neglected,' he declared harshly. 'Don't say that. I love my son dearly.'

'Do you ever tell him? Do you ever show it? Dammit, Andreas, kids aren't kids for long. He'll be grown up before you know it and then you'll wish that you'd spent more time with him.'

His eyes became glacial. 'I didn't bring you out to discuss my son,' he snarled, clearly resenting the home truths.

Peta raised her finely shaped brows. 'So—if it's not to sack me, and it's not because of Nikos, that leaves only one thing. But it won't work, Andreas. I'm not interested in you, not now, not ever.'

He looked at her long and hard, searing her skin with an uncomfortable heat. 'You're an attractive woman, Peta. I find it hard to believe that you won't let a man into your life. Have you had any boyfriends since Ben's father let you down?'

'Not that it's any of your business, but, yes, there have been a couple,' she admitted reluctantly.

'And?'

'And nothing. They didn't work out,' she retorted.

'Because you presented the ice-maiden image, the same as you're trying to do now.'

'Trying has nothing to do with it,' she flashed. 'It's how I feel. I've never yet met a man I can trust.'

She watched as Andreas sucked in a deep breath, straightening his spine, his brown eyes coldly penetrating hers. She had insulted his manhood, but it was true. She would dearly love to meet a man whom she could love deeply and who would never let her down. Andreas wasn't that man. Andreas was still in love with Maria. He wanted her for her body alone and that she could do without.

'How do you know whether or not you can trust a man unless you relax your rigid attitude?' And still those stony brown eyes held hers.

Little did he know it but there had been many times

when she'd been prepared to relax where he was concerned; times when she had indeed let down her guard and almost given in to the clamouring needs of her body. But that wasn't the way to go. And she would be as well to remember it.

'I think when the right man comes along I will know,' she told him bravely, and she was saved from having to elaborate further by their first course arriving in the form of several plates heaped with various appetisers. Some she recognised; some she didn't—baby squid, whitebait, stuffed vine leaves, salads with feta cheese, fresh crusty bread, various dips…so much that it was confusing.

'We'll never get through this lot!' she exclaimed. It was enough to fill her up without the main course.

'Just eat what you fancy,' he said with a wry smile. 'A little of each, perhaps? We can save the salad for later if it's too much.'

Everything was tasty and succulent and Peta tucked in with an appetite she hadn't expected. She drank her water, and when Andreas ordered a carafe of wine she obligingly sipped from her glass. She'd be careful, though, she told herself; she'd drink only enough to help her get through the evening.

Not that it was proving too much of an ordeal. Their conversation had turned to ordinary everyday things and this she could handle. As the evening progressed she could feel herself mellowing, and she even laughed out loud at some of Andreas's anecdotes.

Andreas too had relaxed in his attitude towards her. He was no longer cold and condemning but warm and welcoming. In fact the whole evening was turning into a much more pleasant affair than she'd expected.

'You have a beautiful smile, do you know that?' he asked suddenly.

Peta stopped smiling.

So did Andreas. 'For heaven's sake, Peta, I'm not trying to come on to you. I've already learned that that was a huge mistake.'

'I'm sorry,' she said instantly.

'You're just so used to closing up when a man pays you compliments.'

'I guess so.'

'Then stop it.' He reached out and put his hand over hers where it rested on the table.

Peta felt an incredible heat run through her and she prayed silently that he couldn't feel it, too. This was stupid. He was offering the hand of friendship, nothing more, why couldn't she take it? She'd always used the excuse that it was because Joe had stuffed up on her, but it now occurred to her that it had nothing to do with Joe and everything to do with herself.

She was happy living alone with her son, she didn't want a man in her life—and who was she trying to kid? Andreas was everything she had ever wanted in a man. He was handsome, he was exciting, he was sexy, and once she'd got through the hard tycoon image she had found out that he could be charming and attentive. He would make a good father if he didn't work so hard. Nikos adored him, didn't seem to resent the fact that he didn't see much of him. He was a well-adjusted child who was obviously used to this kind of lifestyle.

But getting too close to Andreas would be like living with a time bomb. It was wrong to be jealous of Maria but Peta was. Andreas didn't talk about her, and it was this fact that was the problem. His mother said he still loved her, and for some reason Peta couldn't even explain to herself she believed the woman.

A *ménage à trois* wouldn't work. He would pay her

attention, he would flatter her, he would take her body and use her—and she like a fool would let him—but he would offer her nothing at the end of it all. His heart was too deeply entrenched in the mother of his child.

All of these thoughts flashed through her mind as his hand held hers and she would have dearly loved to snatch it away, but that would only confirm what he had just said. So she let it lie there, she let the heat course through veins and arteries, she let her pulses and heartbeat quicken, and an incredible need stole over her.

Whether her features softened, whether something happened to alert Andreas to the way she felt, Peta didn't know, but his eyes darkened as though he had picked up on an unspoken message and, lifting her hand to his mouth, he kissed it.

He kissed the back first, trailing feather-light kisses all over, and then her fingers, each one separately, until finally he turned her hand and pressed a kiss into her palm before curling her fingers over it. It was as though he was saying, Hold that kiss. Keep it and think of me.

Unable to help herself, she looked deeply into his eyes, saw a need that reflected her own, held that gaze, and was stupidly disappointed when he was the first to look away.

'More wine?' he asked pleasantly.

Peta shook her head. 'No, thanks.' She hadn't even finished the glass he'd poured her and she didn't intend to. There were going to be no repeats of that fateful night when she'd conceived Ben.

During the rest of the meal, between visits by the attentive, always smiling Stellios—who, she was sure, had already in his own mind got them married—their conversation skirted around everything except the way they felt. But it was there nevertheless, hovering over them like a bad smell, making sure its presence never went away.

The room had filled but neither of them was aware of it, not until Andreas suggested they leave and she looked around. What had happened to her? How had she become so immersed in Andreas that she'd been oblivious to what was going on around her?

He paid the bill and they went out to the car, to a jewelled sky and a crescent moon that promised a new beginning. He opened her door but before she could slide in she found herself enveloped in arms so strong they almost hurt.

'I can't do this,' he growled. 'I can't ignore you. You're driving me crazy, woman, do you know that?' His mouth claimed hers with a suddenness that allowed no retreat. 'I want you; I need you, you have to let me in, Peta. Forget that bastard who screwed you up; let me show you that there's more to life than you're currently experiencing.'

He had been driving her crazy all evening, too. She hadn't been looking forward to crawling into bed without her needs satisfied. So when his mouth swooped on hers Peta made no attempt to stop him.

The kiss sent her senses spinning into orbit and without even a second thought she parted her lips. He seemed to pause, to wonder at her change of heart, and then with a groan his tongue plunged deep inside. He tasted, he explored, he tormented. Peta whimpered.

This was heaven; this was the stuff of dreams. A tall, dark, handsome stranger sweeping her off her feet. Except that he wasn't a stranger, he was her boss. But it made no difference. She wanted him, he wanted her; it was simple.

There was nothing simple about the kiss, though. It

didn't stop at a kiss for long. His hands touched and stroked, sometimes gently, evoking the sweetest, headiest response, sometimes hard and purposeful, pressing her to him so that she couldn't help but feel his throbbing arousal.

Her excitement increased and her arms snaked around him without her being aware of it. She was suddenly full of desperate hunger, didn't care that at the end of the day it would be goodbye and thanks. This was now, this was her deepest desires being satisfied. This was something she had never before experienced, not with this intensity, not with this ferocity.

'This isn't the right place,' he declared gruffly as another car full of diners pulled up, headlights catching their embrace full-beam. 'Let's go home.'

During the drive Peta couldn't help but wonder whether she was doing the right thing. Was this something she would regret come morning? Or was this the beginning of a new and wonderful relationship? He excited her so much, this man. Sitting close to him now kept her senses inflamed, helped by the way he kept darting warm, intimate glances at her, by the way his hand reached across and touched her thigh or her hand.

When they reached the house he moved around the car to open her door, reaching down to help her out, crushing her against him, sending another mindless storm of sensation and need chasing wantonly through her body. But for only a brief moment.

She'd had time to reflect, to decide that this wasn't the way she wanted things to go. It was too soon; he was rushing her. One day, maybe, perhaps in the not too distant future even. But first she needed to come to terms with the new feelings her body was experiencing.

'What's wrong?' he asked as she pulled away from him.

'I can't do this, not yet.'

'Lord,' he exploded. 'I thought you'd got over that. Earlier you—'

'I was intoxicated by the wine and the food and the general ambience. I let myself get carried away,' she answered swiftly. 'But it's not what I want.'

One eyebrow rose. 'No? I think you're kidding yourself, lady. I think you want it very much indeed. Some mistaken sense of reproach for what you did nine years ago is blinding your judgement.'

'Maybe you're right,' she admitted, seizing the excuse. 'But I can't help it.' Adding as they walked into the house, 'I'm going to my room. Alone.'

At that precise moment his mother called out. 'Is that you, Andreas? I'd like a word.'

He swore beneath his breath. 'Your reprieve,' he snarled.

But for how long? she wondered. Andreas wasn't known for his patience. She'd given herself away, shown him that she wasn't exactly resistant to his advances. There'd be no peace now.

And she didn't have to wait long. She'd just come out of the shower and was wearing nothing more than a towel, when, with a mere cursory knock, he burst into her room.

CHAPTER EIGHT

'GET out!' shot a startled Peta. 'Didn't I make myself clear, Andreas? I'm not yet ready to start up a relationship with you. And I certainly don't intend to—'

'Shut up,' he instructed. 'This isn't about you and me, it's about Nikos.'

Peta's hands shot to her mouth. What had happened? She ought never to have gone out and left the boys. Why had she let Andreas persuade her? Why had she put pleasure before duty? Pleasure with a capital P as well, because that was certainly what the kiss had been all about.

Looking at him more closely, she could see that all hunger and desire had gone from his face. It was strained now and pale; she ought to have noticed straight away. Something tragic had happened, and it was all her fault.

'Tell me,' she said quickly.

'The would-be kidnapper—or kidnappers, whatever the case may be—has traced us here.'

'What?' She almost screamed the word and her heart beat a rapid tattoo within her breast. The towel slipped and she strove frantically to save it but failed. Not that Andreas seemed to notice her nakedness. His eyes didn't even flicker. She re-wrapped the towel, tucking the end in firmly, but holding it as well just in case.

'Another threatening letter's arrived,' he informed her. 'My mother's furious that I didn't tell her the real reason we were here.'

'We could move the boys' beds into my room if that would help,' she suggested. 'There's plenty of space.

And you can rest assured I'll keep my eye on Nikos every second of the day.'

'No need,' he said, shaking his head brusquely. 'We're leaving.'

'Again?' she queried, her eyes wide with shock. 'You can't keep running, Andreas, you have to do something. These people must be caught. Have you informed the police?' It didn't seem long since she'd asked him the same question, and yet it must be all of three weeks. Three weeks it had taken whoever it was to find them. Not long. There would be no escape. Wherever they ended up they would be found. Her heart felt as heavy as lead.

'The police suggested it,' he told her shortly. 'At least they're taking this whole thing a lot more seriously than they did in England. Unfortunately they don't have sufficient manpower to protect us while they investigate. So—I'm going to take you and the boys to a mountain hideaway tonight under cover of darkness. We won't be found there.'

An icy shiver raced down Peta's spine. She didn't like the sound of this one little bit. But Andreas wasn't a man you could argue with, especially in this mood.

'If it was myself in danger,' he added, 'I'd stay and face whoever it is that's doing this to me. But where Nikos is concerned I cannot take the risk. So get packing,' he ordered brusquely. 'I'll wake the boys.'

He left the room as quickly as he'd entered. Peta threw on some clothes and heaved out a suitcase. In less than half an hour they were on their way.

Andreas was grim-faced as he drove, and they'd been going well over an hour and a half before he headed up into the blackness of the mountains. The boys had fallen asleep again but he didn't speak, and Peta didn't dare ask any questions.

Eventually they left the mountain road, following what felt like a bumpy cart track going nowhere, and after much twisting and turning the Range Rover's headlights picked out a small stone cabin tucked well into the trees.

'This is it,' he announced tersely. 'Boys, wake up, we're here.'

Ben and Nikos helped carry everything in while Andreas got the generator going. They loved the thought of charging around in the middle of the night, especially when they discovered that they were going to share a bedroom. The trouble was there were only two bedrooms, tiny rooms with a double bed in each, and a dresser and a wardrobe, and not much room to walk around.

Peta looked doubtfully at the second bedroom as she began to unpack the few clothes she'd brought with her. Of one thing she was sure; she wasn't sharing a bed with Andreas Papadakis.

As well as the bedrooms there was a kitchen, a living room and a bathroom. The same amount of space that she'd had at home for herself and Ben, and now there were four of them!

The boys went eagerly to bed and at last she was alone with Andreas. 'We'll be safe now,' he said confidently as they sat down in the tiny living room.

'But for how long?' she wanted to know. 'We can't stay here for ever.'

'Of course not,' he assured her. 'But, whatever you do, don't alarm the boys.'

'What excuse did you give them for leaving at such an ungodly hour?'

He grinned then, his teeth flashing white. 'I told them it was a huge adventure and I had lots of surprises for them. Believe me, they'll love it.'

'It doesn't feel like an adventure to me,' Peta declared sharply. 'For one thing I'm worried stiff, and for another I want to know what the sleeping arrangements are when there's only one bed between the two of us.'

His lips twisted wryly and there was an amazing twinkle in his eye. 'I wondered when you'd get around to that.'

'As a matter of fact, forget I asked,' she retorted quickly. 'I'll take the bed, you can sleep where the hell you like.' She looked doubtfully at the couch on which he was sitting. It didn't look long enough to accommodate a man who was well over six feet, but why should she care? 'Whose cabin is this, anyway?'

'It's mine—my mountain retreat,' he answered. 'Some of my friends use it but it's where I come when things get on top of me.'

Peta lifted her brows. 'How often is that?' She somehow couldn't see anything getting on top of Andreas. He was the most together person she'd ever met. He was perfectly in control of his life—and those around him! It was only now, when his son was in danger, that she'd seen him lose it a little. But not much. He'd quickly worked out a plan of action and put it into operation.

'There have been times,' he admitted, a shadow she was beginning to recognise darkening his eyes.

Like when his wife had died, she quickly surmised. She should have thought of that. 'Has Nikos been here before?'

'No. It's just as much an experience for him as it is for Ben. You'll see, Peta, they'll have the time of their lives.'

'Is there a phone?' What if the kidnapper traced them here? What if the boys fell and seriously hurt themselves?

'No, and my mobile doesn't work up here either. It's what I like best about it.'

The man who was always in touch, always on the phone, always planning and organising, actually liked being cut off?

'You look as though you find it hard to believe.'

'I do,' she said at once. 'You thrive on work; you're never away from it. You'll be bored silly in a couple of days.'

'With two lively youngsters? To say nothing of a very beautiful young woman?' His eyes held hers as he spoke.

Warning bells rang. Peta shook her head. 'I'm here for Nikos's sake, not yours.'

He held up his hands, palms facing her. 'Did I say anything different?'

He was making it sound as though she was the one jumping to conclusions. Peta's blue eyes flashed across the room. 'It's not what you said but the way that you said it.'

'And you're suggesting that I keep well away from you? Not so much as a tiny goodnight kiss? You're going to force me to sleep on this tiny couch while you lie there in my bed and think about me.'

'As if!' A flare of indignant light blazed in Peta's eyes.

'Oh, I think you will,' he said. 'I don't think you'll be able to help yourself, even if it's only to feel guilty.'

'Never!'

His lips quirked. He didn't believe her.

Well, she would show him. She jumped to her feet.

'As a matter of fact I'm going to bed now. Goodnight, Mr Papadakis.'

His eyes narrowed at the formality. 'Sleep tight, Miss James.'

'I will, don't worry.'

She'd just got undressed and into bed, when the door opened.

'Pardon me for intruding,' Andreas said with exaggerated politeness as he snapped on the light, 'but I believe my holdall is in here.'

Her wide blue eyes watched warily as he moved into the room. 'I don't think so,' she snapped, knowing that he was using it as an excuse. 'I'd have seen it if it was.'

'I also need a couple of sheets and a pillow.'

He found what he wanted on a high shelf in the wardrobe, his holdall had been tossed in there, too. Peta's lips thinned. He'd intended sleeping in here all along—until she'd put her foot down. But she didn't care. There was no way he was sharing her bed, even if he did manage to arouse every one of her baser instincts.

Beneath the sheets her body was ready to go up in flames. All her senses had gone into overdrive, and she was so aware of him that she felt sure he must know it. She tried closing her eyes but that was worse, because she didn't know then what he was doing.

Please hurry up and go, she prayed silently. But he seemed in no hurry. He put the holdall down while he slowly and carefully folded the sheets over his arm.

'If you're waiting for an invitation to join me it will be a long night,' she thrust acidly.

'Why are you denying what you really want?' It was a sexual growl, narrowed eyes fixed intently on hers.

It sent a further tingle through her limbs. 'I want more

than anything to be left alone to get some sleep,' she declared shakily. 'I thought it was all sorted.'

'You'd condemn me to that hard, lumpy couch?'

'It didn't look hard and lumpy to me,' she riposted. Goodness, when was he going to get the message? Because the truth was the longer he stood there looking at her, the weaker she was becoming.

'And not even a mite small?'

'So what?' she demanded. 'It was your idea that we come here.'

'Not my idea that we sleep in separate rooms.'

'Then you should have thought about it before we left. You should have known I wouldn't even dream about sleeping with you.'

'Is that so?' Lazy, mocking eyes laughed into hers. 'I think the lady lies. I think you've thought about it a lot. In fact I think you even like the idea.' As he spoke he walked around the foot of the bed to her side.

'No, I don't,' she claimed, shocked to hear how husky her voice sounded.

'OK, if the lady says no then the lady means no. But a goodnight kiss will do no harm, will it?'

Andreas saw the panic in Peta's eyes as he bent over her, and for a brief second wondered whether he ought to back off. But, no, faint heart never won fair lady—wasn't that what they said? And he was certainly not known for being faint-hearted.

She smelled so sweet, looked so lovely, that his male hormones wouldn't behave themselves. And as his lips lightly brushed hers he felt a tremor run through her. Nor was it a tremor of fear; it was desire, he was certain of it. She wasn't as immune as she made out; he'd proved that before when he'd kissed her. No matter how much she protested Peta James was one hell of a sexy lady. An aroused sexy lady!

He'd intended the kiss to be light and friendly, so what was happening to him? Why was he deepening it? Why was he taking the chance of spoiling everything? Because he couldn't help himself, that was why. He wanted to jump into bed with her right now; he wanted to take her into his arms; he wanted to make love to her; he wanted everything!

But he couldn't do that because it would ruin the time they had to spend here. He must never forget that Nikos's safety was his first priority. And he needed Peta to help look after his son. He mustn't antagonise her.

So he raised his head. It took an achingly long time to do so. He felt as though he was held to her by a magnet, and the pull was so strong that it took an enormous effort to break the bond.

He expected a further flow of indignation and anger, was surprised and somewhat pleased when all she did was turn away, letting the back of her head speak for itself. Disapproval, yes, but also an unhappiness within herself for allowing him to kiss her.

He smiled softly as he left the room. It was certainly a step in the right direction.

The couch was as hard and uncomfortable as he had known it would be. It wasn't made for tall men to sleep on—not for anyone to sleep on. Only once before had he attempted to sleep there. The roof had developed a leak during the winter and heavy rain had ruined both beds. He'd hardly slept a wink, and the very next day he'd had the roof fixed and new beds delivered. He'd sworn that he'd never sleep on that couch again.

Until a little minx by the name of Peta James had forced him to do so. He could, of course, have sent Ben in to sleep with his mother while he climbed in beside Nikos, but that would have created a precedent and spoilt any chance he had of ever sharing a bed with the woman who was beginning to drive him insane.

He had thought never to love again after Maria died, had thought it would be disloyal to her memory, especially as he blamed himself, and he wasn't even sure that he was in love now. All he did know was that this very beautiful redhead had got beneath his skin. He wanted her so badly that he was prepared to go to almost any lengths to persuade her into his bed.

When dawn began to streak the purple sky he climbed stiffly from the couch and, picking up a towel, quietly made his way outside. A hundred yards or so higher up the mountain was a natural rock pool deep enough to bathe in. It was a favourite spot of his, always guaranteed to soothe the mind as well as the body.

The chill of the water took his breath away but it did nothing to cool the rampant feelings he had where Peta was concerned. He came out of the pool feeling as hungry for her body as he had when he went in. He was finding it impossible to dismiss the thought of her.

Perhaps it had been a bad idea to bring her up here with him. Maybe he should have come with Nikos alone. Maybe he should never have brought her to Greece in the first place.

Suddenly he sensed that he was being watched and his first thoughts were of the kidnapper.

And he had left the boys alone with a sleeping Peta! Some protection she would be!

Heavens, he had allowed himself to be sidetracked by a pretty woman, forgetting the real reason he was here. He spun around—and in the half-light caught sight of a moving shadowy shape through the trees. Someone was keeping an eye on him while his accomplice did the dirty work!

With a yell, and heedless of the fact that he hadn't a stitch on, he sprinted in the direction of the shape, took a flying leap and landed on top of him. Except that it wasn't a he. 'Peta!' he exclaimed as the awfulness of the situation hit him. 'What the devil are you doing here?'

Peta had thought herself unobserved, had been unprepared when Andreas came charging in her direction, and was now both embarrassed and breathless as he got to his feet and glared down at her. She could hardly avoid looking at him, and at close quarters he was even more magnificent than he had been a dozen yards away. His immediately rampant manhood sent a rapid response through her limbs.

She scrambled with feverish haste to her feet so that at least her eyes could meet his on a level without other things coming between them. 'I—I heard you leave. I wondered where you were going. I—'

'Dammit, I could have killed you, skulking in the undergrowth like that. I thought you were one of the kidnappers. You had no right leaving the boys alone.'

'You said they wouldn't find us here.' She rubbed her shoulder where she had fallen. Already it was beginning to ache.

'You'd better get back to them,' he snarled. 'And if you want to see my naked body all you have to do is ask.' He turned his back on her and tramped to the pool, where he snatched up the towel and wrapped it tightly around his loins.

Peta found it impossible to move. He had the most gorgeous olive-skinned body. Lean hips, muscular shoulders and arms, but not overtly so; whorls of dark chest hair arrowing downwards, disappearing beneath the white towel. She'd been unable to take her eyes off him, had even been tempted to join him in the pool.

Simply looking at him had stirred her senses, sent the blood scorching through her veins. Want and need had taken over and she'd been on the point of making her presence known when he'd spotted her. She hadn't even had time to anticipate his action before he'd sent her crashing to the floor.

'I thought I told you to get back to the boys.' Andreas's eyes were glacially hard, his whole body tense with rejection. 'If Nikos has come to any harm then you'd better look out.'

Peta snapped back to life, but too late; he was already striding down the mountain. She followed more slowly, conscious that she had neglected her duty and he had every right to be angry, but confident that nothing would have happened to the boys.

For most of the night she had tossed and turned, thinking about Andreas, wondering how he was coping on the couch, almost giving in and suggesting they swap places. She had heard him get up and leave. What had made her decide to follow she didn't know, but she had checked Ben and Nikos first and they were both fast asleep.

If she hadn't been so fascinated by his naked body she would have made her presence known, but one look and she'd been hooked, and the longer she'd stood there the harder it had become to call out. It had triggered so many responses that she'd felt as if she was melting on the spot.

As she'd expected, the boys were still asleep, but Andreas didn't apologise. Instead, after pulling on a pair of shorts, he jumped into the Range Rover. 'I'm going to fetch supplies,' he announced. 'What little I brought won't last long. And I'm warning you, don't leave Nikos alone, not for one second.'

Her eyes widened. 'Don't you think you're overreacting?'

'You'd feel the same if it was Ben,' he told her coldly.

'So what was the point in coming up here if you're going to be paranoid? Nikos is an intelligent boy; he's sure to pick up on it.'

He started the engine. 'What I do is my business and you'd do as well to remember that.'

In other words she was here to do as he asked, not to question it. She heaved a sigh as he disappeared down the mountain. Some adventure this was proving to be. His anger was because she'd had the temerity to stare at his naked body, nothing else; not fear for Nikos. Well, he needn't worry, she wouldn't look at him again.

While waiting for the boys to wake she spent her time cleaning the cabin. It was a fairly impersonal place with not much in the way of ornaments or pictures. The uneven stone walls had once been painted white but were now a dingy grey. It needed sprucing up, she felt, although if it was used so infrequently was it worth it? She couldn't see Andreas feeling the need to escape very often.

In the bedroom she finished putting away her things, hanging Andreas's stuff in the wardrobe, too. It was in one of the drawers that she found the snapshot. Peta stared at it for a long time. Maria was beautiful; there was no getting away from it. Even more beautiful here than she was in the portrait done in oils. Rich raven-black hair, sensual lips and wide-spaced almond-shaped eyes. And so like Nikos that it was no wonder Andreas was reminded of his wife every time he looked at him. There was no way she could compete with a woman like this, with her extraordinary beauty and such a wealth of love for the man behind the camera radiating from her eyes.

The sound of voices had her spinning around. 'Mum, we're hungry.'

The spell was broken. And in half an hour Andreas returned.

They spent most of the day wandering through the forest, the children playing hide-and-seek, splashing beneath waterfalls, finding all sorts of natural treasures which they stuffed into their pockets for looking at again later.

Peta deliberately kept all conversation between herself and Andreas impersonal, which wasn't hard when he virtually ignored her. What was hard was ignoring the messages her body kept relaying. It was impossible to stand close and not be aware of him. Impossible to control the quivering sensations he created inside her.

When night-time came she insisted that he take the bed and she the couch.

'If that is your wish,' he said with pained politeness. 'But don't put yourself out on my behalf.'

'I think it will be best,' she answered.

He made no further objections.

As Peta lay there, curled up in the foetal position, she couldn't help thinking how uncomfortable he must have been. It was no wonder he'd got up at the crack of dawn. Amazingly, though, probably because they'd spent the day in the fresh air, she didn't have any trouble dropping off to sleep.

It didn't please her when she got up the following morning to discover that Andreas had beaten her to it and already gone out, because it meant that he'd had to walk past her, might even have stood looking down at her. Her cheeks grew hot at the thought. Her nightie had ended up as usual around her waist, and although the cover had been pulled over her when she awoke, how was she to know that it hadn't slipped off during the night and Andreas had replaced it?

Where was he? At the pool again? She longed to go and look but knew that she dared not. It didn't stop her imagination running riot, though. It was so easy to picture his hard naked body. He'd been perfectly at ease with it, no inhibitions whatsoever, even when he stood right in front of her. Whereas she, Lord help her, had been whipped by a frenzy of unwanted emotions.

If he'd taken her into his arms at that moment she'd have let him undress her, let him lay her on the ground and make love to her. Even the thought of it sent a wild yearning through her body. She shook her head. *Stop this, Peta,* she warned herself. *Stop it this instant. This man is not for you.*

The shower in the cabin was erratic, to say the least, and as she stood beneath it Peta thought longingly of the natural pool. If only she'd woken before Andreas she could have gone up there herself. Tomorrow, she promised herself. Tomorrow she would do it.

The boys had already eaten their breakfast by the time Andreas returned. He looked hot and his hair was dry, so he'd obviously either not bathed or been out of the pool for some time.

'Where have you been?' Nikos posed the question Peta was dying to ask.

Andreas grinned. 'I thought we'd have a treasure hunt today, if that's all right with you boys? I've been setting it up.'

They both jumped up and down and said yes in unison.

'That's settled, then, but I need my breakfast first.'

Peta thought how much younger he looked when he smiled, and how much more relaxed he was with the boys than he was with her. 'We've had toast and cereal,' she said, 'but if you'd like an omelette I can easily—'

'Toast and cereal will do fine for me, too,' he said easily. 'Nikos, I think you'd better put some sturdier shoes on; you, too, Ben.'

As the boys ran off to do his bidding Andreas followed Peta into the kitchen. 'How was the couch?' he asked casually as she placed cereal boxes on the table and filled a jug with milk.

'I slept OK,' she admitted.

'You looked more comfortable than I felt on it.'

'Are you suggesting that I take the couch every night?' she asked sharply as she sliced bread and placed it beneath the grill. 'Because that wasn't my idea when I offered to change places. I think maybe we should do it turn and turn about.'

'And I think maybe if you stopped being so prickly we could share the bed.'

Peta's back was turned to Andreas as he spoke and she unconsciously stiffened, not turning to face him for several long seconds. 'I can't believe you've said that.'

His lips turned down at the corners and his shoulders lifted slightly. 'It seems a perfectly logical decision.'

'Logical, maybe,' she returned huffily, 'but sensible, no. I can't imagine anything worse than sharing a bed with a man who means nothing to me.' Except that he had the ability to set every one of her nerve-ends quivering whenever he was near. Sleeping with him would prove impossible. Sleep she wouldn't. Ignite she most definitely would.

'It's funny,' he said as he sat down at the table and tipped cornflakes into a bowl. 'My impression is very different. I think I do mean something to you, but I also think that you're scared to admit it.'

'Scared?' she echoed. 'Why should I be scared? I'm my own woman. I have full control of my life.' Hell, what a stupid thing to say. She didn't have control of it at all, he did. He'd had it ever since she'd begun to work for him. She'd used to be in control, yes, but not any longer. Everything he'd asked her to do she'd done, even so far as coming here with him. But she was definitely drawing the line at sharing a bed. All he wanted her for was to satisfy his male hunger, and that she could do without.

'If you have control, why do you fall to pieces whenever I look at you in a certain way? Why do you respond to my kisses?'

'Because you're one hell of a sexy man, that's why,' she flared. 'You might not have been aware of it but every woman in the company used to swoon at the mere sight of you.'

Eyebrows rose. 'Did you?'

'Actually, no,' she admitted. 'And because you stir my senses now it doesn't mean that I want to hop into bed with you. Maybe it's because I was once bitten. I don't know. All I do know is that I'm not prepared to let you use my body.'

Her choice of words had him scowling. 'I don't think I've ever been guilty of using a woman for personal gratification. It's always been a two-way thing.'

'Have there been women since Maria?' she dared to ask.

'Yes.'

'And are you telling me that you didn't use them?'

'I had needs,' he admitted, 'but so did they. And so do you,' he added, his voice deepening to a sensual growl.

Just the way he said it caused the pulse at the base of her throat to flutter. 'But my needs are obviously not as great as yours.'

'I think you've burnt the toast.'

Peta swung around quickly. Smoke was rising from the grill. 'Damn!' she exclaimed, adding a few more choice swear words beneath her breath. 'It's your fault.' She tipped the toast smartly into the bin, but when she reached out for the loaf to cut two more slices he stopped her.

'Don't bother. I'm not that hungry anyway.'

Peta began to cough.

'You'd better get out,' he said, flapping a tea towel to try and get rid of the smoke. 'See if the boys are ready. I'll finish up in here.'

She was glad to go, because not only had the toast nearly set on fire, but she was also on fire. All this talk about sleeping together had set off a chain reaction, and each nerve and vein and pulse that it touched jumped louder than the others until her whole body was jangling.

The boys were outside, raring to go, and she drew in much-needed breaths of fresh mountain air. Not that it did a lot of good. It would take more than air to rid her mind and body of Andreas Papadakis. And the longer they were forced together the harder it was going to be.

When Andreas was ready he handed out the first clue, and after studying it for a few minutes Ben and Nikos ran off, laughing. Peta followed more leisurely, conscious of Andreas a few yards away, his eyes ever-watchful on the boys. And probably on herself, too, though she tried not to think of it.

A quarter of an hour passed, and they had all found the second clue and worked it out when Andreas fell into step at her side. 'The boys are enjoying themselves.'

'Yes, indeed,' she agreed. 'It was a good idea of yours.'

'Perhaps now we can finish our conversation.'

Peta frowned as she quickly looked at him. 'What are you talking about?'

'Needs. The fact that you said mine was greater than yours. I don't agree.'

'Not when you're the one who's pushing for an affair?' she asked scornfully.

'Not an affair. You make it sound sordid.'

'So what is it you want?' she demanded. 'You know as well as I do that you're still in love with your wife. No one will ever be able to take her place. What would you do if I let you make love to me? Pretend that I was Maria?'

Oh, Lord, she shouldn't have said that. It was cruel and unasked-for. And when she saw the hurt in his eyes and the angry black shadow across his face she clapped her hands to her mouth. 'I'm sorry,' she said quietly. 'So sorry.'

CHAPTER NINE

ANDREAS walked away from Peta. Her careless words hurt, deeply. If that was the impression he gave then he was doing something wrong. It was true, no one would ever take Maria's place; she would always be very special in his heart. But Peta was different in every way, surely she knew that? He wanted her for herself alone, not as a replacement for Maria.

He strode after the boys; they were having a whale of a time, laughing and running, arguing light-heartedly over the clue, eventually finding the ancient olive tree with the clue tucked into one of its lower branches.

He had thought today would be fun for all of them, had never expected Peta to say something so hurtful. Admittedly she had immediately apologised, but it was the fact that she even thought he would do something like that. If he made love to Peta he certainly wouldn't be thinking about Maria. The two women were as different as chalk from cheese.

'Steady, boys,' he said as they came hurtling back down towards him.

'This is fun,' said Nikos. 'Where's Peta? Why isn't she joining in?'

Andreas turned and was surprised to see that she was nowhere in sight. Surely she hadn't gone back to the house? But he dared not go looking and leave the boys. Although he felt reasonably confident that whoever was threatening to kidnap his son wouldn't trace them up here, he wasn't prepared to take the risk.

'I guess she's still searching for the clue,' he said.

Ben laughed. 'Mummy's not as clever as us, is she?' And he ran off again.

Peta didn't know how she could have been so thoughtless. Andreas felt bad enough about losing his wife without her slamming into him like that. She'd been guilty of thinking of herself alone.

She'd sat down on a boulder when Andreas walked off, burying her head in her hands, wondering how she could rectify the situation. All she could do was apologise again, but the truth was no amount of apology would set the matter right. She'd been completely out of order.

'Mummy, what's the matter?'

Peta looked up as Ben came running towards her, Nikos not far behind.

'I have a headache,' she lied, thinking quickly.

'Does that mean we have to go back?'

'Of course not, darling,' she said, shaking her head. 'All I needed was a few moments to myself. How are you doing?'

'We've found two clues,' he answered importantly, his little chest swelling with pride. 'Will you be all right if we carry on?'

'Of course your mother will be all right.' Andreas spoke over her son's shoulder. 'I'll look after her.'

Peta's mouth twisted wistfully. She'd give anything to be able to retract those thoughtlessly spoken words. There was still pain in Andreas's deep brown eyes, but, thank goodness, he didn't look as though he was going to hold it against her.

'What can I say?' she asked, looking up at him sorrowfully as the boys ran away.

'I think it's best forgotten. Let's follow.'

They chatted as the boys raced around, and on the surface they were friends again, but the intimacy was lost. There were no more suggestions on his part that they share a bed. No innuendoes, no soft, hungry glances. It was gone. Dashed away by a few words.

She ought to be pleased, but she wasn't. Contrarily, she wanted him, wanted to share closeness with him because he excited her. He had awoken long-dead feelings. He had made her feel all woman again. No man had done that in a long time.

Ought she to apologise once more? But one look at his face told her it would do no good. There was a sternness to the beetling brows, a tightness to his mouth, and although when he spoke to her he sounded perfectly normal Peta knew that inside he was hurting like hell.

And she didn't blame him. What she had said was unforgivable.

The boys found the treasure—a carved wooden boat they could play with in the bathing pool—and they all made their way home.

For the rest of the day Andreas played with the boys and Peta busied herself around the little house.

'I think it will be best if you take the bed,' said Andreas later that evening when the boys were asleep and they were sitting outside, enjoying the stillness.

'Why?' she wanted to know. She didn't deserve the bed. 'It's not fair on you. I'll sleep on the couch. I can quite easily manage there.'

'I said, you take the bed,' he answered tersely. 'There's nothing more to be said.'

Peta couldn't understand. If she had to sleep on the couch for the rest of their stay it would be what she deserved. Why wasn't he punishing her? Why was he punishing himself?

'Just for tonight, then,' she agreed.

'Every night, dammit!' he shot back. 'Just do as you're told.'

'But—'

'But nothing.' Stony brown eyes fixed unrelentingly on hers. 'Go to bed, Peta. Go now!'

It was a long and lonely night. Peta tossed and turned, unable to stop thinking about Andreas, wondering whether he was managing to sleep, how comfortable he was. If it hadn't been for her crass insensitivity they might well have been sleeping together.

Her heart pounded at the very thought. But it was one best not delved into. It would never happen, not now. She had well and truly put a stop to any romantic developments.

During the next few days Andreas was friendly enough on the surface. Ben and Nikos never suspected that anything was wrong, but for some unknown reason the fact that he showed not the remotest interest in her made Peta want him all the more.

She was consumed with a hunger she had never felt before. She craved to feel his body against hers, she desperately wanted his kisses, and the longer time went on the more she desired him.

It was becoming an impossible situation.

'How much longer do you plan on staying here?' she asked as they sat outside one evening after the boys were in bed. It was quiet save for the rustle in the trees and the occasional squawk of a bird. 'You can't ignore your business interests for ever.' In fact she was surprised that he had stayed away from them for so long.

'Everything is being well looked after,' he told her

brusquely. 'And I intend to remain here for as long as is necessary.'

'How will you know when the kidnapper has lost interest? What if he's staking out your mother's house, waiting for you to return? What if he kidnaps your mother instead?'

This latter was obviously something that had never occurred to him, for his eyes snapped open. Then he gave a harsh laugh. 'Kidnapping my mother would be their worst nightmare. She'd give them hell. They'd soon realise their mistake.'

'Whatever, we can't stay here indefinitely,' she said.

'Getting fed up, are we?' he asked with a further flash of his magnificent chestnut eyes.

Peta shook her head, auburn hair flying. 'No, but I imagine the boys will get bored soon. There's only so much to do here.'

'They're not showing any signs.'

She shrugged but didn't answer. It was a pointless conversation. She should never have started it.

'I think that you're the one who's finding life dull,' he said softly. And, when there was still no response from her, 'Perhaps it's because I'm not paying you any attention?'

His words had her sucking in a horrified breath and she jumped to her feet and walked a few paces away. Was he saying that he was deliberately leaving her alone? That it wasn't because of what she'd said about his wife?

'It's what you want, isn't it?' he asked.

'Of course.'

'And yet it makes you look miserable.'

'It's not because of—'

Her words were cut off when Andreas whirled her to

face him and his mouth claimed hers in a kiss that sent her spinning into space. Yes, this was what she wanted. *This!*

She felt herself melting, every one of her senses leaping into action. The exciting male smell of him filled her nostrils, teasing and tormenting, making her wriggle against him, inciting him to deepen the kiss, his tongue plunging and thrilling.

He tasted good, oh, so good. This was definitely what she had wanted, had needed, even, over the last few days. She had thought he would never kiss her again, but apparently he had been as miserable as she, and now he was unable to contain his hunger.

When she dared to open her eyes he was looking at her with a smouldering intensity that tightened every one of her muscles and sent shock wave reeling after shock wave. He lifted his mouth for a fraction of a second to utter gruffly, 'You're beautiful.'

And so was he! So was he. Her answer was a mew of satisfaction, and when one hand crept beneath the hem of her cotton top to slide purposefully towards her breast Peta drew in a deep breath of anticipation—and held it. She fitted into the palm of his hand perfectly, but it was not until his thumb grazed across her already erect and expectant nipple that she expelled the air from her body and gave a further cry of pleasure.

Whether he was using her or not, it suddenly didn't matter. She would be a fool to deny what her body so badly wanted. As she involuntarily ground her hips against his she felt the full, exciting extent of his arousal, heard the groan deep in his throat, and gave an answering whimper as his hand tightened over her breast.

'This is no good,' he declared edgily. 'I've been patient long enough.' And with an expertise that sent her mind reeling he whipped her white top over her head and flicked the clasp on her bra. In a matter of seconds her breasts were exposed to his eager eyes.

'Ben and Nikos!' she exclaimed. 'What if—?'

'They're fast asleep,' he assured her, leading her indoors, laying her down on the couch so that he could kneel in front of her. When he began an assault on her breasts with fingers and teeth and tongue Peta very soon grew past caring. This was heaven. This was the stuff dreams were made of. He was quickly transporting her to another world.

She lay back and wallowed in the sensations he was creating. She felt a desperate, urgent, aching hunger to be made love to. No man had ever aroused her to such depths. His tongue flicked the sensitive nub of her breast, his teeth grazed and incited, and she moved uncontrollably beneath him.

'Let's go to bed,' he growled, lifting his head to look into the deep ocean-blue of her eyes.

Peta saw her own raw hunger mirrored on his face. And hunger won. She gave a faint nod and allowed him to lift her effortlessly into his arms. As he walked slowly into the next room he trailed kisses across her brow and over her nose. He kissed each eyelid in turn, each eyebrow, and by the time he put her down her heart was pounding fit to burst.

The vague notion that she was making a grave mistake entered her mind, but she dismissed it instantly and when he kissed her again she entwined her arms around the back of his neck and held him close.

'This is what you want?' he asked roughly.

'Yes!' she whispered urgently. 'Yes, yes, yes!'

'There'll be no regrets?' He began to ease her skirt down over her hips, Peta obligingly lifting her body.

'None at all.'

'You're sure, now?' It was the turn of her panties next, brief triangles of white lace that hid almost nothing.

Peta was beyond answering. Not very long ago she would have felt embarrassed lying in front of Andreas stark naked, but there was something very erotic about having him undress her, especially when he began to strip off his own clothes, too.

When he lay beside her it was not only a joining of bodies but also a joining of senses. They were each hotly aroused, each hungry for the pleasure that lay ahead.

His hands and mouth explored and tormented every inch. 'You're incredible,' he muttered as she heaved and wriggled beneath his touch.

She was fast losing any semblance of self-control, touching him now, stroking and kissing his nipples, his chest; doing to him what he was doing to her. Bodies melded, bodies overheated, bodies grew desperate with need.

He took her hand, urged her to hold him, to feel for herself what she was doing to him. Her touch was almost his undoing. He moved himself over her. She spread her legs instinctively, obligingly. 'Are you sure?' he asked hoarsely. 'There'll be no going back once I—'

'I'm sure, Andreas,' she groaned. 'Take me. Now! Make me yours.'

She felt him hesitate and knew that she had once again spoken without thinking. *Make me yours.* She would never be his. Not in the true sense of the word. He would never ask her to marry him. This was pure sex—pure, unadulterated sex. Two consenting adults behaving in the way that man and woman had since time immemorial.

Now was the time to back out, now was the time to put a stop to it, but she couldn't. Her need was too great. His need was too great.

Already he was entering her, already she was rising to meet him, muscles clenching, holding, urging. It was all and more than she had expected and the final climax lifted them both to another plane. She couldn't help crying out and Andreas groaned his satisfaction too as they collapsed in a heap of slick sweat and pleasure.

But their breathing had not even returned to normal before Nikos came running into the room. 'Daddy, where's Ben?' he asked. 'Where have you taken him?'

CHAPTER TEN

'BEN isn't here, son,' answered Andreas, pushing himself up on one elbow. 'Are you sure you weren't dreaming? I've not been in your room.'

'Yes, you have, I saw you,' Nikos insisted. 'You told him to be quiet. I was awake because I heard noises.'

Peta started to shake as the horror of the situation began to sink in. Andreas shot to his feet and tugged on his trousers. 'How long ago was this, Nikos?'

'Not long. Where is Ben? What's happened?'

'I don't know, but I intend to find out. Peta, you stay here with Nikos.' He was out of the room in two bounds.

Outside, Andreas paused for a second or two, listening. The air up here in the mountains was perfectly still; every little noise carried. But he heard nothing except the scurrying of a tiny animal in the undergrowth.

But then, as his ears became more attuned, he heard what he had most feared—the faint drone of an engine. He swore loudly, dashed back inside for his car keys and was out again in seconds. He ignored Peta's demands that he take her with him, even though he knew what she must be going through. And it was all his fault, dammit.

If he hadn't weakened none of this would have happened. If he hadn't listened to the urges of his body Ben would be safe now. And Lord knew what the kidnapper would do when he realised he had the wrong boy.

It wasn't yet completely dark and he careered down

the mountainside with little heed for his own safety. He needed to catch up with the kidnapper before he reached the main road, because if he didn't he would have no way of knowing which way he had gone.

Peta would never forgive him if anything happened to her son. Ben was her whole life; she idolised him. She'd even shown him, Andreas, the error of his ways. Nikos had almost always been left to his own devices, or to the care of his nanny, before he'd met Peta. Through her he'd realised how much Nikos was missing out on a father's influence. He'd made a pact with himself that in future he'd be different.

Andreas came to the bottom of the track and there was no sign of the other vehicle as he slithered to a halt. Which way should he go? Left or right? He tried the listening technique again but there was other traffic on the road. He took a guess at left, but after a few miles realised it was like searching for a needle in a haystack. He had no idea what sort of vehicle he was looking for.

By the time he got back up the mountain Peta was frantic. She practically fell on him as he climbed out of his vehicle, her face crumpling when she saw that he was alone.

'I'm sorry,' he said, holding her so tightly against him that she couldn't breathe. 'I've done everything I can. It's now in the hands of the police.'

The tears that she had bravely held back in front of Nikos streamed unchecked down her cheeks. She blamed herself. It had been sheer madness giving in to Andreas, except that she'd been equally guilty of wanting to feed her need. They'd been so intent on themselves that they'd heard nothing of what was going on around them.

Quite clearly the kidnapper had been watching the house. He'd probably been staking it out for days, waiting for the right opportunity. He'd seen Andreas half undress her, he'd watched as she was carried into the house, probably even leered through the window as Andreas had sucked and tormented her breasts. It didn't bear thinking about.

And when they'd gone into the bedroom he'd taken his chance, knowing that they were too carried away to hear anything that was going on.

'Oh, God, Andreas,' she sobbed. 'If anything happens to Ben I'll kill myself.'

'Don't talk like that. Nothing will happen to him,' he assured her gently, pulling a clean white handkerchief out of his pocket and pressing it into her hand. 'When they realise they've got the wrong little guy he'll be released, you'll see.'

But Peta wasn't convinced. 'They might not,' she sniffed. 'They might—get rid of him. They could do anything.' Every worst-case scenario was running through her mind.

'The most they'll do is demand money, the same as they would if they'd kidnapped Nikos. It's all they're after, Peta. I know what they're like.'

'How do you know?' she demanded, dabbing her eyes ineffectually because the tears wouldn't stop coming.

His mouth tightened grimly. 'Believe me, I do; it's the way these men work. The police will be here shortly, and after that we're going back down to my mother's.'

'You—you said we'd be s-safe here,' she blubbered.

'I thought we would. I'm so sorry, Peta.' His arms tightened around her once again, trying to reassure her but having little effect. 'I'll do everything I can to ensure Ben is returned to you safely.'

Meaning he'd pay the ransom. Which was the least he could do under the circumstances, she thought bitterly. And yet even as she leaned into his body his strength supported her. The warmth of him consoled her. She had no right to blame Andreas. He couldn't have been more concerned had it been Nikos.

'Oughtn't we to stay?' she asked huskily. 'If—if they're going to return Ben this is where they'll bring him, won't they? And if they send a ransom note it will also come here.'

'I expect so,' he agreed, 'but I think it's no place for you to be now. There'll be a twenty-four-hour guard, don't worry.'

The next few hours passed in a blur. It was embarrassing having to tell the two policemen what they'd been doing while Ben was being kidnapped, even though their faces remained impassive. And they assured her that at first light someone would be back to search the area around the house. She was still tearful when they eventually returned to his parent's home.

Mrs Papadakis, having been warned beforehand what had happened, couldn't have been nicer. The frostiness had gone, the haughtiness had gone, and she hugged Peta as though she was someone very special. 'My son, he tells me about it. I am so sorry that this has happened to you in my country. I hope Ben will be returned to you very soon. Meantime you must not worry. Everything is being done that can be done.'

Peta nodded, not trusting herself to speak.

'I think you should rest; I think you should try to sleep.'

'I won't sleep,' she insisted, shaking her head, 'not until Ben's been found.'

'At least lie down, child. Andreas, take Peta to her room.'

Nikos had already been dispatched to bed and reluctantly Peta allowed herself to be helped. Andreas sat down on the edge of the bed with her. 'When this is all over I'm going to make it up to you, I promise.'

'When this is all over you won't see me again,' she assured him fiercely, ignoring the startled look in his eyes. She had made up her mind that she was going back to England and looking for a new job. Living with Andreas was too dangerous. Not only because of what had happened to Ben but for her own peace of mind, too. She simply wasn't the type who could indulge in an affair. 'If I hadn't allowed myself to be manipulated by you none of this would have happened,' she pointed out. 'I should never have taken the nanny's job.'

'Don't talk like that, Peta,' he said gently. 'It's my fault; I take full responsibility. I more or less said that if you didn't you'd be out of work. It was cruel of me, but I just knew you'd be perfect. I never expected this to happen.' He punched his thigh, not once but several times. 'Here was I, trying to protect Nikos, and now, because some incompetent stuffed up, you are out of your mind with worry. I hold myself entirely responsible.'

'We're both to blame,' amended Peta wearily.

'Who'd have thought that he'd have the audacity to enter the house while we were all there?'

'We left the door open.'

He nodded grimly. 'We were too wrapped up in ourselves.'

'I'd like you to leave,' she said now, lying back on the bed, utterly weary but knowing that she wouldn't sleep, not until Ben was safely returned.

She was mistaken. The moment she closed her eyes she fell asleep, but it wasn't a restful sleep. She dreamt of Ben, dreamt that his kidnappers were torturing him, and she thrashed about on the bed, calling to him, telling him that she was coming. She was woken by Andreas gently shaking her. 'It's all right, Peta, it's just a bad dream.'

'Ben?' She sat bolt upright.

'No news yet, I'm afraid.'

'What time is it? How long have I been asleep?' She felt guilty for daring to drop off while her son's life was in danger.

'It's midday.'

Her eyes shot wide. 'And you've heard nothing?'

'Not yet.'

'No ransom note?'

'No.'

'What's taking so long? I want my son; he'll be terrified. He's never been away from me before.'

'I know.' He held her gently, a finger stroking the hair away from her face, cradling her; trying to soothe her. And it helped—a little! She liked the feel of him; he was strong and powerful and comforting; he'd take care of her; he'd help her find Ben, come hell or high water.

She leaned into him, felt his strength become her strength. 'What can we do?' she asked clearly.

'We're having lunch here, my mother has ordered it, and then I'm going to see the police again. Find out what progress has been made.'

'I'm coming with you,' she said firmly.

She ate only a mouthful of fish and half a grilled tomato before declaring she'd had enough. 'I can't eat while I don't know where Ben is. Do you think he's being looked after, Andreas? Do you think he'll come to any harm?'

Before he could answer Anna tapped on the door and brought in an envelope, which she passed to Andreas, speaking quickly in her own language.

He ripped it open and his eyes hardened as he scanned the contents. Silently he handed it to Peta. It was a demand for the million pounds to be paid in English currency.

'I wonder if he realises that he's got the wrong boy,' mused Andreas.

'Would it make any difference?' she demanded. 'We gave a pretty good indication of how close we are.' Her cheeks flushed as she recalled what they'd been up to.

'I know it's no time to tell you,' he said gruffly, 'but you were magnificent, Peta.'

'No, it's not the right time,' she snapped. 'What are we going to do about this?' She waved the note in front of his face.

'Take it to the police, of course.'

'He says not to.'

'Don't they always?'

'I don't want to do anything that will jeopardise Ben's safety.'

'I wish I knew who was doing this to me,' he said grimly.

'To *you*?' queried Peta. 'What the hell have you got to worry about?' She wished he hadn't reminded her how good it had been in bed. As a matter of fact she never wanted to be reminded of it again. It was a moment in her life that she would regret for as long as she lived.

'Do you think that because he isn't my son I don't

care?' he questioned, brown eyes suddenly hard. 'Hell, Peta, you should know me better than that.'

'I don't know what to think any more,' she replied. 'All I want is my son back.'

The next few days were sheer hell. The waiting drove Peta almost insane. Andreas was a tower of strength, but she couldn't help thinking that if it hadn't been for him none of this would have happened. And she was firm in her resolve that after it was over she would get well out of his life.

Mrs Papadakis walked into the room one day when Peta was sobbing into Andreas's shoulder; his mother motioned him to leave. She sat next to Peta on the sofa and talked calmly and soothingly until finally she stopped crying.

'I can't bear this any longer,' Peta whimpered.

'I know, child. I know, but you must be patient. Let me tell you something.'

Peta scrubbed ineffectually at her face, knowing it would do nothing to help the redness of her nose and eyes. Oh, Lord, when was this nightmare going to end?

'I know how you are feeling. Andreas's brother, he was kidnapped when he was about Ben's age.'

'Oh!' Peta clapped a hand to her mouth. 'Andreas never told me.' Actually, it was just as well; she'd have been paranoid. And it was clearly the reason why he hadn't initially told his mother about the threats. He'd wanted to protect her, to save unhappy memories flooding back. And now she must be hurting, too, reliving that painful time. It accounted for the way her attitude had changed so dramatically. Here was another woman going through exactly the same trauma.

'It would seem,' went on the older woman, 'that anyone who has great wealth is a ready-made target for such ruthless people. I wanted my husband to pay; I would have given up everything, *everything* to get Christos back. But my husband, he thought he knew best. He did not tell the police; he thought he could handle it himself. He did not even tell me when he went to meet the kidnapper. He almost paid for it with his life. Fortunately I got my son back, and my husband; he healed in time. So you see, you must be patient, you must let Andreas and the police work out the best plan of action. It is the only way you can ensure both your son's and my son's safety.'

Through the blur of fresh tears Peta saw that Mrs Papadakis was crying, too.

Finally, after days of waiting, the kidnapper phoned Andreas, giving a time and place where he wanted the money deposited. 'The kid's told me he's not your son, but it makes no difference. One boy is as good as another. And since he's the son of a girl who would appear, from what I saw, to be very special to you—' there was a sickening leer in his voice '—it will be in your best interests to pay. Let the girl bring the money.'

As Peta carried the bag containing the ransom her heart threatened to jump out of her chest. It beat so hard that it was painful and she could hardly breathe. She was supposed to put the bag into a railway-station deposit box—she had the key the kidnapper had sent in her pocket—but she felt like dropping the case now and running. This was the most dangerous thing she'd ever had to do.

Except that it was Ben's life she was carrying in her hand. A million pounds for Ben's life, and Andreas was prepared to pay it! If all went according to plan they'd catch the kidnapper and he'd get his money back. But if it didn't, if she got Ben back but no money, then Andreas would be out of pocket. She would indeed be indebted to him then. She wouldn't be able to walk away.

As she walked into the station Peta knew that she must remain calm. She mustn't draw attention to herself. But she couldn't help wondering whether the kidnapper was watching. Her eyes darted this way and that but no one took any notice of the auburn-haired English girl in a flowered dress and sun-hat, with a battered briefcase tucked under her arm.

She almost expected a gun in her back as she deposited the case, then scolded herself for letting her imagination run away. It was a relief when she was back outside in the hot Greek sunshine, and an even bigger relief when Andreas drew up in his car. 'My brave darling,' he said as she virtually fell into it.

Peta closed her eyes and rested her head on his shoulder for a few seconds. But it wasn't over yet. Already plain-clothes policemen would have moved into the station. The waiting game had begun in earnest.

Twenty-four hours went by and the money hadn't been collected. Peta was inconsolable. And then came the call they were waiting for.

Andreas raced out to his car, Peta close on his heels, and as they reached the station they were in time to see a short, stocky man with light ginger hair being led away by two unsmiling policemen. The man looked across at Andreas with hatred in his eyes. Behind them a policewoman was holding Ben's hand.

As soon as he saw his mother he flew across to her. Peta's relief was so overwhelming that she burst into tears, and it was a moment or two before she realised that Andreas actually knew the man who had stolen her child.

'Craig Eden, no less,' he said.

'You know this man?' asked one of the policemen.

'He knows me all right,' declared the kidnapper fiercely. 'He took everything I owned. Left me with not a penny to support my wife and family.'

Andreas shook his head. 'That's not strictly true, Craig.'

'Seems a pretty reasonable description of the facts to me,' he growled.

'Your company was in trouble. I bought it. I gave you a fair price. End of story.'

'A fair price? Is that what you call it?' sneered Craig Eden, his top lip curled, his eyes brilliantly hard. 'You didn't buy my debts, did you? No, you were too crafty for that. By the time I'd finished paying out there was nothing left. Have you found out what it feels like to be afraid? To be haunted by a fear night and day? It's what I felt when I thought my house was going to be taken off me. You broke me, Andreas Papadakis, and I saw no reason why I should live on the breadline while you lead a life of luxury.'

'Except that it didn't work out, did it?' scorned Andreas. 'Breaking the law never does. You're not quite as clever as you thought you were.'

As the police led the man away Andreas put his arms around Peta and Ben and for a moment none of them spoke, the sheer relief of the moment so overwhelming. Ben was crying, tears streamed down Peta's cheeks, and when Andreas finally said, 'Let's get into the car,' she heard a break in his voice, too.

On the journey back to Andreas's mother's house Peta sat in the back with Ben, her arm tightly around him, never wanting to let him go again. 'Did the man hurt you, sweetheart?' she asked gently.

'No, Mummy, he was a kind man.'

'Did he feed you?'

'Of course. I had lots to eat. I asked him why he had taken me to his house. I told him I wanted to go home. I said that if he didn't take me back Andreas would come and get me. Andreas, were you really going to pay all that money for me?'

'Yes, I was, Ben.'

'Wow, you must be very rich. Are you the richest man in the world?'

Andreas looked at Peta in the interior mirror and smiled gently. 'Yes, I think I must be. If not the richest, the most fortunate.'

It had taken one small child and one very beautiful young woman to make him realise that it was time he let go of the past and got on with his future. He loved Peta. He loved her with all his heart. The discovery was a glorious, uplifting experience. It was as though all the weight of the world had been lifted from his shoulders. He had lost so much in his life that he couldn't bear it if he lost Peta now.

And yet, looking at her in the mirror, he could see that now wasn't the time to tell her. All her love was for her son at this moment, and it probably always would be. She had told him more than once that there was no place in her life for a man.

Somehow he would have to change her mind.

CHAPTER ELEVEN

'YOU deserve a holiday,' Andreas said softly. 'It's time to relax and enjoy yourself once more.'

It was a few days after Ben's release. They'd all, including his mother, talked about nothing else except the kidnapping. About the way Craig Eden had tried to play on their feelings. The way it had been a rerun of Christos's disappearance. The fear the whole thing had engendered. In its own way it had made a deep impact on all three of them.

'We could leave the boys with my mother and—'

'How can you even suggest such a thing?' Peta demanded, blue eyes incredulous. 'Don't you know what I've gone through because of you? I want to go home,' she stormed, shaking her head violently. 'And when I say home I mean back to my own place. You'll have to find another nanny for Nikos. I can't do it any more.'

The shock that ran through him felt like a rocket out of control; it ricocheted through every space in his body. She wanted to leave him! Move out of his life altogether! For the first time in his life he was at a loss for words. 'Why?'

'Do you need to ask?' Her gorgeous eyes flashed, her lovely lips curled, twisting his stomach as he looked at them. 'But apart from the obvious,' she added, 'I'm not cut out to be a nanny. I'm not even sure that I want to do office work any longer.'

In other words she wanted to be free of him! It was like a knife stabbing into his chest. 'So what do you want?' he asked, aware of the gruffness to his tone. 'You need to support Ben. I pay you excellent wages. You won't do better anywhere.' Lord, it sounded as though he was pleading with her, and he was. He couldn't afford to let her go.

'Money isn't everything,' she riposted.

'That isn't what you said to me before.'

'I hadn't discovered then that living with you was like living on the edge of an active volcano. And don't try to change my mind, Andreas, because you'll be wasting your time.'

'Very well, we'll go back,' he said reluctantly, even though he wasn't sure whether letting Peta have her own way was the wisest thing to do. Ought he to tell her now that he loved her? No, it had to be when she was in the right frame of mind. She would think he was using it as a tool to persuade her to stay. She wouldn't believe him.

He was aware that she deeply regretted letting him make love to her, that she constantly blamed herself for Ben being kidnapped; it was a guilt she was going to live with for the rest of her life. But didn't she realise that he felt equally guilty? He couldn't have felt worse had it been his own son. And he wanted to make it up to her. He had thought that a holiday would be the answer, the perfect antidote. Clearly wishful thinking on his part.

Peta had slowly and surely wormed her way into his heart. She had shown him the error of his ways where Nikos was concerned; she had made him see that there was life after the death of a loved one. The trouble was she didn't want a man in her life. She was happy living alone. Occasionally she forgot herself and let her emotions ride high, but almost immediately she regretted it and shut herself back into her ice palace.

Was time and patience the answer? Or should he simply let her go?

But he knew he couldn't do that. If he had to go back to the beginning and pursue her all over again then he would. He would do it differently this time. He would do it the old-fashioned way, with flowers and gifts, and he would never, ever use his authority on her again.

'My mother will be extremely disappointed,' he told her now. 'I think she was looking forward to having the boys.'

Peta's eyes flashed her indignation. 'You spoke to her before me?'

'I needed to make sure she'd have them before I asked you.'

'You mean you thought that you'd *tell* me what we were going to do, the same as always. You never consider anyone else, do you, Andreas? You make up your mind and everyone's supposed to fall in. Well, not this girl, not any longer. I've had enough of following orders. In future I'm going to do what *I* want to do. How soon can we go home?'

He was stunned anew by her outburst. He hadn't realised quite how strongly she felt. He was very tempted to answer in kind. But that would get him nowhere with a woman like Peta. Patience and consideration was the name of the game now.

'I'll make the arrangements,' he said.

Nikos and Ben were as disappointed as he was, and made their feelings very clear, but Peta was adamant.

It was late when they arrived in Southampton. Peta had hardly spoken on the flight. She'd sunk into a world of her own. Most situations he could handle, but for once he didn't know what to do.

'Your property was let on a monthly lease,' he reminded her as he drove to his own house, 'so it might be a little while before you can go back.'

Peta's eyes shot wide. 'I can't wait a whole month.'

'I promise I won't let any harm come to Ben again.'

'It's not that,' she snapped.

No, it was him she didn't want to live with. Because he'd made love to her she'd decided that she wanted nothing more to do with him. She felt that he'd overstepped the mark, even though she herself had been willing. It had been a turning point in their relationship, one that she didn't want to face. That and the fact that Ben had been kidnapped while they were making love. The two would be associated in her mind for ever.

Peta was afraid. Afraid that if she was forced to live in the same house as Andreas for any length of time she would give in to the yearnings of her body. There had to be another solution. She could, of course, spend the time with her parents—they would love to have her and Ben—but she didn't see that as the answer either. Her mother would ask far too many pertinent questions, ones that she wasn't yet ready to answer.

The following morning she was relieved to find that Andreas had already left for Linam's when she got up. The boys played happily with their Scalextric and she helped Bess with the washing. Not that the housekeeper wanted her to, but she needed something to take her mind off Andreas and the love that she felt for him.

'Does Andreas ever mention his wife?' she tentatively asked the other woman.

'Quite often,' she admitted with the widest of smiles. 'There's no escaping the fact that he used to adore that woman. I can't see him ever marrying again. Pity, though. It's all wrong that a man like him should remain single for ever. Why do you ask? Do you fancy him yourself?'

Peta turned her head away so that Bess wouldn't see the quick colour that warmed her cheeks. 'Heavens, no. He's too demanding. Not my type at all.'

'What is your type?' asked the housekeeper, nothing but warm interest on her face.

'I'll know when I meet him,' returned Peta quickly. 'Shall I go and peg these out?' She now knew for sure that Andreas had no serious intentions where she was concerned. An affair was most definitely all that he wanted. It wasn't worth the heartache.

When Andreas returned he was thankfully not alone. 'Peta, I'd like you to meet my brother, Christos. Christos, this is Peta.'

'Nikos's nanny,' informed Peta, taking his hand. She saw Andreas's frown but ignored it. She felt it necessary to make it perfectly clear what her position was in this household.

Christos's handshake was firm and warm, his smile full of genuine interest. He was a couple of inches shorter than Andreas but with the same black hair, although his eyes were a lighter brown and his face less aggressively male. 'I've heard a lot about you from the staff at Linam's. They were sorry to see you go.'

'I was given no choice.' She heard Andreas's indrawn breath but she didn't look at him. 'And I won't be Nikos's nanny for much longer either. I'm looking for work elsewhere.'

'You are?' Christos showed his surprise. 'Why's that? Doesn't my brother pay you enough?' It was meant as a joke but Andreas didn't smile.

'It's not the money. I just don't like being a nanny.'

'You could go back to Linam's. They'd welcome you with open arms.'

He had more of an accent than his brother and she found it very attractive.

Andreas grunted something that sounded like an affirmative but Peta knew that she would never work for him again. She wanted to distance herself as far away as possible.

'Are you joining us for dinner?' asked Christos.

'Of course she is,' said Andreas before she could speak.

There he went again, telling her what to do. Her blue eyes flashed daggers in his direction and if Christos hadn't been there she would have told him exactly what she thought of him. Instead she smiled sweetly at his brother. 'It would be my pleasure.'

During the meal Christos seemed unable to take his eyes off her. 'Tell me all about yourself,' he said. 'My brother here has been remarkably reticent where you're concerned. All I know is that you have an eight-year-old son who was kidnapped. You must have been out of your mind with worry.'

Peta nodded. 'Indeed I was. They were the blackest days of my life.' Blacker even than when Joe had dumped her, and that had been bad enough. 'But all's well that ends well,' she added brightly.

'Do you have any brothers or sisters?'

'No, there's just me—and my parents. They live in Cornwall.'

'Do they know about the kidnapping?' He'd stopped eating and was giving her his undivided attention.

'Goodness, no,' she said with a half-laugh. 'I rang today to let them know I'm back but I didn't want to worry them.'

'They'd think Andreas wasn't looking after you properly, is that it?' he asked with a grin and a sideways glance at his brother.

Andreas scowled, and the longer she talked with Christos the blacker his face got. Peta pretended not to notice. She liked Christos. He was easy to talk to and genuinely friendly and interested. She couldn't see him ever barking orders the way Andreas did. She would like to bet that he got on well with the staff at Linam's.

'How do you like working in England?' she asked.

'Very much. I think I'd like to live here. How about letting me take over Linam's altogether, Andreas?'

Andreas shook his head decisively. 'No go, Christos. I thought you were eager to return to Greece?'

Christos looked at Peta and his dark eyes were meaningful. 'I hadn't reckoned on meeting this charming young lady. How about letting me take you out tomorrow night, Peta?'

'I don't think that would be a good idea,' growled Andreas.

Christos shot him a quick, startled look. 'Am I treading on toes here? I had no idea. I'm—'

'Of course not,' said Peta swiftly. 'And, yes, I'd love to come out with you.' Quite why she had said that she didn't know. But Andreas didn't own her. Why shouldn't she go out with Christos? It would be a fun, no-strings-attached night. She'd be able to relax and let her hair down—something she was finding it increasingly difficult to do with Andreas.

Christos smiled but Andreas's eyes were hard and narrowed, and later that evening he came to Peta's room. She was undressed and ready for bed when he pushed open the door. He didn't even knock, and she didn't have to look at his face to know what he'd come for. Every muscle in her body grew tense.

'What game are you playing?' he demanded. 'What made you say you'd go out with Christos?'

'Why shouldn't I?' she asked with the characteristic lift of her chin. 'You don't own me.'

'I don't own you, no, but I thought we meant something to each other.'

'Then you thought wrong, Andreas. I should never have given in to you. It was a huge mistake. I don't want to get involved with anyone. I thought you knew that.'

'Not ever?' he asked quietly.

'Not ever.'

'Then why are you going out with Christos?'

'Because he looks as though he'll be fun. I need a little lightness in my life at this moment.'

'He fancies you.'

'Nonsense,' she retorted. 'He's only just met me.'

'That doesn't stop it. I too fancied you from the word go. It's a male thing. It's what develops from it that's the problem.'

A shock wave sizzled through Peta's body. Andreas had fancied her from the beginning? He'd sure had a funny way of showing it. He'd done nothing but bark and bawl at her from the very second she'd set foot in his office.

'Let me tell you,' she said, eyeing him boldly, 'nothing will develop between me and Christos. You, above all people, should know that.'

'I know that when a girl meets the right man nothing can stop it.'

'And you think Christos might be the right man for me?'

'Who's to know?' he asked with a very foreign shrug.

'Are you jealous, Andreas?' She knew that he couldn't be, but what other possible reason was there for his behaviour?

'I simply want to make sure that you know what you're doing. Christos is a charmer. Make sure you don't get your fingers burnt.'

And Andreas didn't think he was a charmer himself? Heavens, he had charmed the socks off her. He had made her fall so deeply in love with him that no man would ever interest her again. Christos was merely a diversion, someone to take her mind off her aching heart.

She closed her eyes. 'There's no chance of me doing that,' she said in a soft whisper. And when she opened them again he had taken a step towards her.

Peta backed away, felt the bed behind her legs, and knew that she had nowhere to run. Panic spread through her. 'If you wouldn't mind I'd like to go to bed,' she said sharply.

A slow smile spread across his face. 'That's the best invitation I've had in a long time.'

It took a few seconds for her to realise that he was teasing. A few seconds in which her heart did several somersaults and her legs threatened to give way. Andreas, teasing! That was a first. 'I meant alone,' she stressed.

His smile widened. 'Sleep well, then, my beautiful Peta. I think the boys should go back to school now. I'll take Nikos in the morning and explain to his headmaster. I think you should take Ben.'

Peta nodded.

'And you'll pick them up after school?'

'Of course,' she answered swiftly.

'So I'll see you at breakfast?'

'Yes.'

'May I kiss you goodnight?'

He was asking! Unbelievable! How could she refuse? But fear filled her heart as she gave a little nod.

She need not have worried. It was the lightest of kisses, the sort she gave Ben. A gentle hug and then he was gone, and she was left wondering. Had he taken her at her word? Had he accepted that their little romance was over? Was her time here not going to be the ordeal she'd expected?

As she crawled into bed Peta could find no answer to these questions. Andreas wasn't the type to give in, not when he'd set his sights on something. Even if she couldn't move back into her house maybe she ought to find somewhere else to live temporarily.

She discovered over breakfast that Christos had been living in Andreas's house while they were in Greece. Not that it should have surprised her, but it was something she'd never thought about. And now, as they tucked in to one of Bess's cooked breakfasts, he looked at her with a warmness that made her glance covertly at Andreas.

He was, as she had expected, frowning his disapproval. His eyes were on his brother, not her, as if trying to work out how serious Christos was.

'You haven't forgotten our dinner date tonight?' he asked, pausing as he speared a slice of sausage.

'Of course not.' She glanced again at Andreas and his eyes were on her now. 'Why don't you join us, Andreas?' she suggested, half joking, half serious.

'And tread on my brother's toes?' he asked lightly. 'You know what they say about three being a crowd.'

Christos had frowned when she extended the invitation, now he gave a relieved smile. 'Let Andreas find his own girl,' he said. 'I've never known him to be short. It's about time, brother dear, that you married again. It's wrong for Nikos to keep having nannies. Although,' he added, looking disarmingly at Peta, 'if they're all like Peta then I can see why you do it. A ready-made source of attractive females on tap. You've got it made.'

'You don't know what the hell you're talking about,' snapped Andreas, scraping his chair back from the table. 'I'll go and see if Nikos is ready.' The boys were eating their breakfast in the kitchen, and even though Peta had declared that her place was with them Andreas had insisted that she join him and his brother.

After Andreas had left the room Christos raised his brows. 'What was that all about? He's one seriously touchy man since his return.'

Peta shrugged. She didn't want to get into a discussion about his brother.

'Are you sure there's nothing between you and him? He seems very prickly where you're concerned.'

'Absolutely nothing,' she retorted. 'He's my employer, that's all.'

Christos raised his brows but said no more, although it was clear that he didn't entirely believe her, and she couldn't blame him. She'd been a little too vehement in her denial. And when she left to check on Ben he said, 'Is it still on for tonight?'

'Why shouldn't it be?' she asked sharply from the doorway.

'No reason; just checking.'

But when evening came and Andreas watched them leave Peta began to wish that she hadn't been so eager to accept Christos's invitation. Andreas knew, and she knew, that she was doing it to spite him, and when she returned she would more than likely be subjected to a full-scale interrogation.

'Are you sure you're happy about this?' asked Christos as they set off.

'Perfectly,' she answered smoothly. Except that inside she was filled with several conflicting emotions. She wanted to do this; she wanted to show Andreas that she didn't belong to him and that she had no intention of getting involved with him on a long-term basis. At the same time she wanted to prove to herself that she could date other men and be happy about it. She wanted to confirm that she was a free agent. Except that, being in love with Andreas, she would never be that. Not ever again for as long as she lived. It was a daunting thought.

'Because I believe,' said Christos quietly, 'that there is something going on between Andreas and yourself. I know you've denied it, and my brother won't even speak about you, but neither of you is doing a very good job of concealing your real feelings.'

Peta looked at him wide-eyed, an uncomfortable feeling stirring in her stomach. 'What are you saying?'

'That I think you're in love with each other, but you're either both too stupid to see it, or you have your own reasons for denying it.'

The uncomfortable feeling turned into chilling horror. Surely he couldn't see? 'Andreas doesn't love me,' she scorned.

'You think not?'

'I know not.'

'What makes you so sure?'

'Because of his wife. No one will ever take her place.'

They stopped at a set of traffic lights and he turned to her. 'I used to think that, but since he's met you there's something very different about him. I think he's finally let go.'

Peta's eyes met and held Christos's, then she turned away. 'I can't accept that,' she said. 'He's never given me any reason to believe that he loves me.'

'My brother is not the sort of man who can talk easily about his emotions.' The lights changed and they were off again. 'He can talk on any subject under the sun except love. Some men are like that, Peta. Now, me, I see no reason not to tell a woman that she's beautiful and I adore her and that I'm falling in love with her.' He looked briefly across at her as he spoke and Peta felt a twinge of unease. What if he was trying to tell her something? Things were complicated enough without him adding to it.

'So how about you?' he went on. 'Do you love Andreas?'

Peta hesitated a fraction too long before attempting an answer.

'You give yourself away,' he said on a deep sigh. 'And I'm sorry, because I'd hoped that I was in with a chance.'

'I'm sorry, too,' Peta whispered. This whole conversation was extremely painful. 'Do you still want to take me out to dinner?'

'Of course. Let's give Andreas something to think about.' He reached out and touched her hand and Peta smiled. Perhaps this evening wouldn't be too bad after all.

Andreas couldn't relax. In his mind's eye he kept seeing Peta and Christos walking out of the house together, driving off together, eating dinner in a cosy restaurant, still together. Their conversation would be intimate;

Christos would work his charm on her. He was very good at that, his little brother. While Andreas had been building up his business empire Christos had been captivating the girls. It was surprising he'd never married. He'd been forever coming home declaring that he was in love.

And the instant he'd set eyes on Peta he'd been knocked off his feet. And he, Andreas, had more or less given him *carte blanche* to do as he liked by refusing to discuss his own feelings. He was a fool. He was his own worst enemy. What if Peta fell hook, line and sinker for Christos? How would he be able to win her over then?

He paced from room to room, upstairs, downstairs, upstairs, downstairs. He tried to work at his computer but found it impossible. More pacing, more cursing. He had a photograph of Maria in his bedroom and he looked at it for a long, sober minute. God, but she was beautiful. His stomach churned simply looking at her and he felt the prick of tears at the backs of his eyes. She was an exotic beauty with none of Peta's coyness and delicate English-rose charm. There was a whole world of difference between the two women. And he loved them both!

As he continued holding the picture and looking into Maria's sultry brown eyes he felt her speaking to him. He heard her telling him that the time had come to get on with his life, that he could mourn her no longer. And she told him to hurry or he would lose the woman he had now fallen in love with. *She'll be good for you, Andreas, good for you and good for Nikos. Take her with my blessing.*

Take her with Maria's blessing!

If it were only so easy. He was afraid. A giant in the business world, a man often feared by others, and he was afraid to tell Peta that he loved her. And the reason why? Because he knew he couldn't handle it if she said that she didn't return his love.

The evening remained endless. Ten o'clock came, ten-thirty, eleven, eleven-thirty, and still no sign of Peta and Christos. Jealousy welled like a dam ready to burst. He knew he ought to go to bed, but he wanted to be here to see their faces, to look for any signs of emotional involvement. He needed to know.

And what if he did see it? What if he saw the light of love shining from Peta's eyes? Something he had never seen himself. What if he saw that particular soft radiance a woman had when she'd been well and truly made love to? How would he handle that?

With stoicism, he told himself. He'd give no hint that he was upset. But, he promised himself, he'd go all out to win Peta over, to convince her that he was the better man of the two. He'd tell her that he loved her; he'd get down on his knees if necessary and beg her to marry him. And that would be the most humbling experience of his whole life.

It was almost midnight before they returned. Andreas was pacing the hall when he heard the car and he would have liked nothing better than to stand and face them. But he couldn't do that. Instead he quickly took a seat in the living room, leaving the door open and the lights on so that they'd know he was in there. He picked up a book and pretended to be reading.

Peta had hoped that Andreas would be in bed. She'd had a most enjoyable evening with Christos. Once they'd established that there could be no romantic involvement they'd both let their hair down and set out to have a good time. He'd been excellent company, regaling her with tales of his childhood and his failed love affairs. By all accounts he was quite a ladies man and she could see why.

Both of these Papadakis brothers were gorgeous, with their dark Hellenic looks and strong masculine bodies. Andreas had the edge, though. He had a charisma that Christos didn't. Maybe it was his success, maybe it was because he was older, but, whatever, he was the one who would turn a girl's head first, and he was the one who had captured her heart.

'We didn't expect you to still be up,' said Christos now.

Andreas gave a lazy shrug and pushed himself to his feet. 'I wasn't particularly tired. Have you had a good time, you two?' His eyes rested on Peta as he spoke.

She knew that he had deliberately waited and was trying to assess whether she'd found Christos attractive, whether anything had gone on between them. She smiled warmly at Christos. 'We've had a wonderful time, haven't we?'

'Indeed.' He returned her look with warm affection. 'Am I glad you asked me to come and help you out over here, dear brother. And why you don't fancy Peta yourself I'll never know.'

Andreas's brows beetled into a scowl. 'I'm glad you enjoyed yourselves,' he grated. 'I think I'll go to bed.'

When he had gone Christos turned his lips down and looked at Peta with a questioning look in his eyes.

She shrugged.

'Methinks the man's jealous,' declared Christos.

'I think you're out of your mind,' she returned, 'and I'm going to bed, too. Thank you for a lovely evening.'

'Don't I get a goodnight kiss?'

She smiled slowly and put her arms about his shoulders. But when she leaned towards him all she did was kiss him on the cheek.

'That's cheating,' he growled.

'But it's all you're getting,' she said with a laugh. 'Goodnight, Christos.'

'Goodnight, beautiful lady.'

When Peta turned to leave the room she saw that Andreas had been watching them from the doorway. He'd turned immediately and marched along the corridor leading to their apartment, but he wouldn't have known that the kiss wasn't for real. Good, she thought with grim pleasure. That's the proof he needs that he means nothing to me.

And yet, as she slowly undressed and removed her make-up, as she cleaned her teeth and ran a brush through her hair, she couldn't help wishing that he hadn't seen.

She was not surprised when a few minutes later he tapped on the door and entered her room.

CHAPTER TWELVE

'DON'T tell me. You've come to find out whether I'm attracted to your brother.'

Peta's direct approach caused Andreas's eyes to flicker.

'If you have you're wasting your time, because however I feel towards Christos it's nothing to do with you,' she added firmly.

'So you do find him attractive?' Andreas crossed his arms over his chest and leaned back against the door, watching her intently through narrowed eyes. He was still in his shirt and trousers and it had obviously been his intent all along to come and interrogate her.

Peta's eyes flashed. 'Like I said, it's none of your business.'

'I intend to make it my business,' he countered firmly.

'Oh, yes, and how do you propose to do that?' She too folded her arms, wishing now that she hadn't got undressed. It was difficult trying to project an aloof and proud image wearing only a thin cotton nightie.

'I shall not go away until you give me some definite answers.'

Peta held his gaze for several long, heart-pumping seconds. Lord, he was magnificent. She wanted to haul him over to the bed and let him make love to her. She wanted him so badly that it hurt.

'What's wrong?'

'What do you mean?' she asked with a frown.

'Are you in pain?' He took a half-step towards her.

'No.' Not physical pain. And she cursed herself for letting her innermost feelings show.

'Then what's wrong?'

'You are what's wrong,' she retorted. 'Why won't you leave me alone?'

'Because I care about you.'

'Care!' retorted Peta crossly. 'You don't know the meaning of the word. You don't care about anyone. You didn't even care about your son until he was nearly taken from you.'

Andreas closed his eyes for a second, before saying quietly, 'Nikos means everything to me.'

'I've no doubt. But you never thought to show it. You never had time for him; business always came first.'

Her shot hit home. He winced. 'Not any longer.'

'So what are you going to do when I leave here? Get another nanny? Forget what you've just said? Leave Nikos to amuse himself all over again while you rake in the millions? You can't take it with you, Andreas. What's the point in devoting all your time to work at the expense of your son's happiness?'

'I've not come here to discuss my son.'

'No, you want to know what I think of Christos. Actually—' she allowed her face to soften into a dreamy smile '—he's a charmer. I wasn't sure at first, but the more I got to know him the more I discovered that I really like him. He's asked me out again.'

Andreas's eyes became glacially hard. 'And have you accepted?'

'Why, yes. He's such fun, and he's wonderful company. He makes me forget all my problems.'

'And what problems would those be?'

'As if you didn't know,' she shot back. 'The fact that my son was kidnapped. The fact that I can't get back into my own house. The fact that I'm forced to stay here with a man who wants an affair with me. Is that enough?'

Each barb shot home. She saw him wince. And his mouth grew grimmer and his eyes harder. 'Yes,' he said shortly. 'I can see that you do have problems. Perhaps I, as well as you, will be glad when you've gone.' And with that he spun on his heel and marched out.

Peta wanted to call him back, wanted to ask what he meant, but the door slammed and she hunched her shoulders and clenched her fists. Damn the man! Christos was wrong. Andreas wasn't jealous, not in the slightest. He was simply typically arrogant. Because he paid her wages he thought he owned her. Well, this was—

Her thoughts were interrupted by another knock on the door.

She wrenched it open. 'Andreas, if— Christos!'

'Are you all right?'

'Of course; why?'

'I saw my brother coming out with a face as black as thunder. What happened?'

'You'd better come in,' she said resignedly, and, once the door was closed, 'Like we arranged, I tried to pretend that I was falling for you.'

'And?'

She shook her head slightly. 'It got complicated. I said things I shouldn't have done. He ended up walking out on me. He doesn't love me, he just thinks he owns me. I'm not staying here any longer. I can't put up with any more of this.'

Christos frowned. 'Surely that's a bit hasty?'

'No, it's not. I never planned to stay once we got back.'

'Where will you go?'

'To my parents'.' It wasn't the ideal solution but what other choice had she? She didn't want to spend her hard-earned money on rented accommodation. Her mother and father would love having them for a few weeks. 'It means taking Ben out of school again but there's no alternative.'

'Are you sure you're doing the right thing? Why don't you let me have a word with Andreas? I could—'

'No!' cut in Peta in horror. 'I'll leave while you're both at work tomorrow. Don't say anything to your brother until you come back and find me gone. And even then don't tell him where I am. I'll make arrangements with Bess to have Nikos picked up from school.'

Christos shook his head. 'This isn't the answer.'

'Then what is?' she snapped.

'For you and Andreas to sit down and talk this thing over.'

'There's nothing to say. I'm not telling him I love him if that's what you want.' It would be the ultimate humiliation because, whatever Christos might think, she was absolutely certain that Andreas didn't love her.

'You're an idiot. A very beautiful one, but an idiot all the same.'

He was probably right. She would regret what she had done the moment she walked away. She would most likely tell herself that it would have been better to live with an Andreas who didn't love her rather than subject herself to a life without him.

She had little sleep that night. She lay awake, tossing her problem round and round in her mind. She was up early the next morning, getting the boys ready, having her breakfast with them in the kitchen, doing everything she could to avoid seeing Andreas.

But Andreas had no intention of avoiding her. As she

was leaving the kitchen, the boys having run on ahead, he caught her by the elbow and hustled her into his study. 'You and I have some talking to do.'

Peta feared that Christos had let her down, but Andreas's first words confirmed otherwise.

'What was Christos doing in your room last night?'

Peta felt like laughing—hysterically. She could have lied and said they'd made love, but that would get her nowhere. 'He came to see if I was all right. He saw you leave, heard you slam the door, saw the look on your face. He wondered what was going on.'

'So why didn't he ask me?' snarled Andreas.

'In the mood you were in? You'd have probably snapped his head off and told him it was none of his business.' Peta walked across to the window and pretended to look out at the immaculately manicured lawns.

'You're damn right, it's not,' came his harsh voice over her shoulder. 'What did you tell him?'

He'd moved so close that Peta could feel his breath on the back of her neck. And there was nowhere to go! Her own fault for putting herself into this position. 'That we'd had a few words.'

'He didn't ask what about?'

'Of course he asked. But I could hardly confess that his brother wanted a detailed report of the evening we'd spent together.'

'So what did you say?'

'Nothing much.' She wished he'd move. She wished he wouldn't stand so close. It was unnerving. It was churning her emotions. It was making her ask how could she possibly leave, feeling like this about him?

She continued to look out of the window, but when his hands touched her shoulders she jumped and went as tense as a high wire. He spun her to face him. He looked deep into her eyes. And just when she thought he was going to kiss her he let her go again and walked to the other side of the room. But he still kept looking at her.

'I wish I could meet the man who's done this to you, Peta.'

She shot startled eyes in his direction. 'Done what?' She had no idea what he was talking about.

'He must have hurt you very badly.'

She frowned then as realisation dawned. 'Are you talking about Joe?'

'Of course I'm talking about Joe. And for you to still be afraid of entering into a relationship nine years later then he must have done a real hatchet job.'

Yes, it had made her wary and angry for a very long time, but Joe was most definitely not the reason she was holding Andreas at arm's length. Unknowingly, though, he'd given her the perfect excuse. 'I was at a very vulnerable age,' she said quietly.

'He's a rat, and if I ever set eyes on him I'll kill him.'

There was such vehemence in his tone that Peta was shocked. 'I hardly think it warrants that; it was a long time ago.'

'And you're still suffering.'

Not to the extent he was suggesting, but she wasn't going to admit that. If he knew the truth, if he knew that he was the one who had managed to knock down her defensive wall, she wouldn't have a minute's peace. 'I really don't want to discuss this,' she said, and then made a show of looking at her watch. 'I'd better check the boys are ready for school. Are you taking Nikos or shall I?'

'You do it,' he said brusquely. 'Christos and I need to leave. We have an important meeting first thing.'

Yes, she thought, the same old pattern. He'd never change. He'd always put work before his son.

She didn't tell Ben her plans; she bundled them both into her car and as normal dropped Nikos off first. It was a few minutes before her son realised that they were heading back to the house. 'Have you forgotten something, Mummy?'

'No, darling, we're going down to Nanny and Grandad's for a few days. Won't that be fun?'

His little face lit up. 'I don't have to go to school?'

'No, you don't. But you're not getting out of it; I shall teach you myself, like I did before.'

'That's all right, I like you teaching me. Can Nikos come with us?'

Question followed question all the while she was packing and getting ready. Bess was sorry to see her go, sorry she wasn't getting on with Andreas.

'He knew I was going to leave, I simply didn't tell him when,' explained Peta.

'He'll be sad. You're the best thing that's happened to him in a long time.'

'If you say so,' said Peta, silently disagreeing. If she was the best thing he'd want more from her than an affair. As things stood he wanted a nanny for Nikos and a woman in his bed but no commitment, and as far as she was concerned it simply wasn't enough.

The drive to Cornwall didn't take very long. She hadn't told her parents to expect them and they were both stunned and delighted to see them. Freda and Doug James lived in a coastal village not far from Padstow and Ben was in his element, soon out of the house and down on the beach with his grandfather.

'How long are you staying?' asked her mother as she helped her unpack.

Peta shrugged. 'I don't know. I need a break. And then I'll look for a new job.'

'Why did you leave this one? I thought you liked it. And going to Greece as well. It sounds wonderful. I hope he paid you well?'

Peta nodded. 'Very well.' She had more money in the bank than she'd ever imagined. 'But it wasn't the idyll you imagine. Someone threatened to kidnap his son; that's why we fled.'

'Oh, my goodness! And you never told me,' shrieked her mother. 'You and Ben could have been in danger as well.'

Peta nodded and said as matter-of-factly as she could, so as not to alarm her mother further, 'As it turned out, Ben was kidnapped by mistake.'

Her mother's eyes rolled and she sat down on the edge of the bed. 'Tell me this isn't true.'

By the time Peta had finished explaining Freda James had still not come to terms with what had happened to her precious grandson. 'I don't blame you for leaving the man. It's not safe working for him.'

For the first time in her life Peta felt the need to confide in her mother. 'There's something more, Mum. The kidnapping's not the reason I left. I fell in love with Andreas.'

'I see.' Freda James's brows rose in surprise. 'It does complicate things. Am I right in presuming that he doesn't love you?'

Peta nodded. 'He's still hung up about his dead wife.'

'It's not easy, falling in love,' confided her parent. 'It ought to be, but too often there are complications. Oh, Peta, I've really missed you. It's been so long since you were last here.'

Peta nodded. 'Let's make up for it now.'

But Peta's thoughts were never far away from Andreas, and after lunch the following day, when Ben and her father had gone to the beach, she said, 'You know, Mum, Andreas is the first man I've ever truly loved. I know I thought I loved Joe, and was heartbroken when he dumped me, but, looking back, it wasn't love. He excited me, that was all.'

'And there's no chance of Andreas loving you in return?'

'Not one. I have to accept that he's not meant for me. He'd settle for an affair but I want more than that.'

'Of course you do, love. Best to push him right out of your mind. Ah, the phone, excuse me.'

Easier said than done, thought Peta as she left her mother to her phone call and joined Ben and her father. Andreas simply wouldn't go away.

When they got back to the house several happy if tiring hours later—Ben had run them ragged, racing around the beach and climbing over rocks—her mother seemed to be in an exceptionally good mood. She hummed and sang to herself as she gave Ben his supper, and afterwards, when he was in bed, she announced that she and Dad were going out.

'But you never go out at night,' Peta claimed with a frown.

'Doesn't mean to say we can't,' smiled her mum. 'I've left you a pie and some salad in the fridge. We shan't be late back. Enjoy yourself.'

What did she mean, enjoy herself? Time spent alone perhaps. That must be it. Peta wasn't hungry yet, so she settled herself outside in the back garden with a book and didn't hear the doorbell. She heard nothing until she sensed someone standing a few feet away. When she looked up and saw Andreas Papadakis her heart nearly jumped out of her chest. So who had told?

'Christos?' she enquired.

'No.'

'Bess?'

'That lady has given me one very good talking-to. I didn't know she had it in her.'

'And what exactly did she say?' Peta didn't invite him to sit. She didn't encourage him to take even a step further towards her.

'That she thought I had treated you despicably.'

Peta nodded, agreeing entirely.

'That she didn't blame you for walking out.'

'You left me no choice.'

'She told me I was a fool for not telling you that I loved you.'

'Huh!' she scorned. 'Why would you tell me that when we both know it's not true?' And why had Bess jumped to that conclusion?

'But it is true,' he answered quietly, his eyes darker now than she'd ever seen them, his face totally serious.

Peta's eyes widened. '*You* love *me*? You're joking, of course.'

'I'm not,' he said, shaking his head. 'I'm perfectly serious.'

This was more than she could take in. 'You've told my mother this? It was you on the phone earlier? It's why she's gone out? Hell, Andreas, you had no right.'

'I'm a desperate man,' he admitted, his expression wry.

'And what did my mother say about *my* feelings?' She urgently prayed that her parent hadn't given her away because she wasn't entirely sure that she believed Andreas. If he loved her, if he truly loved her, why couldn't he have said so? Why wait until she had run away and then decide? No, he still wanted her for his own selfish purposes.

'Precisely nothing,' he admitted. 'But she did agree that we ought to talk.' He closed the space between them in a few swift strides, dragging up a wrought-iron chair and positioning it so that he could sit facing her.

'You can talk all you like, it won't make any difference,' she said shortly. 'Words are easy.'

'If it's action you want then—'

'No!' She pulled back in distress as he tried to take her hands. 'Keep away from me, Andreas! I know what you're after. Why do you think I ran away?'

'And exactly what is it you think I'm after?' he asked, his mouth suddenly grim.

'An affair,' she thrust at him, top lip curling. 'It's all you've ever wanted. No commitment, just the use of my body—oh, and a babysitter for Nikos thrown in. Isn't that about right?'

'Maybe.'

'I knew I was right,' Peta claimed triumphantly.

'In the beginning.'

She frowned.

'I did desire you, fiercely. It turned into love without me even recognising it. The care you've shown for Nikos, as well as your own son, has awakened my responsibilities as a father and made me realise that I've loved you all along but tried desperately hard to bury it.'

'Because of Maria?'

He nodded. 'The time has come for me to let go.'

Peta was stunned. She didn't know what to say; she wasn't even sure whether she could believe him, even now, and he could see the doubt on her face.

'It's the truth, Peta.'

'So how did you trace me?'

'I overheard Christos telling Bess where you'd gone. All I had to do then was look on my itemised phone bill for your parents' number. Remember you rang them before we left for Greece?'

Peta closed her eyes. This was something she had never thought of.

'I know you don't return my love, Peta. But you like me, I think.' His brows rose, asking the question. 'And there's no denying the sexual attraction. We could work on it.' His eyes were such a dark brown that they appeared black, and they scanned her face closely, looking for some sign that she was weakening.

Peta felt a rush of emotion and could no longer hide her feelings. She reached out and took his hands into her own. 'Yes, Andreas, we can work on it,' she said softly, her heart beginning to race, her pulses quickening, and a soft heat enveloping her body.

'You really mean that?'

'I do.'

He stood up then and pulled her to her feet. 'May I hold you?'

She nodded, unable now to tear her eyes away from his. And her heart thumped as he urged her gently against the solid hardness of his body. He held her as though she was extremely fragile. 'This is more than I'd hoped for, Peta. I thought I'd have to work on you. I thought I'd have to woo you all over again.'

'It's more than I'd hoped for, too,' she admitted with a wry smile.

He looked down into her upturned face. 'What do you mean?'

'You have no idea how many times I've willed you

to fall in love with me and thought it would never happen. I thought you would never let go of Maria.'

He grew still. 'What are you saying?' And he seemed to be holding his breath as he waited for her answer.

'Can't you guess?'

He touched her chin and then stroked the backs of his fingers down her cheek, looking with almost childish wonder into her luminous blue eyes. 'I think you're saying that you love me, too.' And then he closed his eyes, as if to shut her out in case he was wrong, and she felt a tremor run through him.

'I do.' Her answer was little more than a whisper.

She heard the soft hiss of air as he exhaled, she felt the tension drain out of him, and like two lost souls who'd found each other in the wilderness they clung together, rocking and groaning, rocking and loving, pouring out their emotions in physical contact.

It was many long minutes before she lifted her head and he kissed her. Even then the kiss was gentle, tentative, experimental, as though he might frighten her away again if he asked for too much too soon.

'Tell me I'm not dreaming,' he whispered against her mouth.

'You're not dreaming,' she assured him huskily. 'I'm the one who's dreaming.'

'Oh, no! I love you, Peta. I love you very much. I shall tell you every day of my life. And if only I'd told you earlier then we wouldn't have wasted so much time.' His mouth captured hers again in a mind-drugging kiss that seemed to go on for ever.

When they finally managed to stop she was trembling so much that if he had let her go she would have fallen. He took her two hands into his and held them hard against his chest. She could feel his heart thudding. 'Will you marry me, Peta?' His gorgeous brown eyes held a burning light that threatened to consume her before the day was out.

It took her no more than a second to make up her mind, and her voice was a husky whisper. 'Yes.'

Andreas groaned, and his heart raced now like a mad thing beneath her hands. 'You wove your magic on me, Peta, from the first moment you walked into my office. Such a feisty female. You were entrancing. Don't ever change. And I promise I'll make you the happiest woman in the world.'

'Are you really over Maria?' It was a question she needed to ask.

He nodded. 'I love you in an entirely different way. It will be good between us. I'll never let you down the way Joe did.'

'I'm over Joe,' she told him with a wry smile. 'I used him as a buffer. I was scared of my feelings. I didn't believe that you'd ever love me, not the way I wanted to be loved, or the way I loved you.'

He frowned and looked at her closely. 'Are you saying that you've loved me for a long time?'

Peta gave a wry, guilty smile and nodded. 'Though, like you, I wasn't sure of it until after Ben's kidnapping. It's why I ran away.'

He swore loudly in Greek. 'Do your parents know how you feel about me?'

'My mother does,' she admitted. 'I expect she's told Dad.'

'I wondered why she was so ready to let me see you. Does anyone else know? Am I the last to hear? The one person who should be first?'

'It's your own fault,' she pointed out, though she smiled as she said it.

'I guess it is. But you haven't answered my question. How about Christos? Does he know? Were you talking about me on the night he took you out? I know he fancies you. Did you tell him he stood no chance because you loved me? Did you, Peta? Did you?'

He sounded angry and Peta didn't want to answer, but her expression must have given her away.

With a furious snarl Andreas let her go and put space between them, his eyes blazing accusation.

'He knew that you loved me,' she told him, 'and he wanted to talk to you but I wouldn't let him.'

'Damn! I can't believe I've been so blind, so foolish, so unbelievably ignorant.' He huffed out a sharp breath and paced the patio before coming once again to stand in front of her. 'My darling Peta, I have you to thank for showing me that there is still happiness to be found. My future beckons with all the brightness of a lodestar.'

'Oh, Andreas.' Tears welled and she clung to him, and to her surprise his eyes were suspiciously moist, too. 'This is the happiest day of my life.'

'We'll get married straight away,' he murmured between kisses. 'I'll get a special licence. I can't wait any longer.'

And if she was honest neither could Peta. She had finally found a man she could trust; a man who would never fail her; a man who would look after her for the rest of her life. What more could she ask?

0706/01b V2

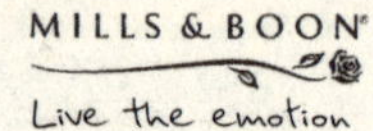

Modern romance™

BEDDED FOR REVENGE *by Sharon Kendrick*

Cesare's pride had been wounded but he planned to bed Sorcha, and then dump her…all for revenge! And revenge was sweet. Sorcha Whittaker was still the sexiest woman he'd ever seen, and their passion was incredible. The hard part now was walking away…

THE SECRET BABY BARGAIN *by Melanie Milburne*

Jake Marriott was clear about the terms of his relationships – no marriage, no babies. So Ashleigh Forrester ran because she was pregnant with his child. But Jake is back, and the striking resemblance to her son is too obvious to ignore. Now Jake wants to buy her as his wife…

MISTRESS FOR A WEEKEND *by Susan Napier*

Nora Lang wants the most dangerous man she can find! Enter top tycoon Blake Macleod. When Nora acquires some business information that he can't risk being leaked, Blake has to keep her in sight – he'll make love to her for the whole weekend!

TAKEN BY THE TYCOON *by Kathryn Ross*

Nicole and her handsome boss Luke Santana work hard and play hard, with no strings attached. But Nicole finds herself wanting more than Luke can give, so she ends their liaison. What will Luke do when he uncovers the secret Nicole carries with her now…?

On sale 4th August 2006

Available at WHSmith, Tesco, ASDA, Borders, Eason, Sainsbury's and most bookshops

www.millsandboon.co.uk